Praise for D.B. Reynolds...

"... a compelling, fast-paced, sexy and exciting story with fantastic and intriguing characters. 5 Warrior Stars!"
—Swept Away by Romance on DRAGAN

"... this is the series to try-if you haven't already. There's always plenty of action, life and death moments, romance and really hot sexy times as well."
—Delightedreaders.com on LACHLAN

"This is a power read, and fans will not be disappointed in the latest installment of Reynolds's tantalizing series. Top Pic! 4 1/2 Stars
—RT Book Reviews of LUCIFER

"Captivating and brimming with brilliance, CHRISTIAN is yet another defining addition to the ever-evolving world of Vampires in America created by D.B. Reynolds."
—KT Book Reviews

"Did I mention that the sizzling sex factor in this book is reaching the combustible stage? It is a wonder my Kindle didn't burn up."
—La Deetda Reads on DECEPTION

"D.B. Reynolds has outdone herself with this exhilarating story; and VINCENT is a worthy addition to Reynolds's always excellent Vampires in America series."
—Fresh Fiction

"Terrific writing, strong characters and world building, excellent storylines all help make Vampires in America a must read. Aden is one of the best so far." A TOP BOOK OF THE YEAR!
—On Top Down Under Book Reviews

Other Books by D. B. Reynolds

VAMPIRES IN AMERICA
Raphael * Jabril * Rajmund * Sophia
Duncan * Lucas * Aden * Vincent

Vampires in America: The Vampire Wars
Deception * Christian * Lucifer

The Cyn and Raphael Novellas
Betrayed * Hunted * Unforgiven
Compelled * Relentless * Detour

Vampires in Europe
Quinn * Lachlan * Xavier

The Stone Warriors
The Stone Warriors: Damian
The Stone Warriors: Kato
The Stone Warriors: Gabriel
The Stone Warriors: Dragan

Xavier

Xavier: Vampires in Europe

by

D. B. Reynolds

ImaJinn Books

This is a work of fiction. Names, characters, places and incidents are either the products of the author's imagination or are used fictitiously. Any resemblance to actual persons (living or dead), events or locations is entirely coincidental.

ImaJinn Books
PO BOX 300921
Memphis, TN 38130
Print ISBN: 978-1-61194-993-3

ImaJinn Books is an Imprint of BelleBooks, Inc.

Copyright © 2020 by D. B. Reynolds

Published in the United States of America.

All rights reserved. No part of this book may be reproduced in any form or by any electronic or mechanical means, including information storage and retrieval systems, without permission in writing from the publisher, except by a reviewer, who may quote brief passages in a review.

ImaJinn Books was founded by Linda Kichline.

We at ImaJinn Books enjoy hearing from readers. Visit our websites
ImaJinnBooks.com
BelleBooks.com
BellBridgeBooks.com

10 9 8 7 6 5 4 3 2 1

Cover design: Debra Dixon
Interior design: Hank Smith
Photo/Art credits:
Background (manipulated) © Michele Kerstholt | Dreamstime.com
Man (manipulated) © Andrey Kiselev & © Vladimirs Poplavskis | Dreamstime.com

:Lxzd:01:

Dedication

Dedicated with love and sorrow in memory of my friend
Sandy Swindell McKenzie

Chapter One

Catalonia, Spain, 1859

XAVIER FLORES Prospero raced into Barcelona far ahead of his companions. He'd been in Madrid when he'd *known*, just *known*, that his Sire was dead. Every vampire on the continent would have known that someone powerful had died, but Xavier had known who it was—Vampire Lord, the Lord of Spain, Josep Alexandre, centuries old, a power beyond reckoning, and in an instant, he was gone. Xavier's grief had been real, his fury unmatched. For if Josep was dead, someone had killed him. And that someone was now Lord of Spain, except . . . . His far-reaching sensitivity to the balance of power told him that the vampire who'd murdered Josep was too weak to rule, unable to contain the power released with the vampire lord's death. And that left the territory leaderless, its vampires desperate and gasping for the strength and leadership they needed to survive.

By all accounts, the murderous fool had managed to escape the city before being killed himself, but the result had been utter carnage, as one vampire after another went on a killing spree in a bid for power. No one had managed to hold the territory—which encompassed all of Spain—for longer than a few days. Xavier hadn't needed anyone to tell him the territory was in crisis. He was powerful enough to sustain himself and his vampire children without a vampire lord's assistance, but most vampires weren't. In every city and village he'd passed through on his race back to Barcelona—every place where one or more vampires had lived—he'd had to linger long enough to revive dying vampires, to share his blood and make them *his,* to save their lives.

And still the challenges and killings continued. It was a constant noise in his head, his instinct straining to forge a connection to one new ruler after another.

But he'd finally reached Barcelona, the center of Spain's vampires because it had been Josep's home for the hundreds of years he'd ruled. Racing down the crowded streets, Xavier ignored angry shouts and thrown objects from pedestrians protesting his horse's thundering passage, until he pounded through the gates of Josep's home, his mount's hooves skidding on the polished stone in front of the dead vampire lord's mansion.

Leaving the horse to the care of his companions, who'd been close behind him when they'd drawn even with the city and would arrive soon enough, he stormed up the steps two at a time and walked into a bloodbath.

The entrance hall, once a gaudy excess of gild and crystal, now stank of old blood and worse, much worse. The pink marble that had been imported from Italy to grace the floor was now dark red with blood stains, the grooves between the huge slabs still slick and shining. *Jesu Crist*, how many had died here? And why? Vampires didn't bleed like that when they died, which meant humans had been slaughtered like cattle to feed . . . hell, he didn't know whom. The instincts that had told him the territory was in turmoil hadn't provided any names. It didn't work like that.

Xavier walked deeper into the mansion, more cautious now. If vampires had been reduced to butchering humans, there was no telling what state they were in. He was confident enough in his ability to destroy anyone who dared attack him, but he wouldn't enjoy having some feral beast of a vampire launch itself at him from hiding and sink fangs into his flesh. *Dios mio*, wasn't that a disgusting thought?

"Sire."

He turned and found Chuy, his lieutenant and the first of his vampire children, moving slowly into the room, his expression reflecting the same revulsion that Xavier himself was feeling.

"Walk carefully, Chuy. I don't know what's going on here, but there are almost certainly a few mad ones lurking about."

"Where will you go, my lord?"

"There's only one choice, my friend. Forward." At a grim nod from his lieutenant, Xavier strode deeper into the wrecked mansion, confident that his back was covered.

"Xavier." A familiar figure appeared in the open doors to what had been Josep's drawing room.

"Dênis." It was an effort to keep the dislike from his voice, for all that he and this vampire shared the same Sire, and had lived in Josep's court at the same time. "You're alive."

Dênis gave an elegant shrug. "The one who killed Josep was not a serious, or even intentional, contender for the territory."

"What does that mean?"

"He attended one of Josep's weekday receptions. You remember the kind. No one of significance ever bothered, but our Sire felt the need to socialize with the common man . . . for reasons of his own," he added in distaste. "The assassin, for that's what he was, maneuvered close to Josep and detonated some sort of magical device. It killed Josep instantly, along with several other vampires. And a few humans," he said offhandedly.

"Magic. Are you certain?"

"Oh, yes. There was another sorcerer in the crowd. You remember, the one who gained such favor with Josep when he restored Sakal's magic."

"Sakal?" he repeated and immediately wondered if the sorcerer was involved in this. He'd never forgiven Josep for making him Vampire. But that had been well over one hundred and fifty years ago. Had Sakal been plotting his revenge all this time? "Was Sakal at the reception that day?" he asked Dênis.

"No, he left two days prior for France, with Josep's permission."

"And where were you?"

Dênis chuckled. "*I* didn't hire the assassin."

"But you didn't try to stop him, either, did you? Why did you not protect our Sire, as I would have?"

"You were always his favorite, Xavier. The one who had free access to the most beautiful women, the best horses and accommodations. Did you ever consider what it was like for the rest of us?"

"You let him die."

"And now Spain is mine."

"Do you believe you can *hold* it?" Xavier sneered. "Against *me*? There was a reason that Josep favored me."

The other vampire's expression hardened. "You'll bow to *me* before the end. I might even make you kiss my feet."

He snorted his opinion of that. "How many challengers have you killed so far?"

"More than I can remember. It's amazing the weaklings who think they can hold power."

Xavier stared at him lazily. "Yes, it is."

Dênis growled, fangs bare. "Leave or challenge, you bastard."

"*I'm* not the bastard here, *Dênis*," he said. "Shall we do this in the courtyard? This building stinks of old blood."

"Those refined senses of yours too delicate for a little blood?"

"Not as long as it's yours." An instant later the defensive shields he'd created from the power of his blood alone sizzled to life, as he deflected the spear of pure energy aimed at his chest. But it hadn't come from Dênis. He swung his gaze to the right and caught a flash of blond hair. Sending a focused rope of his power to wrap about the fleeing vampire's throat, he dragged the attacker back into sight.

The vampire emitted a high-pitched whine, struggling to grip the invisible rope around his neck, his eyes rolling white with terror as he silently begged Dênis for aid. Xavier could have told him no help would be coming. Dênis had never cared for those who looked to him for protection. Not even when the one seeking help had risked his life to help Dênis.

"It was a foolish move," Xavier told the whining vampire. "Did Dênis tell you it would work? That your pitiful attack would be the distraction that gave him the kill? That you'd earn his favor and reward after he was made vampire lord?"

The pathetic vamp had pink tears running down his cheeks, when his gaze switched to Xavier, pleading for his life.

"Will you save him, Dênis? Please, proceed. I'll wait."

Dênis's gaze filled with furious hatred for Xavier. Without so much as a glance, he flicked a hand at the begging vampire. A moment later the pleading vamp fell to the floor, blood soaking his shirt an instant before he collapsed into a greasy pile of skin and bone that betrayed his youth.

"And that," Xavier said, pointing at what was left of a vampire who'd been loyal enough to risk his life for his master, "is why you will never be Lord of Spain."

Dênis's grin was a vicious baring of teeth. "No. *That* is why I will wade through your dust to the throne." A crackling sword of flame shot from his hand as he moved with vampire speed, appearing so close that when he swung the blade, it would have taken Xavier's head had he not snapped his shields up.

"You never did have a sense of honor," Xavier said almost cheerfully as he formed his own blade, this one burning blue and gleaming like the finest carbon steel. "Don't worry. You'll be too dead to crawl."

They fought blade to blade at first, fire against steel, heat against ice. Xavier could have taken his opponent in the first few minutes, but it had been a long ride to get there, and his muscles needed warming. And so he fought until he saw sweat beginning to roll down Dênis's face, until he noted the strikes coming a little slower, carrying a little less force. Until he saw the knowledge in the other vampire's eyes. Death was imminent, and so unnecessary.

"You should have fled in shame after permitting our Sire to die," Xavier said.

"*O diabo te leva*," Dênis snarled.

Xavier laughed. "The devil? It's not me he's after." In an instant, he'd shifted from the almost comfortable strike, parry, strike they'd been exchanging. Knocking Dênis's fiery blade aside with a casual blow, he spun the length of his own gleaming weapon in midair, sliced through his enemy's neck, and stepped back to watch as the vampire's gaze recognized his own death, then disintegrated into dust.

"Sire."

Xavier took the wet cloth Chuy offered him. Dênis had been old enough that his death was fairly tidy. But he'd been a big man—not tall, but thickly built—and Josep's mansion had always been drafty. The dust that had been Dênis floated through the air.

"What now?" Chuy asked, taking the cloth and throwing it aside. This room . . . hell, the entire mansion, was so wrecked that one more piece of debris would hardly matter.

Xavier sighed. He'd hoped to rest in Josep's basement quarters, but though he hadn't yet made it downstairs, he doubted it was safe for anyone—human or vampire. "We'll try my townhouse. It's been some time since I was in this city. It may have escaped notice. The others?" he added, referring to the two vampires and one human who'd accompanied him to the city.

"Waiting outside, my lord. They have your horse."

"Good. Let's go. There's nothing here for anyone." It made him sad to realize that was true. He hadn't cared anything for Josep's riches. But seeing all this destruction somehow brought the loss home to him, made it real. His Sire was forever gone. And he would miss him.

The trip across the city to the townhouse where Xavier had lived for years, before his growing power had forced him to leave Josep's city, was mostly uneventful. One misguided vampire chose to confront him, stepping out from a narrow and dark alley to issue his challenge. Xavier was tired and more than a little sad, but he stepped off his horse, handed the reins to Chuy, then confronted the foolish vamp. Without ceremony, and certainly without any resort to his vampire magic, he took two steps, pulled the excellent, but very ordinary, sword from the tooled, leather sheath at his hip and ran it through the challenger's heart. The vampire's eyes went wide in surprise, and a little betrayal, Xavier thought. Had he expected a magical battle, rather than cold steel? And had he believed he could win?

He sighed, took back the reins from his lieutenant, and mounted his horse. He wondered sometimes at the foolish arrogance of so many vampires, the ones whose Sires seemed to have taught them nothing of the world. Vampirism gave them a bounty of gifts—greater strength, enhanced senses, virtual immortality. But it bestowed those same gifts on *every* vampire. And as with every creature in nature, the strong would always triumph over the weak.

He was relieved, when they arrived at the townhouse, to see it undisturbed and intact. He paid a local retainer to see to it, but when one was absent for months at a time, all manner of destruction could occur.

As the sun rose and he drifted into his much needed daytime rest, he thought about the future, and knew two things. He would face more challenges in the coming days, but in the end, he would triumph and become the new Lord of Spain.

HE WOKE THE next night to a thundering voice that had invaded his sleep and now destroyed the peace of his waking.

"*Fill de puta.*" His own curse filled his thoughts and crashed against the brain of this fresh challenger. He didn't recognize the new vamp's mind and didn't think they'd ever met. Word must have travelled of his battle with Dênis, bringing out fools like the one he'd killed so easily just before dawn. And now this one, though this new challenger was obviously a more serious contender. It would take power to disturb his thoughts during sleep. This vampire had possibly been sitting back and watching the carnage, waiting while the weaker challengers butchered each other and winnowed the field, thinking he would then step up, destroy whoever remained, and claim the territory.

But now Xavier had arrived and blown a hole in his careful plan. Hah! The bastard didn't know it yet, but Xavier was going to do more than just blow a hole in his fucking plan. Josep's territory was *his*, had always been his. By rights, he should have challenged his Sire when it became plain that his own power was the greater. He'd delayed out of love and respect for Josep, but he owed nothing to anyone else.

Rising from his bed, he bathed quickly and went upstairs to enjoy a cup of tea while waiting for the others to wake. He needed blood after the previous night. *Dios mio*, he'd fought and killed—well, more or less *fought* when it came to that last one—three challengers. He needed to feed, and feed well, since this next night promised to be a repeat of the last.

It was almost an hour before the others managed to join him, but they were as eager to do some hunting as he was. They'd all dressed in their best, with a bit of borrowing from Xavier's closet. The trousers were all too big, since Xavier was a much bigger man than most, but the shirts adjusted easily enough. A quick brush of the hair and they were all ready.

"Best luck for blood in this city is a society party," Xavier said. "All those pretty virgins trapped in their papas' houses, and eager for a bit of an evil romp."

"Evil?" Chuy asked. "How's that?"

"You were raised in the Church. You know we're included in the devil's pantheon. Lower than Lucifer himself, naturally."

"Is lower better or worse? Seems to me the ranks in hell would have the worst, and thus the best evil at the bottom."

Xavier and the others laughed as they strolled down the street, eyes on a brightly lit house just ahead, wide open and full of people who were spilling out into the cooler air in the yard.

"*Allà hi aneu, gaudiu.*" Xavier gestured at the crowd of well-dressed men and women, his own eye on a dark-haired beauty who was already casting her gaze his way. Ah, yes. That one was definitely ready for a taste of evil.

Twenty minutes later, he had the dark-haired, and as it turned out, dark-eyed beauty pressed up against a wall, deep in the shadows. She cried out when his fangs slid into her satiny skin and pierced her vein. But her cries soon turned to moans of pleasure when the erotic effect of his bite took hold, and sexual ecstasy took over her body. Xavier had one hand on her rounded, bare ass, and the other on the back of her neck while he slipped his stiff shaft into the silky wetness of her *cony*. There was no virginal bleeding. He'd have smelled it if there was. So this wasn't the sweet thing's first taste of evil. His beauty was a little bit bad. It made her blood all the sweeter.

She shuddered when her body squeezed his cock, the final temptation all that he needed to spill himself inside her. He wondered who'd deflowered her, and if he'd been a vampire. There was no need to worry about disease from a vamp, and no *bebès* either. Maybe she was smart enough to know that. It was an intriguing thought since he'd be in town for a while this time.

Once he'd finished with all these useless challenges, he'd have Josep's estate to deal with. It would take months to transfer the official property records, and then there were his other assets, too many of which he'd have to seek out in order to claim. At some point, he'd no doubt throw up his hands and leave it. Josep's wealth was too far flung. He wouldn't have time for all of it. But there must be a clerk or two among the vampires in this city. He'd lay it all at their feet, while he worked on making a permanent home for his people. He'd claimed an old fortress several miles outside the city and intended to repair it sufficiently, so that he and the bulk of Barcelona's vampires could move into it. It wouldn't be much at first, but they were vampires. They had time.

"What's your name, *bellesa*?"

"Immaculada," she said, wrinkling her pretty nose.

Xavier smiled while he removed his cock from her heat and straightened his clothing. "And what do they call you?"

"Imma. No one calls me the other except my parents."

"Of course. Well, *Imma*, I'm going to be in town a while." He whispered his address in her ear. "Ring the bell any time. There's always someone to answer, and they'll leave you for me."

"Confident, aren't you?"

"I'm better than you've ever met, *bella* Imma. Better than you will ever meet again." He licked the line of blood trailing down her elegant neck. "I'll see you soon." And, feeling bold and well fed, he used a bit of his power to build shadows around himself, so that it would seem to her he'd disappeared into the night. *And thus were tall tales of vampires created*, he thought with grin.

Though he and the others walked down many streets and up a few alleys, no one rose to challenge him. And that was a puzzle. Someone, some *vampire*, was currently holding the territory. Not well, and definitely not with enough power to defeat Xavier, but enough that it grated at his senses like a stone in his boot. His own presence had to be doing the same to whoever this weak vampire lord was, but the vamp was hiding. Recuperating maybe, from what had been weeks of vampire battles. Then again, this one wouldn't have lasted for weeks, so he'd most likely arrived in the city not long before Xavier himself.

Whatever was keeping the pathetic Lord of Spain, who clearly didn't deserve the title, in hiding, there was nothing Xavier could do about it. So he signaled to the others and strode directly home instead. His human servant, Albert, was waiting with tea and wine. Albert had been with him for ten years now, growing from a restless teenager to a responsible man while serving as Xavier's eyes and ears during the day. He seemed content with his position. He had access to a generous household fund, and if he ever decided to take a wife, Xavier hoped they'd remain with him. Even after the children came.

He wanted his *Fortalesa*, which is what he'd decided to call the old citadel, to be a village with humans and vampires living together, creating families by birth or adoption. Whatever it took for *all* of them to feel as if they were *safe* and belonged. That was what he wanted for his headquarters, his lair, when he became the new Lord of Spain.

All he needed now was for the present cowardly lord to show himself and die.

XAVIER WAS FILLED with determination when he rose the following night. Still flush with Imma's generously offered blood, his power was like a feral creature demanding unchained violence. When the others finally rose, they found him pacing the front parlor, unable to remain still.

"He's lost whatever power he was using to hide himself. I know where he is."

Chuy stood in the kitchen with the other two vampires. Rémy and Hadrien were twin brothers whom he'd come across in France, when he'd ventured over that border. It had been done mostly out of curiosity, but finding the two had been a stroke of luck. Especially when they'd proved willing to join him in his search for a permanent home. They looked like they were in their early twenties, and in reality, they were not much beyond that. But they were tall and strong, and together had enough power to fight off any vampires who might think to take advantage of his distraction when he was in the midst of a challenge.

All three put down their evening tea and gave him their full attention. "Is tonight the night, then?" Chuy asked.

"It is. Are you ready?" His question was directed at the group, and they all answered with a bob of the head and single word.

"Sire."

"Victory awaits us."

THE OTHER VAMPIRE was waiting for him. He was older than was typical for a vampire, well into his thirties when he'd been turned, Xavier would guess. But he'd been a vampire long enough for its healing effects to have worked on him. And that wasn't the only aspect of the vamp that drew Xavier's attention. He'd seemed weak the previous night, as if struggling to remain hidden. But Xavier saw now that it had been a ruse, a mask of sorts to fool the challenger he'd known had been searching for him.

Xavier smiled inwardly. That was all right. The power burning inside him had been hungry for violence and it would certainly get it from this one. "Xavier Prospero Flores," he said by way of introduction, when he stood no more than twelve feet from the other vampire.

"Leonardo Gilberto," the vamp replied, letting his true power gleam through his eyes just enough to be seen.

Xavier smiled at the show of power and said, "*Portuguès*. Is there not enough blood in your country to feed its vampires? Or perhaps what remains is too weak?"

The other bared his fangs in a grin. "We'll see whose blood is the weaker tonight."

"No more hiding, Leonardo?"

"I wasn't hiding," he growled. "I had other business."

"A shame to spend your last night on earth conducting business."

"It would be. I trust you were better engaged."

Xavier returned the grin. "Is our little chat sufficient to establish mutual honor?"

Leonardo removed the short cape he'd been wearing and tossed it aside. "Sufficient to me."

"Do you have a blade?" Xavier inquired. The physical blades weren't necessary, but some vampires preferred them, and he *did* want to be a gentleman.

The other vamp held out both hands to show they were empty, and since there was no blade at his hip, Xavier removed his own sword and passed it to Chuy. He looked around. "This seems private enough. Anyone who decides to watch does so at their own peril."

"Suits me." Without further warning, Leonardo raised a rainbow-colored shaft of power and threw it at Xavier like a javelin.

It glittered in the air as it flew . . . and disintegrated into a shower of colors when it crashed against Xavier's rapidly formed shields. It was for attacks just like this one that he'd spent so much time designing and working with his personal shield. It drew away from his power when he fought, and many vampires didn't have the energy to spare. But he did, and it was well worth it.

He grinned at his opponent's look of dismayed surprise, and with practiced ease raised his own blade of power, adding a ray of icy blue to the color show. Stepping forward with vampire speed, he slashed at Leonardo, who managed a last minute riposte with a second, shorter blade that remained stable barely long enough to defend against the strike before shattering into useless sparks.

Xavier plunged closer, taking advantage of Leonardo's shock, hoping to end this one fast, despite the thirst for a bloody victory he'd enjoyed earlier. He'd had his fill of blood and gore when he'd arrived. But it seemed Leonardo wasn't finished yet.

In a burst of multicolored energy, he crossed two big blades in front of his chest, repelling Xavier's strike and shoving him several steps back. Xavier recovered immediately, forming a second blade of his own, shorter but just as deadly. It was the fighting style he'd preferred as a human and perfected as a vampire.

They moved on each other, energy-driven blades flashing like lightning in the black night, filling the air with sizzling magic and the smell of burning energy. Xavier managed to slip his short blade beneath Leonardo's defense and slide it into his gut. The other vamp grunted, but kept fighting. It hadn't been a fatal blow, Xavier knew, but it had been deep enough to cause blood to flow freely down Leonardo's tunic and to his leg. He'd either have to spend power to heal it, or bleed power away uselessly.

Leonardo crossed both blades and shoved Xavier backwards, taking two quick steps back himself to increase the distance between them. He'd chosen to heal the gut wound. But Xavier was under no obligation to give him the time and space to do so. He attacked, taking power from his shield to push closer, wanting to get inside Leonardo's defense and inflict more damage.

But the other vampire saw him coming, and unexpectedly threw both blades into the air, where they dissipated into nothing, while at the same time a huge cudgel of power grew from the grip of his hands. Swinging the new, brutal weapon, he took Xavier on the shoulder, sending him stumbling backward. Xavier's blades flew from his loosened grip, when he matched Leonardo's move and manifested a brutish weapon of his own. Holding it in both hands, he deflected what would have been a fatal strike, then jumped to his feet and hardened his shield as he prepared for the furious and bloody battle his vampire soul longed for.

Blow after blow fell. Cudgels slammed into each other with bone-breaking force as often as they were deflected. Xavier's left shoulder was screaming with pain, but he kept fighting. Barely avoiding a strike that would have broken his leg and probably ended the bout, he swung behind Leonardo and struck him in the shoulder and upper back, then continued his dance to the other side of his opponent, and manifested a knife. Stabbing it quickly into the vamp's other shoulder, he left the blade buried in flesh, to drain power from the bloody wound.

Leonardo's gaze had dimmed from his earlier proud display, and for the first time, Xavier could glimpse the possibility of failure in the other vampire's eyes. He was much like Xavier in that he hadn't expected a real fight from anyone. He'd been so confident in his own strength that failure hadn't even been considered. Unfortunately, Xavier wasn't in this fight to draw, or even to accept surrender. Victory was the only acceptable outcome, and there was no such thing as compassion in a battle to the death. He struck with the cudgel first, a powerful blow that scraped along the similar weapon Leonardo raised in defense. Without pause, Xavier continued with a backward strike, just as he would have if holding a fencing blade, rather than this crude weapon better suited for the brutes who'd first created it, rather than two gentlemen of the aristocracy.

The idea made Xavier laugh. There was nothing gentlemanly about this battle, no matter how they'd begun. It was brute strength vs the same, with the pitiless addition of vampire magic and ambition. Leonardo released one blade, but advanced with a new great sword gripped in both hands, swinging it before him with skill and determination.

Xavier's shoulder protested with tearing pain when his blade and the other met in a horrific shriek of metal and magic that lit the enclosed yard they stood in. He and Leonardo stood almost toe to toe, their eyes meeting over their crossed blades, each knowing that the first to fail would be the first to fall. They were too close to each other, their power too focused on their blades and defense to create a new weapon or shield in time.

Leonardo's eyes were shining orbs of rusty orange, and Xavier could see the dull silver glow of his own gaze glinting off the vampire's sweat-covered skin. Their teeth were bared, fangs displayed, and deep growls rumbled from their chests. Xavier almost regretted having to kill this one. He would have been an excellent warrior to have at his side, a good friend in the centuries ahead. But they'd taken the challenge too far. If he let Leonardo walk away, he'd only end up fighting him again, and he might lose that battle. They were that closely matched.

Using the extra edge of power that made him what he was, he manifested a double-edged knife in his free hand, took an abrupt step back to free enough space, crossed his knife arm over his sword arm, then reclaimed the step he'd taken, and drove the blade into Leonardo's

12

heart, shoving it deeper with a twist of power that shot sparks outward in a circle of magical energy that blew the vampire's heart into a burning ball of shredded flesh.

Leonardo managed a grunt of surprise as he stumbled back and gasped, *"Ut victoriam Xavier."* And in the moment before he dissipated into a dusting that was incredibly fine and complete, Xavier knew he'd been a *very* old vampire.

Xavier released every bit magic that had been hovering around him, and bent over with his good arm braced on one knee. His companions would alert him to any danger, and protect him as necessary. But right now, he just needed to breathe, to let his power settle in his gut and bones, in his—

The blow came so hard that it dropped him to the ground on all fours, a whirlwind of power and memory that slammed through skin and bone to occupy every inch of his body, from his feet to his chest and into his fucking brain until he thought his head would explode from the pressure. At the last moment, it spun out of his head and back to his chest where it took up residence in his heart like a red hot coal.

Letting out a snarl that was half groan, he fell flat to the ground, rolling to his back when memories finally began flooding his brain, telling him what this was, what was happening to him. The thundering power of a vampire lord was now his, the cacophony of what seemed like every vampire living in Spain crying for comfort, demanding protection, demanding to know *who he was*.

As for the memories, they were a gift from his Sire, centuries of living that were now his to draw upon for knowledge, for guidance.

He took time to gaze only at the final moments of his Sire's life. He wanted to know sure that the one who'd killed Josep was dead. If not, Xavier wouldn't rest until he'd hunted the fool down and taken his life. But rather than seeing the face of Josep's killer at the moment of his death, he heard instead his Sire's words of warning.

"Sakal," Josep whispered weakly, as if the death blow had already been struck. "Beware, Xavier. It was Sakal who paid the assassin who killed me. And he will come for you."

Chapter Two

Sant Andreu De Llavaneres Barcelona, Spain, present day

COMMANDER FERRAN Casales slumped behind the thick battlement wall and reloaded his weapon with movements so automatic that they'd become a ritual. *A prayer to the gods of war.* The thought penetrated his exhaustion, making him snort in derision. A prayer to those bastards? Gods had been driving men to kill each other from the moment humans had risen from the primordial ooze. More gods than he could name. It didn't matter. He no longer believed in any of them. At least, not the kind who answered prayers. He'd seen and done too much in his long life. Killed too many.

The renewed metallic chatter of machine weapons shattered the fragile moment of thought. Giving the fresh magazine a final slap, he stood and spun in a single movement, gun raised and firing. Not the long useless free-for-all from the people attacking the *Fortalesa*, but short, controlled three-round bursts that hit every target he aimed at. Young men and women fell to the ground before him. Some screamed, while others went quietly, dead before they knew enough to cry out.

The *Fortalesa* where Ferran stood was as anachronistic as its name, an ancient fortress in a modern world—a fitting home for the most powerful vampire in this country and beyond. Xavier Prospero Flores, Vampire Lord to all of Spain. He'd lived on these two-hundred-plus acres for more than a hundred years, had cleared the forest to expand his fortress, and upgraded various parts every few years. Now, in this age of technology, it was as modern as any palace in the greatest cities on earth. And for most of those years, he and his people—vampire and human—had lived in peace. But now, the *Fortalesa* was being attacked by humans, during daylight hours. The assailants weren't an army—that was too grand a name for what they were. But they were too organized to be called a mob. Someone with a brain was behind this, someone who'd decided his best chance of succeeding was to attack with the sun bright in the sky. He, or she, clearly thought to penetrate the *Fortalesa*, uncover the daylight refuge of every vampire living there, and destroy them, with Lord Xavier himself the most sought-after prize.

Ferran knew all of this. But what he couldn't figure out was why. The attacks seemed pointless, almost suicidal. So many of the attackers had died or were injured, and with nothing to show for it. At least, not yet. Maybe that was its purpose, to wear down the defenders until they made a mistake. But what were the roots of this sudden anti-vampire hysteria? Was it truly human-driven? Or had a powerful vampire from some other territory decided this was his best chance of killing Lord Xavier and taking not only the *Fortalesa*, but the considerable assets that went with it?

His team had held off the day's assault, just as they had the previous day's. Despite the seemingly tireless efforts of their attackers, his people had fought with fierce intensity to defend this place, and not purely out of loyalty to Lord Xavier. The *Fortalesa* was more than a vampire lord's lair—it was their home. Many of his fighters had vampire mates locked away in the dark catacombs, sleeping through the day. Others had husbands or wives among the *Fortalesa*'s human residents, along with children and even grandchildren.

So he knew why *his* people fought. But the attackers seemed driven by old and tired hatreds that had been dormant for decades or longer. What had happened lately, or more likely *who* had happened, to chivy these enemies out of their homes just so they could die outside Lord Xavier's walls? He needed to know. Far better to assassinate one ringleader than to continue mowing down mobs of civilians.

His finger was once more on the release button of his weapon before his brain caught up, his empty magazine dropped and a fresh one slapped into place before the other hit the stone rampart. He wondered how long this lot would keep at it. They wouldn't want to risk the darkness and vampires, but sunset was hours away yet and it seemed likely they'd run out of soldiers before then. Unfortunately, *his* troops were just as human as the enemy's, and growing just as tired. And tired men made mistakes.

He leaned out from the wall's cover and continued firing, picking out the enemy soldiers where they hid among the dense forest surrounding the *Fortalesa*. A flash of a pale face, the spark of a weapon's firing. A shot from his or some other weapon, and the enemy gunman fell.

His arm cramped without warning, a sharp pain that shot from shoulder to elbow, causing his aim to drop. A sudden weakness had him sliding down the wall, while sweat poured down his face and soaked his shirt.

"Commander!" One of his men ran over in a defensive crouch and dropped to his knees. "Are you shot?"

Ferran shook his head. "A chip of stone from the wall, I think. Or maybe a near miss. I'm fine." It was a lie, but a necessary one. He'd told no one about the recurrent pain in his arm, his chest. His people needed him strong, and so he would be. It was that simple.

"Sir, you've been up here for hours. You need to—"

"I need to stay with my fighters. The enemy forces can't last much longer. They'll need time to reach safety before sunset. Wherever the hell their safety lies." The lack of knowledge about the attackers frustrated him. They seemed to melt into the forests like wraiths, which he knew wasn't possible. The enemy was human enough, but Ferran lacked the fighters to both defend the *Fortalesa* and wander the countryside looking for their headquarters, their gathering point. And by the time the vampires woke, giving him freedom to search, there would be no trail for them to follow. That fact alone spoke to a high level of planning. If nothing else, the vamp trackers should have been able to follow the spilled blood from the wounded. But thus far, there'd been nothing, not a trace of trail to pursue. Which was very nearly impossible.

He swore softly, blaming himself for this conundrum. He'd let reconnaissance lag over the past several years, but it had been so long since they'd been attacked. Decades, really. Decades that had aged him beyond what he realized, made him complacent. And though he hadn't yet lost any of his people, he knew he would if these attacks went on much longer.

He needed help before that happened. And not simply more bodies with guns. He needed someone with the intelligence and manpower to investigate and eliminate this threat. Someone to take over a job he was getting too old to perform. Someone to lead the good men and women who had looked to him for leadership all those years. Someone he could trust.

He knew exactly who that person was. The problem would be convincing her to come home.

Chapter Three

Near Bordeaux, France

LAYLA CASALES'S attention flicked from screen to screen as she reviewed video of the hostage exercise her team had just completed. Officially, it had been a success, with the hostage rescued unharmed and none of the bad guys escaping. But she wasn't looking for the "official" outcome. She demanded better than "good" from her people, and usually got it. But not this time.

"You see that?" her lieutenant, Brian Hudson, asked, from where he stood next to her, watching the video just as intently.

"Yeah. Kerry checked the knob on that door, but didn't open it. I wonder why. She knows better."

"That's why." They both watched as Kerry swiveled to take down a bad guy who'd been about to ambush her partner from behind.

"Hmm. But she still should have gone back and checked the door. Too easy for her to become the next ambush victim."

"I'll mention it. Anything else?"

"They're all a bit slower than I'd like," Layla responded. It was nit-picking, but as Captain, she was responsible for every single life on this team. Some would call them mercenaries, but they were more than that. They were a tight band of skilled, disciplined warriors and friends, who chose their battles for reasons that had little to do with politics or greed. They just plain loved to fight, and when that fight occasionally helped the underdog climb to the top, that was icing on the cake.

Unfortunately, their current assignment was leaving dust on their weapons from disuse.

"It's been too long since we've seen real action," Brian commented. "Guarding the rich and beautiful from falling down the garden steps after they've drunk too much wine doesn't exactly reinforce a battle-ready mindset."

Layla nodded silently, then flicked the big display off as the exercise ended. "I know. I'm not sure what I can do about it, though. We can't exactly hire out as mercenaries on the side. Our current contract with Clyde Wilkerson, who happens to *love* these vineyards, doesn't permit it."

Brian chuckled. "That's the only reason why?"

"You know what I mean. We're not allowed to work in any war zones—with a *very* broad definition of war zone."

"Maybe you can persuade Wilkerson to give us a month off, no questions asked. I'm sure we could find a job hot enough to get the juices flowing."

"Maybe. I'll think on it. For now, go ahead and—" Her cell phone's buzz interrupted them. She glanced at the display. "I have to take this. Release the boys and girls. The exercise was fine. I'll have a private word with Kerry."

"Yes, ma'am. See you in the barracks," he said, though their sleeping accommodations hardly qualified as such. The entire team was housed in what Clyde Wilkerson called the "guest cottage," a fucking ten bedroom *house* with a view of the vineyards beautiful enough to grace postcards. It was so big and comfortable that it almost compensated for the absence of *action*. Almost. Her people were all adrenaline junkies, and this assignment just wasn't delivering the necessary rush.

Layla didn't wait for Brian to leave before going back to her call. She didn't care if he overheard. She had no secrets from him. Well, maybe one. But they were best friends, not lovers. Except for anything dealing with the private security firm they'd started together nearly ten years ago, there was no expectation of a midnight confessional. She tapped the screen on her cell phone.

"Mama?" She swung a chair around and straddled it backwards.

"Laylita, *mija*. You are well?"

She knew some people considered it odd, but she and her parents usually spoke English to each other. It had begun when Layla was only six years old—an exercise to help her learn the language, with the side benefit of refreshing her parents' skills at the same time. The habit had only been reinforced when she'd gone off to America for college.

"Of course I'm well, Mama. Tell me what's wrong."

"Why would something be wrong?"

"Because you never call on your own. Papa calls, and you talk."

"Pfft. You think you're so smart."

"I am smart. I'm *your* daughter. Tell me."

"It's your papa. He's . . . "

Alarm spiked. "He's what? Is he sick? Did something happen?"

"*No te preocupes, mija.*"

"Don't worry? What do you mean? Is there something to worry about?"

"*Oy*, I should never have called."

"Mama," Layla said sternly. "It's too late for that. What's going on?"

"He won't admit it," her mother said reluctantly, "but there's something wrong. He's so tired, and I think . . ." She sighed. "I think his chest hurts sometimes."

Fear hardened to a rock in Layla's chest. "What does the doctor say?"

"Laylita, would I be calling you if the old fool had seen a doctor?"

Of course not. "I'm coming home," she declared. "We're not busy here. Brian can handle it."

"I don't know—" Her mother's voice cut off as the familiar deep tones of her father sounded on the other end of the call. "It's Layla, *mi amor*. She called to talk."

Ah ha, so that was the way of it. Her father obviously didn't know her mother had done the calling. The big question was whether he knew her mother suspected he was having chest pains. *Chest pains*, for fuck's sake!

"Layla, *mija*." Her father's voice was as warm and loving as always, no sign of stress. "I was about to call you. How are things among the French, and that foolish billionaire who hired you to do nothing?"

"The same. I was just telling Mama that I'm coming for a visit. We're all going crazy here. It's too boring."

"You never should have signed that stupid contract. You're too good for what he has you doing."

"That's what Brian says. I can't disagree."

"Hmm. How much longer does he own you?"

"Brian?"

Her father *tsked* loudly. "Your billionaire."

"Wilkerson, right. One more year, maybe less. He wants us to sign another contract, but I'm not sure. He needs security, but he doesn't need *us*. I'm beginning to think he considers my team a trophy he can boast about to his guests."

"You could come back here. I'd love to retire and play with my grandchildren instead of going up and down the battlement stairs."

"What are you doing up on the wall? The damn gates are always open."

"Not so much lately. A bad element has moved in."

"Inside the *Fortalesa*?"

"No, no. Lord Xavier would never permit such a thing, you know that."

Privately, she thought *Lord* Xavier was worst element of all, but she wouldn't say so to her father. "You don't have any grandchildren," she reminded him instead.

"I know. I still hope. But for now, I'll settle for advice. When are you coming?"

Layla's eyes squinted in thought. First her mother, with the SOS about her father's health, and now he, himself, was pushing her to visit *soon*. Something was up for sure, and if she wanted to know what it was, she'd have to talk to them in person. Damn it. She loved her parents, but Barcelona was the last place on earth she wanted to be. She'd convinced them to visit her in France last year, but apparently that wasn't an option this time.

She clenched her jaw. *Time to suck it up.* "I'll fly in tomorrow. Don't pick me up. I'll get a car."

"Tomorrow," her father said to her mother.

"Tomorrow, then, *mija*. Safe travels," she called happily.

Chapter Four

Sant Andreu De Llavaneres, Barcelona, Spain

XAVIER WOKE ABRUPTLY as he always did, going from sleep to sharply awake in the space of an eye blink. It had taken him some time to grow accustomed to that aspect of being a vampire. He'd always preferred the Spanish way—the slow, leisurely awareness of voices and aromas drifting up from the kitchens, followed by long, slow muscle stretches, until finally, he'd open his eyes. He sighed. He missed that most, he thought. That and the sunlight warming his bedroom, before his valet knocked and discreetly entered the chamber. He'd never understood how the man knew the moment he woke, or later on, when he'd occasionally entertained an overnight guest, how the valet had known he was *alone*. He'd searched the entire room for spy holes once, when he'd been a teenager with too much energy, though he'd found nothing.

But such things no longer concerned him. He slept in what had been the dungeon of the fortress he'd taken over and made his own. The space no longer deserved the approbation associated with the word, however. It was closer to an elegant hotel than a dank prison, with his quarters larger and more elegant than any of the others. But it was, at the heart of it, still a dungeon, and he felt the cold earth chilling his bones no matter how many lush rugs or elegant tapestries layered the walls and floor. It wasn't the stone or the earth beyond that made it cold. It was a bed that was too big and most nights too empty for one man. Or vampire.

For all that, he was hardly a monk. He'd fucked his share of beautiful women and had sucked the necks of a hell of a lot more. He didn't really have a choice on that last part... unless he wanted to become a monk in truth and drink blood from plastic bags. He snorted. Not likely. Celibacy didn't suit him.

He sat up and swung his legs over the side of the bed, his feet immediately engulfed by the deep rugs. "Right," he muttered, then spat out a long curse in Spanish and faced the night, which brought plenty of problems of its own. He'd been all but unconscious through the day, but that didn't mean he'd been unaware of what was going on. He was a vampire lord. In his own and some others' estimation, he was also the most powerful vampire in Europe. Especially since Raphael from America had done him the favor of destroying that French bitch Mathilde, and then taken out the few others who'd either supported her suicidal scheme, or tried to succeed her when it failed. He'd have to thank Raphael for that, if he ever met him.

That brought a smile to his face, one more cynical than cheery. He'd been in the same room with the powerful western vampire lord, just over a century ago. He'd never felt such overwhelming power from another vampire, and had no desire to cross paths with him again. In point of fact, it was that desire which was at the core of his strategy for Europe.

Xavier had no personal ambitions to rule more than Spain, but he did have plans for greater Europe that mirrored what Raphael had achieved in North America. He'd taken the first step to realize those plans almost a year ago, when he'd convened a meeting of Europe's most powerful vampires in the dimly lit back room of an ordinary French tavern.

But while the gathering had served its purpose, it hadn't insulated him from the kind of petty attacks his *Fortalesa* had endured over the last few days. This was not the work of a powerful vampire, setting up to challenge him for Spain. This was something else, though he hadn't yet figured out *what* exactly it was. It was frustrating and didn't put him in a happy frame of mind as he considered whether he should take the time to feed before pursuing whoever was responsible for the injuries to his daylight guards, and the fucking *insult* to himself.

All he'd ever wanted, from the first moment he'd woken to the terrible craving that would shape the rest of his very long life, was blood. Well, that and sex, though the two commonly went together. He much preferred his blood directly from the vein of a woman drowning in the sexual ecstasy of climax, her pussy hot and wet as she strained beneath him.

His cock stiffened in anticipation before he admitted to himself that while he would enjoy sinking his fangs into a delicate neck, he didn't *need* to. Not tonight. He'd drunk long and lavishly the previous evening from one of the wealthy *esposas* in attendance at a grand party thrown by the mayor of the town below his *Fortalesa*. The *human* mayor, who was wealthy himself, appreciated the role Xavier's presence played in keeping their town safe and free of criminals.

The party had been held for no reason, other than to celebrate the wealth of those attending. Xavier had gone for political reasons of his own, but also because he'd known he would find an attractive and willing meal. So many of the rich women in this part of the countryside spent long weekdays decorating and redecorating their homes, or getting drunk on wine with friends, while their husbands remained in Barcelona until the weekend, conducting all sorts of business, some of which was undoubtedly in the bedroom. So, why shouldn't the ladies enjoy the same? Especially since he was always happy to help.

A chuckle escaped his lips, quickly banished by his recollections of the day he'd just spent sleeping. He'd been aware of the battle raging beyond the walls of his *Fortalesa*, had sensed the fear and pain of those who'd fought or been injured.

These attacks had seemed nothing more than an irritant at first—the kind they'd dealt with in the past, whenever a few local *matones*, bored and restless, had gotten it into their heads to dare each other to harass the vampires in the big stone castle.

But this latest crisis was no idle dare among foolish humans with more courage than brains. Guards had been wounded today, one seriously. He had to stop this before someone was killed. He would have no choice then, but to hunt every enemy fighter to the ground and kill them. He would not, *could* not, tolerate even a petty challenge to his authority, and these assaults had now gone well beyond petty. It didn't matter that this enemy had chosen to strike only in sunlight, when no vampires were at risk—or could be a risk to *them*. He valued the human fighters who'd manned the walls today, some of whom had *bled* for him, just as much as he did the vampires who were sworn to his service—many of whom he'd Sired himself.

He took a quick, hot shower, toweled off without ceremony, then brushed his teeth and got dressed. His fingers served to comb back his long, black hair, and a quick look in the mirror told him he could go another night without shaving. He didn't bother with anything more than a t-shirt and jeans, though he wore combat lace-up boots, despite the warm, humid nights of the Spanish summer.

Xavier returned greetings as he climbed the stairs and walked the halls of the *Fortalesa*, but his thoughts were somber. He was too aware of the scent of spilled blood, of the miasma of fear floating like an unwelcome stench beneath the polite ritual. He stopped one of the men he knew worked closely with his daytime commander, Ferran Casales.

Ferran was growing inevitably older. One of the great tragedies of being a vampire was losing your human friends. In the earliest years after his turning, he'd tried to avoid those friendships, to avoid the inevitable loss. But for one in his position and with his ambitions, it was impossible. And now, there were Ferran and his wife, Ramlah. His long strides faltered briefly when he thought of Ferran's wife, who looked so much like her daughter, Layla. Though looks were all they shared. The fierce and beautiful Layla would never have settled into the role of a commander's wife. No, she'd have insisted on manning the battlements herself, probably ordering about all the other fighters—men and women—just as she no doubt did with that group of mercenaries she'd brought together. Details were sparse when it came to Layla, especially since he was unwilling to probe too obviously. Ferran and Ramlah were clearly proud of their world-traveling daughter, but Layla must have secured their promise to remain silent on any but the most general details of her life. She'd probably told them it had to do with security or some such thing, which would have been a lie.

He wished it was that simple, but he didn't blame Layla for letting her parents believe the convenient fiction. The truth was probably not something she wanted to share. Nor was he anxious to have it known, either. He just wished it hadn't driven her so far away, and for so long. He missed her more than he would admit. She'd been barely out of her teens when she'd left to attend university in the U.S., far too young to be involved with a vampire—a much older vampire. But he'd known from the moment he'd first met the wild and fearless child she'd been that Layla Casales would play an important role in his life. He couldn't have said what that role would be, or why he was so certain of it, though. He'd gained no particular foresight skill when he'd been reborn as a vampire. The gifts bestowed upon newly turned vampires by a seemingly random fate were as varied as the vampires themselves, but his own talents lay in an entirely different direction.

Even so, he'd *known* that Layla was meant to be his, and had cursed the fact that they'd met with such a vast distance in age and experience between them.

"My lord." The raspy voice of Layla's father, Ferran, greeted him as he entered the courtyard. He had to fight the feeling of embarrassment trying to flush his cheeks, knowing he'd been entertaining thoughts of the man's daughter that were decidedly not innocent.

"Ferran," he said warmly, greeting him like the old friend he was. "You're well?"

"Yes, my lord. No casualties from today's attack. They were as determined as ever, but it had the feel of a last-minute strike." He shook his head. "I just don't understand the enemy. They've taken far more casualties than we have, and several deaths, which we have not." The old man crossed himself quickly, a superstitious act aimed at securing the continued blessing of his god.

Xavier didn't mind the gesture. Contrary to popular myth, religious symbols had no effect on vampires.

"Walk with me," Xavier said, as the two of them started across the wide courtyard. "I'm as confused as you are. We need to find out who's driving these attacks. Someone is programming people to risk their lives, but for what? Until we discover who, we won't know the answer to why."

Ferran gave a slow nod, as Xavier's lieutenant, Chuy Bolivar, joined them. "Chuy," Ferran said, echoing Xavier's own greeting.

"My lord. Ferran," he said, then slid into place next to Xavier, without missing a step.

"Ferran was just briefing me on today's attack," Xavier said.

Chuy's lips tightened in anger. "Those people. They die for nothing."

Xavier disagreed. "I've dealt with too many humans in my life to believe that. It's possible they've been brainwashed and don't know the truth, but *they* don't believe it's for nothing when they take up arms against us. Humans don't risk their lives for no reason. Not if they're sane. And there are too many in these assaults—men and women both—for all of them to be insane." He shook his head. "No, someone is behind this."

"Then we must discover who," Chuy insisted, not bothering to conceal his frustration. He'd been sworn to Xavier for over a century, more than long enough to understand that Xavier didn't want sheep among his followers, he wanted wolves. Especially as his lieutenant.

"I've inquired some," Ferran said, as the three men took seats in the commander's office. Ferran sat on a worn leather couch to avoid assuming the seat of authority behind his desk. Xavier ruled this *Fortalesa*, but Ferran had an authority of his own, and they all knew it. "But I must be honest," the human continued. "I'm unwilling to deplete the *Fortalesa*'s daylight security contingent by sending too many fighters out at one time. Whoever these attackers are, they must be living locally—though they aren't necessarily local people. I suspect they've been brought in, perhaps even masquerading as ordinary tourists, to stage these attacks.

Lord Xavier has lived here peacefully for too long to have that many enemies among the locals. Nor does he have any with so much hatred that they're willing to die in the effort."

"You're saying you need more men," Xavier commented. "But how can we trust new recruits? It would be too easy for our enemies to slip some of their own into the mix."

Ferran was nodding. "Agreed, my lord. I'm in discussions with someone I trust to bring in a team of skilled fighters who are also experienced in reconnaissance and investigation."

Xavier gave him a silent, inquisitive look.

But Ferran shook his head. "I'd rather wait until they've agreed. I still might hire someone else, subject to your final approval, of course."

Xavier scowled lightly. "Don't wait too long, Ferran. So far, we've been lucky. That *will not* last. Now, gentlemen, what else do I need to know tonight?"

Barcelona, Eleven years ago

LAYLA'S NERVES danced as she waited in the shelter of the trees for Lord Xavier to return from his patrol around the outside wall of the *Fortalesa*. He and at least one of his vampires did a sweep of the perimeter every night. Usually his lieutenant, Chuy, was with him, sometimes a few other vamps, but he was never alone. She'd made an art form out of eavesdropping on the vampire lord, and so she knew that the others were there for Xavier's protection. She also knew he didn't think their support was necessary, but went along with it for decorum's sake. Apparently, powerful vampire lords never went anywhere without security. Which seemed odd to her, since it was the vampire lords who least needed someone else's protection. Her papa had tried to explain it to her, and she'd listened dutifully. But it seemed there were still things she didn't understand, even though she was always being told how mature she was for her nineteen years of age.

She only wished her so-called maturity extended beyond the assignment of extra duties—*specifically* to the realm of love and relationships. Which was why she was currently lurking in a dark forest, with the night mists swirling as she waited for Xavier to return. Because he was hers. Not formally, not yet. But she'd always known they were meant to be together, even though she'd been too young. She'd accepted their age difference, accepted the truth that had kept them apart for so many years. But now she was an adult. Today was her birthday, her *nineteenth* birthday, old enough to make her own choices, to pick her own boyfriend. Her own . . . lover. She shivered when she thought about what that meant. She'd kissed other boys. She'd even touched a boy's penis two months ago, feeling it grow and harden beneath her fingers, while he squeezed her breasts. It had all been more weird than passionate, but, you know, interesting. She hadn't known boys' penises could do that, but when she'd thought about it later, it had made sense. I mean, she knew where babies came from, for fuck's sake.

And why the hell was she thinking about that? She wasn't waiting in the dark forest for some *boy*. She was waiting for Xavier, Vampire Lord of Spain, and the love of her life. Not like in some fairy tale, either. She wasn't stupid. She knew they had differences—some of them big—like how old he was. But that couldn't change the way she *felt*, the way she'd *always* felt about Xavier. She couldn't even explain it. She'd simply always known he was hers. And tonight, they'd finally be together, the way she'd always known they would be.

Okay, so he was a lot older than she was, but he was older than everyone, even though he didn't look it. He was tall—which was really important, because she was, too. And he was beautiful. One of her friends insisted only women could be beautiful, but that was just stupid. If there'd ever been a beautiful man, it was Xavier. And then, there was his voice. Not harsh or grating, like some men's. Not raspy or high-pitched like others. It was low and melodious, the words flowing from one to the other like a song. A love song just for her. She sighed at the thought, knowing tonight they would finally acknowledge the chemistry between them and admit that their destinies were entwined, that soon she would stand by his side, sharing his responsibilities, lightening the burden of duty that came with being a vampire lord. And not just for the *Fortalesa*, either.

She went to school with kids from the surrounding towns, and they all said how their parents and grandparents thought Xavier and the other vampires in the *Fortalesa* were great neighbors. And how wonderful it was to have such a strong protector on the hill. She'd been so proud of him then, so proud to know he was hers, and that someday, she'd fight by his side, protecting both the *Fortalesa* and the people in the town below.

But though Xavier was the most powerful vampire and had the most responsibility, he'd always made time for her, even when she'd been a little kid. He'd always taken time to ask serious questions, like what was she studying at school, and was she going to university. And then, he'd tell her about events from his own life, especially once he'd discovered she might study history at university, and maybe even become a professor.

Of course, if she *did* teach at a university, it would have to be one close to home. Near her parents, of course, but mostly to Xavier. Because he was. . . . She heard voices and looked around guiltily. No one knew about her and Xavier yet. Not even her best friends. But they would after tonight, after he finally admitted she was old enough. She'd seen Xavier staring at her lately, caught him more than once looking at her in surprise, as if wondering when she'd suddenly grown up. She was tall and long-legged, with long, black hair that fell in big curls down her back. And she had *tetas*, too. Not the tiny ones she'd had at thirteen, but full-on breasts, like her mother's.

She was still younger than the other women Xavier dated. Because of course, he *had* dated while waiting for her to get old enough. But he never kept one woman around for long. And for the record, none of them were more than a few years older than she was now. What did a few years matter when love was involved?

She scowled. A lot apparently, since once her breasts had gotten big enough to matter, he'd stopped hugging her when he visited her parents. Which didn't happen as often as it used to, because Xavier had begun to host formal dinner parties instead. Parties with just the adults. She'd been angry about that at first, and then hurt when it seemed he was avoiding her.

But she knew his heart. He respected her and her parents, and was aware that they were annoyingly old-school when it came to courtship, as they called it. Talk about old-school. Hell, her mama and papa hadn't even been alone together until their wedding night. They never discussed it, obviously, especially not with her, but she got the message. They hadn't had sex until they were married, and thought she should do the same. Like that was going to happen. Hell, most of her friends had already gone almost all the way with their boyfriends. And the only reason she hadn't was because *her* boyfriend was a badass vampire who apparently was just as old-school as her parents. Which made sense, since he was even older than they were. But when he'd dated those other women, they'd always spent the night, or even the day sometimes. And she wasn't stupid enough to think they'd been playing cards and sipping wine.

But tonight would change all that. She could finally show him, once and for all, that she was a woman, and no longer a child he had to shelter from real life. And she was going to do that in the most convincing way possible—she was going to seduce him. She'd already set up everything in an old chapel deep in the forest that her friends all used as a make-out place. She'd been there once, too, with that boy whose penis she'd touched. They'd gone out with friends, but when he'd walked her home, they hadn't taken the road. Instead, they'd walked through the trees and ended up at the old chapel. At least, that's what everyone said it had been. It was so old that no one really knew. It was small, only one room, with crumbling walls and nothing but a makeshift ceiling that someone had fashioned out of tree branches. The cute boy had brought along a blanket, so she knew he'd been planning to take her there all along. And she'd known what he'd wanted.

He hadn't gotten it, of course. And besides, that was history. Tonight was what mattered. She knew the chapel would be empty, because all her friends were at a big soccer tournament. She'd faked an illness to explain her decision to stay behind, and then made her plans. She'd arranged the chapel with a lantern, blankets, and a bottle of wine. She was even (*gulp*) naked under her jacket, so there'd be no need to slow down—no excuse to do so—once she'd begun her seduction. If she kept her hands in her jacket pockets, he shouldn't notice until she was ready, and by then, the mood would be set. Xavier would confess his long-frustrated love for her, she would fall into his arms, and they'd make love.

She heard his voice first, giving Chuy some last-minute orders, probably based on something they'd discovered during their patrol. Just the sound of him made her smile and had butterflies dancing in her stomach. She couldn't believe this was finally going to happen, that *they* were going to happen.

Waiting until Chuy had gone ahead to talk to one of the night sentries, she stepped out of the shadows and called his name softly. "Xavier."

He spun at once, his beautiful eyes shining as they easily located her, despite the dark night.

"Layla? What are you doing out here alone?"

She was suddenly nervous. Her plan had seemed so simple when she'd devised it, and again when she'd been setting up the chapel earlier. But now, confronted with the sheer force of his presence, her hands trembled inside her pockets. "I um . . . there was something I thought you should see, but—"

His voice softened. "What is it? Is something wrong?"

Her pulse raced at his tone, and when he reached out to touch her shoulder, she thought her heart would leap out of her chest. Emboldened by this show of affection, she said, "I found something, some*place* in the forest, deep in the trees, that I think you should see." A small voice inside her head sounded an alarm at this change in plans, from a straightforward seduction to . . . something else. A deception that Xavier might take very badly once he discovered it.

But it was too late.

He was already telling Chuy to go on without him, his arm held out wide in invitation, indicating she should lead the way and saying, "After you."

"Yes," she agreed, afraid if she said anything more that he'd hear her voice quake with nerves. The walk through the forest was quick and quiet. She'd already plotted out the best route to the chapel, and though he attempted once to ask questions about where they were going, she'd said only, "It's not far," then put her head down and concentrated on not tripping. She had her small penlight, which she kept aimed at the ground in front of her, as much to light her way as to avoid blowing out his night vision. She did that instinctively, something every child in the *Fortalesa* was taught, once they were old enough to understand. In a nighttime emergency, it was important not to get in the way of the vampires who might well be fighting for everyone's life.

When the chapel was close enough that she could catch glimpses of it through the trees, she slowed, wondering if she should say something before they got there or—

"Is that the place?"

She jumped at the sound of his voice, but kept walking.

"That's just an old shrine or something, Layla. It's been there for . . . hundreds of years. From before I took over the *Fortalesa*."

"Yes, but—"

"Why are we here?" he demanded, suspicion suddenly blooming in his voice.

"It's inside," she insisted. "The thing you need to see. It's inside."

He studied her a moment. "If you were not the daughter of someone I trusted, I'd think you were trying to set me up for some mischance, to put it kindly. But as you *are*, and since there is no one inside that crumbling bit of stone. . . . Let's see what you have to show me."

Walking ahead of him, she ducked through the low opening and spun to look up at him as he straightened to his full height. She saw his eyes take in the lit lantern, the wine bottle, and the blankets.

"What the fuck—"

"I just wanted to talk to you, and I knew you wouldn't come if I'd asked you plainly. You won't even look at me anymore. It's as if I have a disease or something. But I know it can't be that—" She hated that she'd begun to cry, but couldn't seem to stop. "—because you're a vampire and you can't get sick."

"Layla—"

"Laylita," she corrected, fighting back a sob. "You used to call me Laylita."

"That was before," he muttered, so low that she didn't think she was supposed to hear.

"Before what?" she cried. "Is there something wrong with me?"

"No, no." He took her in his arms . . . finally. "It's just . . . you've grown so much, and . . . you should be talking to boys . . . young men your own age. It's not right for you to—"

"But I don't want them. You're better than they are, and I miss you."

He was holding her so close now that she could feel his penis. Not hard, not yet. But she hugged him back so tightly that their bodies touched, and it began to grow.

"Layla," he whispered. "*Princesa.*"

Her heart soared at the endearment, especially given the physical proof of his attraction, which was now blatantly obvious, despite his weak attempts to put distance between them. He was a vampire and could have pushed much harder, if he'd really wanted to, she reasoned, ignoring the obvious argument that he was trying not to *hurt* her.

"This isn't . . . I'm sorry, but—"

"I know I'm a lot younger than you," she persisted. "But I'll be older soon, and it's not my fault I was born when I was. Besides, all those women I've seen you with are younger than you too, and—"

"But they're older than you are," he said firmly, then set her away from him, so their bodies were no longer touching.

She looked up then, studying his face, trying to think of something, some way she could salvage this. Make him realize . . . hell, make him *admit* his feelings for her. "All right," she said finally. "Just . . . sit down and have a glass of wine with me. Just a glass. So I don't feel like a total loser. Like a monster or something that you can't stand to look at."

"Stop," he snapped. "You're not a fucking monster. You're beautiful and smart and—"

"Then sit with me," she demanded, taking his arm and pulling him down, putting all her weight into it. She didn't look at him when he sat, or when he put enough distance between them that their legs didn't touch. She simply poured the wine and handed him a glass, then raised her own in a toast. "To love," she said, meeting his eyes.

"To friends," he amended sternly.

She smiled and drank, her gaze never leaving his. "You have the most beautiful eyes," she said quietly.

"I shouldn't be here." He drained his glass in one quick toss down his throat and started to rise, but before he could get there, she took his hand, slid it inside her open jacket over her breast, and fell backward, pulling him with her. He was strong, she reminded herself. If he really wanted to stop, he would. More determined than ever, she reached down, quickly unzipped his pants, and wrapped her fingers around his cock with a surprised gasp. He was so much bigger than she'd imagined, and growing even larger as she shaped it with her fingers, feeling it respond to her, reveling in the press of his hand on her breast. She moaned, overwhelmed with unfamiliar sensations, dizzy with joy, wondering if he'd—

"Fuck!" he snarled and shoved himself away, clearly furious.

She didn't understand, didn't know why, because she was still floating on a cloud of delicious sensation. Her whole body was tingling with a pleasure she'd never known was possible. She'd sure as hell never felt anything like this before, which only proved she'd been right about everything. She raised her head and smiled . . . only to find Xavier on his feet, his back turned as he zipped himself up.

"What—" The words caught in her throat when she saw his face. He wasn't trying to be gentle anymore. His eyes were so cold that she shivered and pulled her jacket closed over her naked breasts.

"I apologize, Layla," he said flatly, although his eyes didn't reflect his words. "This was . . . reprehensible on my part. I never should have permitted it to get this far. You needn't be concerned, however. You're in no danger from me in the future. I'm sure you can find your way back," he added. "Good night."

Then he left her there. Cold, half-naked, brokenhearted and thoroughly humiliated.

The next night, she looked, but couldn't find him. Nor was he around the night after that. Until finally, in between bites of breakfast cereal, she asked her father casually, "Is Lord Xavier in town?"

He shook his head without looking up from the reports he was reading. "No, he'll be away for a bit, I'm afraid. One of his people, a good friend, called for help. He's in danger of being overrun by his enemies, so Lord Xavier took several fighters with him. I think he'll be gone a few months. That's what it means to be a vampire lord, you know. He defends the entire territory—all of Spain. He'll probably bring home some new fighters when he comes back. He usually does. In fact, I wouldn't be surprised if he finds a wife this time."

"A mate," she whispered, staring at her cereal. "That's what vampires call it. But . . . why do you think he'll do that? Get a mate, I mean."

"That's not something I want to discuss with *la meva nena,*" he said, stroking a hand down her hair. "Xavier is a man, *mija*. He needs a woman to share his life, just as I have your mama."

Her mother snorted her reaction from where she stood at the counter, chopping meat and vegetables for the stew she'd serve for dinner. "Xavier needs a *vampire* woman," she said. "Someone who's a fighter, not a cook. And not one of those silly women he takes to his bed, either."

Layla hiccupped as she fought back a sob.

"Is something wrong, *mija*?" her father asked. "Are you sick?"

She put down her spoon, convinced she'd throw up if she ate one more bite. Xavier was looking for a mate? "No, I'm just . . . not hungry this morning." Standing, she kissed her father's cheek, then her mother's, and managed to get outside before they could ask any more questions.

She didn't go to school that day. She went to the chapel instead. The wine was gone. She'd thrown the bottle against the wall in a fit of rage after Xavier had left, something she now regretted, since she wouldn't have minded a little help forgetting what he'd done. What he was probably doing right now. The blankets were still there, so she laid down on top of the pile, pulled one over herself, and cried long and hard, unable to stop, even when her chest hurt and her eyes burned from tears that were long past dried up. She'd never known such pain, had never known it was even possible to hurt that much. And she'd never, ever expected Xavier would be the one to cause it.

Approaching Barcelona, Present day

LAYLA WOKE WITH a start, embarrassed to find her cheeks wet, angry that Xavier still had the power to make her cry. She'd left the *Fortalesa* soon after that, had gone to California and UCLA, where she'd met Brian Hudson. He'd been Army ROTC—Reserve Officer Training Corps. It was how he'd managed to attend university. The Army paid his tuition in exchange for him enlisting upon graduation. Layla had been intrigued by the idea, not just the free tuition, but the training. Learning to *fight*. She didn't like to admit Xavier had anything to do with the choice she'd made to enlist, but she couldn't deny, to herself anyway, that she'd experienced a visceral satisfaction with every new strategy she learned, every tactic, every *weapon*. And when she'd proven to be better than the others, better even than the men—stronger, smarter, a better leader—she was promoted above them. Some of them even followed her out of the army and became the core of her own fighting unit. They were respected throughout the world, fighters who garnered the highest price, who took the toughest assignments and always came home victorious. Brian had gone with her, too, without a whisper of reluctance or resentment that *she* was their captain. He was her partner, her lieutenant, her best friend.

But never her lover. Layla hadn't found her mate in all the years she'd been gone. Had never managed to silence the soft voice that whispered from her soul, telling her she'd already met the only man who could be hers. A vampire, who didn't want her.

She jolted upright, angry that Xavier had intruded on her dream, her thoughts, when she'd considered him gone years ago. It must be the situation—the fact that she was returning to Barcelona, to the vampire lord's *Fortalesa*, where she was bound to run into him. She could always stay in the town instead. There were plenty of motels . . . though she'd have to come up with *something* to tell her parents, some excuse for not sleeping in her old bed, in the room they still considered hers.

Damn. She crossed and uncrossed her legs, trying to get comfortable in the lumpy airline seat. She could feel every metal brace and spring in the damn thing, but not an inch of padding, and it pissed her off. Couldn't they at least give her ass a *cushion*?

Okay, so she was in a foul mood. She loved her parents, but hated going back to the *Fortalesa*. Xavier was the reason she'd left Spain all those years ago, and now she had no choice but to go back. She only hoped her heart could take it.

Barcelona, Spain

LAYLA SEARCHED the terminal gate area, convinced she'd find her parents waiting eagerly, though she'd told them not to bother. At one point, she was certain she'd heard her father's booming voice and had spun, expecting his arms to enfold her. But no, it was some other poor soul's family who'd shown up *en masse* to greet their returning scion. She breathed a sigh of relief and kept walking, but couldn't shake the perverse feeling that their absence worried her. Her father had always come to pick her up. Sometimes her mother wasn't with him, but *he* was always there. Damn it, maybe something was *seriously* wrong with his health. The idea had her chest tightening with worry. Her parents were the only constant in her life. They'd always been there for her. Hell, they worked with vampires. There was no reason they couldn't *always* be there, if they wanted. Surely the great and powerful *Xavier* could spare the occasional ounce of blood to prolong the lives of two people who'd devoted their lives to him? Selfish asshole.

She marched down the rows of rental cars and schooled herself into the right mindset for this visit. Xavier wasn't the asshole who'd charmed an impressionable young teenager just because he could. He wasn't the arrogant jerk who'd broken that teenager's heart without so much as a casual thought. For this visit, he was someone her parents respected and probably loved nearly as much as they loved her. Someone they'd served for their entire adult lives. A good man, an honest man.

Hah!

She slammed the trunk on the mid-sized rental sedan, already missing the big SUVs her team used. But it made no sense to get anything bigger when it was just her. Still, she felt as if there was a target painted on the flimsy vehicle door, with a big sign that said "Hit me!" in bright red letters.

She made a sound of disgust, as much at herself as the situation. She was a grown ass woman with a grown ass job, and a kick *ass* team of her own, every one of whom considered *her* the kick ass-iest of them all. So what the fuck was wrong with her?

She managed a smile for the nice man standing watch over the garage exit, and turned toward the *Fortalesa*. Toward home. But was it really that, after all this time? She rolled her eyes in disgust . . . at herself. Of course it was. Her *parents* were there. Hell, why else had she been pushing them to join her in France? Because *they* were her home.

"Suck it up, babe," she muttered, then veered onto the highway that would take her to Xavier.

LESS THAN AN hour later—and far too soon—Layla turned onto the long narrow road leading up to the ancient hillside fortress that housed Spain's vampire lord and a good part of the country's population of vampires. Her parents had been living there when she was born, although thankfully, the blessed event had taken place in a Barcelona hospital. When she'd been a child, she'd assumed that was because the vampires would have been drawn to all the blood from the birthing and endangered her life. But she'd discovered later that it was simply due to the absence of a qualified physician in the *Fortalesa*, and nothing to do with blood or vampires. She'd found that vastly irritating in its simplicity. Talk about perverse thinking.

She'd only been back here once in the dozen years she'd been gone, and that time was only a single daytime visit after she'd graduated university. Since then, she'd persuaded her parents to meet her at one elegant hotel or other—some in Barcelona, some not. And after she'd contracted with Clyde Wilkerson to live on his French vineyard and *theoretically* protect it from she didn't know what, her parents had visited France twice.

But this time . . . this time she'd have to suck it up and stay at the *Fortalesa*. It was the only way to ensure she learned what was really happening with her father's health. "Don't be a coward," she muttered as she rounded the final curve of green forest. "It was more than ten years ago, for fuck's sake. He probably doesn't even remember it." *It* being the night she'd humiliated herself. The night the fucking vampire had made it clear she was nothing special.

"What did he know?" she muttered and shoved aside all thoughts of "that night," while she looked up at the huge fortress in front of her. She automatically scanned the *Fortalesa*'s walls, taking in the thick walls and battlements, the modifications to accommodate modern weapons. The solid merlons of the battlement walls had been built up to form a series of square bunkers which surrounded the defending shooters, and provided two windows suitable for weapons up to and including machine guns. Her eye caught on some work being carried out on the portion of wall alongside the road, and closest to the surrounding forest. A three-man team was up there performing repairs of some kind. She squinted, trying to see more clearly in the morning glare, and frowned. That sure as hell looked like fresh damage, as if the wall had been struck by something heavy. Her frown deepened. It could be old damage that had recently become a problem. The *Fortalesa* was very, very old, after all. But it sure as hell didn't look old. She'd seen enough fighting, including the kind of heavy bombardment that could inflict that sort of damage to a strong wall. She also recognized fresh stone when she saw it. And this was damn fresh. It made her reconsider her mother's warning, and her father's easy cheer in response. Had her father been injured in battle? Had the *Fortalesa* been attacked? Was that what her mother had been warning her about?

She drove the final fifty yards to the entrance, expecting the huge gates to open before she got there. But they remained solidly shut, and she didn't like that any more than she did the damaged wall.

A man on the wall above the gate watched her approach and stop at an electronic call box that hadn't been there on her last visit—which admittedly had been years ago. Without saying a word, the guard studied her through her windshield as she pushed the intercom button and announced her name.

"Layla Casales. I'm here to see my parents, Ferran and Ramlah Casales," she added deliberately.

The guard had ducked back while she was speaking, so she hadn't caught his reaction to her name, or her father's, who also happened to be the guard's commander. But the gates immediately rolled back to either side, moving along metal rails that were inside the wall and looked to have been replaced recently. Security clearly had been improved, and she wondered about the reason as she drove through and into the *Fortalesa*'s huge main yard. There was a well-concealed parking garage around back for the many full-time residents, both vampire and human. But visitors parked at the far end of the yard, near the barracks, where there were several parking spots lined out for that purpose. It felt odd to be a visitor in the place where she'd grown up, but it shouldn't have. She no longer considered the *Fortalesa* her home, and never would again. If not for her parents, she'd never have been there at all.

She was already parked and out of the car, the back door half open while she reached inside for her backpack, when the scent of her mother's perfume filled the air. She turned into Ramlah's embrace, dipping her head to cover the tears that filled her eyes. It didn't matter that she was now a head taller than her mother. In an instant, she was transformed into a child finding comfort in the embrace, in the familiar scents and sounds of home. She hadn't realized how much she'd missed it all until that moment. *Damn it. I am not going to cry like a fucking baby.*

"*Laylita, mija,*" her mother crooned, wrapping her arms around Layla as if she truly was still a little girl.

Layla straightened, which made her so much taller that she had to bend over to hug her mother again. "Mama. How's Papa? How's everything?"

"Perfect now that my daughter has come home. Come, close that door. We'll have tea." Ramlah waited while she slung her backpack over one shoulder, then locked and closed the door of the rental car. Linking their arms together, the two women strolled across the mostly dirt-covered yard.

Layla glanced into her father's office as they passed. It was full daylight, and he was in charge of the *Fortalesa*, but the room was empty. Not a great surprise. He rarely spent time in his office. Ferran Casales liked to be on the wall with his troops, not *sitting behind a damn computer*, as he'd often said.

"Where's Papa?" she asked, as they started up the stairs to the family quarters.

"Oh, he's around somewhere. Now that you're here, he'll join us soon enough."

"He still knows everything that's happening inside these walls, huh?"

"I tell you, *mija*, he's worse than ever. He's hired many people to take over some of his duties, but I swear he's busier than he was before he hired them."

Layla dropped her pack in her childhood bedroom, then settled at the small table in the warm and sunny kitchen. "And what about his heart?"

Her mother didn't meet her eyes. "His heart?"

"Mama, you said he was having chest pains. He should have his heart checked."

Your father insists it was only a pulled muscle."

"Did he see the doctor? Is that what the doctor said?"

"No. He did *finally* agree to see a doctor, and the doctor said . . . " Her mother's lips pursed as if fighting back the next words.

"What? What's wrong?" She couldn't believe even her stubborn father would ignore the most obvious signs of a serious problem. As for her mother . . . she'd always been too willing to go along with what her father wanted. It had always frustrated Layla that her strong and intelligent mother lost half her brain cells and most of her backbone when it came to dealing with her father. Ferran was not a garrulous man, but he *was* perverse enough to enjoy a good argument. And yet she'd never seen or heard a serious disagreement between her parents. "Chest pains could be serious, Mama. We need to catch it as soon as we can. Postponing will only make it worse."

"Make what worse?" her father demanded, his boots thudding on the landing outside the door.

"Papa!" Layla went into his arms, just as she had her mother's, but with a lot less care. Whereas her mother was a petite beauty, her father was big and gruff, with a deep chest and a voice to go with it. His arms tightened around her, still strong and hard with muscle despite his years. "Finally, you come to visit us! It's a wonder you remember how to get here."

She laughed. "A lot's changed, that's for sure. What's with the new gate? At first, I didn't think they were going to let me in."

"You exaggerate. My people all knew you were coming, as does Lord Xavier. He'll be happy to see you."

That was one reunion that was never going to happen, but Layla didn't say anything. If she mentioned it to her parents, they'd insist on knowing why. She hadn't talked about her reasons when she'd left, and she wasn't about to start now.

"Sit, *amor meu*," her mother said, hustling her father over to the table. "I'll pour you a cup."

"A moment, no more," Ferran said, sitting with a weary sigh.

"Busy?" Layla asked casually, dropping down onto the chair next to him.

"*Oy*," he responded fervently. "I've got four fighters still too wounded to fight, and there's so much to do."

"Wounded? How?" she demanded.

Her parents exchanged a silent look. "You might as well tell her," Ramlah said, switching on the gas flame under a freshly filled kettle.

"Tell me what?" She looked at her father. "You got me here with whispered half-secrets, and now it looks as if you're gearing up for the zombie apocalypse. What's going on?"

"Zombies," Ferran muttered, shaking his head.

"Papa. Tell me."

Her father heaved a deep sigh. "I'm getting old, *mija*." He raised his hand when she would have protested. "Don't argue. For once, just listen."

She was shocked into stillness by his words. She'd been his shadow most of her life, the son he'd never had. She'd followed him around, learning everything he did, everything he thought. And he'd been just as devoted to her. He'd never ever criticized her, never told her to *listen for once*. Her reaction must have shown on her face, because he immediately wrapped his arm around her shoulders and pulled her close enough to kiss the side of her head.

"I love you, you know that. But you do love to argue, Laylita. I know," he continued, cutting off her protest. "You get it from me, and I raised you that way. Life can be hard on a woman, and I wanted you strong enough to fight." He chuckled. "I succeeded in that, didn't I? But now, I'm an old man, and I need you to listen."

"I'm listening," she assured him and zipped her lips shut with a finger to make him smile, terrified now by whatever he was about to say. What would she do if her father were seriously ill?

"I've commanded this *Fortalesa* for over forty years, since before you were born. Only the day guard, to be sure. But we all know that's the greatest danger for Lord Xavier and the others, and I'm proud that he's trusted me for so long. But now . . . ." His mouth tightened in irritation. "I made a mistake. We've had peace for so long and we get along well with the humans in the town, with all our neighbors. Lord Xavier is powerful, but fair to his people. They respect that and return it twofold by respecting his rules, and being honest with him." He paused when her mother slipped a cup of tea in front of him, looking up with a smile of thanks, then sipping slowly while she walked around and sat across from him at the table.

"As I said, it's been peaceful, and I took for granted that it would stay that way."

Layla was dying to ask questions, but held back and waited.

"My team here is a good one. They're well-trained and loyal. I haven't slipped that badly. But they're not enough. Their quality is good, but I need twice as many of them to deal with what's happening."

She was all but biting her tongue to keep from demanding to know what the *fuck* was going on. But she was still feeling the sting of his earlier comment, and knew he'd get to it. Eventually.

"We're under attack. Humans," he added, sounding genuinely confused. "Three separate attacks in the last two and half weeks, and only during the daylight. They come out of the trees, armed with good weapons—rifles mostly, a few automatic pistols, and plenty of ammo. They're decent shooters, but not professional. I'm certain they're not trained soldiers—more like civilians who've been given a few lessons."

"Has anyone been hurt?" she asked quietly. She'd grown up with some of the fighters who worked for her father.

He shook his head. "Nothing at first. They seemed to aim at the wall instead of the people, and there weren't that many of them. There were more when they attacked the second time, a week later. More of them and some minor injuries for us. Lord Xavier became concerned then. One attack was a nuisance, a hate crime against vampires. But two? That was something else."

Layla had to fight against the urge to make a face every time he said, "*Lord* Xavier." Not just Xavier. Oh, no. It had to be *Lord*. As if the bastard vampire wasn't just a man like any other.

"But the second attack represented a *major* shift in the battle. Not for us, but for them, because *their fighters* began to die," her father continued, seeming puzzled by their willingness to accept casualties. "My fighters are not like the enemy's. They are well-trained and disciplined and they *will* use the full capability of their weapons in defense of this *Fortalesa*. We have families living here, women and children, civilians. When the guards are under attack, so are *they*. And we fight back." He met her gaze.

"What do they want? And why do they think this will get it for them?" she asked.

"I don't know yet. But someone has to be doing the organizing, getting them those weapons, providing enough training to use them. Unless there's now a store selling MP5s at the *Plaça del Mercadal*." He shook his head. "But so far, I haven't been able to find who is behind the attacks. The coward doesn't lead his people into battle. He huddles somewhere far away."

"Have you followed—?"

He nodded. "We've tried, but they slip away into the forest and hide"—he shrugged—"long enough that my soldiers lose their trail. And this is my own failure. I don't have enough people, much less trained investigators, to track them down. The fighters may be simply returning to their homes. But why are they attacking? They must regroup with their leader at least some time, but I can find no evidence of such meetings. And yet, how else would they coordinate their movements, or know where to pick up fresh ammunition?" He threw his hands up in frustration. "None of it makes sense."

Layla considered everything he'd said. He was right about the terrain. The forest surrounding the *Fortalesa* was nearly endless, covering hills that dipped and rose again with no break in the tree cover. Xavier owned some seventy-two of the surrounding acres, and as far as she knew, had no intention of clearing any of it. He liked the coverage it provided, the privacy and the defense. Now that she had education and training of her own, both from the university and from years spent on battlefields around the world, she understood why Xavier liked his trees, liked the privacy and the defensibility. It would have been even more defensible if he'd cleared a mile-wide killing zone all around the *Fortalesa*, giving the enemy nowhere to hide. But she understood why he hadn't done it. He would have achieved greater defensibility, but the price would have been a near total absence of privacy. Not to mention the splendor of the tree-covered hills, their cool shade in summer and fresh scent in winter. They were simply too beautiful to despoil.

It seemed a fanciful reason for a hard-ass vampire lord, which Xavier definitely was. But he'd always been more than that, for most of her life at least. It was part of why she'd fallen so hard for him.

Her thoughts screeched to a halt. *Had* fallen, she reminded herself. Past tense. She'd been young and stupid. But she wasn't anymore.

"I can recommend some very good people from Madrid," she told her father. "Good fighters who can help you—"

"I don't want *very good* people, *mija*. I want the best."

Her gaze narrowed. Oh no. She got it now. She was absolutely *not* going to fall for this. "The local fighters are excellent, Papa. I've worked with them. I'll give them a call while I'm here." She reached for her cell phone.

It was her mother who stopped her. "Your papa needs your help," Ramlah said in her soft voice. "Not from strangers, Laylita. From you. His daughter."

"Mama. I signed a contract in France. I cannot just—"

"The doctor says he might need an operation."

Layla froze. "Operation?" She looked from one to the other. "Papa?"

"*Sí.*" Her father all but spat the single word. "They want to cut open my heart and—"

"They're not cutting open your heart, Ferran," her mother corrected mildly. "They don't know yet what is wrong. That's why they want more tests. You might need only those stents they talked about. To open your arteries."

Layla's heart was still beating too fast, and she knew her mother was much more stressed than her calm words revealed. It was an act for her father, and Layla tried to do the same. "And if they can't?" she asked. "Put in the stents, I mean."

"Then heart surgery," her mother admitted.

"And they will cut my heart open, as I said."

"Papa," Layla said in exasperation. "Even if you need surgery, that's not how they do it. When are the tests?"

"We have an appointment with the specialist in two days. But only if this stubborn old goat agrees to go."

"Of course you're going," Layla said, genuinely surprised.

"Am I?" her father demanded. "And who will take care of all of this"—he gestured out the window, with its view of the courtyard and the high surrounding wall—"while I'm sick? It might be several weeks before I can do my job the way it needs doing. And who will take care of the *Fortalesa* until then?"

Layla made a *tsking* noise. "Gabino is perfectly capable of—"

"Gabino left two months ago. He moved his family to Madrid to be closer to his wife's parents. They're getting too old to be alone, and her brother lives in Portugal."

"Then who's doing his job while . . . No wonder you're exhausted, Papa. You're trying to do it all yourself, aren't you?"

"No," he said firmly. "I am *not*. I've promoted Danilo from the ranks. She's very smart and very capable. If this were a regular time, a peaceful time, as it's been for fifty years, she'd be fine. But it's not, and Danilo is not yet experienced enough to handle a true crisis. The situation with these human attackers could blow up at any moment."

Layla knew what she had to do. She didn't *want* to, but there was no choice. She was no doctor, but she knew enough. Her father needed his heart looked after, whether with stents or something more serious. Without treatment, he could have a major heart attack, and possibly die. What was the inconvenience and *embarrassment* of dealing with Xavier when measured against her father's life?

She had to help, had to cover for him until he was at least well enough to walk the battlements and order everyone else around.

Layla closed her eyes, trying to steady her stomach. She wanted to throw up at the very idea of staying in the *Fortalesa*, of dealing with Xavier night after night. But she swallowed it down, put her arm around her father's broad shoulders, and said, "Have the tests, Papa. I'll stay until you're better again. I can do this."

Her mother's eyes filled with gratitude, but her father gave her a stubborn look. "You have your own job, and your own people to worry about."

"Brian can handle them, especially now. The man who hired us, Clyde Wilkerson, is in residence at the vineyard for now, and is planning to stay for the next few months. The most that will happen is that drunken party guests will try to walk through the vineyards after dark, and fall in the dirt. Every one of my people is bored to tears. We've been running drills just to stay busy and keep our skills up. My guys will be fighting each other for the chance to fly here and help out. What do you say, Papa? You think I'm good enough to fill your shoes for a while?"

Her father didn't answer right away. He was studying his hands, his fingers as scarred as her own, as battle-marked as any full-time warrior's would be. He seemed to be considering her words, and for a moment, she worried that he *didn't* think she could do the job and was trying to find a way to tell her so. When he finally raised his head, it was to look at her mother. Layla did the same and saw fear shadowing the love in Ramlah's dark brown eyes, fear that she'd lose him, begging him to save himself for her, if for no other reason.

He took his wife's hand across the table, and spoke without looking at Layla. "All right," he croaked, his voice rough with the same emotion that had filled Ramlah's eyes with tears. "When?"

Layla sighed deeply, mostly from relief that her father would go through with seeking help. But a small part of her was sighing because she didn't want to stay in this place. Not even for a single night, much less the weeks it might be before her father was well enough to return to full duties.

"I'll need some time to get up to speed on your personnel and routines. I know a lot's changed since I left. I'll also be bringing some of my people in. They can be here tomorrow. And in the meantime, *you* need to call that specialist and tell him you'll be there."

Her father's jaw tightened for a moment before he cracked it open and said, "Tell me what you need. I'll see you have it."

Chapter Five

THE SKY WAS STILL streaked with the glorious colors of a sun barely fallen behind the horizon when Xavier woke. It was well before any of his vampires, as he was old enough and strong enough to withstand the sun's reflected light, although not even he could have walked beneath the sky before full dark. His early wakening did, however, permit him to take stock of his surroundings, to play back in his mind any daytime events which had penetrated his sleep, giving him time to consider consequences.

He knew there'd been another attack. Though he wasn't convinced that was the right word to describe these assaults. Suicide missions seemed more apt. It was as if the humans *wanted* to sacrifice themselves to achieve some greater goal. Did they think if enough humans were supposedly killed by the vicious vampire lord and his minions, that the local population would rise up and wipe out him and every other vampire in his stronghold? Would they then butcher the humans who lived there, too? Punish them for allying with the bloodthirsty monsters?

He sat up and stood in a single movement, tossing aside the thin sheet which was his only cover. He didn't get cold, not in any season, and not even in his most secure underground chamber. It was a benefit of his vampire blood, or so he assumed, although few of his vampires shared—

His reflections skidded to a halt as a familiar mind abruptly made itself known. He paused his headlong march to the shower and sent his awareness soaring upward, passing through stone floors and thick walls, following the trail of a mind he knew nearly as well as his own, though it had been years since he'd touched it.

When he found her, he smiled slowly. She'd changed in the years since he'd last seen her. But then, of *course* she had. She'd been . . . very young then. Barely an adult. Some might have argued she'd still been a child. But she was definitely an adult now. The taste of her mind was as exhilarating as it had ever been. As sweet, too, despite the discipline that had made her harder and more careful than she'd once been. Even so, there was no mistaking the sense of her. Layla had come home.

He rushed through his shower and dressed quickly, wanting to get upstairs before she left, probably trying to avoid *him*. In all the years she'd been gone, the damn woman hadn't lingered so much as a minute past sunset on the rare occasions when she visited her parents. Mostly she hadn't come to the *Fortalesa* at all, but had met them in the city, or in some other country. He'd kept track of her, despite her avoidance of him. He'd known where she was living, where she traveled, and where she and her fellow mercenary fighters were deployed. There'd also been Ferran's proud updates on her progress through university and later, when she'd been an officer in the U.S. military, and later still when she'd brought together a small group of experienced fighters to form her own group. Ferran worried, but the warrior in him was proud of his only child, proud of her prowess in battle, of her skill as a leader.

But for all that, Xavier was certain that Layla had never confessed to her father her true reasons for staying away.

He took an extra few minutes to check his appearance in the mirror, to brush his shoulder-length black hair and make sure the dark beard covering his jaw was still a fashionable scrub. After all, it had been years. He wanted Layla to appreciate what she'd missed. His smile flashed white on a laugh. Oh yeah, he was vain as sin. But then, if one believed the teachings of the religion he'd grown up with, he was already condemned to the devil's realm. So he might as well enjoy the journey.

"I'LL NEED ALL your records. Personnel—past and present, including *former* employees—reconnaissance, any investigation you've conducted trying to pin down the enemy or the leaders. Interviews, observations, that sort of thing. There've been some new buildings added to the *Fortalesa* since the last time I was here. I'll need blueprints and layouts as it is now. Armory audits, inventory. And I'll need to work closely with you until you leave, which gives me less than two days, but I'll deal with it. Anything I need after that"—she shrugged—"that's what cell phones are for. I'd like another—"

She froze as someone came up behind her, standing too close. She knew who it was even before his smooth, deep voice said, "Welcome home, Layla."

She reacted without thought, jamming her elbow into his stomach hard, even though she'd be the one carrying bruises the next day. The asshole's body was like a fucking rock.

Taking a quick step away, she spun to find him laughing. *Laughing.* If she'd hit any other man that hard, he'd be bent over, gasping for breath and trying not to vomit. Of course, Xavier wasn't exactly a man. Though he was definitely male, and just as fucking beautiful as he'd ever been. Damn it.

"Sorry," she said, smiling sweetly. "I didn't know it was you. You startled me."

He stopped laughing. "*Dios mio*, woman. Who'd you think it was? If it had been anyone else, you'd have ruptured something." He grinned, which only made him more devastating. "It's good to finally see you, Layla. We've missed each other the few times you've visited since college."

"I know," she said with a regret as false as her smile. "But the roads are so dark. I wanted to get back to the city before the light faded."

His eyes sparkled with humor. He wasn't fooled for an instant. She hadn't expected him to be. She hadn't *wanted* him to be, either. She might be here a while, until her father was well enough to return to full duty, and she didn't want Lord-fucking-Xavier to think there was anything friendly about her presence. It was a business arrangement, nothing more. And she was only doing it for her father, not the vampire lord.

"Layla's filling in for a few weeks, while I deal with doctors," Ferran said proudly. "She has a lot of experience—in both the army and private security—and since she already knows this place, she'll be perfect."

"She always was," Xavier agreed, his sexy mouth curved into a smile that was too knowing for what they had between them.

Stop, she told herself. *I don't care if he's beautiful and his mouth is sexy, so just stop thinking about it.* "Was there something you needed, my lord?" she asked, her tone utterly professional.

"I was looking for Ferran," he said, dismissing her in an instant, as if that knowing smile had never happened. Turning to her father, he said, "There was another attack today."

He'd only just risen from his sleep, and couldn't have been briefed yet, but he hadn't been asking a question. She was reminded once again that Xavier wasn't an ordinary vampire. He was *the* Vampire Lord of Spain, one of the most powerful vampires in Europe. Maybe even the world. She couldn't have said how many vampire lords there were in the world these days, but she knew there weren't very many. And she definitely didn't know Xavier's strength compared to the others. She could have found that information if she'd really wanted, but she'd intentionally avoided anything to do with vampires since she'd gone away to school.

Xavier was uncommonly powerful, which made him a deadly weapon in her arsenal. Nothing more. Her job was the defense of his *Fortalesa*. Officially only during daylight, but wars didn't follow a clock these days. What began in sunlight could easily carry into the night.

She looked at her father and said, "If you point me to the right files, Papa, I can find the information I need, while you brief Lord Xavier on today's attack. I also need to—"

"I want you in on this briefing," Xavier said. "You're already my temporary daylight commander. You need the latest intel."

Temporary, she reminded herself, biting her tongue to keep from telling him what he could do with his fucking commands. Besides, the beautiful bastard was right. No. The *bastard* was right. No more beautiful or any other unnecessary observations. "Very well," she agreed briskly. "Here or—"

"We have a nightly briefing in Lord Xavier's office, Laylita," her father said. "His lieutenant and any others he feels should attend will join us."

"Makes sense. Shall I stop and tell Mama—"

"Ramlah knows the routine. We'll be finished in time for dinner."

"Okay," she muttered, feeling like the odd man out, even though she was the one who'd be in command when the sun rose. "But I do need to contact Brian, and tell him about the situation here. I'll run upstairs, get a few things I'll need for the meeting, and call him on the way. I'll see you there."

XAVIER STOOD WITH Ferran, waiting until Layla was out of sight, her footsteps fading as she rounded the second flight of stairs.

"Who's Brian?" Xavier asked, keeping the growl from his voice with an effort.

"Brian? He's an officer on her team. They work together," Ferran said walking with him across the courtyard to the vampire wing and the office from which Xavier ran not just this *Fortalesa*, but the country's entire vampire population.

"Have you met him?"

"Oh, yes. Both times we visited her in France, and once when she was in college."

"She's known him a long time, then."

"She met him her first year in the United States, I think. Or maybe it was the second. It was a while ago. My lord," he said when they reached Xavier's office, "are you comfortable with this? With having Layla assist you in my place, while I'm gone? I can postpone—"

"No need, my friend. You're too important to everyone in the *Fortalesa*. I need you healthy. Besides, Ramlah would stake me in my sleep if I said anything else." They both laughed as Xavier poured two rounded snifters of a Portuguese port, and handed one to Ferran. "I trust you. If you say she's up to the task, then she is. It's as simple as that. Now, tell me about today's attack."

LAYLA SAT ON HER bed in the same bedroom where she'd slept for most her life. The bed had been changed when she'd turned thirteen. They'd lost the white princess headboard and fluffy canopy in favor of what had passed for more mature décor in her teenage girl's mind. Thankfully, her mother had changed it again when she'd gone off to college, so she was no longer subjected to staring at posters of Enrique Iglesias and Ryan Cabrera while she tried to sleep.

Leaving her boots on, she hit Brian's number on her cell, then put her feet up and leaned against the pillows while she waited for him to pick up.

"Yes, ma'am," he answered.

Such a smartass. "I've told you not to call me 'ma'am.' It makes me sound like some old bulldog of a sergeant."

"You could never be that, my lady."

"Be serious. I don't have much time."

"What's up?" He was abruptly all business, clearly having picked up on her mood. They'd been friends for years—never lovers, which was probably why they were still such good friends. Brian knew her better than anybody.

"My dad's going in the hospital."

"Layla, I'm sorry. What is it?"

"Heart."

"Ah shit. What're they doing?"

Tears stung her eyes. She'd needed to tell someone else, someone who could understand how devastating this whole situation was to her. Not the thing with Xavier. *No one* knew about him. It was her dad. She was an only child, and her parents were everything to her. Her only family. She'd never even had a serious relationship, never truly loved or been loved by anyone else. Except Brian, which was the real reason she'd needed to call him.

"Surgery, maybe," she said, managing to keep her voice casual.

"They need to do some tests. Possibly just stents, which would be a lot less intrusive. But either way, he'll need me here to fill in until he recovers. Apparently, his longtime lieutenant left two months ago to move to Madrid and be closer to family. So, there's no one else here who's qualified—"

"But you are, and you're going to stay." No complaints, no questions, just of course she was staying. This was family. Brian understood.

"Looks like it," she sighed. "I haven't seen any numbers or personnel files yet, but from what my dad tells me, they're either understaffed, or improperly deployed. I'll know more once I get a chance to review."

"Hey, say the word and we'll be on a jet headed your way."

"Mmm, not yet. There's something weird going on with what sounds like a local fringe group who object to vampires, and think the answer is to hide in the woods and take pot shots at the guards. Or at least, that seems to be how it *started*. But with this last attack, they're escalating. Some of the guards were injured today. Nothing fatal, and only one or two that required medical attention. But if this group is ramping up for something bigger, we need to be prepared. I'm heading for a briefing now. I'll know more after that, including if I need some of you with me."

"Come on, Layla. Throw us a bone."

She laughed. "Right, because you're living in squalor over there in France."

"You know we're not, but it's fucking boring. You need us, we're there."

"I know. Look, I have to go. I just wanted to give you a head's up. I'll call tomorrow, give you the update. Give the boys and girls my love, and don't drink too much wine."

They hung up at the same time, as Layla swung her legs off the bed and shoved the phone into a pocket. She grabbed her leather portfolio with its supply of writing pads and pens, kissed her mother as she hurried through the living room, then marched off to her first meeting as the temporary daylight commander for Lord fucking Xavier.

Chapter Six

XAVIER LISTENED to the multiple conversations going on in his office, and longed for the days when no one expected or worried about democracy. Everyone around the table wanted their say, then wanted *their* say on the other guy's say, and on and on. They all agreed on the basics, but each wanted their opinion to be the final word. And fuck, if he didn't shut this down, he'd either start killing people, or walk out and leave them to it. The former would be more satisfying, but he'd probably lose some useful voices in the process. And in some cases, he might lose a lot more than that.

Like Layla. He liked *her*. Hell, he'd liked her a little too much before she went away to college, and had thought he'd kept it to himself. Until she'd come on to him. To this day, he regretted that night and the way he'd handled it. Though there'd been no *good* way. She'd been nineteen years old for fuck's sake. He'd been too old even before he'd been made Vampire, and then . . . Well shit. She'd been about to begin the biggest adventure of her life, maybe even meet the man she'd marry, and have a family. That was what humans did.

While *his* plans at the time had all included crafting alliances and increasing his personal power in preparation for what he'd known, since the night he'd woken as a vampire, was his destiny. He'd been created to rule, to build beyond what any previous Spanish vampire lord had achieved. To rule all of Spain, not the fractured country it had been when his Sire ruled. And he'd done it. The human residents might fight over interior borders and rights, but those lines didn't exist for Spain's vampires. He ruled them all.

His ambitions didn't end there, however. He was well-positioned to become the kingmaker of continental Europe. He'd met every one of his fellow vampire lords in the surrounding countries, and was stronger than any of them. He didn't count Scotland's Lachlan or Ireland's Quinn in that calculation. They had their own countries, their own territories, but they also had strong links back to North America. He didn't care overmuch, however. As long as they left the continent alone, he'd leave *them* alone.

But what he wanted for continental Europe was what Raphael had in North America. He wanted the strength of an alliance of vampire lords, the prosperity of peace between them. And the only way to achieve that was one country at a time, one neighbor at a time.

But now it seemed as though someone didn't want him to succeed. He could think of no other explanation for this sudden outbreak of human hostilities against him. These guerilla-style tactics of attack and fade into the woods had to be more than a fresh wave of human hatred. There was something more behind it, some*one* more driving it. He had his suspicions, or more like a list of possible enemies. The problem was, it just didn't seem logical for any of them to attack him directly. Maybe they would lobby the others, whisper against him, but his plan of alliance hadn't gotten far enough to pose a real threat to anyone. And if he had his say about it, it never would. He didn't want to conquer the other countries. He didn't want to fight them at all. He wanted to be ready in the face of outside enemies. He wasn't even sure they *had* outside enemies. Not yet. But ever since Mathilde had gathered her strongest vampires, then set out to destroy Raphael and put herself in his place, Raphael—who'd survived quite handily—had begun meddling in the affairs of European vampires.

He'd begun by killing Mathilde and every one of the vampires who'd left France with her. He'd then completed the destruction by visiting France and killing the strongest potential successors to her territory. And then he'd installed his own allies in Ireland and Scotland. If continental Europe's vampire lords didn't unite, any one of them could be next.

Except him. He had no intention of falling to any challenger. Not for a very long time.

His gaze strayed to the beautiful Layla. She could make a vampire's life worth continuing. But only if he could get her to talk to him first. What was her problem anyway? She'd been gone more than ten years, had barely visited her parents, and then only in daytime so as to avoid *him*, he was certain. He hadn't received a letter, or a postcard—not even in the first months after her departure when she might have written just to tell him to go fuck himself. In the deafening silence, he'd assumed with good reason that she'd moved past whatever feelings she'd had for him. It had scraped his ego some. He wasn't usually forgotten that easily. But hadn't he told himself that it was what he wanted for her? And really, there'd been nothing between them before that night. So why was she acting like he was the biggest villain in her life?

He shifted his gaze away from her, tuned back into the discussion, and finally said what he'd been thinking. "I think we agree on the basics. I'll make the final decision in consultation with my commanders, including Layla Casales, whom I think you all know." He glanced over with a smile for Layla, and she glared back at him. *That* was growing old.

"The detailed plan will be ready tomorrow night." He stood, signaling that the meeting was over, then waited while there was a general shuffle toward the door, before saying, "Layla, could you hold back a moment, please?"

LAYLA FUMED PRIVATELY at the thinly veiled order for her to remain. It had been a while since she'd had a commanding officer, and she hadn't missed it. But her father was watching, and he needed to know that she could do his job while he was gone. Otherwise, he wouldn't go. His devotion to Xavier was that strong. So she kissed him on the cheek and said, "I'll be up in a minute, Papa. We'll brainstorm all of this before morning."

He hugged her, then gave Xavier a respectful nod and walked out with Danilo, his new lieutenant who had skill and determination, but not a lot of experience. The younger woman had spoken little during the discussions, but she'd listened to everything and had taken more than a few notes. It was the right thing for a junior officer to do, and Layla had been impressed. She'd been impressed in an entirely different way to discover that Danilo was older than she looked. She'd served in both Iraq and Afghanistan with Spain's UN forces, and was fluent in Arabic, German, and English, in addition to her native Spanish. The language skills might not be necessary to her job at the *Fortalesa*, but the English was handy, and linguistic ability spoke to a sharp mind and a receptive intellect. In fact, if Danilo ever tired of working for vampires, Layla would happily recruit her for her own team.

"Would you like a drink?"

She managed not to startle visibly at the question. She hadn't forgotten he was there. He was far too dangerous for that. It was just his *voice*. It was . . . hypnotic. As deep and smooth as the best whiskey ever made, it was pure seduction. *Pure fucking lies*, she reminded herself bitterly.

"No thank you," she told him. "What's this about?"

He tsked softly and strolled past her to the door. She laid a hand on her sidearm, watching with suspicious eyes as he closed the door and walked behind his desk. He didn't sit, but stood there with both hands raised, palm out, and smirked. "Just closing the door, *cariño*."

She stared at him. *Cariño?* Oh, hell no. He'd lost the right to call her that a long time ago. But if they waded into *that* fucking mess, they'd be there all night. "Why close the door?" she demanded.

His dark eyebrows rose. "For privacy, of course. Some things—"

"We don't need privacy for *any* things." She would have stormed out, but his next words stopped her.

"Why are you so angry, Layla?"

She turned to stare at him in disbelief. He was serious. "Are you kidding me?"

He shrugged gracefully. "Not unless I misunderstand the American phrase."

"If you don't know, then . . . " *Then what?* she asked herself. She wasn't about to bare her soul and tell him the truth. It was bad enough that she'd trusted him when she'd been young and stupid. She wasn't going to make *that* mistake again. "Look, I'm here because my father asked me to stay," she snarled. "I'll do the job, give it everything I've got. But it's a job, nothing else. So, good night, Lord Xavier," she finished.

She snatched open the door quickly, before he could stop her. Though if he'd really wanted, he could have been in front of the door before she'd even reached for the handle. That knowledge did nothing to improve her mood as she exited the vampire wing and strode across the main courtyard at a brisk, hard pace, stopping only when she reached the stairs to her parents' apartment. If she went up there in this mood, they'd notice immediately, and then she'd have to come up with a convenient lie to explain. And what would she say? She couldn't say she'd fought with someone else in the *Fortalesa*, because it might come back to bite her in the ass. She had to live with these people—human and vampire both—maybe even for two or three months. She could always say she'd had an argument with Brian, or someone else from her team, but that seemed disloyal to *them*.

Fucking Xavier, she fumed and turned instead for the wall, climbing the stairs and walking the long length of the *Fortalesa* until she was above the gate and looking down at the town far below. It was the same direction from which the humans must have come, and yet somehow, they'd managed to disappear into the forest, according to her father who wasn't a fanciful man, as if they'd never been there.

How was that possible? Sure, people from the town knew the forests well. So did those who lived in the *Fortalesa*. So had *she*, once upon a time. Even now, she'd never get lost out there. The trees had gotten taller, the forest thicker, but the land remained the same.

And then there were the vampires. Many of them were old enough to have been with Xavier when he'd first claimed the *Fortalesa* more than two hundred years ago, even before he'd become Spain's vampire lord.

So how the hell were a bunch of humans managing to disappear so completely that even the vampires couldn't seem to track them? It worried her, though it would have worried her *more* if she hadn't been certain that Xavier knew something. Something he wasn't telling anyone. It might be more suspicion than knowledge, but he was still keeping whatever it was to himself. She didn't think even her father knew, certain that he, at least, would have told her.

Damn. She needed to have another meeting with the vampire, after all.

"Fuck."

LAYLA WOKE TO the scent of fresh coffee, which wasn't that unusual. Someone was always brewing coffee in the team's kitchen. What *was* unusual was the accompanying scent of fresh bread and olive oil. After all these years, her mother still baked for her father every morning. The bread would be served at lunch and dinner, as well. Except that by the time lunch rolled around today, her parents would be at a hotel in Barcelona, where they'd stay until her father had received whatever treatment he needed.

She tossed the blankets aside, wondering whether her mama had baked the bread for *her,* or if she was taking it with them to the city.

"Papa." She kissed him on the head where he sat at the table, crossed to hug her mother, then sat across from them at the table. "I stayed up late last night, reading files," she told him, as she smeared marmalade over her still-warm bread. "You have a good team."

"Good," he agreed, "but too young, and with no serious fighting experience. They mostly grew up here, in the *Fortalesa*, and they've never seen anything like these attacks. Hell, before this started, we left the gates open most days. Guarded," he added, "but open."

"In reading the files, I didn't see much in the way of an investigation into who's behind all this."

He gave her an even look over his coffee cup, then set it down. "That's because I haven't done much. I don't have people with that kind of experience. I've made a few queries in town, asking after any visitors acting strangely, carrying guns, or coming and going at odd hours."

"Good luck with that."

"Precisely. This is a tourist area, and it's early summer. Every town on the coast is filled with strangers. Lord Xavier was checking into something else, an idea he had about these people. He hasn't shared any information with me yet, which might mean there was nothing to find, and his idea came to nothing."

"Or he's still working on it," she suggested.

"That, too."

"I'll ask him at the next briefing. By the way, does he meet with you every night? Or only when something big happens?"

"Every night, though if nothing 'big' as you say, happens, it's more in the way of a drink among friends, with only Lord Xavier, his lieutenant Chuy, and his security chief, Joaquim. Along with myself."

"Thank God for that. You and Mama ready to go?" she asked, intentionally changing the subject. It was time for both her parents, but her father especially, to forget about the *Fortalesa* for a while and think about his health instead.

"Soon. Are we crowding you in this apartment?"

She laughed. "Hardly. Besides, I'll probably move to the barracks. I'm bringing Brian and a couple of the others here from France. I'll need them if things get any uglier, and they can always give your newbies a few pointers."

"Brian's coming? I'm sorry we'll miss him."

"Normally we'd split the two assignments, but they don't need him there. He's pitifully bored. And who knows? He might still be here when you get back. So when are you leaving?"

"In a couple of hours. I want to walk the wall with you today, introduce you to as many people as I can."

"Good idea. I'm not here to shake anything up. I want to slide into your routine as smoothly as possible."

"Good. I'm sure people will have questions, and I don't like unnecessary surprises. So, I'll tell them as much as I can. Especially after the meeting last night."

Layla didn't want to talk about last night's meeting, so she changed the subject. "I thought I'd check inventory, too. Danilo was in charge of that, but I'm guessing she's not anymore, since you've promoted her."

"No, she's still in charge, but one of the others does the actual counting. The job rotates along with the patrol assignments, so that everyone knows what we have on hand in a crisis."

Layla nodded her agreement. "Always best. Mama, are you leaving any of this bread for me?"

Her mother laughed. "What do you think, *mija*? That I'd leave you to make your own?"

That made Layla laugh, too, as she stood and gulped down the rest of her coffee. "You ready, Papa?"

He nodded. "I've been waiting for *you*. Do you always get up this late?"

"Oh, Papa, that hurts. This was supposed to be a vacation."

"Not anymore, *mija*. You've been hired."

AN HOUR LATER, the morning sun was beating down on Layla's unprotected head as she stood next to her father and Danilo. She had a cap in her duffle, which was sitting in her father's office, because she was an idiot. She'd never have left the team's barracks without a hat. In fact, she'd have berated any member of her team who'd forgotten one. Wars were rarely fought in cool, comfortable climates anymore. Especially not the kind of wars that employed mercenaries, like hers.

"Looks quiet so far this morning," she observed, as she pushed up her sunglasses and raised high-powered binoculars to her eyes. They didn't do much to reassure her, since an entire army could have been sheltering in the surrounding forest, and they'd have been effectively invisible. At night, a good infrared scope would sort them out, but in daytime, especially on hot days like this, there wasn't enough variation between human body temperature and the surrounding air. Infrared wouldn't work.

That might even be a factor in choosing to attack during the day. Though if so, it was a minor one. She had a lot of doubts about this situation, but one thing she knew for sure—the attacks were coming in daylight in order to keep the vampires out of it. Hell, Xavier's vampires didn't need infrared. They didn't even need to see you. They could just follow the sound of your heartbeat.

"Here you go," a male voice said from behind her, as a baseball style cap was propped on her head. "You'll fall over in this heat, *hermosa*."

Layla grabbed the hat and turned to find a young man whose soulful brown eyes carried a teasing glint over a bright, white smile. He was maybe an inch taller than she was, which put him around six feet, with a sturdy, muscular build, and an attitude that said he knew just how pretty he was. It was also obvious that he was accustomed to sweeping women off their feet with a single glance.

Too bad Layla preferred men, rather than overreaching boys, since this one was certainly several years younger than she was.

"This is my daughter, Layla Casales," her father growled. "Your new commanding officer."

The boy/man's grin only widened. "How wonderful. Welcome to the *Fortalesa*, my lady."

"Just plain Captain will do," she said dryly and handed back the hat. "I have a hat. Where are you supposed to be?"

He blinked in surprise, clearly taken aback by her reaction. Or the lack of one.

"Aww, did your charm fail you this morning?" she wanted to coo. But he needed to understand that she was not his *hermosa* or anything else. She was his commanding officer. She studied him, waiting.

"I'm, that is, I have a message for the commander," he said, stumbling only a bit before he straightened and turned to her father. "A body has been found, sir. Southeast, half mile back in the trees. They're bringing it in now."

Layla looked at her father, all thoughts of the boy/man forgotten. "Is this a first?"

He nodded silently. "We'll give Łucja an hour or so to get the— Male or female?" he asked the pretty messenger.

"Uh." He winced. "I didn't see the body myself, sir. But I understand the animals had been at it."

"Ah. Tell Dr. Nowak we'll be there shortly."

"Sir. Ma'am?" he added uncertainly in Layla's direction, then quick-stepped toward the nearest stairs.

"He's a good man," her father said.

She turned from watching the messenger disappear down the stone steps. "Is he? A man, I mean. What is he, eighteen?"

Danilo snorted at the same time Layla's father said, "Twenty-five on his last birthday, and he served three years in the military."

Layla wondered if she was just that *old*, or if her idea of the perfect male had been forever skewed by growing up surrounded by gorgeous vampires who appeared forever twenty-five. On the other hand, while they might look twenty-five, their eyes always told the real story. There were multiple lifetimes of living in their eyes. She thought of Xavier's dark, depthless eyes, the way they gleamed like polished pewter whenever he— Oh fuck, no. She was not going to go all dreamy about him and his freaky vampire eyes. He was the reason she'd never had a serious relationship. Not because no man could measure up to his looks, but because he'd taught her from the very beginning that men couldn't be trusted.

"Is *Woosha* the same person as Dr. Novak?" she asked, pronouncing the doctor's first name the way her father had, since she didn't know the nationality of the name, or even how it was spelled.

Her father nodded. "Łucja Nowak." He pulled a pencil from his pocket, took her notebook and wrote the name out. "Not spelled the way it's pronounced, obviously. Not by our alphabet. It's Polish. *She's* Polish. Visited Barcelona on vacation and never went back. She's been here seven years now. We were looking for a full-time medical doctor, and she was looking for a job. So we met a few times, and she's worked out great. Treats everyone from *abuelas* to newborn babies. She works with the vamps, too, though they don't need much from her."

"Guess I'll be meeting her this morning. But I'd like to do another circuit before we go look at dead people. Is that okay?"

"Only *one* dead person, *mija*. Don't tempt the gods."

She gave a smiling wave to Danilo as they set off down the broad top of the wall. The wall itself was four feet wide and constructed of solid stone. The floor of the walkway was the top of the main wall, though additional, narrow walls had been built up on the sides and served as both a safety against falling, and more importantly, as a barrier for defenders to shelter behind. In addition to the barrier wall, stone battlements occurred at regular intervals, jutting out a full foot over the front of the wall, and narrowing the walkway by half, so that the walkway was briefly two feet wide, and the battlement enclosure itself had a full three feet of maneuvering space inside. At the time it had been built, and later when Xavier was refurbishing and rebuilding, fortress designs took into account the need to prevent attackers from breaching the walls with ladders. That obviously was no longer the case, since an enemy could simply lob explosive charges over the wall from a safe distance, or blow a hole in the wall with a mortar charge.

But Xavier liked his walls, liked the privacy and separation they afforded from the human world. So, he'd reinforced and repaired them over the years and made them even stronger. His communication and surveillance gear was cutting edge technology, but when it came to walls, he was still an eighteenth century man. Not that Layla was knocking it. She'd wished more than once for a good, solid wall when she'd been fighting. The thought had her wondering idly whether Xavier had been in the military as a human. He was well-versed in military history, she knew that. And in retrospect, she knew he had a strong sense of strategy. Fortunately, that was a question she didn't need an answer to.

Pulling out her cell, while her father talked to one of the guards, she punched Brian's speed dial number.

"You must be really bored," he answered this time. "Either that or you've forgotten how little action we see here in the vineyards."

"No, just checking in."

"Ah, you're homesick, then. You miss us!" he added cheerfully.

"Don't flatter yourself. Nothing on the horizon?"

"Nada. I've checked all four directions, and not a grape thief in sight. What about there?"

"They're understaffed, though not as bad as I thought. The problem is more one of experience, and maybe a little complacence. To hear everyone tell it, they've barely fired their weapons except on the practice range. On the other hand, we've had a bit of excitement this morning. They found a dead body not far from the *Fortalesa*."

"Who?" Brian's tone was all business.

"No one from here, I don't think. Whoever found the DB couldn't do an ID, and this place is like a small town. Everyone knows everyone else."

"They have a coroner, medical examiner? Anyone who can do a post-mortem?"

"A medical doctor who's a jack-of-all-trades, apparently. I don't think they have much need for a full-fledged coroner. We'll be dropping by there in a bit, to see what she found out."

"Christ, we lead boring lives, don't we? Was this what we had in mind when we enlisted in the army, all bright-eyed and eager after graduating UCLA? The excitement of finding dead bodies?"

"No, I think our eagerness had mostly to do with them paying off our student loans."

"Oh, right. So, how long will you be there?"

"I already told you. A few weeks."

"Ah, but some of the boys and girls are threatening to visit you. They want to get there before it's too late."

"Why would they do that?"

"I don't know, it's warm and sunny?"

"It's warm there, too. Besides it's hot as hell today, and I forgot my hat."

Brian laughed. "That'll be ten demerits, Captain."

"Don't remind me. I was in a hurry. My dad was up and back down from the wall before I even woke up."

"Wow. You're really slacking off on your vacation."

"Fuck you. I have to go see a dead person. Talk to you later."

THE DEAD PERSON turned out to be a very young woman, barely more than a teenager, with black hair to her waist, coffee brown skin, and what would have been lovely and delicate hands if the fingertips hadn't been chewed off. Her eyes were also missing, along with her lips, which made identification nearly impossible without DNA. Although maybe the doc could salvage enough of a fingertip or three to assist an ID. She had nothing in her pockets—no wallet, no money, no ID—but was dressed in stylishly distressed blue jeans and expensive athletic shoes. Her teeth were intact, and she'd benefited from excellent dental care during her short life, with no cavities, and evidence that orthodontic work had probably given her a pretty smile. She wouldn't be smiling ever again, unfortunately. They'd be lucky if they even managed to identify her.

"I'll have to call the authorities on this," Dr. Nowak said, pulling the sheet back over the young woman's ruined face. "She definitely has dental records somewhere, and she's been taken care of, but even if there's a missing person report, it could be from anywhere in Europe. Hell, we don't know for sure that she's even European."

"Cause of death?" Layla asked.

"Gunshot chewed up her heart and lungs—9mm, which I believe is what we use."

"So does everyone else, so that doesn't mean much. Could be someone just wanted to dispose of a body and decided to lay it at our feet." She turned to her father. "Have we had any fighting in the rear quadrant lately?"

He shook his head. "No, it's been a straight up frontal strategy."

"She could have been shot and crawled away, I guess. Or someone dragged her there to get her away from the fight, but she died first. It sure doesn't help us figure out who's behind this. Not without ID."

Dr. Nowak looked up at her. "That's a cold way of looking at it."

Layla shrugged. "That's reality, doc. Tell me, when you call the local authorities, do they come here? Or do we take the body to them?"

"I don't know," the doctor said. "This is a first." She looked over at Layla's father who shrugged.

"I don't think it's ever happened before," he said. "The vamps don't usually die, and when they do . . . " He made a *phttt* noise to indicate a vampire dusting. "As for the human population, they mostly choose cremation, which we do onsite. It comes from living with vampires, I guess."

"Right, then," Nowak said. "I'll make the calls and let you know what I find out."

"Thank you, Łucja. I know this isn't what you signed up for," her father said.

"Not true, sir. Death is a part of life, and I signed up for all of it." With that, she pulled off her gloves, dropped them in the biohazard disposal, and walked over to her desk, turning her back on Layla and her father.

"Well," Layla said, as she walked into the courtyard with him. "I believe we've been dismissed, Commander."

"Ah, Łucja's okay. It's just the culture she was raised with. Not everyone lives in everyone else's underwear like we do."

"Papa! That's disgusting. I think it's time for you to leave for Barcelona."

"Why? You want the dead body all to yourself?"

"No." She pointed upward. "Because your wife is standing on the balcony surrounded by suitcases."

He looked up and waved. Such a simple thing, a wave. But there was so much love on her father's face as he waved to her mother. They'd been together nearly forty years, and he still smiled at her as if she brought the sunlight to his day. Layla wanted that. Wanted someone she could still love just as much after four decades as they had the first time they'd held each other.

She sighed and looked away. Fat chance she had of that.

THINGS MOVED QUICKLY after that. Layla's mom made sure of it. She knew her husband, knew he'd delay until it was so late that he'd postpone their departure to the next morning. Fortunately, Ramlah was the one person who could order Ferran around and get things done.

Less than an hour later, Layla was waving at their car from her perch on the wall above the gate. And when they were finally swallowed by the dusty twists and turns of the road, she felt . . . empty. And alone. Fuck that. Every person in the *Fortalesa* was depending on her to do her job. And that didn't include moping around like a teenager.

She headed for the stairs. She needed to check in with Dr. Novak, and then finish her review of the *Fortalesa*'s personnel. They'd been running the same duty schedule for too long. People became complacent and not as sharp as they needed to be.

And then maybe she'd call Brian, just to hear a friendly voice. Even if all he did was complain about France.

Chapter Seven

THE SKY WAS brilliant that evening. An entire palette of pink and red, with the occasional spike of blue sky shining through. It was the kind of sunset that tourists travelled to Barcelona to witness at the end of a long day of sightseeing.

Layla appreciated the beauty. Appreciated even more the end of a peaceful day, with no Rambo wannabes hiding in the trees, taking potshots at the *Fortalesa* or its people. The gates remained shut, as they'd been all day, and Layla had doubled the guard contingent on the gate controls so that no one person could admit the enemy. Some would call her paranoid for taking that step. But these attacks felt like a prelude to her—as if they were softening up the *Fortalesa*'s defenders, letting them think the enemy was nothing but some vampire-hating troublemakers.

But Layla believed there was something more. She just didn't know what. Not yet. But she'd figure it out. And in the meantime, she wanted security tight and the guards on alert.

What she wanted, what she *needed* right now, however, was food. She'd skipped lunch and was starving. She could take thirty minutes for dinner, if she hurried. After that was the nightly briefing with Xavier, which she assumed would be more thorough, since this was her first day on the job.

She completed a final walk around the wall, and finding no immediate threats, met Danilo above the gate.

"The watch is yours," Layla said, formally putting Danilo in charge. They'd agreed that Layla would take the day shift, and Danilo the nighttime, when only a few human guards remained, mostly to supplement the vampires who took over after sunset. Danilo wouldn't have any authority over the vamps, but Layla would need a detailed report every morning on anything that happened during the night. Layla knew she'd be fighting her inner control freak the whole time, stopping herself from constantly checking by phone, or just *dropping by* for some cool night air. She'd read every page of Danilo's file, and knew that she hadn't seen the kind of fighting that Layla had. Nor anything close to the hostage rescues or bodyguard jobs that turned violent, which she and her team were frequently contracted for. The French vineyard was an aberration, not their usual duty.

But Danilo did have field experience, and had been promoted twice before completing her active service with the Spanish military. There was also the fact that Layla's father had hired her, and she trusted his knowledge and judgment more than anyone else's.

She checked her watch with a hissed curse. The thirty minutes she'd planned for dinner had somehow shrunk to less than twenty. But she had to eat. Xavier could just wait a few damn minutes. It wasn't as if he had nothing to do while he waited. Hell, he could use the time to set up his own dinner for later on. Some buxom beauty who spent all her time looking beautiful and wouldn't know what to do with a gun to save her life. She'd probably never cracked open a serious book either, but spent all her time studying fashion magazines.

Layla shook her head, amused by her own thoughts. She had no idea where Xavier got his blood fixes. She'd watched women come and go when she'd been younger, before she'd left for the U.S. But there'd been too many of them to pinpoint which one was Xavier's. If he even had one. More likely, he selected from the buffet each night.

"Stop," she said out loud as she walked into her parents' apartment. It was odd being there without them. Plus there was no Mama at the stove, no wonderful smells filling the kitchen. Shit. She had to fix her own dinner. She hadn't done that in years. Ever since graduating from university, she'd been living communally, one way or the other. And on the rare occasions when she had an evening all alone, she'd order take-out, or walk to the nearest bistro. Fuck.

"Please tell me you left food, Mama," she said, still talking to herself. Crossing her fingers, she opened the refrigerator and found a casserole just waiting to be heated. "Yes!" She threw it in the microwave, which her mother would never have done, picked a number of minutes at random, then went to wash the day's sweat from her face and hands.

She gobbled down her dinner right out of the dish. She was already late for the meeting with Xavier, and feeling . . . not guilty. She had nothing to feel guilty about. But since she'd taken on this job, she was compelled to do it right, just as she did every other assignment.

Even worse was the image dawning in her brain of an impatient Xavier showing up at the apartment door and . . . Correction. He wouldn't stop at the door. He'd simply stroll in and demand her attention. Xavier didn't get angry. He just did what he wanted and assumed everyone else would go along with it.

"*Merde!*" She'd been working in France long enough that the curse came easily to her tongue. Grabbing the dirty dish, she dropped it into the sink with some soap and water, ran wet hands over her face and dried it with the dish towel. (Her mother would be appalled!) Then, tossing a breath mint into her mouth, she ran out the door.

XAVIER SIPPED A glass of red wine, liberally seasoned with blood, and waited for Layla. He'd kept track of her through the day. Not in detail, not the way he could have if they'd shared blood. But in monitoring the general ebb and flow of the *Fortalesa* and its people, he was confident in his assessment of her activities. She'd been diligent, which was nothing more than he'd expected. He'd known her for most of her life. She'd been born in the *Fortalesa*, though she hadn't come to his attention until her father had been elevated to Commander of his daylight guard. He'd noticed her more after she was old enough to follow her father around, announcing to anyone who would listen that she was going to be a soldier just like her papa. No one had believed her then, not even her father. Her ambition had been dismissed as a young girl's fancy, grown out of love for her father.

Xavier hadn't dismissed it, though. He'd known she meant it. Even as a small child, she'd had a core of steel, a strength of character that drove her to excel at everything she did. And when she persisted in her determination to be a soldier, her parents winced and said nothing, hoping she'd leave it behind once she went to university and understood the full variety of professions available to her.

Even Xavier had privately hoped she'd seek a quieter vocation. Not because he'd thought she couldn't do anything else, but because, above all, he'd wanted her safe. Humans were too fragile, too easy to kill. And no one knew better than he that even in the safest countries, the most secure cities, the world was a violent place. It was enough to survive a normal life of home and family, without courting death by throwing yourself in its path. Not that what he wanted mattered, in this case. Layla had always nodded and smiled at those who urged her to choose another path, that she was much too smart to become a common soldier.

There'd never been anything common about Layla. He'd seen her in a way that others didn't—not even her parents. And though he'd fought the knowledge until the day she left for the U.S., he'd always sensed an indefinable something special about Layla. A connection that shouldn't have been there, something unique to her and no one else.

Human mystics—those who claimed to speak to the dead or to see the future—would have said he'd known her in a past life, that their souls were drawn to each other. Xavier believed in magic. How could he not? He was a vampire who could stop a man's heart with a thought, or tear that same heart from his enemy's chest and force him to watch it burn. Maybe vampire abilities weren't magic the way humans understood it. Maybe people simply hadn't advanced enough to understand it for what it was. Some vampires believed that vampirism was an evolutionary change in the human race, that they were more advanced beings than ordinary humans.

Xavier didn't know about evolution and didn't spend much time worrying about it either. He knew who his parents were, knew who his Sire was, and how he'd changed from human to vampire. After that, he'd been too busy learning to use the new powers he'd been given, and then finding his place in a world dominated by a few extraordinarily powerful vampires. Because he was one of them. No one knew what factors determined which vampires would rule and which would go about their lives in much the same way they had before being turned, except for a few specific changes. For his part, Xavier had always known his destiny and had pursued it with the same single-minded ambition he saw in Layla.

Layla. The flame inside him flared with heat every time he thought of her. The unique connection he'd felt when she'd been a child hadn't disappeared as he'd thought it would, when he'd dismissed it as a protectiveness for the child of close friends, which Ferran and Ramlah had grown to be.

His feelings for her had instead grown stronger. And he'd been forced to look for other explanations. He'd even considered the possibility that she was a danger to him, that his vampire senses, which far exceeded those of a regular human's, were trying to warn him. He hadn't been able to make himself believe the logic of that one. How could even the most finely tuned vampire brain know that a young girl would grow up to assassinate him? It made no sense.

He'd cautiously explored the topic with another vampire or two, those whose discretion he could count on. But he'd never told even them whom it concerned, or even if he was the one involved, not willing to risk drawing the wrong kind of attention to Layla. The unique was always desired by certain people—both vampire and human—but especially by vampires whose long lives sometimes made them subject to a desperate kind of ennui which lusted after anything to relieve the boredom.

But the inquiries turned out to be useless anyway, since none of those he'd spoken to had experienced anything like it, nor even heard of it happening to anyone else. So Xavier stopped worrying about it, deciding it was the product of a long-forgotten hindbrain fart that humans were no longer able to utilize, much less explain.

He looked up at the muted sound of a door closing far down the hallway and smiled. Layla had arrived at last. Standing, he picked up his wine and walked around his desk to the conference table where he took a seat facing the door. She'd be angry when she walked in, knowing she was late and choosing to take it out on him. He wondered if she treated others the same. If, for example, she'd snarled at her commanding officer when she'd been in the army. He doubted it. He'd observed her enough before she left to know her ire was reserved for him.

The door swung open without a knock and Layla rushed in, stopping short when she saw him sitting alone. She scowled and asked, "Is everybody late? I wish I'd known that. I have a million other things I need to take care of. You could have just texted when you were ready to start."

He grinned. He'd certainly called that one. "No one else is coming," he said calmly. "Since this was your first full day as commander, I thought you might have questions, or want to go over details that don't concern the others."

Her scowl deepened. "What about the attacks? Don't they *concern* everyone?"

His grin widened. "Of course. But my people are fully capable of making any necessary preparations, and even launching reconnaissance teams, without consulting me on every detail."

"And I'm not?"

He sighed. "Get yourself a drink, Layla, and sit down. I'm not your enemy here."

Her eyes narrowed, but she came close enough to drop a few files on the table, then went and poured herself a glass of whiskey. But not until she'd sniffed the wine decanter, then grimaced and shot him a suspicious glance. Xavier could have told her there was unopened wine on the shelf, but didn't see the point once she'd decided on whiskey instead.

Walking back to the table, she pulled out the chair opposite his, sat down, and took a long sip of her drink before lifting her gaze to his. "So, what's this all about?"

He shrugged, feeling the same sensory tug from her that he always had. The only difference was that he knew what it was now. He'd figured it out before she'd left for university. It was one of the main reasons he'd let her go. And, yes, he *had* let her go, because he could have stopped her with a single word if he'd chosen to.

"It's as I said. This was your first full day. I thought we might discuss it."

It was her turn to shrug. "It's not like I haven't been doing the same job for years. The location changes, but nothing else does. People are people. Buildings are buildings."

He raised a skeptical eyebrow.

She rolled her eyes and said, "Fine. Buildings change. A lot. Which affects tactical planning. But I deal with that on every new assignment."

"Like the vineyard? What are you doing there? No, the real question is what Clyde Wilkerson is doing that requires a special forces level of military protection."

"You know Wilkerson?"

"We've met."

"Before we started working for him obviously, since I never heard of it."

"What's the answer?"

She tilted her head, then said, "Oh, right. Wilkerson's not doing anything except having a lot house guests and parties with the rich and famous. I'm sure there are illegal substances making the rounds during both of those activities, but we have nothing to do with it. Besides, he's too rich to get picked up on a drug charge. You're rich—you understand that."

His mood had softened along with her attitude, though he remained cautious. "I don't give or attend parties anymore. I never enjoyed them, and haven't seen the need for a very long time."

She gave him a real smile. "You'll get a reputation if you keep that up. The billionaire vampire recluse. They'll make movies about you if you're not careful."

"I'll keep that in mind." He sipped his wine and said, "No new attack today."

"No, not so much as a single head popping up to spy on us. I'm not sure what that means, though, since we can't figure out what they want, and they don't seem inclined to tell us. I've decided to bring in a couple of the people from my team to help out. Not—" She held up a hand to forestall his objection. "Not for regular guard duties. You don't need that. The *Fortalesa* is well-fortified and relatively easy to defend with the number of daylight guards you already have. Not to mention your vampires if these assailants are stupid enough to continue past sunset. Which they haven't been, so far.

"But my colleagues bring some specific talents of their own, including a wealth of battlefield experience that your people simply don't have. And I wouldn't expect them to. They've been trained to defend this very defensible *stationary* position. My team specializes in maneuvering through and behind enemy lines for both reconnaissance and sabotage, which is both effective and demoralizing. Also—and don't brush this off without listening first—I want to bring in one of the women on my team. Kerry Nask. She gets very reliable . . . hunches, I guess you could call them."

He drew a slow breath and let it out. "I am not one to discount the possibility of *hunches*, though humans tend to see magic where it's not. Many of you assume the process of becoming vampire is itself a function of magic. It is not, in fact, but the mistaken belief among humans serves us well."

Her eyes went wide with curiosity. "If the vampire thing doesn't use magic, then what happens to you guys? What's the truth?"

"A secret. One which we only share with those very few humans we trust absolutely."

She frowned. "Does my father know?"

He wanted to laugh. She was so predictably competitive, even with her own father whose job she'd now taken over, which she took to mean that she should know everything *he* did. Xavier almost regretted disappointing her. "Ferran does not know. There's no reason he needs to."

"Oh. Damn." She laughed and every nerve, every blood cell in his body paid attention.

It was such a *free* sound, the laugh of a small child who hadn't yet learned that the world was a dangerous place. And for the briefest moment, it transformed her features, making her resemble the young woman she'd been before she left. Before she'd not only learned of the world's danger, but had gone out and dealt with it in some of the most brutal conflicts around the globe.

"You're staring," she said softly. "Did I get too close to some secret?"

He shook his head and forced himself to relax. "No, I was just . . . surprised. You haven't seemed very happy to be back. You've been mostly angry . . . at me."

She regarded him silently, then said, "I was. I've been nursing hurt feelings from that last night for years—probably blowing it up in my mind to be more than it was. But now . . . I hate to say it—your ego's big enough—but—" She made a slight shrugging motion with one shoulder. "You were right. I was a stupid teenager, which is redundant, I know. But you could have taken advantage of my stupidity. A lot of men would have. And you didn't. I should probably thank you." She grinned abruptly. "But I'm not that evolved yet."

He grinned back at her, more relieved than she could possibly know that they'd achieved, if not friendship, then at least a détente. "And now?" he asked, knowing he was pushing her, but unwilling to let it go.

"And now I'm here, and we're working together. I'd be stupid to sit around sulking instead of doing my job."

So. She wasn't yet ready to accept what was between them. He could wait.

He nodded once and said, "Bring whichever colleagues you think are necessary or useful while we figure this out. Did your father tell you how to invoice the *Fortalesa* for the services or supplies you need?"

"He left notes. I'm sure I can figure it out, but if not, one of the guys I'm bringing in is a mathematical genius. How difficult can it be?"

"Not at all. Or so I'm told. I don't do accounts payable."

She chuckled. "Was that a *joke*, Lord Xavier? Did you hurt anything?"

"Very funny," he said dryly. "There's much you don't know about me."

She gathered her papers and stood. "I'm sure that's true." But then she looked at him in chagrin. "I'm sorry. I'm getting ready to leave here, and I didn't even ask if there was something else you wanted to address."

"No, that was everything. When will your people arrive?"

"Tomorrow probably, the next day at the latest. I'm not asking for the whole team, just a few specialists who *really* aren't necessary at the damn vineyard."

"If you all dislike the assignment in France, why are you still there?"

"We signed a contract for eighteen months, covering two harvests. That's the big party time in the world of vineyards, apparently. Especially the ones that are nothing but vanity properties for billionaires. It pays well, and Wilkerson isn't a bad guy. When I took the contract, we'd just come off a brutal assignment. Every one of us was injured and exhausted, a couple of the guys pretty seriously. A peaceful cruise of a job sounded pretty good, so we took it." She sighed. "You know what they say, right? Be careful what you wish for? Yeah, well, turns out we're a bunch of adrenaline junkies who, after three months of sitting around the vineyard, started getting stir crazy. It's been over a year now, and we've begun inventing dangerous things to do."

"And now you're here, where people are shooting at you."

She made a dismissive noise. "This barely qualifies as being shot at, believe me. You don't know some of the places we've all been."

Actually he did, but he didn't tell her that.

She picked up her whiskey and drained the glass. "Same time tomorrow?" she asked.

He nodded. "Same."

She gave a little salute and said, "See you then."

XAVIER LISTENED to her footsteps moving down the hall, heard the heavy door open as she took the stairs up to the shaded courtyard outside the *Fortalesa*'s vampire wing. She was only able to come and go freely because he'd inputted her likeness into the biometric database controlling the various locks. It gave her access to most of the vampire wing, but not all. There were vaults on the floor beneath this one. A second basement level where he and his vampires slept during the day. Very few humans ever gained access to that floor, much less to the vaults themselves. And no one did so without his personal approval.

Layla would eventually be one of those people, although she didn't know it yet. She probably didn't even know, didn't understand, that she very likely would become important to *him*, that she'd be given extraordinary access. That someday she might even hold the very lives of his vampires in her hands. She would hold *his* life, too. And he had never sufficiently trusted anyone, vampire or human, to put his life in their hands.

But he would do it for Layla. Because he'd finally figured out what the pull was that he felt toward her. The same kind of pull that he'd bet millions she also felt toward him. Because Layla was the one woman whom he could truly love, the woman who was destined to be his mate. He hadn't believed in destiny when he'd been human. The church taught free will and he'd believed, helped by the fact that he'd come from two loving parents and enough wealth to determine his own future.

Now, centuries later, fate seemed determined to prove its power. He and Layla were both either totally fucked, or incredibly lucky. From the vantage point of his much greater lifespan, as well as the fact that he'd figured out what was between them a long time ago, he knew he had no choice. He loved Layla as much as he always had, but those feelings had matured over the years. She'd become a woman and gained experience of life and death. Layla was the love of his life, his mate.

But only if she made the same choice. And he had no fucking clue whether she would or not.

LAYLA WAS GLAD for the moonless night when she opened the outside door and stepped into the courtyard. She'd managed to make it up the stairs and out of the building without crying, but as if opening the damn door had flicked a switch, a silent flood of tears began flowing over her cheeks to drip off her jaw. She didn't want anyone to see, didn't want anyone to ask her what was wrong.

What could she tell them? That she was fool enough to fall in love with a vampire? Hell, there wasn't any falling involved. She'd fallen a long time ago, but had worked so hard convincing herself that she hated him that she'd begun to believe it.

But not any longer. One look at him and she'd known it had been a mistake to come back. It hurt to sit across the table from him without touching, to talk about inventory and weapons, and training and all the other bullshit that was so important, but wasn't what she wanted to say. Wasn't what she wanted to *do*. She wasn't a teenager anymore, with no knowledge of what it meant to have sex. That it could be so much more than an athletic exercise. That your soul was laid bare and the only barrier you had was the *absence* of any deeper emotion. Love. She'd never loved any of the men she'd dated, had sex with. Hell, some of them had been more sex than dating. They simply hadn't mattered to her, any more than she'd mattered to them. And she'd been fine with that.

But she had no barriers with Xavier. He was so circumspect with her, so *damn* careful to maintain his distance, to limit their exchanges to professional concerns. That smooth whiskey voice of his that could be so warm and inviting with others, remained cool and distant with her. Just the sound of it was like a knife in her chest.

She wanted to think it had been a mistake to come back, after all. That she could have found someone else to step in until her father returned, excusing her reluctance by insisting she wanted to be in Barcelona *with* her father and mother. Hell, Brian would have done it, and with a lot less drama on both sides. Would Xavier have approved Brian, she wondered? Or was there a perverse part of him that had wanted *her* to be the one to come, so he could prove, without a doubt, that there could never be anything between them, that he'd done the honorable thing, the *moral* thing by turning her away all those years ago.

Well, if that's what he'd wanted, he'd gotten it. She'd admitted he'd been right back then. Maybe she should leave now, after all. Maybe Xavier wouldn't even object if she did so. Brian would be arriving soon enough. He could easily take over, and she could go back to France and the vineyard.

That's what she'd do. She'd call Brian tonight, before she fell asleep, so he and Kerry and one or two others could catch a morning flight and be here by tomorrow afternoon. That would allow twenty-four hours to transition between the two of them, and she could leave for France the next day.

Her eyes ached from the combination of tears and not enough sleep by the time she let herself into the apartment. Dropping everything on the kitchen table, she made her way to the bathroom, where she soaked a washcloth in cold water, then laid down on her bed with it over her eyes. She'd just rest there for a few minutes, until her eyes felt better. Then she'd brush her teeth and call Brian before going to sleep. That was the plan.

The next thing she knew, the sun was in her eyes.

Chapter Eight

LAYLA HATED running late, especially when it was only her second day on a job. She couldn't remember the last time she'd slept through her alarm. That had to be what had happened, she thought as she climbed the stairs to the top of the wall, taking them two at a time. She hadn't so much as checked her phone this morning, to see if her regular alarm was still set, or if she'd somehow switched it off. Why the hell would she do that? No, she'd slept right through the damn thing.

When Layla stepped out onto the wall, Danilo was there, standing with legs braced in a resting position as she stared out over the gate.

"Sorry I'm late," Layla said, joining the other woman.

Danilo glanced at her watch, then looked at Layla in surprise. "Five whole minutes," she said.

"Still, it won't happen again. Let's walk. You can give me your report."

They started off at a slow pace, taking time to scan the surrounding forests, giving special attention to the trees beyond the kill zone in the rear of the *Fortalesa*, where they'd found the young woman's body the previous day. No missing person reports had come in, which wasn't a surprise. If she lived out of the area, or even worse, in another country, it could take weeks or months before the report made it this far. Xavier's data gathering operation had all the advantages the latest tech could give them, but law enforcement didn't always share. Or if they did, it was low priority. Especially for one missing young woman. Now, if she'd been wanted for murder or something equally heinous, the process would have worked more efficiently. Hell, for all they knew, no one had even missed her yet. Her family might assume she was still away at college, working hard.

"We didn't have as many vamps as usual with us last night," Danilo commented. "Lord Xavier apparently has them combing the streets looking for weapons, as well as the people who've been using them against us. Joaquim, who I'm assuming you know is Xavier's security chief, kept watch with me for part of the night. He's pissed as hell that we haven't found the enemy yet."

"I can imagine. I can *also* imagine his lord and master is doubly pissed."

Danilo studied her for a moment and said, "You mean Lord Xavier?"

Layla knew she'd made a mistake. She had to stop thinking of Xavier in the familiar mindset of her childhood, or as her father's good friend. To Danilo and everyone else on this wall, he was Lord with a capital "L" Xavier. Vampire lord of the entire country.

"Yeah, sorry," she said immediately. "I've been away too long. I grew up here, and Lord Xavier was always very approachable when I was kid. But I can tell you firsthand that he's definitely pissed as hell that it's taking so long to find answers. With my father gone, I'm the one in the nightly briefings, even though you probably know more than I do at this point. Maybe you should come too?"

"Oh no," Danilo said quickly. "You're not sticking me with *that* assignment. I'm happy to skip mornings with the family, but if I missed dinner, I'd never hear the end of it. My mama's in charge of *that* table."

Layla grinned. "Sounds like my mother, except she's so happy to have me home that I can get away with almost anything. For a while anyway."

Danilo shared the grin. "We didn't miss the absent vamps much. Don't tell anyone I said this, but nothing happened all night. The vamps who *were* up here with us could have run races on top of the wall and it wouldn't have mattered."

"I was surprised when my father said the night guard was human and vamp both. Is that usual, or a reaction to the recent hostilities?"

"Only since the first attack. We always have a few humans up here at night, in case the vamps get called away, or in the event we need to rouse the entire *Fortalesa*. If that happened, it would make more sense to use the human guards as runners, to sound the alarm, and knock on every door."

"There's a general alarm for that, isn't there? Something zapped out to every cell phone in the *Fortalesa*?"

"Absolutely, but some people—civilians mostly—mute their phones at night. I'd do it myself, if I could. There are too many notifications and shit, not to mention messages from people who stay up late, or even all night, and forget that the rest of us don't. But we also have the grandparents who simply don't hear as well as they used to."

"I hate to be a doomsayer, but this sudden quiet worries me."

"Why?"

"All day yesterday, it was perfectly calm. And now you tell me that last night was, too. I have trouble believing our enemy, whoever it is, has suddenly decided to stop and go home."

"The attacks were disorganized, not well executed. Almost amateurish. And their shooters suffered far more casualties that we did. Even apart from the dead girl, we're fairly confident they had at least one fatality, and probably more. Maybe they decided it wasn't worth the cost."

"Maybe. That doesn't feel right, though. More likely, they wanted us to believe they were amateurs. My gut's telling me there's more coming, and my gut's visited a lot of war zones with me."

"What if they weren't supposed to be here at all? What if they *are* part of something bigger, but they jumped the gun on the greater plan and got called back into line."

"In that case, I want to know what the plan was, and probably still is. I don't trust unlooked-for good luck."

"You sound like my *avi*, Commander."

"Your grandfather's a smart man then, and I have good reasons for not trusting luck." She stepped away from the front wall, ready to finish their walk, but suddenly remembered she hadn't called Brian the previous night. Because she'd fallen asleep for fuck's sake. "Listen," she said to Danilo. "I hate to ask, but I need to make one phone call before I forget it . . . *again*. Can you wait five more minutes?"

"Sure. If I wait long enough, my husband will have the kids fed and the kitchen cleaned by the time I get there."

Layla started to laugh as she pulled out her phone, but before her hand left her pocket, she was running for the gate as well-trained reflexes reacted to the sound of gunfire before her brain managed to process the sound. She grabbed Danilo's arm when she would have run alongside her. "No," she said and pointed in the other direction. "They might be hitting more than one quarter."

Danila nodded and ran back the way they'd come, while Layla stretched out her legs and ran full tilt until the gate was in sight. She slowed then, just enough to assess the situation and take precautions. The wall wasn't high enough to conceal her full height, so she stopped at the first battlement she came to and grabbed the MP5 submachine gun the day guard had waiting for her. Waiting only long enough to check the magazine and sling the extra ammo belt over her shoulder, she bent into a crouch and kept running until she reached a battlement much closer to the gate where another guard was firing short, controlled bursts through one of the openings in the stone enclosure. He glanced back when Layla ducked into the narrow space, putting his back against the firing shelter's stone wall, while Layla did the same on the opposite side. The two of them took up most of the limited space, their feet nearly touching between them.

"Same strategy they used before," the man said, breathing heavily. "But twice as many shooters. Radio reports two serious injuries on our side already. They're double-teaming us when we step up to fire, so we have less time to aim properly and are scoring fewer hits."

Layla nodded her understanding, then clicked the comm to Danilo. "New strategy. We're going to work in teams. When they pop up to fire at our first shooter, our Number Two steps out of the enclosure and fires at them. First shooter gets better coverage, better results. Our second should be able to take out at least one before they can switch targets. The teams take turns randomly, and space their actions in seconds, so the enemy can't identify a pattern."

"Roger that. I'll comm the other teams."

"Roger out." She met the guard's gaze across the small space, wanting to be sure he'd been listening. "What's your name?"

"Tony Tosell, ma'am. Who goes first?"

Tony was older than she'd first thought, which she was glad to see. Some of the day guards were too young to have had real world experience. Xavier's territory had been too peaceful for too long. "You stay inside. I'll step out to your left and start firing two seconds after you."

He nodded, checked his weapon, and gave her a single, sharp nod.

She did the same, then crouching as low as she could, she slipped around the battlement and crept up to the wall. Hearing Tony's weapon scrape on the stone in the instant before he began firing, she stood, aimed, and got off two controlled bursts before slamming her back against the battlement wall. As Tony's weapon went live a second time, she shouted, "Moving," and spun around the battlement to the opposite side. Popping up immediately to fire a second time, she dropped straight down to her knees to avoid return fire that came at her a lot faster—not because the enemy had ascertained the defenders' new strategy, but because she was now on the gate side of the battlement.

Duckwalking back into the enclosure, she met Tony's concerned gaze across the tight space.

"You're bleeding, ma'am."

Layla blinked and touched her cheek, suddenly aware of a sharp stinging sensation. "Damn stone wall. A shard must have been chipped off. And it's Layla, not ma'am. Not when we've become so close." She grinned when she said that, which had Tony grinning in return. "Ready?" she asked as she counted the seconds in her head. "Switch positions." She indicated the right-hand gun slot on the enclosure, establishing the routine on this first round.

"I'm up," he said and disappeared as she stepped up to the narrow window, aimed as she moved, and was firing while the barrel of her MP5 was still sliding forward. Two sharp bursts, duck. Two more bursts while Tony was still firing, and she dropped to a crouch, her back against the wall beneath the gun slot. Tony was in the narrow doorway an instant later, checked her position, and slipped inside the battlement.

Layla counted three seconds in her head, and they started all over again. Shoot, wait, move. They continued that way for what seemed like hours, though she had more than enough combat experience to know it had been nowhere near that long. The *Fortalesa* teams kept up a steady, but random pattern of fire, moving and shooting all up and down the wall, taking turns inside the shelter and out. By the time the enemy's fire began to slow, she and Tony were both soaked with sweat. Layla's collar was wet with blood that colored the sweat dripping from her jaw, while Tony had a rough bandage around one arm that was more red than white where he'd been shot.

As always, Layla's jaw ached like a son of bitch, because she'd never managed to break the habit of clenching her teeth when shit got heavy. She worked the jaw as she slammed in her fifth thirty-round magazine. She had one more mag after that, and had called for additional ammo from the runners stationed along the base of the wall for that purpose. But with the enemy's rate of fire slowing, she hoped she wouldn't need it.

"Is it me, or are those assholes covering their retreat?" she asked Tony, meaning the enemy fire had shifted from active targeting to undirected sprays which seemed intended to force the wall's defenders to stay down.

Tony nodded his agreement, and she inched toward the doorway. "I'm taking a look. From the left," she added wryly. The left was the side which provided better cover from enemy fire. She fired three more bursts, to test the enemy's mood, but by the time her final round got off, the enemy's fire had ceased completely.

"Damn it," she swore and ran for the stairs. This might be her best chance to follow those assholes, to see where they went and discover how they managed to disappear so completely that not even vampires could track them.

Tony followed without being asked, and they both caught fresh mags as they ran, all but falling down the stairs. Somehow landing on her feet, she raced for the sally port, the small, heavily secured door twenty-five yards left of the gate. No one else was moving in the yard, except the *Fortalesa*'s small team of medics who were gradually being joined and assisted by exhausted fighters. A quick survey as she ran told her the enemy's new, much larger attack force had done serious damage.

Furious, she swung the MP5 over her shoulder to rest on her back, pressed her thumb against the biometric scanner, sighed a relieved breath when it worked, then used both hands to lift the heavy metal riot bar. Swinging her weapon back to the ready position, she glanced once at Tony, then cracked open the thick door. When a quick glance told her there was no one waiting to pounce, she opened the door farther and rushed out, heading straight for the tree cover. She paused only long enough to scan the immediate area, then continued. There was a trail of sorts this time. More shooters meant more feet stomping the detritus-covered ground, and more bodies crashing into branches and through undergrowth. They were quiet, she'd give them that. There were no cries or moans, no curses. She stopped suddenly, taking cover behind a trio of entwined tree trunks.

Tony appeared confused, but stopped next to her, crouching low.

Layla held one finger to her lips and just listened. The silence was so absolute that even the normal sounds of the forest were absent. No birds, no rustling rodents, not a breath of wind moving through the trees.

What the actual fuck?

She stepped out and continued following the trail which was still as plain as a blinking red sign. Until it just . . . stopped. She stared at the ground, saw the leaves and dirt flattened as if several pairs of feet had passed, and then the trail just disappeared, as if the fleeing people had been lifted into the air, or vanished into an invisible fairy mound.

"Impossible," she muttered, and paced to the left and right of the truncated trail, looking for something to indicate where the retreating enemy had gone. People didn't simply disappear mid-step. They had to have gone somewhere.

But though she and Tony both searched for more than an hour, not only along the line of the break, but traveling deeper into the trees, searching for renewed sign of a trail that *had* to be there, they found nothing. The two of them exchanged a look, as if each was doubting the sanity of the other.

Layla broke the gaze first, with a shake of her head. "We're not imagining this. It happened."

He frowned and said, "Magic, Layla."

She smiled. "Magic? Really?"

It was his turn to smile, to give her a look that said she was being naïve. "We sleep surrounded by vampires, but you doubt the existence of magic?"

"Vampires are natural, just like you and me. Not exactly like us, because they're . . . higher on the evolutionary chart, but they bleed, they die. That's not magic."

His smile widened. "Perhaps you should speak to Lord Xavier about this. You meet with him, yes? Just as the commander did?"

"Yes."

"Ask him. If I'm wrong, no matter. But if I'm right, he needs to know."

Layla thought about that as they walked back to the *Fortalesa*. She'd assumed—Xavier had *let* her assume—that he'd been waiting for new information, for his vampires to find the evil genius behind these attacks, and then he'd take action. But waiting wasn't Xavier's usual *modus operandi*, was it?

No, Xavier was a fucking vampire lord and far more powerful than anyone else she knew. And that asshole knew more than he was telling her. God damn him.

She walked faster, her boots thumping the ground, while Tony—not having been privy to her thought process—shot worried glances her way. When they broke out from under the trees, with the *Fortalesa* in sight, the sun immediately tried to burn a hole in the top of her head, and she remembered it was still morning. Which meant she'd have to wait *hours* to confront that lying bloodsucking asshole.

"Well, fuck."

"Layla?" Tony asked cautiously.

Geez, did she look that deranged? "Come on," she said on a sigh. "We can't do any more with this, and there are wounded to tend to."

AFTER LAYLA HAD made sure the last of her injured fighters had been taken care of, and had her own minor wound treated, she walked every inch of the *Fortalesa*'s wall, both on top and at ground level, including the far back wall, where the forest was so dense as to be impassable. She was tired. More tired than she should have been. She'd fought harder and longer battles with her team. And sure, they collapsed at the end of it, but while they were in the grinder, they ran on pure adrenaline, pushing each other to keep going.

And that was the difference. She missed her team. She knew what each of them was capable of, knew whom she could count on for what, with no questions, no doubts. Tony had been great, but she didn't *know* him.

"Well, fuck," she muttered and climbed the stairs to her parents' apartment to do what she should have done the previous night. She called Brian.

"Ma'am?" he answered.

"Don't start that," she said wearily.

"You sound tired, Layla."

She sighed. "It's been a hell of a day."

"More fighting?" He sounded surprised. She supposed he had good reason to be, since the last time they'd spoken, everything had quieted down.

"More and worse. They doubled their number. We fought them off, with no fatalities, although we sustained a few nasty wounds. But they're disappearing into thin air once they retreat. I tracked them myself this time, and their trail simply vanished."

"People don't disappear."

"No, they don't. And I have a strong suspicion that Xavier either knows or has a damn good idea of what's going on."

"What's he told you?"

"Nothing. But that's going to change. It's time for some answers."

"Uh. Vampire lord. Maybe you shouldn't piss him off."

"Fuck that. I grew up with vamps, remember? The worst he can do is fire me."

"Say the word, Layla, and we're there."

"I'm saying it, Brian. My dad's got a good group, but I need more experience and my team's specific talents. I don't want to short-staff the Wilkerson estate, though."

"No problem. I'll call in a team of boy scouts yearning for their combat badge."

She laughed. "Okay, then. You, River and Kerry."

"Excellent, we'll be there tomorrow . . . early morning, possibly before dawn. That okay with your vampire?"

"He's not *my* vampire."

"Okaaay. See you then." And he hung up.

A check of the time told Layla she still had the better part of two hours before her nightly meeting with Xavier. And this meeting was going to be more than a briefing. She wondered if the others would be invited and hoped for the first time since she'd arrived that she'd be alone with Xavier. The other vampires, especially Joaquim and Chuy, were bound to be super protective and slavishly loyal to Xavier. They wouldn't have been elevated to the position of his highest advisers if they weren't.

She gave a mental shrug as she stripped off her sweat-stained and dirty clothes. It would be better if the others weren't there, but their presence wouldn't stop her. She'd either get answers or she'd walk. She couldn't lead, couldn't make good decisions if she didn't have all the information. Especially not when it was deliberately being kept from her, and she didn't know why.

Tossing her dirty clothes aside, she stepped under the shower while it was still cold. She felt as though she'd been sweating for days, rather than a few hours. The water warmed quickly enough that it still felt good, and even better once she'd washed her hair, then soaped and rinsed her body twice over.

She toweled dry with brisk movements, pulled on fresh clothes, and her same boots. Clothes were important, but the right boots could make all the difference in the world when you were fighting for your life.

Feeling reasonably human again, she grabbed a ripe pear and headed back downstairs to the *Fortalesa*'s small hospital. Most days it had four beds and served as a first-aid and emergency room for everyone who lived there. Today, they'd crammed four cots in with the beds and set up triage in a tent outside. Layla stopped in the tent first, where three cots had been set up and used for those who could be treated and sent home to rest. Now, the cots had been turned into beds and held two fighters who were still receiving IV fluids of one sort or another, and a third who was still groggy from the painkillers Nowak had given him after treatment for a wounded shoulder. She stopped at each of the three bunks to exchange a word with the men. They were in surprisingly high spirits and feeling good about having successfully fought off the larger enemy force. She matched their cheer for a while, since it would do no good to diminish their victory with her concerns, and then walked into the hospital itself.

She waited just inside the door until Doctor Nowak noticed her, then tipped her head toward the only private space left, which was a short hall in the back where two unisex bathrooms were located. Neither room was occupied, so she grabbed a couple bottles of water, then leaned against the back wall and waited. When Nowak joined her, she held up one of the bottles. The doctor took it with a tired but grateful smile, then propped her back against the same wall.

"You get any rest yet?" Layla asked.

Nowak drained the bottle, then took the second one Layla offered. "Thirty minutes on a cot in the office next door. So far, I've been rotating my staff every two hours. But if none of our patients crash in the next hour, I'll probably let everyone except two of my medics go home and sleep for six hours, keeping the ones who stay on the two hour rest shifts. If that works out after six hours, I'll increase their sleep shifts to four. At that point, I'll bring in two of the ones I sent home, and let the original two take their own turn at home."

Layla gave her a dry look. "Did you need to write all those numbers down?"

She looked puzzled. "No, that's standard crisis mode."

"Guess my crises have all been non-standard. I notice you didn't include yourself in that schedule."

"Oh, I'll rotate with the others next door, adding more time when the fresh medics start back."

"I hate to ask, lest you accuse me of being cold again, but what's the prognosis?"

"We're looking at a minimum three to five days before any of these patients are mobile, including the three in the tent. After that, I'll evaluate their progress daily, and give you a report. When they *are* able to report back, they'll have to be on restricted duty."

She took another long drink of water then continued, "And what do I mean by restricted duty, you ask? If you're lucky, two or three will be able to sit on the wall and fire a weapon, rather than jumping around all the time, like they were today. The others are looking at a longer recovery. Hopefully long enough that this fighting will be done and over with."

"I see. Thank you. I'll brief Lord Xavier."

"Layla."

She turned.

"I don't think you're cold. You have one of the hardest jobs around here. You fight when all the others do, but you don't go home. Instead, you work in my hospital, and now you're going to brief Lord Xavier, and try to decide how to keep everyone alive. Not just the people on the wall, but all those sheltering inside the *Fortalesa*, too. I, at least, can heal all of my patients"—she gestured toward the packed hospital bay—"given the tiniest bit of luck. You have to send your fighters out to die, the next time those fools attack. Whether that's tomorrow, or two months from now."

"No," Layla disagreed urgently. "I *never* send them out to die. I train them, arm them, support them to the very best of my ability. I send them out there to fight and then come home to their families alive and well. If I believed otherwise, I couldn't do my job."

"I suppose not," Nowak said thoughtfully. "And if you could, no one would follow you."

Layla gave a tired sigh and said, "I'll check back after I brief Xavier."

"Just call," Novak said simply. "It's pointless for you to spend your energy running up and down those stairs, when you could just call. Even you need rest," she added, indicating Layla's bandaged arm.

"I'll do that. Thank you."

XAVIER LOOKED up when Layla walked into his office. Joaquim and Chuy were already there. They'd come early, both having information to exchange that, while bearing on the existing conflict, had little to do with the active fighting that took place during the day.

But Xavier was very aware of the day's attack. He'd been anticipating her arrival this evening, hoping the détente of sorts that they'd reached the previous night would not only hold, but even improve her attitude toward him. He saw her take note of the empty wine glasses in front of the two vampires before lifting her gaze to him, and knew this wasn't going to be a friendly briefing.

"Give us the room," he said quietly. Joaquim and Chuy stood without protest. Their business with him was done, and they both had sources of their own who would provide details of the day's fighting.

"Sire," they said simultaneously as they pushed in their chairs and headed for the door, both of them greeting Layla briefly before leaving the office.

As she had the night before, Layla poured two fingers of whiskey in a glass and sat across from him at the table. She didn't say anything, but studied him silently, as if waiting for him to speak.

"It was a difficult day," he said, starting with something neutral, and confident that if she was angry or upset about something that had happened, she'd get to it soon enough.

She sipped her whiskey, without shifting her gaze away from him. "You could say that, yes."

"Dr. Nowak reports no fatalities, and while there are injuries, some serious, none that require my intervention."

That surprised her into saying, "You donate blood to injured guards?"

"When needed. Why does that surprise you?"

She avoided looking at him, setting down her phone, and arranging a few pages of handwritten notes in what appeared to be a nervous gesture. "There was no conflict when I left, so I guess there was never an opportunity for you to . . . heal anybody."

He smiled slightly. "You think not? You were *very* young."

Anger flashed in her eyes. "Well, I'm not young now, and I don't like being lied to."

Xavier gave her a quizzical look. She'd been tense when she'd arrived, so it couldn't be his healing efforts that precipitated what was essentially an accusation that *he* had lied to her. And she clearly wanted a confrontation, so there was no point in avoiding it. "And what have I lied about, Layla?"

"You lied by omission," she snapped. "You know more than you're telling me about the people attacking the *Fortalesa*, and the person behind it. Including the supposed *mystery* of how they're escaping without a trace. I tracked their retreat today—"

His reaction, which had been lazily curious about her mood, sharpened abruptly. "How far did you go?"

She stopped mid-sentence and stared at him. "You *do* know something, you bastard. Why wasn't I told? How the hell am I supposed to defend this place and these people if you're keeping secrets from me?"

"How far did you go, Layla?" he repeated in a hard demand.

"Until the trail cut off in fucking mid-step. So tell me, *Lord Xavier*, what does it mean?"

He stood without warning and said, "We're taking a walk."

She stood at the same time. "I'm not going anywhere with you, until you explain—"

"Walk with me, Commander."

It was an order, and from the rebellious look on her face, she knew it. "Fine." Leaving her notes on the table, she slid her phone into a pocket and waited.

Xavier came around the table and gestured for her to precede him to the door.

"No thanks. You lead the way."

"I've no plans to assault you from behind," he said dryly. "I was being polite."

"Fuck polite. I don't trust you."

He sighed and wondered if he'd ever met a more difficult woman, and then wondered why the hell he found that attractive. "Very well," he said with a sigh, then grinned. "But you should know that if you attempt to assault *me*, I'll fight back."

"Ha ha. Just walk."

THEY WALKED SIDE by side, through the inner courtyard, and past the hospital which was quiet and dark. He took that as a good sign, noting there was no smell of death—which would have been unmistakable—but only the usual scents he associated with human sick rooms. Layla might not credit it, but he and Dr. Nowak spoke daily on a regular basis, and during a crisis such as this, even more often. He probably knew more about the people injured than Layla did, though he wouldn't bother to confront her with that fact. She hardly needed another reason to dislike him. Or pretend that she did.

The spark that had drawn them together was still there. He felt it, and so did she, whether she'd admit or not. He was a damn vampire, for fuck's sake. He knew when a woman wanted him. Her heart was beating a little too fast, her cheeks were warm with a flush of awareness, her pupils dilated. And he knew if he stripped her bare, her breasts would be heavy with desire, her nipples . . . Fuck. He had to rein in his thoughts before *his* body became too aroused to conceal.

Damn, but he wanted this woman. When she'd left before, he'd seen the potential for what she could become, but now . . . She had a fire deep inside that drove her to challenge every rule, every attempt to rein her in. It was a fire he wanted to touch, to stroke to life until it became an inferno whose only purpose was to drive them both mad with desire. He wanted to feel that heat burning in his own veins as he sank his fangs into her flesh, with her bucking beneath him in helpless orgasm.

God knew he wanted her. But for more than just sex, more than just her body—though that body was enough to tempt the saints. It was the force of her intellect when turned on a problem, the confidence that saw competition at every turn and had to do more than simply succeed.

Layla had always had to *win*.

He knew he'd wounded her all those years ago, when he'd rejected her innocent seduction. Wounded more than just her heart. She'd insist, as she had the previous night, that she'd gotten over it, over *him*, a long time ago. That she'd grown out of the young girl's crush that had been between them. But she'd have been lying. Just as he'd lied when he'd sent her away.

She didn't seem surprised when they exited through the sally port next to the big, main gate, which was securely closed. And when she finally spoke, it was to say, "I called France earlier. Danilo's good, but I needed to talk to someone with more strategic experience than she has."

"I would rather you not discuss my affairs outside the *Fortalesa*." He didn't know why it irritated him that she'd called someone else to discuss her day. Someone who was not *him*. Or maybe he did.

"And I'd rather you not lie to me about what's going on," she responded sweetly.

"And am I allowed to ask what your French friend had to say?"

"He's not French, just working there for now."

"Ah. Someone you work with, then."

"Yeah. A friend."

"And?"

"He and two others are flying in tomorrow. They have skills that your people don't—at least your human guards don't. Skills that I need, if I'm going to figure out who's behind all this and what they want. They're also experienced enough to command, in case I find it necessary to send one or more smaller contingents of fighters into the field. We can't just sit here and wait for the next attack."

"Is that what you think I'm doing? Sitting and waiting for my ene--mies to attack?" he demanded, angry and letting it show. Did she think he'd become Lord of Spain by sitting behind high walls and doing *nothing*? That he'd never fought a real battle, with blood flying while vampires screamed as decades—sometimes centuries—worth of lives ended in an instant?

She stopped walking and stared at him. "No, in fact I'm pretty God damned sure that's *not* what you've been doing. Which, I assume, is why we're out here in the woods in the middle of the fucking night, with barely a sliver of moon to see by. Not that it makes much difference in the fucking forest!"

One half of his mouth quirked into a smile. He didn't remember her cursing quite this much before. "Can you find the place where the trail terminated?"

"What?"

"The trail. You said you followed the enemy's retreat. Can you show me where it ended?"

She looked around slowly, then down at the ground. "It's a lot darker than it was. One tree looks a lot like another. But..." She scanned the surrounding forest again. "Yeah, I think so. And if this is some kind of test, just so you can show me up by walking right to it, tell me now and don't waste my time."

He *could* find it without her. But he was rather enjoying their walk. "I'll know when we get closer," he said ambiguously. It was the truth. Just not all of it.

She studied him a moment, then pulled out a small flashlight and turned it on.

"Continue to aim that downward."

"I know the drill." They walked a few more steps, when she said, "You're paying for the people coming in tomorrow."

"Am I?"

"I have a budget for the daylight guard. I'm using it."

He didn't really care what they cost. He was more interested in *who* they were, and what they meant to her. But he wasn't going to admit that. "Tell me, Laylita," he said, using the nickname he hadn't spoken in all the years she'd been gone, "what will you give me if I let these people of yours come to my *Fortalesa*?"

"They're not coming for a fucking sleepover," she gritted out. "They're professional and highly skilled, the best in the world at what they do. And they're coming here to help pull *your* ass out of the fire. My father's people are damn good, and they have courage and heart. But one of my fighters is worth ten of them. It's not an insult, nor a criticism. It's simple reality. My guys have fought and survived some of the meanest, most dangerous conflicts in the world, frequently while hired by assholes they didn't particularly like or respect. So you don't need to worry about that. You *need* them. So suck it up, *my lord*."

His smile widened. He so loved swatting at her temper. "There are people, and places, I'd much rather suck," he crooned.

She stopped to stare at him, nostrils flaring and eyes widening in outrage, but she forced it back and smiled sweetly. "I'm sure there is no shortage of volunteers for that activity. I, however, have a job to do."

He laughed, really *laughed*, for the first time in weeks. "I *have* missed you, *cariño*."

She glared. "Well I haven't missed you, and I'm not your fucking *cariño*."

"Not yet," he replied. He *always* won—always got what and whom he wanted. And he definitely wanted *her*.

She eyed him steadily. "Are we going to continue or what?"

Ah. His Layla had definitely matured while she'd been gone. She still had the fire that had drawn him back then, but she'd learned to bank it to a simmer until it would be most effective. "No need. Wait here a moment."

She held out her hands in a "What the fuck?" gesture and shook her head in disgust, but watched silently as he continued in the general direction they'd been heading. He took several more steps, needing to distance himself from the waves of emotion she was throwing off. He'd learned enough from her father about her career—both formal military and later freelancing—to know she was as good as she claimed her associates were, the ones coming in tomorrow and the others, too. The fact that she was boiling over with emotion had little to do with her typical behavior on the job and more to do with him, and her conflicted love/hate feelings toward him.

"Layla," he said softly.

He'd moved far enough away that she had to search for just a moment. He knew the moment she spotted the dark silver gleam of his eyes, as her own went wide with a soft gasp.

"Come here, please."

She did, moving silently as she followed the path he'd taken. She flicked her flashlight on again, once she reached his side, slowly panning the narrow beam around the area. First the trees, then the spaces between them, and finally the ground. "This is it," she said softly. "See how the trail just . . . ends?"

She looked up at him, but he wasn't looking at her, or anything else. Not in this world. He held out his hands as if feeling an invisible wall.

"Did you find something?"

"Magic," he murmured, lifting his head slightly and inhaling, as if it was a scent in the air. "You want to know how they're vanishing so completely," he continued, barely loud enough to be heard. "Our enemy is a sorcerer, and he's using magic to whisk his fighters away."

"Excuse me? A sorcerer?"

He heard the skepticism in her voice and gave her a surprised look.

"You put faith in your Kerry and her hunches, and yet you doubt the existence of sorcerers and their magic?"

"Well, yeah? I mean, Kerry's hunches are one thing, and I've seen you do some pretty cool tricks, but—"

"I don't do *tricks*, Layla. I am a vampire lord, which means I have considerable power that neither you nor your science can explain. As for what sorcerers are capable of, what is that, if not what you would call magic?"

She bit the inside of her cheek for a moment, then admitted, "I don't know. I want to say it's impossible, but clearly it's not. I guess I never really thought of it much at all."

"No sorcerers in your armies, or that of your enemy?"

"Not that I know of."

"The key word being, 'know.' I imagine your leaders prefer to keep that sort of thing secret from the general public. And it would seem, from its soldiers, as well."

She stared. "So you're saying magic is real? And there are *sorcerers* who can . . . what?"

"That would depend on the sorcerer. I must admit, they are rare in the world now, though at one time they were plentiful enough that they went to war against vampires."

"You're kidding. Were you—?"

"No. That was long before my birth. There are still sorcerers alive, though I'm told they've dwindled in number due to the small amount of magic left in this world."

She closed her eyes for a moment, then opened them wide and said slowly, "So you're saying there's some sorcerer who has a hard-on for you . . . personally? Or is he, or she, just looking for any vampire to shoot at?"

"That's what I've been trying to discover—the secret that you claim I've kept from you. Though I can't see how knowing that would have changed your defensive strategy at all."

"Defensively, you're probably right. But if I'd known there was some wacko sorcerer lurking around who could . . . what? Open a magical door for his people to walk through? Where are they going, by the way? How far?"

"To know that, I need to discover who this sorcerer is."

"Have you made any progress?"

"Not yet, but he has to have a hiding place nearby. I've consulted a few others, who are older and more knowledgeable about such things, and they all tell me the same thing—that the sorcerer has to be *here* in order to send his people to safety."

"So he can't *open the door* from the other side?"

"Not that my associates are aware."

"Are any of these *associates* that you consulted sorcerers themselves?"

"Regrettably, no. One is a magic user, but not powerful enough to be considered a sorcerer. The others are vampires—one old enough to remember the war and the other a historian who has studied the sorcery of that time."

"I know you've been sending your vampires out, looking for something. What is it?"

"Not some*thing*, but someone. It takes a great deal of power for a sorcerer to transport others, rather than just himself. I suspect that's why the initial attacks used so few people. But even those few could not have been carried far. He has to have a headquarters in the city. There's no other possibility. But Barcelona is a big city with many buildings."

She studied the ground pensively for a moment, then said, "I told you about Kerry Nask, the woman coming in tomorrow with the others. I told you she gets *hunches* about stuff. Like telling us to take this street, instead of that one, when we're on a mission. Or warning us not to launch a particular operation that we've sometimes spent a lot of time planning. And we've learned to listen to her. I don't care how much time or money we've put into a specific op, if Kerry says don't do it, we don't. Sometimes it's cancelled completely, other times we just shift the timetable or the specifics around. But we never, and I mean *never*, ignore what she says."

"Is she a vampire?"

"No. Her mother's a witch, whatever that means. She heads up a coven in Pennsylvania. But Kerry's not. A witch, I mean. She's not even sure how she knows to warn us about stuff. It's not something she works at. It just comes to her."

"She's clearly a sensitive, but that can include any number of abilities."

"Well, I was just wondering if she might be helpful in tracking down this sorcerer of yours. Would he give off enough of a . . . sign or whatever that she could pick it up? Like if we drive up and down the streets of Barcelona?"

He didn't dismiss the idea out of hand, but considered it. "Doubtful," he said finally. "But if I or my vampires managed to pick up a trace, she might be useful in confirming it. What I'd really like is to capture one of his people and *persuade* them to talk."

LAYLA KNEW WHAT *persuade* meant when he said it like that. He'd pry into the person's head and dig around until he found what he needed. And she had *no* problem with him doing that. These people, whoever they were, were shooting at *her* people. Or her parents' people, which was close enough. After all, she'd grown up here.

She took a step closer to Xavier. "See, now, that's something I could have helped you with, if you'd told me. Capturing one fighter is very different than stopping an entire retreat."

She regretted that step when he took a step of his own, putting them bare inches apart. Which was way too close. But if she backed up, she'd be admitting it bothered her to have him there.

He was looking down at her, his eyes once more filled with that eerie pewter gleam. She had to tilt her head back to look at him. He was so damn tall. She was very nearly six feet—*was* that tall in her boots. But he still towered over her. Well, not *towered*. It just seemed that way since she was accustomed to being taller than most people. She really liked that about him, though. Liked that he was taller, that she had to stretch to put her arms around his neck, that he'd probably completely dominate her in bed . . .

"*Stop that!*" her inner voice screeched. He was still watching her. "Yes?" she asked calmly, as if she'd spent the last few seconds waiting patiently and not spinning sensual images of the two of them.

His lips curved the tiniest bit. "Is the absence of vampires on your team deliberate?"

She shook her head. "No. One of our original members was a vampire. Great guy, excellent scout. He fell in love, and his girlfriend wanted him out. Wanted him to stay alive, I guess. He was a damn good fighter, and a very good friend. He still is. And he was damn near irreplaceable on the team. The best we could do was fill the hole he left."

His gaze changed, as if he was seeing a part of her he hadn't known existed. He probably was. Her years in the army hadn't been spent at a desk, and notwithstanding the damn vineyard, neither were the jobs she did with her team. She'd done things both in the army and after that she'd rather forget, but they'd changed her, made her harder, more skeptical, less trusting. All of that. But they'd also taught her how to survive the worst humanity had to offer, how to protect the people who fought at your side, and how to walk away when it was over.

Xavier's eyes never left her face, but the sense of him changed. The air was just the air, no longer filled with the stark awareness of him that had her thinking hot, sweaty thoughts that she shouldn't.

"When are your people arriving?" he asked, somehow stepping back psychologically, without physical moving.

She blinked as the world returned to its normal state, feeling as if she'd been stretched too tight. She licked dry lips, much too aware of his eyes dropping to her mouth, following the movement of her tongue.

No, no, no. They were *not* going to do this.

"Tomorrow," she said, hearing the rasp in her own voice. "I'm not sure what time. But definitely in the morning."

His eyes lifted from her mouth to meet her gaze. "I'll want to meet them tomorrow night."

"Everyone? Or just Kerry?"

"All of them. Three, you said. You trust them, but I need to meet them, Layla. I need to be sure."

He said it so calmly. There was no insult intended. Just the truth. She couldn't get angry about that. He had ways of judging people that she couldn't match.

"All right," she said just as quietly. "Where?"

"They'll be bunking in the barracks?"

"Yes. The barracks are empty, so there's more than enough room."

"Will you stay with them, too?"

"Yeah, it's what we're used to. We get more done that way."

He nodded. "Good. I'll come to you, then. One hour after sunset. I'm assuming you know when that is?"

She smiled slightly. The sun's schedule was something you just *knew* when you lived inside the *Fortalesa*. It had been a while for her, but it was posted in her mother's kitchen, in her father's office, and pretty much everywhere else. "I know it." She would have turned away then, but he touched her wounded cheek, his fingers stroking her skin so gently that she didn't feel it until he was turning her to face him. "Does this hurt?"

"Not really." She was far too aware of how close he was. She wanted to jerk away, to tell him not to touch her. So why didn't she?

She was still trying to work that out when he said, "Look at me, Layla."

Oh, no. That way lay madness. But a stubborn part of her refused to stand there with lowered eyes as if she was afraid of him, afraid of what she might do if she looked into those strangely lit eyes. She lifted her head.

"I can heal this." His fingers touched the injury with tender care.

She shook her head, her eyes still locked with his. "Don't waste your energy. It's not that bad. It just stings a little."

"Then perhaps this will help." Her face was still upturned to meet his gaze, when he lowered his head and put his mouth close to hers. She had a moment of panicked indecision. Her heart raced in eager anticipation, and she was so damn hungry for his touch, despite the years she'd spent cursing his name. But she'd sworn she wouldn't do this. He couldn't be trusted, not when her heart still ached sometimes in the dark of night. When she was cold and exhausted from a day that had seen too much blood and death. When she longed for memories she could wrap around herself, memories that would convince her to keep going.

Before she could decide, before she could say anything, his lips were touching hers, and they were so sensuous and warm, so unlike the cold face he showed to the world—the hard-ass vampire lord who took no shit and gave no quarter. She moaned in soft surrender as her mouth opened against his, as his other arm circled her waist and pulled her closer . . .

"No!" she cried, and shoved herself away from every part of him. Not just his mouth or his body, but the memories of that last night before she'd left for good. The night he'd broken her heart, told her she was too young, too inexperienced to know what she wanted. Too young. Right. As if a two-hundred-year-old vampire was going to a find woman more his age to suck on. She'd cursed herself then, for being stupid enough to fall for him. For believing that she was somehow different, that he'd love *her* when he'd never loved anyone.

"Layla—"

He reached for her, but she held out a hand palm first. "No. I'm sorry. I didn't mean to . . . Just no." She walked away from him, trying not to run, not wanting to fall. It was so fucking dark. She reminded herself who she was—no longer a heartbroken nineteen-year-old girl, but a strong, accomplished woman. A deadly fighter who commanded not only the respect of some of the best soldiers in the field, but their friendship, and their love. She didn't need Xavier in her life. She didn't need anyone but the people who were already there.

Chapter Nine

THE NEXT DAY dawned hot and clear, and too fucking early. Layla rolled out of bed and went straight to the shower she'd skipped the night before, because she'd been too tired. She was moving to the barracks today, and reminded herself to strip the sheets so her mother didn't come home to blood and dirt. She never worried about this stuff in the field, where everyone was in the same condition, and where a bit of bloody filth was the very last thing one was concerned about. But her mother would be aghast, and even more so if Layla explained they did it all the time.

She grabbed the sheets and yanked them off the bed as she walked away, dumping the pile near the door to take with her. There was a laundry room in the barracks. She could wash them there, and if she pulled up the comforter on her bed and closed the door, maybe her mother wouldn't notice the sheets were gone.

She shook her head. What was she? A teenager again? Trying to cover up evidence of her many misdeeds? Christ, she was a grown ass woman. She didn't need to explain her shower habits to her mother. But she was still going to take the sheets with her to the damn barracks. Coward.

She checked out the wound on her cheek before stepping under the shower's hot spray. It was ugly and would leave a scar. But it was more like a deep tissue burn than a bullet wound. It didn't even sting when the water hit it . . . "Fuck!" Well, not much. She should have just let Xavier heal the damn thing.

She soaped her body quickly and efficiently, then washed and conditioned her hair even though she would just braid it back for the day, probably while it was still wet. Gorgeous hair wasn't on her list of priorities either.

Was it ever? She tipped her head back to rinse out the conditioner and tried to remember the last time she'd cared what her hair looked like. There'd been the trip the team had taken to Paris, before settling down into the vineyard. Yeah, they'd all gotten spiffed up for one of their nights there. They'd gone to a Michelin-starred restaurant and everything. And before that? She couldn't remember, which was an answer in itself. Layla Casales was not exactly Miss Universe material.

Shrugging, because she really didn't care, she stepped out of the shower, toweled off, and pulled on some underwear along with her usual sports bra, then combed and braided her hair. Deodorant, and moisturizer with a strong sun screen, because while she didn't do primping, she also didn't want to end up a wrinkled old crone by the age of fifty.

Khaki-colored pants, combat-style with multiple pockets, and a tan tank top completed her ensemble along with a long-sleeved shirt in the same color, which she wore unbuttoned. She did a final walk-through to be sure everything she needed was back in her duffel, then for about two minutes, she considered making herself some breakfast. *That* thought was discarded immediately in favor of a quick trip to the communal kitchen, which was handily located right next to the barracks. It wasn't her mama's cooking, but it wasn't bad either.

She was just hitting the outside stairs when her phone rang. She looked down at the display and smiled. "Casales."

"We're on the ground in Barcelona," Brian said, not bothering with niceties. He and the others had been activated, which meant it was time for business, and *their* business was deadly serious. "On our way to you. I figure an hour, no more."

"Good."

"Anything new happen?"

"No. It's quiet here so far, but my instincts are telling me that won't last." She considered warning him about the involvement of magic, but that was a longer conversation. She imagined his reaction not only to the *existence* of sorcerers, but to the idea that one was tied up in this affair, would be the same as hers.

"Understood. See you soonest."

She disconnected and shoved the phone into a pocket, then began her morning survey of the wall, stopping to answer questions, or just talk. She made a point of seeking out the walking wounded who'd recovered enough, or whose injuries had been light enough, to resume their duties. She'd stopped at the hospital and heard Nowak's report on yesterday's injured—both hospitalized and not. She'd been relieved to learn that the most seriously wounded were all making excellent recoveries, thanks in no small part to a late night visit by Xavier, even though he'd told her he wasn't going. And damn if that didn't make it more difficult to hate him.

It irritated her that she was even thinking about him, much less having trouble hating him. She wanted to put it down to exhaustion, but knew it was more. She was bothered by their trek into the forest last night, and how easy it had been to remain civil, even when he'd told her about his investigation into the use of magic by their enemy. She had to admit that her initial anger that he'd withheld such an important piece of intel had been blown away by the revelation that sorcerers and magic were real. For fuck's sake, could this operation get any more complicated? And then she'd gone and kissed him. It was as if the universe had decided to have a bit of fun at her expense, to push her and Xavier together and see what happened. The chemistry between them was as electric as ever. She'd have sworn there were literal sparks flying whenever they got too close. As if they each gave off a different chemical, and when circumstance brought them within a certain physical distance . . . boom! Sparks flew and an explosion ensued, resulting in bad decisions and unwise sexual intercourse. She supposed for some people, chemistry was a good thing, but all she'd ever gotten was a broken heart.

She stopped at the back wall and studied the distant trees, looking for anyone who shouldn't have been there. She couldn't see all of it. Xavier's property stretched for acres and while he was a good neighbor, he was also very particular about maintaining his privacy. Vampires had long memories to go with their long lives, and it wasn't that long ago that they'd been hunted and murdered in their sleep.

Finding nothing, which was no more than she'd expected, she exchanged a quick word with the two guards patrolling that quadrant, then continued around the other side until she'd walked the entire distance around the *Fortalesa's* wall and was approaching the gate. A rush of childish voices had her turning to look down into the courtyard. The morning cluster of children were heading for the fifteen-passenger van that was the *Fortalesa's* version of a school bus. These were the youngest students, nine of them who looked to be from around six to eleven years of age. There were older students, too, but their school day began much earlier, and since a few of them were able to drive, they took turns ferrying each other in a fire-engine red minivan. They all could have been educated privately within the *Fortalesa*, rather than traveling to the nearest town, but the parents and Xavier had long ago decided in favor of the socialization provided by the schools, along with a decent education.

The number of children living within the *Fortalesa* was small compared to, say, a modest town of the same population. But the *Fortalesa* wasn't typical. At any given time, at least a third of the people living there were vampires, and even a few of them had children, either adopted or brought into the family by their chosen mates. Being a vampire didn't automatically take away the desire to raise a family.

In a very real sense, however, the vampires themselves functioned as a large family. Vamps tended to prefer living in groups, for protection if nothing else, but within those groups there was a connection as strong as any human familial bond. And within the *Fortalesa*, that bond had been extended to include most human residents, but especially the children.

Vampires were the product of their making and socialization after they were turned. And *that* was largely a function of the vampire who turned them, which in this case was Xavier. There were definitely some in the *Fortalesa* who'd been turned by someone else, but those few had taken blood oaths to Xavier, which bound them to him as their master in a very real sense, as in literal life or death. But the oaths were more than that. For all that Layla thought Xavier was an asshole, she acknowledged the powerful sense of loyalty that tied him to his people. If the vampires of the *Fortalesa* ever went to war, Xavier wouldn't be in a secure place giving orders over the radio. He'd be leading them from the very front of the pack.

Smiling at the children's happy chatter, she set aside thoughts of Xavier and turned to study the surrounding forest and the long, empty road beyond the gate. It was so quiet this morning, in contrast to yesterday's battle—the non-stop rattle of gunfire, the cries of the wounded and curses of the fighters. And then the abrupt silence as the attackers simply faded away. Before last night, she'd very briefly considered, and immediately discarded, the fantastic idea that the attackers were ghosts.

But now, she wasn't sure the reality was any better. Their enemy wasn't a ghost, but he *was* a sorcerer who could . . . teleport, she supposed one could call it, his fighters out of danger in such a way that not even Xavier could follow. She wondered if Xavier had enough power to stop the teleport from occurring. After all, magical energy was still energy. Maybe Xavier could toss a virtual grenade of his own power against the sorcerer's and break up the . . . spell or whatever it was that created the teleport. That could be one of the reasons their enemy only attacked in daytime. Magic or not, if the attack had come during the night, the vamps would have wiped the field clean in a matter of hours. But daytime attacks also stopped Xavier from matching his strength against that of the sorcerer. Did Xavier know who the sorcerer was? He'd said his vamps were looking, but he'd never *specifically* said he didn't know the enemy.

That gave her more to think about, and more questions for Xavier, which she frustratingly couldn't deal with until sunset, a long day away. Climbing up to the slightly higher guard post above the gate, she studied the postcard perfect scene outside—the seemingly endless flow of trees over the surrounding hills, the winding road that dipped and disappeared on its way to the distant town, which was a charming cluster of colorful rooftops, with sun shining on the blue Mediterranean beyond.

It was lovely, and so peaceful this morning. It should have been soothing. Instead it was making her instincts twitch, and she wasn't alone. There was no *peace* up on the wall. Every defender gripped their weapons tightly, their eyes searching the surrounding forest for some sign of an attack they all knew was coming.

Movement and the sound of an engine had her turning back to see the school van heading for the gate. It was driven by an armed guard, while another sat inside near the back emergency exit. A second vehicle, carrying two more armed guards, followed behind. Layla stopped pacing when the small convoy passed under her feet, then turned and kept watch as they disappeared down the hill, until even the dust cloud of their passage had settled.

She stood a moment longer, contrasting all that surrounding beauty with whatever evil had chosen to set poorly trained humans against a powerful and well-defended vampire lord. As always, her thoughts continued to circle back to the same question: what was their enemy after? What did he hope to gain?

Shaking her head in frustration when the answer continued to elude her, she left the guard post to resume her route along the thick wall and tried to stop thinking about their enemy. Maybe if she stopped obsessing about motivation, the answer would come to her. It sure as hell wasn't doing her any good to continually stress over it. Determined to follow her own advice, and to do what she could to bolster the morale of her fighters, she maintained a relaxed pose as she stopped to speak with every guard she came to—answering their questions and asking some of her own, wanting to get to know these people much better than she did. Most of them were strangers to her, and that could be a problem in the midst of a battle. A few seconds' delay at some order they didn't understand could mean life or death. Better to do what she could on this peaceful and too-fucking-hot morning. She tried to recall if it had always been this hot and humid during the summers when she'd been growing up. She didn't remember it that way, but no one else seemed bothered, so maybe she'd simply been gone too long. Or maybe her patience with the world had been tested too often, her willingness to accept the situation rather than kick someone's ass and change it.

And maybe she'd been a mercenary for too long. There were some things that a gun couldn't change any more than wishful thinking could. She stopped and surveyed the landscape once more from the different angle. Why the hell was it so quiet this morning? An intentional strategy by their enemy? Was he or she trying to rattle them, to keep them guessing and eventually putting them off their game? No army—no matter the size—could remain on high alert forever.

Her phone rang, startling her out of her thoughts with a sharp jerk that she immediately tried to cover. A jumpy commander didn't exactly inspire confidence. She snatched up the phone, expecting it to be Brian calling with an update, but when she looked, the ID wasn't one she recognized. Frowning, she answered with a sharp, "Casales."

"Something bad's happened. The kids, my sister. I can't get anyone to tell me—" The girl's voice cut off with a loud sob, as she fought to get her voice back.

"All right," Layla soothed. "We'll take care of it. What's your name, *mija*?"

"Alícia."

"Okay, Alícia. Can you answer some questions for me?" As she spoke she was running for the nearest stairway and waving frantically at Danilo who was at a battlement fifty yards away, helping one of the fighters adjust the sights on his MP5. The fighter caught Layla's excited gesturing first, but Danilo was running to join her a minute later, as Layla returned to the terrified Alícia. "Are you hurt?" she asked the girl.

"No, no. None of us older kids, just the little ones."

"The little ones? Did the bus crash? Can you see it?"

"No," she wailed. "It's gone."

"All right," Layla said calmly. "I want you and all the other big kids to get inside the school and stay there together, until I can get someone down there to pick you up. And keep your phone on, in case I need to contact you. You got all that?"

"Yeah, yes. Okay." She turned away from the phone and Layla heard her calling a name she vaguely remembered as one of the other teenagers. And then she disconnected without another word.

Reminding herself that Alícia wasn't one of her fighters and couldn't know about comm procedures, she quickly punched in the number for the lead guard on the children's van, while explaining the situation to Danilo who'd joined her, standing above the stairway. When there was no answer on the guard's phone, she called the driver instead, but got the same lack of a response. No answer, no voicemail.

"Shit!" She quickly updated Danilo, while they both ran down the stairs and headed for Layla's rental car, still parked outside the barracks. "I'm going down there," she said. "You're in charge—" Her phone rang. "Casales," she snapped. "Who is this?"

"What's happened?" Brian's response was sharp, no bullshit, right to the point.

"The kids' bus . . . I don't know exactly what, but it sounds like a hijacking. Maybe an accident, but I don't think so. I'm on my way there. Where are you?"

"We just rolled into town."

"Stay there, don't come up. And try to look harmless until I get there."

"Roger that." Years of joint combat experience had them both hanging up at the same time. There was no need to say more.

Layla was running across the wide main yard when a shout from one of the guards, followed by a loud, metal creak, told her the gate was opening. She spun without slowing and ran that way instead, shouting orders for the fighters above to stop staring and maintain their watch. It would be too easy to use a distracting entry to toss enough explosive through the open gate to clear a path for their attack.

Her own MP5 was on a sling around her neck, and she was never without her side arm and knives, but she didn't pull any of them as she raced for the gate. The guards had seen something, or more likely some*one*, that had them opening the gate, and she feared who or what it might be.

Two men stumbled into view, both bloody, though one was in much worse shape, leaning heavily on his companion, being carried as much as walking on his own. Everyone raced to help, including Dr. Nowak whose assistant ran next to her, stretcher under one arm. Nowak stopped the guards when they would have lowered both men to the ground, gesturing sharply for the weaker one to be placed on the now deployed stretcher, while the other was supported on both sides and walked through the open gate and to the small hospital.

Layla altered her trajectory to follow Nowak, aware of a small crowd gathering behind them, demanding answers. Like a small town, word travelled fast in the *Fortalesa*, and the families of the missing children were already gathering to demand answers. Layla glanced back to see two guards moving in to prevent the terrified families from storming the hospital, or rushing out the open gate to search for their children.

Layla slowed to a walk when she neared the hospital. Nowak and the stretcher went one way, but she followed the bloody but conscious guard who was being hustled to a bed and surrounded by caregivers. They eased him back and immediately began cutting away his clothes, while a nurse asked questions and gave orders to the others. Layla waited as long as she could, not wanting to get in the way, but lives were at stake, and she needed answers.

"What's his name?" she asked one of the soldiers who'd helped the injured man into the infirmary.

"Jeremy," the man said. "His wife was raised here."

Layla nodded, then moved to stand at the foot of the bed, ignoring a scowl from the woman who seemed to be in charge. Raising her voice to be heard, she added the sharp crack of authority to get his attention. "Jeremy."

He responded at once, his eyes slitting open to focus on her. "Commander."

"What happened?" she demanded. "From the beginning."

His chin dipped when he swallowed hard before beginning to speak. "Ambush," he said, his voice harsh with pain. "They hit Dario and Edgard at the same time, shooting through the glass front and back, and nearly crashing the van. They're both dead." His eyes were glassy, his expression one of disbelief. "Dead," he repeated faintly, then swallowed again and kept going. "Ruben and I were in the backup car. We fought to reach the van's emergency door, to get the kids out, but those bastards walked right up to us, as though they weren't even worried about us shooting back. There were a lot of them, a dozen, maybe. We fired on them, but . . . They must have been wearing body armor or . . . I don't know. Ruben went down before me. I covered him, but there were so many," he added in a whisper. "And they were fearless. They just didn't care."

"Jeremy," Layla snapped, needing whatever he could tell her, before he passed out. "What about the kids?"

"Not hurt, I don't think. The gunmen, women, too," he clarified, frowning. "That's all they wanted was the kids, but they didn't seem to want them hurt. Once Dario and Edgard were down, none of their fire was aimed at the van, just at the two of us. I thought I was dead." He looked up in confusion, as if not understanding why he was still alive.

"Did they say anything?" she asked.

"No," he said, obviously puzzled. "They took our weapons, shot our car to hell, then drove away in the van and left us alive. I don't know why."

"All of them left? With the kids?"

"Not all the attackers."

"Just three of them went with the kids. The rest just . . . disappeared like they do. Left our men behind, in the dirt. Just dragged them out of the van and left them there. Dead," he repeated again. He stared at her. "I tried to follow, Commander, but . . . Ruben needed help, and they were gone so fast. The car was useless, and Ruben . . . I didn't know what to do."

"That's all right, Jeremy. You did the right thing, helping Ruben, coming here. They made a mistake taking our kids. And we're going to get them back. Every one of them."

A rough sound escaped Jeremy's lips. It might have been a sob, but Layla pretended not to notice. The man had lost friends in that attack. Even worse, he'd lost the *Fortalesa*'s most vulnerable asset—their children. "Rest now," she told him. "And I'll let your wife know where you are."

Layla told one of the techs to make sure both Jeremy's and Ruben's families were told where to find them, then turned and strode from the building. The two dead guards would need to be retrieved, but she had to go after those kids. Several guards were milling around outside the hospital, waiting for word. She grabbed one at random and said, "We have two dead at the crash site. Take two guards and a vehicle and get them back here, before their families try to do it themselves."

Danilo was waiting when she left the crowd behind and started for her car again. "Where are you going?" she asked.

"To get those kids back."

"Who's going with you?"

"No one," Layla responded, raising a hand to forestall any protest. "Three of my people just arrived down below, and time is critical. By the time I get there, they'll already be scouring the city for any sign of the van. The damn thing shouldn't be hard for the locals to miss, with the windows shot out. And the blood. You don't shoot two men point blank without leaving a trace. We'll find it."

"Are you sure?" Danilo asked, meeting her gaze. "You haven't been here in a long time. You don't know the area—"

"I grew up here. It hasn't changed that much. Besides, I have a lot of experience sneaking around in places I don't know." She opened the car door and threw her MP5 across the seat before sliding in. She'd have liked an extra magazine or two, but her people would have brought plenty with them. She'd get some from them. All those years she'd spent fighting other people's wars . . . They'd prepared her for this moment, and she was glad. "The *Fortalesa* is yours to command," she told Danilo, then closed the door and drove to the gate.

But she'd no sooner paused to let the gate swing open, than a warning shout rang out from above. She left the car where it was and raced up the stairs. Standing next to the guard who'd called to her, she lifted a hand to shield her eyes from the bright mid-morning sun and stared in disbelief. A lone person, a teenaged girl she saw, was approaching from below, her long-legged stride as casual as if she was arriving to visit a friend. A white cloth hung limply from the stick she carried propped over her shoulder, and as she drew closer, she shifted to swing it back and forth in front of her like a flag.

"What the fuck?" Layla muttered. "Don't open that gate," she commanded. "I'll take the sally port." Without another word, she took the stairs down two at a time and ran for the small door once more. Danilo saw where she was heading and raced after her.

"I should go," the younger woman insisted. "You're needed here."

"Not how I operate. I lead my people, I don't follow them."

"Damn it, Layla," Danilo swore, any semblance of discipline gone. "You know I'm right."

Layla stopped long enough to face her directly. "No, you're not," she said plainly. "Not in my army, okay? Now, help me lift this fucking riot bar, and lock it after me." Once the door was open, she smiled at the younger woman. "Stop worrying. I've survived far worse than this."

The gate thudded shut behind her as she strode out to meet the messenger, who was even younger than she'd first thought. Drawing her sidearm, holding it in both hands, she aimed at the smiling teenager, and called, "Stop right there," as soon as they were within speaking distance. "Who are you?"

"I am the messenger, and I bring word from the lord of us all." She held out a white envelope.

"I don't know who the fuck you're talking about," Layla growled. "But he sure as hell isn't *my* lord."

The messenger smiled in smug bliss. It was the only way to describe it. It was the smile of a true believer, one who was certain she knew truths that Layla didn't and pitied her for her ignorance. "You will learn," she said softly. "But you will bleed first. He told us this would happen."

Layla could *hear* the capital "H" on "he." Who the fuck? She started

105

to rip open the envelope, then glared at the creepy messenger. "Are you waiting for a reply? Or are you just hanging around?"

Another placid smile. "My duty is done. Will you respect the—"

"Yeah, I'll hold to white flag protocol. Just remember, I'm not the one stealing children from their families and putting their lives in danger to make a damn point. It's your fucking lord doing that. You have ten seconds to start walking, or I start shooting."

The girl's façade cracked as anger flared in those calm eyes, the first real emotion she'd shown.

Layla saw it and arched her brows in question. "Problem?"

"You'll learn," the messenger said again, but it was a sharp hiss of sound this time, all pretense of blissful calm gone. She spun on her heel and started back down the hill, her stride no longer the relaxed stroll that had brought her there.

Layla waited, backing a few cautious steps closer to the gate, until she was sure the teenager was truly leaving. Shooting a quick glance over her shoulder to verify that the guards above the gate had their attention, and their weapons, focused on the departing teenager, she made her way back to the sally port. A shout rose from the wall when she was a few feet away, and Danilo opened the gate for her.

Once the sally port was barred behind her, she ducked into her father's unused office and studied the sealed envelope. She was no crime scene investigator like they had everywhere on TV these days. Though it was possible Xavier had one on staff. Maybe one of his vamps had that special skill. She didn't like the idea of opening a sealed message from a known enemy, but on the other hand, it couldn't be coincidence that the messenger had shown up so soon after the kidnapping. If this message, whatever it was, contained details or demands relevant to the missing children, she couldn't wait until sunset to deal with it. And maybe that's what the enemy was counting on. Just one more incidence of them avoiding any direct confrontation with the vampires.

She turned it over and stared at the wax seal holding the flap shut. "Pretentious fuck," she muttered. Who used wax seals anymore?

She drew a long, deep breath and blew it out, then slipped a fingertip under the loose side of the envelope flap, and slowly slid it all the way down, until she'd dislodged the seal without cracking it. She'd save that for Xavier. He might recognize it.

The message inside was a single folded piece of thick paper, the kind used for letters back before everyone switched to email, and then text messages. Tipping the envelope so the page slid to the desk, she set the envelope aside and picked up the message. Holding it with two fingers and at arm's length, she turned her face away, and flipped the page open. When nothing happened, she began to read.

> *Xavier,*
>
> *I have rescued these poor children from the servitude they were innocently born into. I'd like to believe their parents were ignorant of the damage they were doing, but I cannot take that chance with their young lives, cannot stand by when their future is to be used as food for your vampires. Or worse, to be turned into one of the very demons who have destroyed their lives. If you look for them, they will die. Better a quick death at my hand, than endless suffering at yours.*
>
> *—Sakal*

"Sakal?" Layla said. "Who the fuck is Sakal?" Damn, she wished Xavier was awake. Or that at least Brian and the others were here instead of down in the town, even though what they were doing down there was more important. She needed someone she trusted to bounce this off.

One thing she knew for sure—this Sakal wanted them to wait. And there was a hard and fast rule against ever acting on the enemy's timetable. Give the kidnappers the several hours until darkness, and they would disappear with the children forever.

She slid the message back into the envelope, then put the whole thing in the top drawer of her father's desk and secured it, using the key hanging from the open lock. She was out the door two minutes later, and double timing it back to the gate.

Her car was there, but instead of sliding into the driver's seat, she opened the passenger door, grabbed her MP5, and strode to the sally port, which had probably seen more use in the last two days than in the entire time Xavier had lived in the *Fortalesa*.

She found Tony, the guard from the last firefight, waiting for her there, and said, "I'm going down the hill."

"Need backup?" he asked, his expression both sharp and eager.

She shook her head, said, "No," but glanced up at the billed cap he was wearing. "I need this," she said, taking it without asking.

He gave her a bemused look. "It's yours. Anything else?"

She shoved the cap low on her forehead. "I need everyone to stay here on alert. Right here. I know they're worried and terrified, but I don't want an angry mob of parents coming after me. Tell them I'm on it, and I have a skilled hostage rescue team waiting below."

"Is it true?"

"Yes, it is. Sometime, I'll tell you the stories. Give me your cell number," she said as an afterthought, thinking it would be good to have a second way of reaching the *Fortalesa*.

He rattled it off as Layla tapped in the numbers, then called him to be sure it stayed in her cell's memory.

The gate was already open and waiting for her. "Lock it behind me," she said, then stepped out onto the apron of empty space below the wall. Pausing for no more than a heartbeat, she ran at an easy lope for the trees, walked in several yards, until she doubted anyone could see her, then started downhill on foot.

WHILE LAYLA MADE her way through the forest and down the hill, Xavier lay trapped, fighting the unbreakable bonds of a sleep that held him prisoner while his people suffered. The most vulnerable and easily wounded of them all—the children who ran to hold his hand when he visited their homes or attended their holiday plays and parties, the ones who counted on him to keep them safe—those children had been taken in an act so violent, it would scar them forever. Just as it would him. He would never forget, could never forgive anyone who'd played even the smallest part in its planning. Everyone involved in this heinous crime would suffer before he was through with them. Every godforsaken one of them. He swore it.

For all the good his oaths did, he thought viciously. It frustrated him, *infuriated* him, that he couldn't see the details, couldn't know exactly what had been done, or even who'd done it. His mind could only read the horror of the guards' brutal deaths, the frantic terror of the children.

He knew that Layla would already be on task, doing everything she could to find the kidnappers and get a rescue underway. He knew what she was capable of. Knew things that even her father didn't know, things she'd never shared, because she didn't want him to think his only child, his *daughter*, was a brute capable of monstrous acts of cruelty. Xavier only knew because he had contacts among the vampire community in the U.S., vampires who'd mated or married humans from that country, including several who'd moved to the U.S. to be with their lover or mate when they'd gone home. Those vampires in turn either worked, or had friends who worked, in places where they could be of assistance, and remembering friendship or loyalty to Xavier, were willing to help when he asked. Which he did only rarely.

In this case, they had, on his behalf, gained access to details involving both Layla's military record and the jobs her current team had undertaken as private security consultants. Those records, both government and private, had often included so-called after-action reports, which frequently revealed the most extreme details of the undertaken missions. This was especially true for the privately funded jobs, since those were more likely to involve people who'd wanted to punish the ones who'd crossed them in one way or another, and would demand proof. They were most often hostage rescue and ransom cases, since neither Layla nor those she worked with were simple murderers for hire. But that didn't mean they followed every law. When a child or children had been taken or abused, Layla's team worried only about the hostages, and did whatever it took—killing or torturing *whomever* necessary—to return the children safely.

So he knew the extremes to which his Layla would go to rescue the ones who'd been kidnapped. He only wished he'd managed to get closer to her, faster. Their eventual bonding was inevitable in his mind, but if he'd already taken her blood, or if she'd already taken even the smallest amount of his, there would have been a chance that he could link with her, so they could communicate even when he slept and she hunted.

But all he could do now was lie in this dark room and curse the fate that had not only given him the gift of vampirism, but had made him a power with it. The same fate that now extracted a daily price in exchange.

Even worse, he had received fresh information just before sunrise that might have helped Layla and the others locate the missing children. Two of his scouts had identified a possible nest of rogue vampires hidden in the city. He didn't know yet who was behind this attack, but if unknown vampires were moving around freely in Barcelona, it was always possible they were somehow involved. His vamps didn't yet have a number, but even five strange vampires in his city were too many for Xavier to remain unaware of their presence for long.

By design, most of Barcelona's vampires lived inside the *Fortalesa* because he liked it that way. The fact that these newly arrived vampires were trying to conceal themselves from him, even knowing he would inevitably sniff them out, was enough to suggest they were working for one of his enemies. Maybe even the same one who'd attacked his lair and kidnapped its children.

But for all that their discovery was a welcome development, he'd been left cursing, because the news had come too late for him to act on until the next night. As it was, the two scouts had barely reached the basement loading dock of the vampire wing before collapsing into their daylight sleep. They'd had to be carried to their vault bedrooms by Xavier whose age and strength permitted him to remain awake and strong well past the time when most vampires were soundly asleep.

And still, while the children suffered, while Layla walked into danger, he could do nothing but lie there and curse in silence.

LAYLA WALKED slowly at first, aware of every footfall, every branch in her way, though she doubted the enemy—*Sakal*, she corrected—had posted anyone in the forest to waylay possible rescuers from the *Fortalesa*. If he—or she, the name was unfamiliar and could be anyone—decided to conceal an ambush somewhere, it was more likely to be on the road itself. It would be logical on his part to assume that a rescue operation would include several armed guards and a vehicle in order to mobilize as quickly as possible. Sakal might know that her father was gone, and that she was filling in, but he couldn't know that Brian and the others were in town waiting for her. Or that she'd hike down to meet them.

Let him think they were obeying his command not to look for the kidnapped children. Or waiting until darkness when Xavier could make the decision. That was his mistake, and one she was going to take advantage of. Whoever had thought it a good idea to get Xavier's attention by taking the *Fortalesa's* children didn't understand what they'd done. She'd been raised here. She knew what it was like to grow up in a place where every child was treasured, where every adult—human and vampire—treated each child as their own. It had taken her a while to understand why, especially since the *Fortalesa* was a place for vampires. They were virtually immortal, but the price of that immortality was the inability to breed, even with human partners. As a result, a lot of vamps became obsessed with death, or with acquiring wealth to ease their immortal lives.

But Xavier had made the decision early on, that his lair, as he called it, his *Fortalesa* would be a true community, where humans and vampires dwelled together. Where vampires could live with their human mates, and be part of a family unit if that's what they chose. The result was a close-knit community with humans and vampires protecting *each other*, and where families were the center of the social fabric.

She didn't envy Danilo's job right now. Keeping the parents and grandparents, the neighbors and friends from forming a hunting party to search for their children would be a monstrous chore, especially when some of the missing kids were certain to have parents within the guard ranks. She counted on her father's reputation as their long-time commander—and hoped enough of it would transfer to her—that they'd wait, knowing good men and women were on the kidnappers' trail. And that they wouldn't stop until every child was safe, and the kidnappers were no longer breathing on this earth.

She was nearing the town now, moving easily, her clothing blending into the surrounding foliage, her footsteps nearly silent. She was good at this, at remaining unseen and unheard when moving through enemy territory. It was a skill she'd had to learn early on when she'd been chosen for reconnaissance missions, not only for her ability to perfectly recall everything she'd seen and heard, but because she was a woman and thus seen as less threatening. She and her teammates, before they even *were* a team, had spent a lot of time in countries where women were the property of men—fathers, husbands, even brothers. When the women were permitted to go out, they were often covered head to toe, which was a very convenient camouflage not only for Layla, but sometimes for a male companion as well. Layla had known enough of the regional dialect to pass if she'd been called upon to speak, but she was more often inserted or extracted at night. And for that reason, she'd learned how to move quietly through dried brush and weeds. Animals ignored her for the most part, rustling in the underbrush, while birds continued to sing in the treetops. Layla was part of the forest, no threat, raising no alarms.

She was, however, armed for bear, as the saying went, though there were no bears in this part of Spain. She carried her MP5 in the ready position, though still wishing she had an extra mag or two. A 9mm Glock 19 rode on her hip, and she had two knives—one at her waist, one in her boot. And just for kicks, she had a taser on her belt. Armed and pissed off as she was, she was almost disappointed at the lack of enemies along her route, and by the time she could hear the occasional car or truck passing by, she was actively hoping that her team had found someone to attack. She wanted to hurt the bastards who'd thought terrorizing children was in any way acceptable.

It struck her then that the kidnappers hadn't demanded anything for a safe return. No ransom, no reciprocal action of any kind. Did they truly plan to whisk the *Fortalesa*'s children away forever? Did they think

Xavier, or anyone else, would permit that?

She hit the edge of the forest, then, and hunkered down in the shadows to consider her next steps. Sakal had to know Xavier would come for the children. So why take them? Something itched at her brain about that letter. It struck her as too familiar, almost taunting. Too much of a one-up shot aimed at Xavier, to be from an unknown. And he'd addressed Xavier by his first name, signing his own the same way. This felt personal.

It would be interesting to see Xavier's reaction to Sakal's letter. But she couldn't wait for that. She had to act based on what she knew at this moment, so she went ahead and texted Brian, asking his position. As she was typing, her phone vibrated with a call from him.

"Can you talk?" he asked, his voice low, but not stealthily so.

"Give me a minute," she murmured, and moved deeper back under the trees, finding a spot that would shield her from casual listeners, but not blind her to anyone coming up on her position. "All right, go."

"We're set up at a place called *Vista Bonica*. It's a rundown motel that probably rents rooms by the hour, but it was right on the edge of town as we drove in. Figured we'd keep a low profile until we heard from you."

"Good choice. And you're right. They do rent rooms by the hour, so don't sit anywhere."

Brian chuckled briefly. "Oh hell, Cap. You know River. First thing he did was strip the beds and dump everything in a pile along with the towels."

"This is one time I agree with him. What's the situation now?"

"I'm on my own, Kerry and Riv are together, checking in every thirty. Should be hearing from them in a few."

Layla studied her current location, mentally calculating time and route to reach the *Vista Bonica*. It wasn't far, but armed and dressed as she was, she wouldn't blend in with locals *or* tourists. Spain's gun policy was very restrictive, and civilians simply didn't carry guns of any kind, much less a damn MP5. She cursed herself for not thinking of that sooner, and then immediately moved past it. She needed her weapons. "I figure thirty minutes for me to reach you," she told Brian. "It's going to take some maneuvering to avoid notice. Let me know if anything pops before then."

"Roger that. Out."

She tucked her phone in a pocket, then walked silently to where the forest gave way to houses and streets. The neighborhood was working class, quiet this time of day with children in school and parents working. She'd bet there were more than a few grandparents caring for grandchildren too young for school. But in this heat, they'd stay inside if they could.

Layla unhooked the MP5 from its sling around her neck, then quickly removed her shirt, baring toned and suntanned arms in a plain tank-top. Using her belt and shirt she rigged a shapeless, hobo-style shoulder bag and slid the gun inside so that the collapsed shoulder stock was tucked into her armpit. It wasn't comfortable, but it hid the gun from casual notice, while keeping it reasonably accessible. Next, she untucked her tank top and pulled it over the Glock at her hip. Again, not perfect concealment, but she wanted it handy. Her knives she left in place. Her boots she could do nothing about, since she wasn't about to go barefoot, but figured wearing combat boots as a fashion statement was still common enough that no one would think it worth noticing.

With a final scan of the quiet streets, she fixed the route in her head and began walking. She'd been gone for a lot of years and things had changed, so she wasn't confident about the street layout. But she had an excellent sense of direction and knew where the hotel was. As long as she maintained a rough southerly heading, she'd end up close enough to that side of town to spot the hotel.

She'd been walking more than twenty minutes, and the combination of her fast pace and the hot sun was causing sweat to pool along her sides and between her breasts. The billed cap she'd grabbed from Tony was pulled low on her forehead and combined with her sunglasses, shielded her face from both sun and detection. So when she approached a corner just as a familiar fire-engine red Ford minivan slowed next to her, she saw *them* before they recognized *her*.

Scowling, she stepped off the curb and knocked on the passenger side window of the front seat. Six startled faces turned as one to stare at her while she gestured for the front passenger to lower his window.

"Commander," he said, voice cracking nervously.

Layla scanned the guilty faces of the *Fortalesa*'s teenage population. "Alícia," she said, spying the girl in the second row of seats. "I might be confused, but I don't think this is the way to school."

"No, ma'am."

"It's not her fault," the driver said, before Layla could respond. "Miri's sister is one of the missing kids, so we took a vote and agreed to look for them."

"You took a vote? Well, then, carry on."

The driver gave her wide eyes. "Really?"

"No, you idiot," she snapped. "But since you're here, I'm going to make use of you. Or at least your van. You," she said, gesturing at the front passenger. "Go sit in the back."

The boy, who couldn't have been more than thirteen, didn't say a word. He simply opened the door, jumped out, and ran around to climb into the cargo space of the minivan, even though there was room in the third-row seat. Apparently, she was intimidating. Who knew?

She walked over and checked that the back hatch had been secured behind Alícia's defender, not wanting to lose anyone. Then she slid into the passenger seat and eyed the driver. "What's your name?"

"Marcos Quintana, Commander."

Layla snorted at the polite address. "Just call me Layla, kid."

"Yes, Commander."

She sighed, certain she'd been that young once, though she couldn't remember when. "Okay, Marcos. You know the *Vista Bonica*?"

"Yes." A blush pinked the golden skin on his cheeks.

Nope, Layla reconsidered. She'd never been that young. She sighed. "Just get us there. No need to speed," she added when the car jerked into motion. "We don't want to draw any attention to ourselves. And you kids in the back," she called over her shoulder. "Cell phones off."

She had Marcos drive past the motel first, while she called Brian.

"Cap, where—"

"I just drove past. Are we clear to come in?"

"We?"

"Long story. Are we?"

"Yes. Two rooms on the east end, ground floor."

"Be there in five."

"Okay you guys, listen up," she said in her best commanding officer voice. "Once we hit that parking lot, we need to *move*. Do what I say, exactly as I say it. Same goes for whoever opens the door to that room."

"What room?" a girl's voice asked from what sounded like the third row.

"It'll be obvious once we get there. Your *only* duty right now is to do what I *say*, when I say it. Got it?"

"Yes, ma'am," echoed in several voices.

"Good enough. Marcos, turn into the parking lot and go all the way to the end." She pointed. "Park on the far side of that black SUV." She glanced at the teen to see him nodding, eyes blinking rapidly, throat moving as he swallowed his nerves. "Easy stuff, kid. Don't worry."

"Okay."

The van bumped over the rough driveway, and Marcos had to swerve around some very serious potholes, but soon enough they were pulling to a stop, just as the door in front of them opened and Brian stood waiting. He had a forbidding presence, Layla had to admit, all six feet, four inches of him, standing there in full battle dress, bristling with weapons.

"Everyone out," she called. "No squeals, no screams. Quick and quiet, stay low."

In the doorway, Brian stood back as the teens scurried past him into the room, while River barked orders in Spanish with a bit of British accent leaking through. Layla meanwhile snagged the keys from Marcos as he bailed out, locked the minivan's doors, and followed them in.

"Good to have you here, Captain," Brian said as he closed the door.

River was hustling the teens into an adjoining room. "You don't move without my permission," he ordered. "Head's over there. The bathroom," he added in a longsuffering tone, then explained, "Soft drinks in the cooler, sandwiches, too. Now stay. And don't touch that fucking door. Got it?"

There was a chorus of agreement, and then Riv walked back to rejoin the others. He was tall and deceptively lean, his brown hair still worn military short. He was good-looking enough that she'd seen one or two of the girls giving him wide eyes, and Layla loved him like a brother. But he was a fiend for neatness and always had sanitizing wipes in his pack. He was also a damn good pilot and could fly anything with wings or without. He'd been flying a helicopter for the British SSA, when she and Brian had crossed paths with him at a bar in Istanbul. And when they'd decided to put together their own team, he'd been the first one they'd called.

Kerry of the lucky hunches was sitting in the first room, hunched over a computer, with a paper map of the town sitting next to her. She was five feet, four inches of muscle, with a sniper's eye and a sixth degree black belt in Shotokan karate. Her blond hair was cut short, and she had soulful brown eyes that she frequently used to her advantage.

"Anything from recon?" Layla asked, after exchanging greetings with everyone and rescuing her weapons from the makeshift purse. She settled back against the headboard and accepted the cold soda River brought her, while ignoring his frown of disapproval over the feet she had propped on the bed.

Kerry nodded without looking up. "We followed a different gossip trail than Brian, but ended up at the same house." She looked up at Layla abruptly. "What are we doing with them?" she asked, jerking her head toward the other room.

"They were out looking on their own. I decided they'd be safer with us. Once we have the littles, we'll take them all home."

Kerry shrugged. Shit always happened and they dealt with it. It was what they did. "Riv, why don't you provide details, so I can finish this?"

"Right. Kerry and I tracked the van, figuring that was our best lead. If it's used all the time to shuttle the kids to school, people in this town have to know it, recognize it, know where it's supposed to be, and where it's not. We wore civvies, just another vacationing couple stopping in for coffee and pastry. A lot of people were doing the same, talking to each other, and we listened. Word's gotten out about the missing kids. Mostly via pals at the school, where their absence had been noticed. Apparently, gossip begins at an early age. Some kid was in the director's office, and overhead a conversation. Another boy's mom came to pick him up, worried her kid would be next. And on and on.

"Upshot is word got out and people noticed when the van drove by a place it shouldn't be. One guy, former military, noticed the shattered window, the blood on the door. A gran paid attention because the kids were too quiet. Gotta admit, I was impressed."

"So you followed the bread crumbs," Layla said. "What'd you find?"

"Brian, waiting for us. He got there first."

"That's because *I* didn't stay to finish my coffee before acting on what I'd heard."

River just shrugged.

"Where's the house?" Layla asked.

"South of here," Riv replied. "Just past the town proper. Van was concealed under an awning. They tried to camouflage it with branches and shit. Maybe they thought we had air support." He made a what-the-fuck gesture and continued. "Their camo might have passed a casual look, but we're not casual, Cap. Small house," he continued. "Windows all covered with blinds mostly, but some brown paper taped over, probably where they didn't have anything else. I moved in for a closer look while Brian headed back here to meet you, and Kerry kept watch on the street. Got one good look where the curtains didn't quite close. I don't know your kids," he said, meeting Layla's gaze. "But there were too many little ones in the room I saw. Most of them were or had been crying, and all of them looked scared and huddled together. Pissed me off, but definitely our PC," he finished, using the abbreviation for "precious cargo" which was what people like those on her team used to describe the hostages they'd been sent to rescue.

"See anyone else?" she asked.

"No older kids, or adults, either. But I couldn't see much beyond one part of one room. It needs a closer look, but I'd say at least some of your missing are there." He tapped the phone which was attached to the cross-strapped gear belt over his chest. "I set up a couple mini-cams front and back. Quality will be for shit, but we should pick up if anyone else arrives or if they try to move the kids."

Layla glanced at Brian. "What do you think?"

"I say we go in, take down any hostiles, and get those kids home."

"Agreed, but I'd sure love to grab at least one of those fuckers alive and talking. I don't care who it is, but one of them is going to squeal. Understood?" She looked around, received three identical nods, and stood. "Kerry, I assume that's the map you're studying. How far is this place? And what's the fastest route there? We'll need to drive, so we can transport the kids fast."

"Better to drive anyway. All of us geared up would draw too much attention. Kidnappers might have friends looking out for them. Ten minute drive, fifteen tops. Only one traffic signal."

"Right," Layla said. "We leave in ten. Riv, everyone's on comms. Make it happen."

"Yes, ma'am."

"Okay, we're on the clock. Let's move."

While the others did last minute gear checks, she stepped into the second room and faced down the teenagers. *Kill me now,* she thought as she met a variety of expressions, from frightened to bored, and all the way to sulky. What the fuck?

"We're heading out to recover the PC—"

"What does that mean?" Marcos demanded. His was the sulky face.

She blinked, not understanding the question at first. "Oh. Precious cargo. PC. The kids." She eyed him. "What'd you think I meant?"

"Nothing," he muttered, not meeting her gaze.

"Uh huh. Anyway, we're heading out, and *you* all are staying here. You can sit in the other room, too. But you are not to touch anything," she said, enunciating every word. "You understand?"

"Can we touch the TV?" someone asked in a snide tone. The others snickered, but no one claimed responsibility.

Layla rolled her eyes. "Sure. Although I expect the only channel it gets is porn, which you can watch, as long as it's free. But if I get a huge movie bill when we check out, or if any parents complain, someone's going to pay."

"Can we turn our cell phones back on now?" someone asked.

Layla gave them a hard stare, to make sure they were paying attention. "Are you safe at home in your little bed? No, you are *not*. So cell phones may be on, but ringers are off." She glanced over her shoulder and found her team about ready to depart. "All right. We're leaving. Remember what I said. Lock the door, don't answer it, don't even call out." She turned away as Brian opened the door and led the way to the SUV, but then she swung back at the last moment to say, "And no fucking on the beds."

Ten seconds later, she was in the SUV and pulling the door shut as River sped them out of the parking lot and on the road to undertake one of the most important rescues they'd ever had to do.

Chapter Ten

THE BIG SUVS THAT Layla's team habitually rented when necessary weren't as common in Europe as in the US, but they weren't unheard of either. Money was money, everywhere in the world. One didn't call Hertz for that kind of rental, however. Fortunately, the team did enough work around the world that they had a network of suppliers, including one very happy contact in Barcelona, who'd been waiting for them with a Mercedes SUV that could comfortably hold the four of them and their gear. Layla wasn't as broadly muscled as the guys, but her legs made up for it. Kerry, on the other hand, was pretty and petite, and utterly harmless. Yeah, right. Bad guys frequently took her as an easy mark, which was the last mistake they made, before she killed them. Pound for pound, she was stronger than any of the guys, and vicious as a rabid squirrel.

They parked at a house across the street from where the children were being held. Brian had verified it was uninhabited, but not vacant. The area was mostly upscale, with walls surrounding several homes just like it. Layla reasoned these were primarily vacation homes for wealthy owners from all over Europe. Winter visitors from the northern countries were common in Spain. The one they'd chosen as a staging location had a good-sized wall around the front, with no gate across the driveway. River pulled onto the circular drive in front of the house, taking them out of sight from the street, and stopping under several good-sized shade trees. He then maneuvered the SUV until they were facing outward for a quick exit, without sacrificing any of their cover.

"I want to see the house before we make any plans," Layla said quietly.

They all wore standard Bluetooth comms, which were uplinked to a private communications satellite network, for which they paid an access fee. It wasn't cheap, but it was worth every dime and had saved their asses more than once.

"No movement on the cams I set up," River commented. "Not since we found the place."

"Okay. You and me, River. Let's go."

They didn't bother concealing their weapons when they made their way back to the kidnappers' house. They hadn't seen a single person on the street or in a yard. The hottest part of the day was fast approaching and, being sensible people, the Spanish favored the siesta. The traditional start of that practice wouldn't be for two hours yet, but for stay-at-home parents and grandparents, especially with younger children, they'd already have called the little ones in for a light lunch before sending them off to sleep.

Nonetheless, she and River paused in the shade of a bent pine tree near where the van had been concealed, in front of a closed and locked garage. It made Layla wonder if the kidnappers had broken into the house, knowing no one would be around. What were they doing in there? Why take the kids, only to sit on them so close to the *Fortalesa?*

River caught her gaze and gestured toward the back of the house, then took off low and quiet, leading Layla to the window where he'd sighted the children.

Once there, he pointed at the right window, then held back, maintaining watch while Layla drifted over to take a look. She found it pretty much as River had described, except none of the children were awake any longer. They slept huddled together for comfort, visibly sweating, which told her the air-conditioning wasn't on, and supported her idea that the kidnappers had no right to be in the house.

There wasn't much else she could do at that moment, except watch, so she rejoined River and silently gestured that she wanted to do a complete circle of the building before heading back to the others. With that accomplished, and no new information gathered, they slipped through an opening in the hedge to the next yard, ducked around patio furniture to reach the far side, then snuck between houses to the street. They crossed, and arrived at the house where they'd parked by walking through an unlocked pedestrian gate which led to a curving path to the front door.

Between the ungated driveway and this unlocked gate, it was obvious that the owners had the front wall for privacy from the street, not for security.

"So what's the plan?" Brian asked, while Layla and River downed cold bottles of water. The humidity was killer.

"I counted nine kids in that room—that should be all of them."

"SUV's going to be crowded on the way back," River commented. "You planning to use the van?"

"No. Too many people noticed it this morning, and I don't want anyone seeing us drive away. Besides, it's not far to the motel, and we have the older kids' minivan there. They had some empty space. One of us can drive that, and take the three biggest hostages, along with the teens. We'll take the littlest ones in the SUV, on our laps if we need to."

When the others nodded, she said, "All right. We go in fast and quiet, enter through the back. Kerry and River, you go straight for the kids. Brian and I will search the house and eliminate any hostiles. But I want to keep one alive for questioning back at the *Fortalesa*."

"You don't want to just do it while we're there, then leave the body?" Kerry asked.

Layla eyed her. "Is that a question, or something else?"

"Just a question. I'm curious why you'd want to bother dragging anyone back."

"So Xavier can do the questioning," she replied flatly.

"Ah. I keep forgetting this gig's got vampires involved. *Big* vampires. The kind *we* never work with."

"True," Layla admitted. "But I grew up with them, so . . . at least we know they won't have us for dinner. Not without consent, anyway." She grinned, knowing that Kerry had—and she suspected Brian had, too—enjoyed sex with at least one vampire in the past. *Enjoyed* being the operative word there. Or so she'd heard. She herself had never partaken, which now that she thought about it, probably seemed strange to the others.

"Questions?" she asked and when no one responded, she said. "Okay, Kerry and River you cross first. I don't want all four of us out there at the same time."

The two of them took off and while Brian watched, Layla checked back with the teens waiting at the motel. Luckily, she had Alícia's number from when the girl had called to tell them about the kidnapping. The call rang four times, and she was already calculating how long it would take to get back there and whom she could send, when the girl answered with a worried, "Yes?"

"Alícia, it's Layla. Everything okay there?" More than one TV seemed to be blaring in the background, with lots of porn-quality moans rising above the general noise.

"Oh, yeah. It just took me a while to figure out my phone was vibrating."

Layla didn't want to imagine what *that* meant. "Just tell me if everyone's still healthy. No blood, no broken bones, no bad guys with a knife at your throat."

"*Dios mio,*" the girl said with the ages-old disgust of a teenager. "We're watching gross movies. And eating junk from someone's stash."

Thinking Brian wasn't going to happy, she said, "Good. We won't be long now."

Her comm clicked once, signaling the other two were in place, so she and Brian took off, moving quickly, but not speed walking, across the street and around to the back of the house. A quick peek through the small, curtained window on the door, showed an empty kitchen. Three seconds later, they'd picked the flimsy lock and were inside.

Kerry and River headed right toward the room where the kids were, while she and Brian took the hallway.

Noise came from the kids, crying when they woke up to more strangers.

Startled cries followed from behind a partially closed door just ahead and to the left as she and Brian approached, and a woman shouted in Spanish, not Catalan. "Wake up. Someone's here!"

A sub-machine gun on full auto filled the air with lead as the door swung open, but Layla and Brian held back, waiting until the gun went quiet before rolling into the room to come up firing their own weapons to much better effect. There were two hostiles—one male, one female, both teenagers, the girl just barely. The boy was already down, from three shots to the chest. But Brian had switched his aim at the last minute, taking the girl in the legs.

Layla figured the gunfire and the wounded girl's resulting screams would have brought any other hostiles running. But wanting to be sure, she left Brian to play medic, and hopefully shut up the girl before she roused the neighbors, while she went to check out the rest of the house. It was small compared to some of the others, but had a big yard and a long driveway with a detached garage at the end. It was probably what all the houses had looked like, before wealth moved in and took advantage of the large lots to upscale.

Once she was sure the house was empty, and after listening at a front window to be sure that no neighbors had gathered in response to the screamer, and no sirens were signaling the approach of authorities, she walked back to where Kerry and River were gathered in the kitchen with the kids.

"Brian knocked her out," Kerry said, pointing to where the wounded girl was lying on a lounger outside the back door. "He's gone for the SUV," she continued. "Simpler and faster than trying to get these poor little ones across the street. He can back right up to the where the van is concealed. If no one's noticed *that* so far, they're not going to notice us parked for the few minutes it'll take to evac."

Once Brian returned with the SUV, they loaded the older children into the cargo space, then River went back for their prisoner. Meanwhile Kerry and Layla climbed into the back seat and, with Brian's assistance, distributed the little ones onto laps. The smallest girl, who'd been inconsolable, crying in hard hiccupping sobs through the whole process, immediately stood on the back seat and stretched her arms over to a boy who reached up from the cargo space and pulled her onto his lap. He couldn't have been more than nine years old himself, but he held her close, kissing the top of her head and making soothing sounds.

Siblings, Layla thought, as the little girl's sobs died down to soft cries, and then quieted altogether. She watched River return with the prisoner, whom he stuffed into the front passenger seat well, and then maneuvered himself inside with one leg bent and his foot on the seat. It had to be uncomfortable, but it made more sense for her and Kerry to be in back, leaving more room for the kids, and not traumatizing them any further at the sight of a bloody, unconscious body.

Brian closed his door and cruised down the slight slope of the drive, not hitting the gas until he was on the street, leaving the empty house and a dead teenage boy behind.

Arriving at the motel, Layla's team moved like the well-oiled machine they were. In a change of plans, Layla and River exited the SUV to load up the teenagers in the minivan, and drive back with them, while Brian and Kerry would go straight back to the *Fortalesa* with the smaller children already in the SUV.

The prisoner remained stuffed into the seat well, but no one cared about her comfort.

Brian had wanted to wait, so they could all drive back together. But Layla wanted those kids returned as soon as possible. She also figured the SUV, with Kerry and Brian, was more secure than the minivan, and certainly less of a familiar vehicle to anyone who saw it. So, after Brian took off, she and River opened the motel room door to find a bunch of guilty looks, while on the TV screen a very buxom woman was making herself *very* available to three men at the same time. Or "air tight," as it was called in the porn industry.

"What the bloody hell?" River demanded.

"They're teenagers," Layla said, as if that explained everything.

"Christ. I'm not touching a single God damned thing in this room.

You mob are loading your stuff *and* ours. Get on with it."

Layla, feeling cautiously more relaxed now that the children were at least no longer in the clutches of their captors, chuckled and clapped to get the kids' attention. "You heard the man, boys and girls. Load up everything that doesn't belong here. We'll sort it out later."

"Wait," Miri cried, jumping to her feet. "What about my sister and the others?"

"Safe and on their way home," Layla said belatedly. She should have started off with that, damn it. "The sooner you get everything loaded, the sooner we'll join them. So, chop chop. Let's get moving."

River gave the room a single disgusted look, then marched out to stare at the minivan—most likely in despair that he'd soon be driving it. "Whose fucking idea was that color?" he asked.

"My father's actually. He figured the kids couldn't get up to too much trouble, since everyone in town would recognize the vehicle."

"Well, shite. He was probably right about that. I'm embarrassed to drive it."

"You can ride in cargo, if you want. No one'll see you back there."

"Yeah, like that's going to happen. Get in, you lot," he said to kids. "I'm evac'ing this cesspool of bacteria permanently. If you're not in the vehicle in two minutes, I'm leaving you behind."

Layla made sure everyone was in and belted where possible. It was a tight squeeze, and poor Marcos bit the bullet and volunteered to sit with the cargo, which had her forgiving his earlier bout of teenage sulkiness. When she slid into the front passenger seat and closed the door, she said, "Let's boogie, Riv."

"You wound my fine British ears with that ghastly American slang," he said in his poshest accent, then swung a grin in her direction and took off.

Layla texted both Danilo and Tony once they were out of the busiest part of town, letting them know that Brian would be arriving first. And that all the children *and* the teens were safe and unharmed. That last was probably a bit of wishful thinking, since the children who'd been kidnapped would probably have nightmares for a very long time. But she knew Xavier would spare no cost to secure whatever counseling or other help they needed. He was a good leader, a good man . . . even if he was a vampire.

Chapter Eleven

THEY PULLED THROUGH the gates of the *Fortalesa* to the expected sounds of a joyous homecoming, with tears and laughter overriding the few angry demands to know everything she and the others had learned about the kidnappers, and what was going to be done about it.

Layla had to jump out of the minivan, stand on top of the wall above the closed gates, and yell to get their attention, until finally Brian joined her with a bullhorn that he must have dug out of his own gear, or been provided with by someone wise enough to see that all the shouting was getting nothing done. With the bullhorn amplifying his strong male tones, he ordered everyone to shut the fuck up. And when they did, he apologized to the ladies and children, then turned it over to Layla who told them she'd arrange a town hall with everyone invited, as soon as she'd briefed Lord Xavier. He, of course, would be the one making any decision as to what they would do next.

Layla knew he wouldn't tell them *everything*—just enough to ease their minds. Certainly, he wouldn't announce whatever actions he was going to take to hunt down and destroy Sakal and whoever had helped him. But by reminding the people that Xavier would be taking charge, Layla had calmed the crowds enough that they followed her suggestion to use the intervening time to care for their families, while specific arrangements were gotten underway for the town hall.

She remained on the wall until almost everyone had dispersed. Then leaving Danilo and Tony to answer any remaining questions, she joined her teammates. Brian had parked the SUV so that the front passenger door was even with the open door of the barracks. That door was wider than usual to allow various pieces of equipment and weapons to be easily maneuvered in and out. More importantly, it also made it easy to sneak a bleeding and unconscious prisoner inside without anyone noticing that the four fighters who'd rescued the children had also brought home a present for Lord Xavier.

XAVIER SHATTERED the final chain holding him to sleep and

sprang off the bed with a roar of rage that had every one of his vampires shivering where they lay sleeping up and down the hallways of the vault. Fresh information flowed to his thoughts, driven by his awareness of every soul who lived within the *Fortalesa*, every person who was his to protect. From the eldest *avi* to the youngest *nena*, Xavier was aware of them all on a gut level that was difficult to describe to one who'd never experienced it. He simply *knew*.

And that was how he knew that all of the children were home and safe. He could sense the mood of his people, and while there was anger simmering below the surface, the dominant emotions were joy and relief, tempered by a lingering concern. He shared all those emotions, but it was anger that drove him.

He paused a moment, standing perfectly still as his power swept the entire *Fortalesa* once more, skimming over the familiar, searching for the unknown. Of which there were several.

Concentrating, he reached out to a mind that was as familiar as his own. "*Chuy,*" he said, jolting his lieutenant out of his daylight sleep an hour or more before he would have done so naturally. The older and stronger the vampire, the earlier he woke and the later he was driven to sleep. As a powerful vampire of nearly four hundred years, Xavier wasn't forced into his daylight sleep until the sun was fully over the horizon, just as he woke while the evening sky was still bright and the sun's orb barely visible below the earth's edge. Chuy was one of his own children, nearly two hundred years old and a powerful master vampire in his own right. He couldn't match Xavier's strength, but he was closer than any other in the *Fortalesa*.

"*Sire.*" Chuy's mental voice was slightly groggy, but alert to the fact that something was very wrong. Xavier wouldn't have wakened him otherwise.

"We were attacked today, and the children kidnapped. They've been rescued and returned, but there are strangers inside the Fortalesa. I want every vampire up and alert within the hour. Meet me in my office in thirty minutes. That should give me enough time to discover the identity of our visitors and gather in Layla for a briefing."

"Sire."

Xavier cut the connection without useless niceties. There was a time for politesse. This was not it. His first impulse was to damn the niceties, throw on clothes, and storm upstairs to assess the situation. But reason stopped him on the verge of opening the vault door. If he appeared among his people raging and incoherent, it would only add to the terror of the day, and do nothing to assure them that their families were safe and the criminals would pay.

He kept the black jeans he'd already pulled on, but ripped off the T-shirt and walked back to the bathroom. He ignored the shower. Reason hadn't prevailed to that extent. But he did brush his teeth and give his face a brisk wash with cold water, then ran wet hands back through his long black hair, which tended toward unruliness if left to its natural state. His beard, he decided, was just long enough to pass for an intentional scruff, which was a good thing because he had no intention of taking the time to shave.

Now marginally more presentable, he went to his closet and donned a long-sleeved black T-shirt, then sat to pull on socks and lace up combat-style boots. He'd be hunting tonight, one way or another.

He walked down an empty hallway in the vampire wing, the only vampire powerful enough to already be fully alert and functional, although Chuy and Joaquim were both awake and had communicated their readiness. Having gotten a better sense of the mood in the *Fortalesa* and knowing there was no immediate danger, Xavier sent them additional orders regarding the scouts' information and the need to clean out the rogue vampire nest they'd found.

As for the strangers he'd detected inside the *Fortalesa*, he was beginning to believe they were Layla's fellow fighters, although there was one . . . a young female, he thought, who was giving off such strong and violent emotions that she had to be someone *other*. Not a friend. A prisoner, perhaps, he thought with vicious satisfaction. He would enjoy nothing more than interrogating an enemy prisoner. He would scrub her brain, until he'd discovered every hope, every secret, every *fear* she possessed. Until there was nothing left but spongy scars in a hollow skull.

His first thought upon emerging into the fresh herb smell of the courtyard outside the vampire wing was to search for Layla. A glance up at her parents' second floor apartment found it dark and unoccupied. He strode into the small, protected courtyard, leaving it behind where it merged with the larger main yard. He passed the hospital—quiet and dimly lit with no fresh agony flavoring the emotions of either patients or medics. Stepping farther into the yard, he immediately caught the scent of fresh blood and looked right, toward the far end, where an unfamiliar vehicle was parked in front of the barracks. It was completely black, with tinted windows, and wheels that had been blackened until there wasn't even a glimmer of light to betray its presence. Tonight, however, the cargo door was open, the interior light revealing three people, including Layla, who were unloading various bags and pieces of gear.

He turned in that direction, but paused when he saw a big, blond man exit the barracks, put his arms around Layla, and bend his head to murmur something against her ear. She laughed and shoved him away, but they were both grinning when she swung a canvas duffle over her shoulder and entered the barracks, turning right beyond the door, where the sleeping quarters were located.

Brian, Xavier thought. Layla's *good friend.* And she'd brought him here, to *his Fortalesa.* If it had been any other day, he'd have considered the man's presence a mild irritant and let it go, confident in the knowledge that Layla was his. But it was *this* day—a day he'd spent helplessly trapped in sleep while his people were attacked, their children taken. And it had been this *Brian* who'd gone with Layla to rescue the children who were *his* to protect.

Just as Layla was, quite simply, *his.*

"INCOMING," BRIAN said softly, when Layla returned for a second load.

"What?" she asked, then looked up to see trouble with a capital X striding down the long length of the yard. Wanting to put some distance between what looked like an enraged vampire lord and her people, she took several steps in his direction before she was drawn up short by his appearance. His eyes were shining with power, that odd pewter glow eclipsing his irises completely. But it wasn't only his eyes that told her he was angry. Xavier was a big man. Three inches over six feet, with a broad chest and thickly muscled shoulders and thighs. And every one of those muscles was taut with rage, his powerful hands clenched to highlight the strength in his arms and shoulders. He was still beautiful, maybe more than she'd ever seen him. But then, she'd never seen him this angry.

He didn't speak to her at first, but looked over her shoulder to where Brian stood watching, his stance ready to defend her if necessary.

"Rémy," Xavier said, and a lone male vampire appeared out of the shadows as if he had been conjured there by the sound of his master's voice. "There's a prisoner in the barracks. Take her to my interrogation room."

"Yes, my lord," Rémy said, and walked past Layla without a glance.

Turning, she signaled an "okay" to Brian and Kerry, who both stood watching with wary expressions as the vampire drew closer. Rémy didn't acknowledge them at all, simply walked past and emerged a moment later with the still-unconscious prisoner over his shoulder. He walked past her and Xavier without a word, just going about his master's bidding.

"Where are you taking her?" Layla asked, more out of curiosity than anything else, since she'd already decided to let Xavier do the questioning.

"The vampire wing," he said, as if he wondered why she was asking. "Feel free to observe, although I warn you, it won't be pretty. And she won't survive."

Layla concealed her wince at the matter-of-fact way he said that, even though she honestly had no problem with the judgment.

"Layla." Brian touched her shoulder lightly as he came to stand next to her.

He stared at Xavier for a moment, then introduced himself. "Brian Hudson," he said simply. Between the stories Layla had told him and the few vampires they'd encountered in their various assignments, he knew better than to offer a handshake.

Xavier's already cold expression went positively frigid while he eyed Brian up and down, his glittering eyes slowly shuttered behind a lazy blink as his gaze shifted to Layla. "This is your commanding officer?" he asked her.

It was Brian who answered with a low chuckle that didn't win him any points. "No, sir," he said. "She's mine."

"Your what?" Xavier growled.

"My commanding officer."

Xavier's lip curled. "Then why are you standing here?"

"I thought my captain might need some help."

"And you thought *you* could help her? Against me?"

"I don't know," Brian admitted. "But I'd have to try."

All but forgotten in the escalating testosterone battle between the two males, Layla sighed and stepped between them, breaking their stare-down. "Thank you, Brian, but I don't require assistance. You should join the others and get settled in the barracks. You guys have more gear to deal with than I do."

Brian studied her for an unhappy moment, turned and shot Xavier a hard look, then snapped a sharp salute—which had to be for the vampire lord's benefit, since they *never* saluted—and strolled into the barracks with deliberate ease.

Xavier watched him go, then looked back to Layla. "My office, now," he growled.

She shook her head. "I have to make sure—"

He moved so fast, she didn't see it coming. Suddenly, he was no more than an inch away, his head lowered until they were practically nose to nose, those gleaming eyes staring into hers. "Don't push me tonight, Layla," he hissed. "I need a briefing, and you're going to deliver it."

"You took my prisoner," she accused.

"She's my prisoner, not yours."

"Bastard."

"Hardly. My mother was a lady of the court, and my father was her husband under Church law. I'll thank you not to sully her good name."

She glowered, wondering if any of that was true, or if he was just being an arrogant ass.

"No comeback," he gloated. "How very disappointing . . . for *you*." He took another look around and apparently didn't like what he saw. "We're taking this to my office," he said, looking down at her. "The only question is how you're going to get there."

"You wouldn't dare," she muttered.

"You've been gone far too long, if you think that's true. And you wouldn't be able to stop me any more than your boyfriend would."

And they'd been getting along so well, she thought, gritting her jaw hard enough that her teeth hurt. "Fuck," she snapped.

Xavier gave her a look she couldn't interpret, a cross between gloating and indulgence. And what the hell was that supposed to mean? "Walk with me," he said, his tone so gentle that it completely disarmed her.

"Ugh," she groaned, but began walking in the right direction while he turned to join her.

They'd taken only a few steps, when Xavier said, "He's in love with you."

It was such a non sequitur that she gave him a startled look. "What? Who?"

"Your man Brian. He's in love with you."

"No, he's not," she said, letting him hear, in her voice, what an absurd idea that was. "Brian loves me, yes. But as a friend, a brother. There's never been anything else between us."

"So you say."

"So I *know*. We've known each other for years. We served in the military together, before creating this team. Trust me, there's nothing between us."

"Captain." Brian's shout drew her attention with impeccable timing. She looked up at Xavier. "I'll catch up."

"I'll wait," he snarled.

She walked back, meeting Brian halfway. "What's up?"

"You okay?" he asked softly, glancing at Xavier over her shoulder, making his meaning clear.

"Fine. He was angry, but he'd never hurt me."

"So what's the story between you two?"

"What? There is no story," she lied.

"Yeah, right," he scoffed. "Tell that to someone who hasn't known you for ten years. You have a thing for him."

"Did. Past tense. As in, no longer."

"Uh huh. For what it's worth, he likes you, too."

"He likes everything with a pussy."

Brian laughed. "Now I *know* you like him."

"Drop it, Hudson. Get yourself and the others settled and fed. The communal kitchen's *that* way. They'll just be serving dinner. And stop dissecting my non-existent love life."

"Sure thing, Cap. I take it you're heading for a debriefing and strategy session with the vampire gang," he said with way too much enthusiasm.

"Unfortunately. I'm hungry, too, you know."

"Want me to save you something? I imagine there won't be much to eat among the vamps."

She sighed. "You're right about that. Maybe I can persuade his highness to order something. But just in case, put something in the refrigerator for me."

"Will do, but hey, as long as you're all plotting the future, remind the vamp about the kids. All of them, young and old, need to stay out of school until we've neutralized this threat. They failed this time, but that doesn't mean they won't try again."

"Good point. I'll get someone to call the schools, get assignments or whatever. Xavier's a good politician, always supports the town government, contributes to pet projects and the like. They won't fight on home-schooling the kids until we can guarantee their safety again." She shot a look back to where Xavier waited, probably hearing every word they were saying. Damn vampire. "I have to get to this meeting while I can still keep my eyes open. Don't forget to save me some food, and don't try swapping bedrooms while I'm gone either."

Brian snorted. "Your stuff's already in the biggest room. Too much trouble to move it."

She slapped his arm with a grin, then spun on her heel and rejoined Xavier.

XAVIER HAD WAITED in silence while Layla and her subordinate spoke, presumably including his orders for the next few hours. They sure as hell didn't look as if that was the only thing going on, though. They stood as close as lovers and touched easily. What the fuck was that? It was obvious that *Brian* loved Layla, and he couldn't believe she was so blind that she didn't see it. She'd always been smarter than the others in her age group, and nothing he'd seen so far indicated that had changed. She was also incredibly observant, especially of the people around her, with an intuitive sense of human behavior—something he obviously lacked. She hadn't been so quick to notice though, when she'd denied there was anything more to her relationship with the human. She had a big blind spot there.

Not that it mattered. In the end, she would be his. It had taken all his strength to walk away once. He wasn't going to do it again. Not now that she'd returned, with all the beauty and sensuality that had been only a promise in the teenager, and was now fully realized in the woman. Not even her physical strength and military experience could take away from her desirability. She was lush and curvy, despite the lean muscles and battle-hardened gaze. And damn if he didn't want her more than ever.

Layla joined him, her dark eyes raised to meet his. "What's with the scowl, oh great one?"

He closed his eyes briefly. She could push him as no one else could. Mostly because he wouldn't have tolerated it from anyone else. "The day's events don't lend themselves to laughter," he growled. "May we leave now?"

She made a noise that was half laugh and half snort—nothing that a *lady* would have permitted to escape her delicate lips. And yet he found it charming.

"I'm hungry," she said simply. "And since I'm probably going to be the only human at this meeting, I need one of your minions to bring me some food. A sandwich will be fine. A big sandwich, with no onions. Everything else is good."

"I don't have minions, but I will be happy to request a sandwich for you, especially one with no onions."

She laughed, and they walked the rest of the way in a comfortable silence.

CHUY STOOD WHEN they entered, and gave Xavier a slight bow from the waist. "Sire."

Xavier waved his lieutenant back down, and Layla noticed that he was drinking rum tonight, rather than wine. She personally despised the stuff, but since the vampire symbiote metabolized alcohol too rapidly for it to have any real effect, vamps mostly drank for the taste. And rum had a very distinct taste. Blech.

Joaquim walked in a moment later, while she was pouring herself a good old-fashioned whiskey.

"Good evening, my lord," Joaquim said, then added, "Commander," with a look in her direction. He ignored the bar, going straight to the conference table, where he sat facing the room.

"Layla?" Xavier said, once they were both seated at the table, with him at one end, and her sitting next to him—a seat, she couldn't help noticing, that both his vampires had left carefully open. "Tell us what happened today. In detail, if you would."

She looked up, ready to begin, but paused when one of Xavier's vampire guards walked in and set a plate in front of her, with the requested sandwich, along with some sliced fruit, and an unopened bottle of water.

"*Gràcies,*" Xavier said. "*I sense visitants,*" he added, indicating there were to be no visitors, no interruptions.

"Sire," the vamp said and closed the door behind him as he left.

Layla gave the sandwich a longing look, but settled for a slice of fruit and a sip of water before beginning her report. "It started with a call from one of the teenagers, Alícia Vilar. There was a rumor running around the school that the children's van had been attacked, and the children taken. I want to add at this point that I don't think whoever took them expected us to respond as quickly or effectively as we did."

She leaned forward, warming to the topic. The kidnappers' motivation had bothered her almost from the beginning, but especially after her team had found the children practically unguarded, and had freed them easily. It certainly had been different than other hostage rescues they'd executed over the years.

"First, the kidnapping was not just daytime, but morning. They could just as easily have taken the kids on their way home in the early afternoon. They knew my *father* was gone, but they didn't know that I'd replaced him, or that I'd immediately go after them. And they sure as hell didn't know that some of my team had arrived in town on the very heels of the kidnapping."

She sipped some water before continuing. "We found the children drugged to sleep, and guarded by two inexperienced teenagers who were also sound asleep. Why were the children being held in a house thirty minutes from here? Why hadn't they immediately left town, or at least taken the hostages to Barcelona, where they wouldn't have every person on the street noticing the damn van driving by with its windows all shot to hell? Because they expected *you* and your vampires to respond, expected to have the entire *day* to take the children to wherever their plan was. Granted, it was simple good luck that my guys showed up when they did, and were able to pinpoint the kidnappers' house so fast.

She swallowed a piece of melon, letting the sweet juice wet her throat, although it only served to make her more hungry.

"And then there's this." She handed Xavier the note that had been delivered under a white flag, just as she'd been taking off to meet her team.

Xavier froze when she laid the envelope on the table in front of him, with the note inside, and the seal intact. "Where'd you get this?" he demanded, his eyes flaring with power for an instant, before they went back to normal. Or *his* normal.

"Another teenager, a little older than the prisoner and her dead friend—certainly bolder and more confident than either of them—arrived at the *Fortalesa*. She was walking, though when we search tomorrow, we'll probably find indications that somebody had driven her most of the way, and they'd later left together. She was carrying a white flag and specifically asked whether we would honor it before she handed that letter over."

"What do you think she'd have done if you'd refused?"

"Good question. I wouldn't be surprised if whoever had brought her here had a long-range rifle aimed at me, or whoever else might have come out to speak to her. You know the guard and driver from the van were butchered, both of them dead. And the two guards in the escort vehicle were severely wounded. These people clearly don't have any qualms about killing to get what they want."

"Which is what?" Joaquim asked.

Layla would have shared her own confusion as to that, but she was staring at Xavier and realized that he *knew* who Sakal was. "Xavier?" she asked softly. "Does that name mean something to you?"

"*Fill de puta*," he swore softly, then looked at her and added, "Something," in a voice hoarse with an emotion.

Anger she would have understood. But this was more than that.

There was a history there, one she needed to know if she was to have a hope in hell of understanding what was going on.

"Sire?" Chuy said, concern in his voice. "Who is it?"

Xavier spun the note down the table where both vampires could read it. And when they did, they looked up with expressions every bit as distraught as his.

Recognizing that this was something more than just secret-keeping between them, Layla swallowed her frustration, and even took a long drink of water before she touched Xavier's hand where it lay on the table and said quietly, "I need to know what this means. I can't defend the *Fortalesa* and its people if I don't know what to expect."

He'd been staring at the empty envelope which lay with its wax seal face up, but now he lifted his head and spoke to his vampires in a furious voice. "We're taking that nest tonight. We'll leave well after midnight, when they'll assume we're staying home and licking our wounds. When *they'll* be returning to their beds, confident that they're safe for another night. But in the meantime, be visible. Walk throughout the *Fortalesa*, let everyone—vampire and human—see your confidence that the enemy will soon pay the ultimate price."

Then he stood. "I'll call you when I'm ready to interrogate the prisoner."

The vampires rose and left without another word, while Xavier followed them to the door and locked it. Then he returned to the table and held out a hand to her.

She took it and stood without question, hoping this meant he was going to tell her who the fuck Sakal was, and why his involvement had all of them looking as though the devil himself had shown up at their front gate.

XAVIER LED AN unresisting Layla through the door to his bedroom, surprised when, though her fingers tightened on his, she didn't offer an immediate protest. What had he been thinking earlier, that she was unusually sensitive to the moods of people around her? Perhaps she'd read his and known that he wasn't planning to throw her on the bed and fuck her until he felt better, and she no longer had the strength to ask questions.

"Drink?" he asked, lifting a crystal decanter identical to the one in his office, and with the same whiskey inside.

"Sure, though . . . is it okay if I eat my sandwich? If I drink any more on an empty stomach, I'll probably get sick instead of drunk."

"Get your food," he said, gesturing toward the door. "If you're to understand who Sakal is, I've a long story to tell."

She blinked in surprise, probably at the idea that he would tell her anything about his past. But she hadn't been around long enough as an adult to hear his stories. They certainly weren't fit for anyone younger.

He poured two drinks, left one on the side table closest to the door, then walked around to the side of the bed and stretched out, his own drink in hand. Sipping slowly, he waited until she sat cross-legged on the bed next to him, her plate of food carefully sitting on the cloth napkin that had been wrapped around the fork and knife delivered with the meal. Presumably, she'd taken that precaution to protect the bed's comforter, although he would have told her not to bother.

"Okay, if I start eating?"

"Of course. I'm not that delicate, *cariño*. You, more than anyone, surely know that."

"True, but I'm trying to be polite. I've never been in your bedroom."

She'd probably meant that to lighten his mood, but knowing that Sakal was even *alive*, much less returning to trouble him again, it would take a hell of a lot more than a casual quip to cheer him up. The bastard's death would be a good place to start.

He shook his head at that and muttered, "He should be two hundred years dead already. At least. How is it possible that he's survived this long?"

"Sakal?" she asked around a mouthful of sandwich.

"His full name is *Ori* Sakal, and he's a vampire, though weaker than a strong human. He should have starved, unable to enthrall a human well enough to feed. That is, if he wasn't killed by some other vampire first."

He let a sigh come then, sipping his whiskey for a while before continuing. "Sakal was a sorcerer of considerable skill before he was turned. I was just past my hundredth year, and my power had already eclipsed that of my Sire, Josep Alexandre. I no longer lived under Josep's roof, but we were allies of a sort. There was plenty of territory to go around then, unlike now, which made it possible for us to coexist peaceably, as long as we saw each other rarely and only for short visits.

"I remember when my Sire first approached me about this sorcerer he'd met. The man was not the *most* powerful sorcerer in our world, but he was uncommonly strong, and my Sire wanted him in his court in a way that ensured no other could make use of his talents. That, of course, meant making him a vampire, loyal only to my Sire." Xavier paused to take a sip before continuing. "You might think that made it simple. Turn the sorcerer, make him yours for eternity. The problem, and the reason my Sire hesitated enough to seek my opinion, was twofold. First, there was always the chance that the newly-turned vampire would end up as I had, more powerful than the Sire. That didn't happen often, however, and so it wasn't the major concern.

"No, the biggest problem was that attempts to make a vampire out of a sorcerer were so rare that most believed them to be the stuff of fable. What was taken as fact, however, was that no vampire had ever succeeded in turning a sorcerer . . . without that sorcerer *also* losing his magical abilities. They retained not even the small amount of magic that most vampires are capable of. Or at least, that was the accepted truth."

He paused again, thinking back to those days with his Sire. They'd been friends as well as allies, something that was still uncommon. Powerful vampires were known to murder any of their children who surpassed them. Not all vampires, of course, since *he* was still alive, but still, most strong offspring were usually eliminated. He drew another long sip from his glass and caught Layla's wide-eyed expression, not of eagerness for the rest of his tale, but exasperation, wanting him to get on with it. He smiled slightly in her direction, and took one sip more than he would have otherwise before continuing.

"As I said, it's a long story."

1796, Catalonia, Spain

XAVIER PROSPERO Flores strode into his Sire's drawing room, every aspect of his bearing conveying not only the confidence of a man born to wealth and nobility, but of a vampire even more powerful than his Sire, whom he was visiting. Power burned in his veins and had, ever since the night he'd been turned. He had the strength, the *immortality* of a vampire, but not just any vampire. Xavier had the strength to rule, to become a lord. A *vampire* lord, with the power of life and death over hundreds, even thousands of lesser vampires.

He grinned at the Catalonian ladies he passed, seeing the admiration in their gazes, the lust that would scandalize their mothers and grandmothers had they been there to see it. He winked at the one or two he knew . . . *intimately*, but didn't stop for any of them. His Sire had summoned him. And while he was no longer bound to respond, he chose to do so, out love and loyalty for this man who had given him the gift of life itself.

He might partake later of the festivities—and the ladies—to be had this evening, but for now, his purpose was clear. His Sire required his service, and he had come for the man who'd given him a gift beyond measure. He'd been dying when he'd been turned, riddled with infection from a wound that had seemed minor, but had swept through his body leaving him on the very precipice of death. His parents, desperate to do anything that would save their son's life, had requested the intervention of Lord Josep Alexandre, a powerful vampire who lived in Catalonia, and partook on occasion of invitations to court offered by royals and others who found him a pleasing companion. Josep had agreed, seeing in Xavier a permanent grasp on his family's extensive wealth and holdings, since he was their only child. It hadn't worked out that way for Josep, given Xavier's strength, but he nonetheless felt both gratitude and loyalty to the vampire who'd saved his life.

Catching sight of his Sire entering from the front of the room, Xavier caught the vampire lord's eye and exchanged a quick telepathic acknowledgement. By the time he reached Josep's side, the vampire lord had turned and was leading him to a small chamber behind the large drawing room, one that was used for a variety of private exchanges.

"Sire," Xavier said, taking Josep's proffered hand and bending to kiss it. "How may I serve you?"

The vampire lord smiled warmly. "You serve simply by existing, Xavier."

He dipped his head in a way that was meant to be humble, but didn't quite meet that standard. Xavier was far too arrogant, far too sure of his power and skills, to be truly humble. But his Sire either didn't notice or didn't care.

"A drink?" Josep asked, as he served himself, pouring dark red liquid into a small crystal glass.

"No, thank you, my lord."

"Sit, then. I want to discuss a matter with you. I need your advice."

"Any wisdom I may possess is yours."

Josep chuckled. "Your mother taught you well, Xavier. But modesty sits uneasily on your tongue."

Xavier had nothing to say to that, as it was the simple truth, and so he sat when Josep did, then waited.

Josep took another full sip of the blooded wine before saying, "What do you know of the war we vampires fought against the magic wielders some centuries ago?"

He tipped his head curiously, taken aback by the unexpected question. If he had the right of it, the war between vampires and sorcerers was more than mere centuries past. It had occurred in the previous millennium, maybe even the one before that, which as far as he knew, was well before his Sire had been born. "I know somewhat of it, my lord. It was brutal, with terrible losses on both sides. More so in the early months, when the magicians, lacking honor and courage both, rallied humans to seek out and kill vampires as they lay helpless in their daytime sleep."

"Just so," Josep agreed. "You're wondering if I was alive then." His smile widened. "I was not, though there are others still alive—both vampires and sorcerers—who were. Not many anymore, but enough that a wise vampire needs to beware."

"Is there some new danger on the horizon, my lord?"

"Not specifically. But let me not play with words. A sorcerer has arrived in my territory. He comes from France, and while I've no reason to believe his home is elsewhere, it would seem that he thinks to settle with *us* in Spain."

"Why?"

Josep raised a single finger. "Exactly. Why? And what use can I make of him?"

"Is he powerful enough to be useful?"

"My spies tell me so."

Xavier considered the problem for a moment, his thoughts raising and rejecting possibilities in a whirlwind of calculation. "You wish to turn him," he said in dawning realization.

Josep threw back his head in a delighted laugh. "It is no wonder that you're my favorite child. You understand my thoughts as well as I do myself."

"You honor me, Sire."

He waved away the comment. "It is no more than you deserve. Now, what do you think of my idea?"

Xavier hesitated, thinking how best to convey his opinion. "If it is possible, it would seem an excellent strategy. It must be said that I'm unaware of any threat from those who currently use magic, and indeed it is my understanding that the number of sorcerers is dwindling, just as you said. But, while it is always best to anticipate your enemy's moves, rather than react to them, I have heard from others that when a magic user, or sorcerer as the case may be, is made vampire, he loses any shred of magical ability."

"That is no more than superstition. No one has ever attempted to turn a sorcerer, certainly not in my lifetime, which is a fair number of centuries, nor can my scholars find any mention of it in their books and scrolls."

Xavier frowned. "Perhaps you're right in this, but does the sorcerer believe the same? And if not, will he consent?"

"That is why you must bring him to me, so that I may ask. I cannot go to him myself—it wouldn't be seemly. But while you are powerful, you live far from this city and are less likely to be known by a sorcerer from France."

Xavier stood immediately, ready to undertake this rather simple mission. But Josep waved him back down.

"Not this instant, Xavier. Enjoy the reception, and the many lovely *guests*. Tomorrow will be soon enough to begin."

XAVIER HAD LITTLE trouble locating Sakal the next night. Unlike many, if not most, magic users, this sorcerer had set himself up in an elegant townhouse, which spoke to his success, if nothing else. Ignoring the line of petitioners, Xavier strode up the stairs and into the small foyer. Few argued his right to do so, and those who did were quickly silenced by the pewter gleam of his dark eyes. People knew what it meant when a vampire's eyes possessed that eerie glow—power, and a lot of it.

A servant appeared in front of him when he started down the hallway of the small, but well-appointed home. The man was human, but then why wouldn't he be? Sakal was also human . . . for now.

"My lord." The servant spoke quietly, as if to avoid disturbing whoever was behind the door he'd just closed and now stood in front of. "I am unaware of your appointment."

"That's because I didn't make one." Xavier smiled, fangs on full display. "But your master will see me now."

The servant froze, quivering like a terrified rabbit under the force of Xavier's gaze. "Yes," he whispered at last. "One moment, if you would." He fumbled for the handle behind him, nearly falling inward when the door opened.

Xavier was amused by the servant's terrified reaction, and didn't immediately shove into the room where Sakal was receiving petitioners.

For money, of course. He had no doubt the sorcerer charged a handsome fee for his services. His amusement was not infinite, however. He decided to wait three minutes before entering the room with or without an invitation.

The door opened again as a well-fed merchant hurried out, face paling when he saw Xavier waiting. The man squeaked a greeting of some sort, or perhaps it was an apology. Xavier barely glanced his way, his attention already drawn to the tableau inside the room. Sakal—it could be no one else—sat on a gilt-backed chair dramatically placed between two tall candelabras, each bearing six fat, wax candles. The sorcerer's robes were black velvet with glyphs embroidered in silver thread. Xavier glanced at the glyphs, but made no attempt to reason them out. Chances were they meant nothing and were simply there to impress the ignorant. But if not, then he wasn't about to trap himself by foolishly reading the wrong thing and getting caught up in some spell.

Sakal stood when Xavier entered, his outwardly calm expression betrayed by the wariness hiding behind his gaze. "I'm told you require an audience," he said. "You've been quite insistent."

An audience, Xavier thought scornfully. The last thing he needed or wanted was an *audience* with a fucking sorcerer. If not for his loyalty to Josep, he'd have killed the human on the spot for daring such arrogance. But what he said was, "Lord Josep would speak to you. Come with me."

The sorcerer appeared taken aback at the brusque command, but recovered quickly. "And if I choose not to go with you, do you believe you can take me against my will?"

Xavier regarded him with a cold stare. "Do you believe I cannot?"

Sakal made a slight moue, as if the answer was uncertain, but said only, "I am intrigued. I will go."

Xavier snorted dismissively and gestured at the door, for Sakal to lead the way.

"Surely if we are to be colleagues, we should trust each other," the sorcerer observed.

"You've much to learn of the world, if you believe *that* to be likely."

Sakal scowled at the ambiguous response, fussed pretentiously with his robe, but finally surrendered and marched out of the room, with Xavier a dark presence at his back.

Xavier telepathed his Sire when he and Sakal arrived at Josep's home. His telepathic reach was considerably greater than most, but he'd have been able to contact Josep regardless. The bond between Sire and child was very strong.

The vampire lord was not waiting when Xavier hustled Sakal into his receiving room. He wasn't some common line vamp, or even a powerful master. He was the fucking Lord of Spain and didn't lower himself to wait in eager attendance upon a mere human, no matter that this particular human styled himself a sorcerer.

Sakal searched the large room, plainly surprised to find it empty. He aimed a glance at Xavier that was part question and part arrogance. Xavier ignored him and simply took up position near the entrance to keep others out. Josep didn't require his protection, although if Sakal became a threat, Xavier could kill the bastard in a heartbeat without taking a step closer.

"Ori Sakal, I presume."

Sakal spun at the sound of Josep's voice. He recovered quickly, but Xavier caught the moment of shock that he hadn't sensed the vampire lord's arrival.

"Lord Josep Alexandre," Sakal said smoothly, as if he hadn't been summoned as one would a servant. "To what do I owe the honor?"

Josep shot Xavier an amused glance, sharing his view of the sorcerer. *Except for his magical skills,* Xavier reminded himself. There was a reason Sakal stood in this room.

"I have plans for you," the vampire lord informed him.

The sorcerer's brow shot up in unconcealed surprise, but he held his tongue. Perhaps he wasn't so ignorant, after all.

"And I have a gift for you, as well," Josep continued. "A great gift."

"Might I inquire as to the nature of this gift?"

Josep laughed. "So cautious and courtly. You'll do well amongst us."

Sakal stilled. "Amongst whom, my lord?"

"Don't be coy. You know who and what I am."

"Vampire," the sorcerer whispered. "But what does that have to do with me?"

"I'm going to make you one of us. A vampire sorcerer. You'll be the first."

"And if I choose to refuse this . . . *gift?*"

It was Josep's turn to look surprised. "Why would you? You're a sorcerer, and I'm offering to add the power of a vampire to the magic you already possess."

Sakal took a cautious step back from the vampire lord who'd drawn steadily closer as he spoke. "Lord Josep, I am greatly honored that you would consider such a thing, but you surely remember the war between our peoples, and the carnage that resulted. Vampires and sorcerers are both creatures of magic, that's true. But the two magics are opposed to one another. The best outcome would be that I wake from"—he gestured in agitation, clearly uncertain as to precisely what action was necessary to make him a vampire—"the ceremony," he said finally. "To find myself with no power at all."

Josep seemed amused. "If that is the best, what would then be worst?"

"That the two powers would battle within me until the conflict caused such pressure that my body exploded into a fine paste of blood and entrails."

Xavier smirked. In his opinion, that was the *least* likely outcome, though Sakal couldn't know it. The magic that turned a man into a vampire was more than powerful, it was possessive. It might do battle with the sorcerer's magic, but it would win, and would then rebuild whatever parts of Sakal's body had been damaged in the process. It could take months, or even years, he supposed. But eventually vampire magic would claim the body.

"That scenario is highly unlikely, for reasons you cannot yet be trusted with." Josep shrugged, as if either outcome was acceptable, to him anyway. "The *best* case, however, would be that you wake as a powerful vampire, with your sorcery intact. A sorcerer vampire. Something this world has never seen."

Sakal couldn't hide the greedy gleam in his gaze. He was also unable to hide his thoughts from the two vampires, though he probably didn't realize it. The fool magic user actually saw only two possibilities, one of which was his death. But the other.... He saw himself with a power equal to Josep's. Saw his future as the ruler of Spain with greater power than any vampire or sorcerer in the world.

He pretended to ponder Josep's offer, not knowing that he would be turned before the night was over, whether he agreed or not. Josep wasn't interested in Sakal's future, only his own. If Sakal proved a useful tool, he would be kept. If not, he would be discarded, one way or the other.

Xavier wanted to bare his fangs in a grin. If Josep decided the sorcerer needed to be killed, the task would fall to him. And he would most definitely enjoy it.

"Very well." Sakal somehow managed to imbue the simple words with an overload of pomposity. "I agree."

Josep's lip curled in an amused smile, but he said nothing. He simply crooked a finger in Sakal's direction, then turned and led them all through an open door into a small sitting chamber, with a richly brocaded lounge and plenty of shadows. Xavier secured the door behind them with his own magic, then stood guard over his Sire, just in case the sorcerer was stupid enough to attack during the ceremony.

Sakal discarded his elaborate robe and loosened the neck of his tunic willingly enough, seeming intrigued more than anything else. At least, until Josep sank his fangs into his throat. Then the almighty sorcerer whimpered like a child, until he finally spared himself further humiliation and passed out.

The blood exchange took some considerable time. It wasn't a simple thing to drain a human's blood until he stood on the knife's edge of death, and then to replace that blood with the vampire lord's own. But eventually it was complete, and Sakal was lying unconscious and limp on the elaborate lounge.

"He'll be moved to the cellar before sunrise." Josep poured himself a glass of blood-dosed wine.

"And then?"

"And then we'll see how he wakes." He spoked dismissively, uncaring of the outcome. "Go, Xavier. Enjoy your night. Only, return after sunset tomorrow. I'll want you with me when he wakes."

"Of course, my lord."

"And thank you, Xavier."

"My honor, Sire." Xavier managed a slight smile, but in his heart, he was worried. It wasn't his to agree or not with whatever Josep chose to do, but he thought this evening had been unwise, and even foolishly arrogant. This "experiment" could go terribly wrong.

XAVIER STOOD IN a dank basement room the next night, waiting for Sakal to wake to his first night as a vampire. The first night of a vampire's life was disorienting for everyone, just as his own had been. When the sorcerer finally stirred, Xavier knew at once that Sakal was definitely now a vampire, but did he have any power? While the new vampire lay blinking in confusion, Xavier sent a narrow thread of his own power searching for the same in Sakal. But though he twined his probe through flesh and thought, he found *no* measurable power, beyond the small amount necessary to keep him alive. No *vampire* power. But what of his sorcery?

"Is it done?" Sakal's question was little more than a croak of sound.

"Yes," Xavier said evenly, not wanting to reveal what he'd learned.

The sorcerer turned bleary eyes his way. "What is the outcome?"

"That is for Lord Josep to determine."

Sakal sighed heavily, but managed to swing his legs over to sit on the side of the bed. At which point, he looked around in mingled confusion and disgust. "What is this place? It's *primitive*. And cold as the grave." His eyes widened. "Is that what this is? Am I in a grave?"

Xavier laughed, despite himself. "That is a tale for children. You're in the basement of Josep's home. Vampires require darkness and safety during the day. This basement provides that."

"Surely a blanket or two would be appropriate," he said, fingering the rough, cotton cover with distaste.

"Now that you've survived, the accommodations will improve."

Sakal gave him a shocked glance that was quickly shuttered, to be replaced by his seemingly habitual sneer. "When is my audience with Josep?"

"As soon as you can stand on your own."

Sakal was shaky, but determined, as they climbed the stairs, though he seemed to be growing more agitated with every step.

"Are you well?" Xavier asked, sympathetic to the sorcerer's plight, for all that he was an unlikeable ass.

"My magic," Sakal whispered. "Where is—?" He shot Xavier a suspicious glance and didn't finish what he'd been about to say as they finally reached the room where Josep waited.

Xavier knew the instant Josep realized that the sorcerer had no power as a vampire. His thoughts, when they met Xavier's, were disappointed, but accepting of the failure.

"Lord Josep," Sakal snapped, demanding his Sire's attention. "What is the outcome? I'm told only you would know."

Amusement drifted from Josep's mind, before he pinned the sorcerer with his eyes blazing power and said, "You are a vampire."

"But what of the rest?" Sakal insisted.

"What is the state of your sorcery?"

Sakal was silent for a moment, as if searching within himself. But when he looked up again, his words were hard and accusing. "Weak," he growled. "Weak as I haven't been since childhood. *What* have you done to me, vampire?"

Josep's smile bared his fangs. "Careful, sorcerer—if you can still call yourself that. Regardless, however, you *are* a vampire, and a pitifully weak one of those, too. Either of us in this room could slap you down with a thought."

"You did this to me," Sakal hissed, and threw one arm forward as if tossing a toy. Josep laughed, but Xavier saw it for what it was. With a burst of speed, he placed himself in front of his Sire so that the twisting sphere of magic struck him full in the chest. The shock of it dropped him to his knees as he waited for the magic to chew into his chest and destroy his heart.

And he waited.

He stared down at the blackened spot on his tunic where the magic had hit, but felt nothing. Gripping both sides of the neckline, he ripped downward until his chest was bare, and found no mark, not even the redness that a human fist would have caused.

"Your gift has revealed itself at last," Josep said, chuckling. "And with excellent timing."

Xavier looked from his uninjured chest to his Sire. "Gift, my lord?"

"Every powerful vampire has a talent unique to him alone. And yours, it would seem, has just saved my life." He clapped a hand on Xavier's shoulder. "Congratulations, my child. You're immune to magic."

Xavier heard a gasp and swung around to find Sakal backing away in shock, and more than a little fear.

"You'll pay for this," the sorcerer whispered, hate-filled eyes lifted to Josep, before shifting to include Xavier. "Both of you will pay before the end."

And then he ran, chased by the sound of Josep's delighted laughter.

Sant Andreu De Llavaneres, Barcelona, Spain, present day

"YOU LET HIM GO?" Layla asked in disbelief.

Xavier sighed. "It was a mistake, but the decision wasn't mine."

"That's a cop-out."

He scowled at her. "It was a different time. It was Josep's home—his territory, not mine."

"You already said you were more powerful than he was. Why should you have to pay for his mistake?"

"You can't understand. You're not a vampire."

"And thank God for that, if it means standing by while some full-of-himself vampire lord decides *my* future."

"You were in the army. Did you agree with every decision your generals made? Decisions that sent you and others out to be killed?"

Layla grimaced. "Okay, I see your point." She twisted to set the now-empty plate on the side table, then settled back, took the glass of whiskey from his hand, drank, and returned it. "So that's why Sakal's after you. Why'd you think he was dead?"

"Sakal thought he could leave Spain whenever he wanted. He didn't understand that as a vampire, he was now bound to his Sire, who was Josep. He couldn't leave Josep's territory. Not because Josep wouldn't permit it, though he wouldn't, but because by entering a rival vampire lord's territory without permission, he would be subject to immediate execution. No questions asked."

"Josep would kill him?"

"No, Layla, the rival vampire lord would. You don't fully comprehend the power a vampire lord wields over those who live within his authority. I know every vampire in Spain. Not personally, that's impossible, though I have met a good number of them. But I know their . . . " He fought for the right word. "Their taste in my mind, the sense of them. Now, someone as weak as Sakal could slip beneath the radar, as we say now, for some period of time. But eventually, he would be discovered. Not by me, but by one of those loyal to me. I have master vampires in every city, keeping track of who lives there and keeping them in line. Every other vampire lord has the same."

"Sounds feudal, which wasn't a great thing for the serfs."

"It is. Vampires have been around a long time, and they live a long time, too. There's been very little change in the rules that govern vampire society in thousands of years."

"*Fuck* me."

He shot her a grin.

"That was an expression," she snapped, as heat spread over her face.

"Don't worry, *cariño*. When I fuck you, it will be because you want it."

She snorted. "Like that's going to happen."

"Oh, it is. But not tonight."

And what the hell was with that pang of regret she was feeling? Damn it. "So what happened?" she asked grumpily.

"My Sire, Josep, ignored Sakal for months while he considered the situation. It was common for a sorcerer to travel in those days. They were scholars as much as magic-users, and Sakal was convinced he could find a way to restore his full magical talents. Josep liked that possibility, because he would have been left with a strong sorcerer who had an unbreakable bond to *him*, as his Sire. The Sire-child bond is one of the strongest there is among vampires. Only the mate bond is stronger."

Layla found that bit of truth interesting and maybe something more. But it was something she wasn't ready to think about yet, so she said, "But if Sakal left, and managed to avoid getting killed, could Josep somehow call him back?"

"It was a possibility, but in the end, it wasn't necessary. A second sorcerer, one more powerful than Sakal, happened to wander through Barcelona. He met with Josep, which was not unusual since many, if not most, sorcerers at the time were always looking for patrons to support them while they conducted their research. And with a vampire lord, there was no need to pretend that magic didn't exist.

"But it wasn't long before this sorcerer learned of Sakal's predicament, probably from Sakal himself. They approached Josep soon after, asking for a chance to allow the new sorcerer to restore the full measure of Sakal's magical power." He sighed in regret. "And Josep agreed."

"But something went wrong."

"Yes, it did. If I'd been there, I would have reminded Josep how well his meddling in magic had turned out the first time. As it was, the spell did work, after a fashion. Sakal recovered virtually all of his sorcerous power. Unfortunately, what he lost was his sanity."

"He's not crazy," Layla insisted. "No nutjob could have orchestrated this campaign, these guerilla-style tactics. They don't even care if they inflict casualties on our side. It's enough that they keep us on edge, wondering when the next attack is going to come. And then there's the disappearing act with his troops that he pulls off every time."

"They're not disappearing," he corrected mildly.

"I know that, but anything else sounds too much like, "Beam me up, Scotty."

He studied her as if worried she'd lost her mind.

"*Star Trek*, dude. It's a TV show, where they teleport people"—she shrugged—"using some electronic, computer thing. I'm not sure how it worked, but it was definitely not magic. And we're getting off the point. Today's kidnapping is a clear escalation, even if it didn't work out for them. We need to figure out his next step, before it happens."

"I agree. But first . . . "

Without warning, he rolled in her direction, reaching out as he did to wrap her in one arm and pull her under his body. It all happened so fast that the next thing she knew, he was kissing her, his lips firm but soft, his mouth demanding as he urged her lips apart and his tongue slid against hers like warm silk, seducing and claiming in turn.

Layla knew she should fight the seduction. She was strong. She should throw him off, then toss some whiskey in his face to cool him down. Who the hell did he think he was?

Except... she didn't want to do any of that. What she wanted was... every touch of his lips against hers, every stroke of his tongue... the strength in his fingers as he gripped her hip, holding her in place. And God save her, the weight of his rigid cock against her thigh.

Her heart was racing, her nipples stiff against the confinement of her sports bra. She wanted to be naked with him, wanted him to—

As fast as it had begun, it was over. He gave her one, final hard kiss, then jumped from the bed and said, "I have a prisoner to question. Want to watch?"

If she'd had a gun in her hand, she'd have shot him at that moment. She didn't even care that it wouldn't kill him, or that he'd heal in no time. It would *hurt*. Hell, maybe she'd shoot him anyway. She only had to roll a tiny bit to reach the Glock stabbing her in the kidney right now, because she was lying on the damn thing. Thanks to *him*.

But before she could act, he grinned and said, "Now, now, Commander. You don't want to shoot your employer. Besides, if you do that, *I'll* recover easily enough, but *you'll* miss the interrogation."

She got to her feet and growled. "You can just tell me about it later."

"Maybe. Maybe not."

"You're such an asshole. Where is this interrogation?"

Chapter Twelve

JOAQUIM AND CHUY were both waiting when Xavier led Layla through the office and out to the hallway. Walking back toward the stairs and then beyond, the four continued down a section of bare walls until they reached a square, deeply recessed alcove that contained a thick metal door.

"I didn't know this existed," she said.

"Why would you? This is a place that very few *vampires* are free to access."

"Has my father been here?"

"Only once, long ago."

"He never talked about it."

"And neither will you."

"Ah. I see."

"Not yet you don't. But you will."

He placed all five fingers on a biometric scanner to one side, and heard the door open with a soft buzz. Not long ago, that release would have been much louder and less sophisticated, but he believed in making use of modern technology, whether it was individual keys for the doors, or electronic locks.

"This way," he said, pointing to the left, where he could smell the human's fear waiting for him. He opened an unlocked door and entered a small observation room. It contained three plain chairs and a small, narrow table on which sat several notepads and pens. There was also a compact refrigerator and a small microwave sitting on top of it. The refrigerator would hold a few pints of blood, which Rémy would have seen to when he'd stowed the prisoner in the adjoining cell. It was there for Xavier's use, or any other vampire accompanying him. And sometimes when the prisoner was vampire, it was used on him as well, for both benefit and torment.

"You'll remain here," Xavier told Layla, then nodded at Chuy to indicate that he would remain also, and put a hand on the cell door, ready to open its lock.

"Why can't I go in with you?" Layla demanded.

"Because you can't," he responded simply, then released a small burst of his personal power into the door, freeing it to crack open a bare inch. He could sense Layla's anger, but ignored it, and without so much as a glance back at her, he opened the door all the way and walked into the cell, with Joaquim stepping inside as well, before closing the door behind them.

Xavier studied the girl. She was strapped down, lying on a thinly padded metal table, and seemed to be out cold, but he searched her consciousness, wanting to be sure. His main concern wasn't that she might be faking her insensible state, but that she could be carrying magical booby traps that might be triggered if he used coercive power to interrogate her. What he found confirmed her allegiance, or at least alliance, with Sakal, or some other sorcerer of considerable power. But the trap he found wasn't for him. Rather, it was a failsafe to protect Sakal by destroying her heart and killing her before she could divulge any secrets. He wondered if she was aware of the fatal device, and if her allegiance was that strong.

Well, he'd soon find out, but first he had to remove that damn magical explosive.

He deepened her unconscious state to avoid a sudden and unwanted awakening. He had the power to nullify the magical failsafe, but it would be a delicate operation. If she woke abruptly and began thrashing about, she could die anyway, before he could question her.

After a quick nod to Joaquim—who would understand what Xavier was about to do and defend him against the rare possibility of an intrusion—he closed his eyes, and rested his hand flat on her chest, fingers spread wide. Sinking down into her flesh, through the bone of her ribcage, he caught a mental image of her heart beating steadily, slowly. He'd studied human anatomy in detail once he'd discovered he could do this. It was dangerous for humans. They were so much more delicate than the vampires he "operated" on. But the skill came in handy for healing the weaker members of his vampire cohort living within his *Fortalesa*.

Searching beyond the physical heart, he saw the sorcerer's spell waiting. It was a small thing, no more than a blurry blotch on her heart. But it responded to his magic which made it visible to his scan. This was the delicate part. If he touched the spell's blotch before surrounding the entire heart, it could still do terrible damage. He didn't worry about the various veins and arteries running in and out. Once he had the entire thing contained, his particular magic would nullify the spell, causing it to dissipate into harmless bits of nothing, like all the other bits of nothing that swam in the human body and were eventually excreted with other waste.

When he was certain the entire organ was contained, along with the murderous spell, he touched the barest extension of the blotchy thing and watched as it fell apart under the gift of his magic. When he'd first discovered his unique gift, he'd thought it of limited use, but no longer. Apart from his ability to use his power in a non-lethal way on vampires, it seemed almost prophetic for him to have this gift when his most deadly enemy had turned out to be not just a vampire, but a sorcerer vampire.

He withdrew his magic, thinking it perverse that he had just saved the girl's life only so that he could torture the truth out of her, if necessary. There was a possibility that she would hold out and refuse to tell the truth, causing him to resort to more extreme forms of torture. He was willing to use whatever force necessary to get the information he wanted. And he thought it likely that Sakal had conditioned her psychologically to withstand torture and not betray him. That alone would have worked under human torture, but knowing what vampires were capable of and willing to do, Sakal had needed the failsafe spell to protect himself against the possibility that one of his followers would undergo vampire questioning.

Xavier did a final scan of the girl's body searching for anything he might have missed, and when he found nothing, he sent a miniscule shock of power into her brain to bring to her back to consciousness.

"Stop!" The girl's eyes flashed open, and she tried to sit up, straining so frantically at the straps holding her arms down that they dug into her flesh deep enough to draw blood.

"You're awake," Xavier commented.

Her head twisted around and she stared up at him in defiance. "No drugs," she snapped, twisting against the tight bonds as much as she could. "Lord Sakal says drugs pollute the mind, and we must remain coherent at all times if we are to serve his plan."

Xavier glanced over at Layla and caught her satisfied smile. She'd known this girl would be a talker. That's why she'd kept her alive. His own smile was grimmer, however. He had to persuade her to talk about the right things.

Giving her one of his most dashing smiles, he asked, "What's your name?"

Her first reaction was a mutinous glare, followed by a full-face frown that seemed to indicate deep thought. "Cláudia. And that's all I'm going to tell you."

Making a sound of regret, he said "I'm afraid you couldn't be more wrong."

She returned a smug smile and said, "Lord Sakal gifted me with his magic. You cannot coerce or torture me into revealing our secrets to you, *vampire*." She said the last word as a curse.

"You need to be less trusting, *nena*," he murmured. "Did your master also tell you that his *magic* would stop you by killing you?"

She appeared doubtful for a moment, but then the smug smile returned. "My lord wouldn't do that. He loves all of us who follow him, and treats us well. He gathered us from the streets, where we were beggars and worse, treated like the dirt underfoot. He brought us to a safe place and takes care of us when no one else would."

More curious than anything else, he asked, "The attacks on me, the weapons. Did he teach you that, too?"

"Yes. And we were eager to serve him, to rid the world of you and your bloodthirsty vampires. You're little better than animals, all of you."

He chuckled. "Did he tell you that he, too, is a vampire?"

"You lie. He told us you would. You tried to change him into one of your own, but his magic fought back and refused to permit it. But you had already poisoned his blood like an incurable disease, so that the sun harms him terribly."

"And the blood?" Xavier pushed.

"His blood flows like any other," she answered quizzically, as if not understanding the question.

"He requires blood to remain alive. He drinks blood like any other vampire."

"More lies," she hissed.

Interesting, he thought. So Sakal wasn't using his flock of followers as food. He might be roaming the streets hiding among the vamps in a rogue nest, like the one his vampires would root out tonight. But that wasn't Sakal's style. He considered himself far above the common man, whether peasant or aristocrat. He wasn't about to troll the streets and pay some whore to let him feed from her. And he wasn't powerful enough to entrance an unwilling victim.

Sakal could be using magic to erase the memory of his bite from whomever he selected for the night. But that would be cumbersome and time-consuming if he wanted to erase only the biting and none of the other mind controls he'd already planted. Not to mention that others would eventually notice bite marks on one or more of their fellow acolytes' necks and be curious.

It would be much easier to pay a whore, except that this was Sakal. So he must have a small stable of willing donors whom he kept close, but didn't reveal to his followers. Interesting, but not helpful for tonight's interrogation.

"I'm sorry, Cláudia, but this is going to hurt. I feel compelled to remind you that the sooner you talk, the sooner the pain will end. Just think of me as a truth seeker, like you."

She gave him a puzzled but frightened look, as if believing him, but not wanting to. "Lord Sakal is our teacher," she said in hesitant voice. "*He* is the source of all truth."

"Did he tell you that?"

"Yes. We were fooled by our parents and their government. But he's taught us the real truth, and we love him for that."

"What did he teach you? I'd like to learn."

"We can only be free when we break away from the chains of authority, revolting against those who want to enslave us to serve their interests."

"And what do I or my people have to do with this? Why kidnap the children who look to me for safety just as you look to Sakal?"

"Because you're a monster," she spat back at him. "A demon who would enslave us all to feed his unholy hunger and nourish the vampires he's created."

"Is that why you took the children?"

"We took them to *save* them."

She was so earnest that he believed *she* believed, though he knew better. Sakal would have killed those children if forced to it, if only for the pain it would have caused Xavier. He wouldn't have cared about the pain of their parents, their families.

"They have parents, Cláudia. Families who love them and would miss them." He didn't know why he was trying reason with her. But she was so young. It was a shame she'd been used by Sakal, and would now die at Xavier's hands.

"It's too late for their parents, but the children can still be saved."

"I see," he said, sighing. "Then tell me. Where is Lord Sakal?"

She clamped her lips tight and glared up at him.

"I'm sorry," he said, then gripped her arm and gave her *pain*.

She screamed, going stiff within the bonds, too terrified to thrash, in too much agony to move the slightest muscle. Tears were streaming down her face when he released her, and when she sobbed, it was as if she would empty her chest, the sound she made was so hard and so full of pain.

"Where is Lord Sakal?" he repeated softly and waited until her sobs let up enough that she could breathe, knowing that the pain would have lessened just enough to permit her to speak, while lying in wait in a way that she would feel it lurking, would know it could pounce at any moment.

"He saved me. I don't want to betray him," she said in a pitiful voice, as if hoping that Xavier would release her out of pity.

She knew too little of vampires, if she thought that. Xavier had no pity left for any but the ones he loved. And even they would diminish in his eyes if they ever betrayed him.

"You love him," Xavier said reasonably. "But he is hurting the ones *I* love. He is willing to kill, or send *you* to kill to further his goals. And *I* am willing to kill anyone who would hurt those whom I love, including every man, woman, and child who lives within my *Fortalesa*, and looks to me for protection."

"I can't," she pleaded, straining against her bonds as much as she could. He gripped her arm again and before he'd even begun to increase the pain, she screamed, "Please! I can't!"

"But you can, *nena*. And you will."

Blood was pouring from her eyes, from her nose, and the arm where he'd gripped her was burned as if from a fire, but she eventually told him everything he needed to know.

"He comes to us every night," she whispered, shivering from the pain, now utterly defeated.

"He comes to you," Xavier repeated. "But he doesn't live with you, doesn't *stay* with you."

"No. We have a farm of our own. We grow food, and we have animals for meat and cheese."

"Where does he go at night then?"

"I don't know," she said, then stared up at him in sudden terror. "I *don't*. It's the truth. None of us knows. He has guards who are always with him. They take down his words when he teaches us, so that we may study and learn."

"They live with him?" he asked, suddenly knowing exactly where Sakal's blood was coming from.

"I think they must."

Xavier's mouth quirked up in a cynical smile. "These assistants . . . are they women?"

"Yes. His very first students," she said eagerly. "They've been with him from the beginning of his journey to teach the truth."

"*Where* do they live with him?"

Fear clouded her eyes again. "I don't know. I told you. I don't *know*." She began crying again.

"Cláudia." His voice was cold and demanding as he stared down at her. "Tell me the truth."

She shuddered, choking on a final sob as she tried to hold them back. "They leave every night," she said, her voice hitching on the final words. "But I don't know—Wait!" she screamed when he lifted his hand. "Barcelona. He lives in Barcelona. In a, a *building*, not a house."

Xavier tilted his head curiously. "How did you discover that?"

"I didn't, not by myself. One of the others told me. He described a beautiful, gold building like a temple, where he first learned of Lord Sakal's truth."

"He remembered being there?" Xavier thought that odd, either that, or very negligent. Surely Sakal wasn't stupid enough to recruit new acolytes where he lived.

"It was his first night on the farm," she whispered, barely audible. "He, he disappeared after that."

"Of course, he did. When Sakal and the women leave you, *how* do they leave? Helicopter? Do they drive away in a vehicle?"

"Vehicle," she said in that same bare whisper. "A big one. Black . . . all over, windows, too."

He glanced at Joachim who jerked his chin at the girl and mouthed the word, "Where?"

Nodding his understanding and irritated that he hadn't thought of it, he asked, "Where do you and the others live, Cláudia? We'll give you a ride home."

Her expression when she looked at him was so full of hope that he hated himself for deceiving her, but only for an instant. If he set her free, she would go straight back to her friends and they'd report to Sakal. Better the damn sorcerer not know that Xavier had any idea what he was up to.

And even better that he not know Xavier was coming for him.

LAYLA WAS BOTH uneasy and curious when she accompanied Xavier out of the interrogation area and back along the way they'd come.

Joachim and Chuy had remained with the prisoner, and she had to ask the question, even though she wasn't at all sure she wanted to know the answer.

Steeling herself, she asked, "What will happen to her?"

"What do you think? What would you do with a prisoner who had revealed too much, and who, if set free, would go right back to her master and tell *him* everything we'd learned?"

Layla clenched her jaw unhappily, but gave him the truth. "Kill him."

He glanced down at her. "Kill *him*. Do you refer to the master, or the prisoner? Are you reluctant to kill a woman? Especially a very young one, who is nonetheless as capable as a man of betraying you."

She lowered her head to avoid his gaze, not because she didn't know the truth, but because she did. And she wondered what he would think of *her* once she told him. "Man or woman, there is no difference. A young child, I would try to save if I could."

Xavier was smiling when she finally dared to look up at him.

"What?" she demanded. "You asked, I gave you the truth."

"We are very much alike, *cariño*. That is why you are mine."

"I told you, I don't *belong* to anyone."

"So you did," he agreed pleasantly.

Frustrated at the non-answer, she looked for something to change the subject. "I didn't know the vampire wing was so big."

"Why would you? Few humans are ever permitted inside."

That was true. Like everyone else, she was familiar with the above-ground offices and facilities occupying the elaborate structure that rose above the rest of the *Fortalesa*. But the rest of this, Xavier's offices and that hall with the interrogation room—probably more than one—that was all new to her. And she'd seen more stairs than just the ones that she'd taken to get down to Xavier's office. Stairs that continued even farther down from where they'd exited to this floor. There had to be at least one sub-basement down there, maybe more.

Xavier had gone quiet, not offering any additional details about the vampire wing or what might lie beneath it. Instead, he led her back to his office, walked in ahead of her, and then held the door politely until she'd passed.

She turned when he closed the door and asked, "So where is Joachim taking her?" She didn't add "to be killed," although she was thinking it.

"To a cell which will be her home for the next while."

"How long? And why?"

He considered the question for some time. Probably because he wasn't used to anyone questioning his decisions. "As long as it takes," he growled finally.

"To do what?" she pushed.

"To kill Sakal, and negate the threat he represents."

Layla thought about that. He probably expected her to demand more from him, more details maybe, more about what he'd do to the rest of Sakal's sycophants. She did none of that. "Okay."

He was so surprised that he didn't manage to conceal it.

She chuckled. "My life for the last six years has been war of one kind or another. There is no gray on the battlefield. Only black and white."

"I can't say I'm happy you chose that path, but I'm glad you understand." He'd circled around the map table and was studying it intently. "Come here. We need to discuss what we do next."

"I think that's obvious. We have the location of the farm compound, and Sakal supposedly visits there every night. I'll take my people and check it out."

He regarded her for several minutes, and she was convinced he was about to order her to stand down, that she and her team were not to do a recon of the farm. She would have ignored him, but it still would have pissed her off.

She didn't know which of them was more surprised when instead of rejecting the idea out of hand, he said, "You would do this during the day, I assume?"

"Late afternoon," she corrected. "Cláudia said Sakal visits every night. I want to know if that's true."

"It's not worth the risk. He's dangerous, Layla. And we have other ways of gaining information, if we need it."

"We're dangerous, too. I'll let you know what we find."

"YOU SURE ABOUT this?" Brian asked the next morning, standing with legs spread wide so she didn't have to look up at him.

"Of course, I'm sure. Why would you ask that?" Layla scowled. "Do I usually give my people orders I'm not sure about?"

"Cheap shot, Cap. You know that's not what I meant."

"What *did* you mean?"

He took her arm, and with a glance back at the others who were dutifully not listening, pulled her farther into the trees on the hill above the farm compound. "I *mean* are you doing this for the right reasons? Or just to get back at your fanged boyfriend."

"He's not my boyfriend. He never was. And this has nothing to do with him. If we're going to run an op against that building"—she pointed at the main structure below—"we need better intel than we can get sitting a hundred yards away on a hillside. We've already been watching the place for two hours, and we've learned everything we can from this position. We know they all come out to work in the morning, that they don't wear uniforms or stupid robes. And since their glorious leader will be arriving after sunset, plus them being farmers and all, it's good bet that they'll stop for the day close to sunset, put away their tools, and return inside for the night."

"And we learned all that sitting right here, where they can't see us."

"I don't get it, Brian. This is a standard recon op. What's your problem with it?"

"My problem is you're going in blind. For all we know, they have checkpoints inside every door. Maybe they all have a secret tattoo, or a fluorescent stamp, like in a bar. For that matter, they might have pressure plates outside all the windows, and most of the doors."

"That's pretty extreme for a kids' farm compound, don't you think? Besides, Cláudia didn't have a tattoo or a bar stamp, and she didn't say anything about the kind of security measures you're thinking of," she dismissed.

"So you stripped her down, searched her head to toe? Did you scan her with a black light?"

"You know we didn't."

"So how do you know—?"

"I don't, okay? Are you saying we've never scouted an unknown location before? Have you been working with the same team I have for six years? Come on, Brian."

"Who's going with you on this intel gathering mission? Because I know *you're* going."

"Kerry. We're the only two women, and if we have to, we can play the part of adoring servants long enough to get out of there."

"Fuck. You're going to do this, no matter what I say."

She shrugged. "Unless you can come up with a good reason why we shouldn't. We need better intel on the interior of that building. Is it one big room inside? A warren of hallways? Who the fuck knows? But don't you think we should?"

He sighed. "You really think we're going to assault that place?"

"I don't know. I *do* know that Xavier wants Sakal, not a bunch of teenage truth seekers. So any op we do run will have to be at night, to be sure the asshole vamp is there."

He dropped his head, jaw clenched as he studied his boots, before looking back up. "All right. But you're not going in unarmed, and you're wearing comms. River and I will move in closer, but we'll still need to know if you're in trouble before it happens, not after they drag your dead bodies out into the dirt."

"You really think that Kerry and I couldn't take a bunch of kids, if we had to? Have some faith."

"I have *plenty* of faith. I just know you too well. Let's get this damn thing organized."

AN HOUR LATER, LAYLA and Kerry were ready. The grounds of the compound had been crowded with acolytes until maybe fifteen minutes ago, performing a variety of tasks, including farming and maintenance. But then, a soft chime had sounded outside the building, and the workers had responded instantly. They patted the dirt around a final plant, put away their tools, and headed for a row of outdoor faucets to wash their hands. They'd been orderly about it, but not horror movie creepy orderly. There'd been no falling into line and marching in silent lock-step to the sinks and through the open doors. After washing up, they'd walked into the building in small groups of quiet conversation, and that was it.

Layla glanced at the time. They had another hour until true sunset, maybe an hour after that before Sakal would arrive, since according to Xavier, the vampire was weak and wouldn't rise until well after dark. If she and Kerry were going to infiltrate the compound, it had to be now. They wanted to be in and gone before Sakal arrived. Weak or not, if he had anything close to the kind of enhanced senses that Xavier and his people exhibited, Sakal might sense their presence, and they'd be cooked. She glanced at the other woman and found her staring back, waiting.

"We go now," Layla said softly. "They're probably settling in for their evening meal down there, before prepping for the vamp's arrival. If they eat communally—and why wouldn't they, with the whole group-think mentality—they'll all be in one room, so we can snoop some."

"Right, but make it fast," Brian said, crouching next to them. "You need to be out before they finish eating."

"We'll be careful. I'm not going to get caught by a bunch of brainwashed teenagers." As she spoke, she was removing her ballistic vest, followed by her boots, which she exchanged for a pair of well-used sneakers. Her weapons had been removed, except for her Glock pistol with a thirty-round mag, and her belt knife. She and Kerry were both dressed in tank tops and khaki pants, which they'd rolled up to mid-calf.

When they'd checked their comm units and were ready to go, Layla looked at Kerry and said, "You've got our route fixed, right?"

"Yes, ma'am."

"Good, you lead. And you guys stay frosty and alert up here."

Brian and River chuckled at the favorite movie quote, but their nods were serious. This mission had been a cakewalk when all they'd been doing was talking about it. But now shit might go down.

The two women moved with practiced ease through the thick shrubs and stunted trees covering the hillside between them and the compound. They'd marched twice as fast through much more hellish environments on other battlefields, but the tough part of tonight's approach was still ahead of them. Once they paused to lie flat on the ground and brought up scopes to check out the building, looking for cameras or watchers they might not have spotted from above. Layla found it impossible to believe there was no security at all on this place.

"Maybe the doors are locked," Kerry murmured, as she continued to scan.

"Probably. From the little I could see, they looked like push-bar fire doors. Easy open from the inside, easy lock from the outside."

"Not an easy lock to by-pass, though. Not with a crowd inside. If we open a door and they're all sitting there eating dinner, they just *might* notice us."

"Roger that. I say we go in a window."

"I'd sure like to get a look inside before we pick an entry point," Kerry commented.

"Yeah. No ground level windows on this side, though. Let's go down a bit more, take a stroll around the building, see if we can get a peek into where they all are."

"Agreed. On three."

They ran across the open ground, crouched low and moving fast. If they were wrong, and someone was perched in a crow's nest outlook on top of the building, they were fucked. But there hadn't been any sign of that. So it was a risk, but a good one.

And it worked. In minutes, their backs were pressed up against a windowless wall, listening to nothing but silence. Looking over, Layla lifted her chin ahead of them, got a confirming nod from Kerry, and took off down the length of one wall to the corner, where they paused long enough to verify there was no one on the next side of the building, then moved along that wall in the same fashion.

They were about to give up on the idea of windows, when they peeked around next corner and found a long row of them starting about waist height and stopping a foot from the roof eaves. They could hear a steady hum of noise coming through those windows—lively conversations, with an occasional shout of laughter, the clank of flatware on cups and plates, the random scrape of a chair on a tiled floor. It was the sound of a large group of people having a meal. There were no amplified voices, no announcements or speaker that they could detect. Not yet, anyway.

Dropping to their hands and knees, they crawled below the windows, careful to remain close to the wall to avoid anyone catching a glimpse of movement. It was unlikely, but why take the risk? Once past the final window, there was a short expanse of wall—three feet maybe—and then an apparent portico, which Layla verified led to another closed, push-bar fire door.

Using hand-signals, she told Kerry they were going to go past the door to the next stretch of wall, which also had windows, but not as many. By now, they were completely out of sight of Brian and River keeping watch up on the hill. They couldn't risk a verbal message over their comms, but before moving on, Layla sent a high frequency squelch to signal that she and Kerry were secure and undetected.

Moving past the door—which was too close to the dining hall, even if they'd managed to get through it—they went down on all-fours once more and passed under the first double window on the next stretch of wall. They stopped there and listened. Their eyes met, and Kerry pulled out a small mirror on a telescoping wand. Expanding the wand to its greatest length, she slid it very slowly up over the window frame until it was even with the corner of the glass. Then turning it at a slight angle, they both studied what it showed of the room, which turned out to be a rather boring office, with cheap metal shelves against one wall and a closed door.

Retracting the mirror and tucking it into a pocket, Kerry stood very slowly until her eye level was where the mirror had been a moment earlier. When she'd dropped down next to Layla once more, she spoke in a barely detectable voice. "Office. Cheap furniture, piles of what look like pamphlets or handouts on metal shelves. Sakal's not wasting his money on furnishings, that's for sure. The room's empty, door's closed, but looks like it *is* used on a regular basis. There's trash in the can, empty coffee cup on the desk, jacket on back of the door. The window's very doable."

Decision time, Layla thought. Could they risk going through the window? Did they have time? She wished she knew how long their dinner took, and if the meal was just a precursor to an evening brainwashing session. That was probably too much to hope for, but they wouldn't need much time. They already knew what the cult was about, so they weren't there to steal propaganda or financial data. Their only purpose was to get the lay of the building. That big dining hall, for example, took up a good third of the interior space, which meant they probably *slept* communally, too. The building was a single floor, with a pitched roof. It was possible some people slept in the attic, but space would be limited.

"We're going in," she decided, speaking softly. "I want to open the office door, get a look both ways, then get out. We'll exit down this side," she added, pointing to the far wall which they hadn't covered yet. "I want to know if it's all offices, or if there are bedrooms on this side."

Kerry nodded, then stood and went to work on the window. The frame was weathered metal, not built to withstand the summer humidity or the long, cold and wet winters—more evidence that Sakal's compound had been cheaply, and probably quickly, constructed. Kerry had the lock open and the glass removed in minutes. There was no screen, and the office was predictably warm once they got inside.

Neither of them bothered with the desk or metal shelves. They went right to the door and, with Kerry standing behind it, Layla twisted the knob slowly, then barely cracked it open. She stood and listened until she was satisfied that no one was near. Slipping her cell phone from a pants pocket, she widened the opening, stepped into the hall, and immediately began videoing the hallway from left to right. She was deeply tempted to hurry to the opposite end of the hall from the dining room, to grab shots of stairwells or cross hallways, but she'd no sooner had the thought, than a chime sounded from the dining hall and the persistent hum of people talking and eating cut off like a switch being thrown.

Knowing their time was up, she quickly stepped back into the office, closed the door, and signaled with a jerk of her head that it was time to make their exit.

Kerry was already moving. She was at the window and outside

before Layla had the door closed and crossed the room herself. Once she was out, as well, Kerry popped the window back into place, but didn't bother locking it. It would take too much time, and an unlocked window with no signs of intrusion was easily excused and forgotten. It wasn't worth the effort or the delay.

Layla led the way down the rest of the building side, slowing at every window interval for a quick glance, then moving on. When they reached the end of building, they ran directly to the hillside with its covering greenery and began climbing, wanting to put as much distance between them and the building as quickly as possible.

They'd climbed a good seventy or so yards into the increasingly dense foliage before they stopped long enough to send another high frequency squelch to signal the others that they were out and safe. After that, it was simply a matter of time and a lot of scratched skin before they made their way back to the observation post.

When they returned, Brian gave them a relieved once-over. The op was done, everyone was back unharmed, and the enemy was none the wiser—the very definition of a successful infiltration.

"Pictures and vid," Layla said simply, then glanced at the horizon where a brilliant sunset bathed the sky. "Let's hang around until Sakal shows, so we can get photos and a time record. Xavier will want to see what we've got." She handed Brian her phone. "Air drop my files to your phone, then upload to our private server once we get back. I don't want this to be our only record."

"You don't trust the vamp?"

"Depends on what I'm trusting him for. Will he betray us? No. Will he think he knows better and try to leave us out of the action? Abso-fucking-lutely."

And *that* finally brought a grin to his face.

Chapter Thirteen

THE SUN WAS BARELY an hour past setting when they arrived back at the *Fortalesa*. Layla knew the vamps would be awake, but not necessarily up and around yet. They had to shower and shave just like anyone else, and at least some of them would take the time to feed—especially if the food was in bed with them. She pictured Xavier sinking his fangs into some dark beauty sharing his bed, and immediately banished the image from her mind. The women he chose for food were none of her business.

"Even if he fucks them?" She ignored that stupid voice in her head, focusing instead on stripping off her clothes and stepping into a shower hot enough to wipe every thought from her brain. It would have been nice to linger, but she wanted to catch Xavier before he set anything in motion without the intel she and Kerry had secured that afternoon. She turned off the water, did a quick rubdown with a towel, then brushed out and braided her wet hair. Pulling some combat-style pants from her duffle, she realized it was her last clean pair. Damn it. She'd run out of clean clothes. That meant laundry. Ugh. When she reached for her socks, she was weirdly pleased to see several fresh pairs still waiting for her.

That's what her life had come to since being back here—the joy of clean socks.

"Fuck. I need to get away from this place."

"What was that, Cap?"

She snarled at the closed door which provided visual privacy, but let every fart and moan drift into the hallway. "Go away," she yelled and was rewarded by the sound of laughter trailing down the hallway.

Once fully dressed, she grabbed her phone and marched back to the common area of the barracks, where her teammates were chowing down on grilled steak and fried peppers and potatoes. It smelled heavenly, and Layla's stomach growled on cue. But she forced herself to settle for a few grabbed slices of steak and strode for the door.

"No dinner, Cap?"

"Save some for me. I want to brief Xavier before the night gets started."

"No guarantees."

"Assholes," she called over her shoulder. They'd save something. She hoped.

Activity in the vampire wing was in full swing when she approached the first guard point. The vamp either recognized her, or had been told to let her pass, because though his eyes lit with a red glow for a moment or two, he stood aside before she reached him and let her walk by.

Xavier's office door stood open, which seemed innocent enough. But she still hesitated before walking slowly into the room, every sense on alert.

"Whom did you expect?"

The velvety dark voice came from the open door behind her, making her whirl, knife in hand. Xavier stood there alone, head tilted curiously as he gave the knife a pointed glance and lifted his gaze to her face. "What do you think you could do with that?"

"Nothing. You startled me, that's all. It's automatic."

He closed the door behind him and strolled past her to the small bar. "Drink?" he asked, pouring himself some of the wine.

"No, thanks."

He spun as gracefully as a dancer and took a sip from his glass. "I assume you wanted to see me."

She did, but now that she was there, now that he'd reminded her oh-so-subtly of the overwhelming power he possessed, she considered what his reaction might be to her information. Not the information itself, but her method of retrieving it. She gave a mental shrug. She'd known all of that going in, and it hadn't stopped her. Her team was hers to command. Besides, he hadn't explicitly forbidden the mission. Mostly because he'd been asleep and unable to consult on it, but still . . .

Oh, get on with it, Layla. When did you become such a wuss?

He said nothing, just stood there looking gorgeous, while regarding her with slightly amused indulgence. Her back and her resolve stiffened. Smug bastard.

"We acquired some useful intel today," she said, retrieving her phone from a pants pocket. Unlocking it, she pulled up the interior images and held out the phone to him.

His expression once more curious, he set down his drink and took the phone. He didn't say anything as he scrolled through the images, stopping more than once to study a particular image more closely.

"I've worked up a sketch of the layout based on what we saw today, and what we judge from the exterior. It's on my tablet, but I can send it to you, if you give me the number or email where you want it."

He handed her phone back, picked up his drink, took another sip, and set it down again. "That's excellent . . . if I planned to take the compound," he added, eyes no longer amused.

She stared for a moment, trying to understand what he meant. "Of course, we're hitting the compound. That's the only sure location for Sakal."

"Is it?"

She noticed for the first time that he'd gone still, muscles flexing under a tight, long-sleeved T-shirt, and eyes flat with anger.

"You're not going to attack him there," she said slowly. "When was this decided? And don't you think that's something I should have known?"

"You wouldn't have needed to know, if you'd *informed* me of your plans ahead of time," he said in a calm, rational voice that was utterly belied by the growing pewter fire in his eyes.

A matching fire began to burn in her gut as her own anger rose to meet his. "My team is not under your command."

"Aren't they?" he snarled right back. "Aren't they, *and you,* living in *my Fortalesa?*"

"Yes, of course, but—"

"And am I not in sole command of the *entire Fortalesa?* Or were the barracks exempted from my rule, and I've forgotten?"

She ground her teeth at the snide addition. "You know damn well—"

He took two steps closer so quickly that he was standing a breath away before she saw him move. "Then tell me, Layla, why did you conduct this mission without telling me?"

She stared up at him with narrowed eyes and spoke slowly, enunciating every word. "It was an opportunity to gain intel. We took advantage of it. It happens."

"Not in my world," he replied the same way.

"I hate you," she hissed.

An unexpected grin lit his face. "No, you don't."

And before she could stop him, he'd wrapped one powerful arm around her waist, and the other over her shoulder, hand fisted around her braid, as he lowered his head and took her mouth in a hot, demanding kiss.

She wanted to shove him away, to punch that rock-hard gut and curse at him. Instead, she met his mouth with a hungry groan, going up on her toes and opening her lips to deepen the kiss. His arms tightened until there wasn't a millimeter of space between them, while her arms wrapped around his neck, fingers tugging his hair.

His hold firmed as he walked her backwards, all but carrying her until the edge of the conference table hit her thighs. He kept moving, settling her on the table, spreading her legs, and stepping between them—all without releasing her mouth, his kiss destroying any lingering resistance beneath a wave of desire. Layla had never felt as alive as she did in that moment. Every inch of her body, from her skin down to muscle and bone, and oh God, her heart, was so full of need, so full of . . . love, damn it. Tears burned the backs of her eyes, and she was grateful he couldn't see. Had she thought she could walk away from this man? That she hated him? What a fool she'd been. She never should have come back here, but it was too late now. Too late.

She must have whispered that last against his lips, because he pulled back to see her face, his gaze searching her eyes. "Layla?" he murmured, even as he gave her mouth a look so blatantly carnal that she felt a rush of hot desire pulse between her thighs. She moaned, her eyes closing against a staggering tide of need for this man. This vampire.

Her only answer to his unvoiced question was a shake of her head. She couldn't even remember what she'd whispered only a few seconds ago. It didn't matter. All that mattered was him. "Xavier," she breathed, and closed the small distance between them, her tongue sliding between his sexy lips, using his distraction to explore his warm mouth, his tongue as it stroked hers. Strong, claiming.

A wordless snarl said her explorations were over as he gripped the bottom of her shirt and tugged it over her head, tossing it to the side while he fisted a big hand in her hair and slammed his mouth against hers in a growling, vicious kiss of possession. His fingers were already at the front of her bra.

Not a pretty bra. The thought floated through her thoughts and was gone before she could remember why it mattered, when he unhooked the front closure of the tight sports bra and let her breasts spill free. He caught them one at a time, squeezing, pinching, his calloused thumb strumming her nipples with firm strokes that hurt so good. She almost came in that moment, the release of her breasts from their tight confinement, the rasp of his skin against hers, the aching need filling her every pore.

But Xavier pulled back with a guttural oath and ripped her pants open to the sound of tearing fabric, then yanked them down her legs, taking her panties with them, cursing when he realized they wouldn't go over her boots, then splitting them right down the center seam with a roar of furious impatience.

Layla laughed, desperate to have him inside her, crazy with it and him. She spread her legs wider, bending her knees, and grabbing his shirt to pull him down on top of her until their mouths crashed together, blood flowing as his fangs cut into her lips, and he licked it up greedily.

Muscles flexed when he reached between them to rip his own pants open. She had a moment to enjoy the hard length of his arousal against her thigh, and then he was gripping her hips and pulling her onto his erection, slamming deep inside her with a determined thrust.

She cried out when he filled her, shocked by the sharp ache of flesh that hadn't felt any man's cock in a very long time, much less one as big and thick as Xavier's. *Xavier,* her mind whispered. Finally, he was hers. *But for how long?* that same whisper asked.

Before the last word of doubt penetrated her thoughts, he was pulling out and slamming in again, his hips driving with a force so desperate that she had to cross her legs behind his back to keep their bodies together.

He leaned down, bringing their faces close, and the eyes that met hers were now fully engulfed in the pewter gleam of his power. He bent to lick the side of her neck, his tongue rough and hot against the delicate skin below her ear lobe. When he lifted his head, his fangs were on full display, slick and white below his snarling lips. "Say, 'yes,' Layla. Say, 'yes'."

Her stomach clenched at the realization of what he was asking. Blood. Of course. He wanted to take her blood. She should have known. She *did* know. Sex and blood were linked for a vampire. She'd never let one take her, had never even had sex with a vampire. But still, she *knew.* His eyes darkened with emotion at her hesitation. Could he read the fear in her eyes? The doubt?

For one second, she thought his arms stiffened, bracing to lift himself off her, to pull back from the connection they'd finally made. No. No, she wasn't letting him go again.

She looked into those amazing eyes and said, "Yes."

He sank onto her with a hard groan, his cock seeming to pulse inside her, growing impossibly longer, thicker when she felt the hard press of his fangs, the sharp pain as they sliced into her skin, the pressure when he pierced her vein, and then . . . .

She screamed as her entire body seemed to convulse at once, every muscle flexing and stretching, every nerve coming alive while her pussy pulsed in hard contractions, and hot juices ran down her thighs. The orgasm was magnitudes above any she'd experienced before, rippling over and through her as it rolled on and on. She was aware of Xavier's breath hot against her neck, his chest a heavy weight on her breasts, crushing her against the table . . . and then the rushing heat of his climax, while he lifted his head in a rumbling growl of triumph.

She must have passed out then, because when she opened her eyes, she was on his lap, cradled against his chest while he stroked her hair and murmured sweet words, saying she was beautiful, that he loved her . . .

Wait, what? She sat up enough to look at him.

"Are you well, *cariño*? I was rough."

She blinked, feeling . . . foggy. Out of it. She must have dreamed that part about him saying he loved her. Xavier had never said anything like that to her before, not even close.

"Layla?"

She gave a weak smile. "I'm recovering."

His grin was pure male pride.

Good grief. He was over three hundred years old and still proud of his dick. She rested her head on his shoulder. How could she describe sex with Xavier? Amazing? Exponentially better than any lover she'd ever had before? She swallowed a tired sigh. If he heard, she'd have to explain, and maybe soothe his ego. And sad to say, she was simply too tired for another mind-blowing orgasm.

Xavier's deep chuckle made her frown. Where did that come from? Had he read her mind? Could he? She'd never really asked. Eh, most likely it was more of that male ego preening at his ability to wear her out. Hah. Little did he know. Yeah, sure she was exhausted from him and a truly mind-blowing climax. But before that, the op at the compound had been both stressful and demanding. She kissed his neck with a smile. She'd never tell.

She dozed a bit on his lap, coming awake to a bed that was not hers, with a delicious male body crushed against her back, a hard-muscled arm curved around her waist, and a *very* hard cock sliding into her pussy. He lowered his mouth to her neck, and she moaned, his kiss hot and open-mouthed, his tongue scraping over the big vein beneath her ear, as if plumping it for penetration. She pulled his hand from her waist to her breasts, crying out when strong fingers pinched her nipples to the edge of pain when he cupped one full mound and then the other. Reaching back, she stroked her hand over his hip and his ass, urging him even closer, feeling his cock swell when he shoved impossibly deeper inside her. She writhed under the weight of desire crushing the breath from her lungs and struggled to remain conscious, to make the moment last, even while her mind was lost in a flood of sensation that threatened to drown her.

"Xavier." She heard herself whimper his name and wanted to pull back, to retreat from the dangerous edge of an emotion she'd buried long ago . . . locked away behind steel doors and too many years of denial.

"I love you." The words were whispered directly into her ear, impossible to deny, to pretend she hadn't heard, that it had all been a dream.

Tears flowed as relief and terror fought for dominance. She couldn't do this again. Couldn't lose him all over again. She'd never survive. Her teeth dug into her lip as she forced back a sob, and warm blood dribbled over her chin.

Xavier's thunderous snarl vibrated through her body. He gripped her jaw, stroked his tongue over her chin, and locked his lips against hers, sucking every drop of blood as he crushed her mouth under the strength of his demand. His hand drifted over her belly and between her thighs, thick fingers scraping along the skin of her pussy where it stretched tight around the width of his shaft, teasing her swollen clit, circling round and round, until finally he plunged into her hard and deep from behind, and pressed a firm thumb directly onto the engorged nub.

Her cry was high and desperate as the orgasm swept over and through her body, as she drowned in a fresh wave of sensation when his fangs sank into her vein. The heat of his release expanded his cock until she thought the delicate nerves and tissues of her sheath would tear under the overwhelming pressure as he bucked inside her, climaxing over and over while her inner muscles gripped him tight.

His deep groan of pleasure rumbled along her neck, his chest rising and falling against her back as she struggled to breathe. He collapsed on top of her, folding her nearly sideways under his weight, until he slid from inside her and rolled to his back, yanking her up and onto his chest.

When she'd recovered enough to speak again, she asked, "Did you take my clothes off?" She'd intended to raise her head and deliver a glare with the question, but had decided it was too much work. So her breath drifted over his chest as she spoke, and she felt the deep rumble of his voice when he responded.

"What was left of them. Would you rather have slept with them on?"

She caught the laughter in his voice and looked up in time to catch the edge of a smile on his lips. Unfortunately, she also caught the glowing numbers of the digital clock on his bedside and groaned. "I can't sleep here today. I'm supposed to be your daylight commander, for fuck's sake."

"I want you to do something for me. Or have some of your people do it."

"Really?" She raised up on one elbow to stare at him. "You've never asked me for anything before."

"Things change. You made note of Sakal's arrival last night. I want to know if he's on a schedule, and if he shows up there at the same time tonight."

She thought about that request for a moment. Why would he want to know that, unless he needed to know where Sakal was at a certain time? Unable to restrain her curiosity, she asked, "Why?"

"Because I want to know when he arrives."

"Funny," she said, not at all amused by the evasion. "Seriously, why does it matter tonight? Is there something I need to know? Some new development my people should look for?"

"No. I just want to know he's there."

She narrowed her eyes at him. "You're planning something. What is it? If it involves an attack, I need to know about it. My *people* need to know about it, so they don't get stuck unprepared in the middle of something."

He rose up on one elbow to study her. "I'm sending a vampire scout team to reconnoiter his lair in the city. Is that a problem?" he asked with the cool arrogance he wore so well.

"Probably not. I assume they know their jobs, but . . . why send vamps? Why not have my guys check it in daytime? Wouldn't that be safer all around?"

"Yes, if safety was the only issue. But it's not. My vampires can go places that your people cannot, can *sense* things that your people cannot. And in the event of unanticipated attack, they can also handle and *survive* a significantly greater level of violence."

She tilted her head to one side and studied him with open curiosity. "You think he has a troop of vampires living somewhere—in either the city or the compound."

"It's certainly something we would need to know."

Well, that answer that told her nothing, and certainly didn't answer the question either. She considered repeating herself, using more direct language, but decided against it. It would be an exercise in futility. There was obviously something he didn't want her to know and wasn't going to tell her, no matter how many different ways she phrased it.

She sat up and swung her legs off the side of the bed, grateful they were long enough to touch the floor. It was a very high bed, and she didn't relish the idea of having her legs swing in midair like a child's. "Okay," she agreed. "I still need to get up, though. I want to walk the wall and check in on your daylight troops. After that I'll go by the hospital, before we head over to the farm compound."

"I'll stop by the hospital before sunrise." He started to say more, but his phone rang. He picked it up, checked the display. "It's Chuy," he said, naming his lieutenant. He answered, but said only, "I'll call you shortly," and hung up.

"Right." She stood. "I'll leave you to your people, then, and go check in with mine. She was pissed at the way he'd brushed off her questions, but didn't want to make it more than that, so she leaned across the bed to kiss him. He immediately pulled her down for a deeper kiss, which very quickly turned into something more when his hands began doing delicious things to her body, which made *his* body respond in ways that made her want to stay right where she was.

She groaned. "No, no. There's no time. I have to shower and—"

He swung out of the bed with her in his arms, his mouth locked on hers in a deep, seductive kiss that sucked her in until she didn't care about anything else. When they came up for air, his eyes were wild, drowning in the deep pewter glow of his power. "We're showering together," he announced, his voice deeper than usual and his gaze as predatory as a wild animal tracking his prey. She shivered under the weight of that stare and kissed him again, as he carried her to his shower.

Oh well, how long could it take? She needed to shower anyway, so why not add a quick fuck?

Layla thought about those words when she walked back to the barracks, comfortably relaxed and sore at the same time. The last few hours had involved more sex than she'd had in years. She hadn't been celibate, but she'd been cautious, and she never stayed with the same guy for long, preferring to avoid the inevitable complications of a serious relationship—complications that always seemed to expect a greater career sacrifice on her part. She was, after all, a woman in a field of men.

Surely, she'd prefer something more . . . suitable?

"Fuck that," she muttered as she entered the barracks and headed for her small private room. She'd told Xavier she needed to check in on the daylight troops, but they remained tucked warmly in their beds for now, and wouldn't show up for duty until just before sunrise, when the vamps went off to sleep. Which meant *she* could grab a few hours of shut-eye before it was necessary for her to be awake and thinking rationally.

XAVIER WAITED UNTIL Layla had left the bedroom and then his office, until she'd exited into the hallway and closed the office door, and then waited even longer, until he could no longer sense her mental signature in the vampire wing. He'd taken her blood twice during the hours they'd spent together, and though she'd done no more than unintentionally lick a taste of *his* blood, the combination was enough that he could track her at this range.

She would have been unhappy, to say the least, to discover his plans for the rest of the night. And probably beyond angry at what those plans meant for the not too distant future. He could have confided in her. She'd been in the American military for several years, and involved in more than one highly sensitive mission. Add to that the obvious loyalty of the fighters she now commanded, and it equaled a person who could be trusted with confidential details. But it wasn't only his life at stake if the plan went wrong, and so he'd made the decision to keep his plans secret. She could be angry at him later. And he had no doubt that there *would* be a later for them. He'd let her go once, and it had been the right thing to do. If she'd never returned to the *Fortalesa*, his long life would have gone on, very possibly with another woman eventually becoming his mate.

But she *had* returned. And this time, he was going to let fate take its own path.

Stepping into the hallway, he listened carefully to be certain he was alone. It wasn't only Layla he wanted to keep in the dark. Only two other vampires knew of this mission, no one else.

Striding down the dark halls under the vampire wing, he kept his senses attuned to the presence of others. Two hours from now, these same hallways would be busy with his vampires seeking the safety of their unground quarters before sunrise. But now they were nearly deserted, his vamps all out with whatever their night's plans had been, whether work or play.

He made a final turn into a short, dark hallway, with a lone door at its end. The enhanced sight granted by his vampire blood showed him the details clearly, especially since he knew the door, and the room beyond, were there. Most would have dismissed it as nothing more than a supply closet, if they'd found it at all. And even then, they would have been unable to open the door, since the well-concealed biometric lock was keyed only to him and the two others who knew of tonight's mission.

Chuy and Joaquim stood when he slipped inside and closed the door behind him. He waved them down and took a chair for himself, grateful that one of them—probably Chuy—had thought to bring a thermos of warm blood wine. He didn't need the blood after what he'd taken from Layla, but he took the glass anyway, when Chuy poured and handed it to him.

Taking a long sip, Xavier leaned back to face the others. "The raid on the rogue vampire nest? Did it turn up anything useful?"

Joaquim frowned. "Our people discovered six vampires living in what was supposed to be an empty building, not far from the docks. They were all questioned and executed, but had no knowledge of Sakal. They were renegades from Poland. They mistook the relative scarcity of vampires in downtown Barcelona as an indicator of lax oversight on your part."

"You're certain of their story?"

"Yes, my lord. I questioned them myself."

Xavier scowled. "That's disappointing, though not entirely surprising. Sakal is much too weak to control any vampires on his own. His followers will be human, just like those we've already uncovered." He sipped his wine before continuing. "Are we all set for tonight, then?"

"We are," Joaquim confirmed. "Though I'm still not convinced it's wise for you to go alone."

"I'm not going alone. Chuy will be with me."

"And if Chuy"—he glanced at the lieutenant and said, "No offense, my friend," before continuing—"is out of the picture for one of a million reasons that could pull him away during a mission like this, you'll be alone. And we still have no idea of who's really inside the damn sorcerer's lair. He could have an entire army of vampires in there with him."

It was much the same scenario that Layla had posed, but Xavier's response was very different. "I appreciate your concern, but as I said, Sakal simply doesn't have the juice to control an army of vampires. He's not even strong enough to be a *member* of my personal guard, much less to command the equivalent of one."

"And what of his sorcery?"

"It doesn't work on me. You know that. And while I hesitate to remind you of the obvious, I *am* a vampire lord, and a more than ordinarily powerful one. If Sakal has somehow used sorcery to corral an army of vampires under his command, there is no question that I could seize control and turn them against him."

"All true, Sire. But why not take both of us, as insurance."

"Because I need you here to give the appearance that this is an ordinary night in the *Fortalesa*. It's not at all unusual for me not to be seen for hours after sunset, and Chuy is frequently out pursuing some task or other on my behalf. But you, my friend, are on the wall, in the armory, the hospital, and always available if called to the gate. You're visible and would be missed. Plus, I need you to verify Sakal's arrival at and departure from the compound. Another vampire could do that, but he would have questions and might even have to be told about the mission. And every new person adds a new layer of danger."

Joaquim sighed gustily. He was still unhappy, Xavier knew. But he'd resigned himself to the reality. It was critical that this mission be carried out with the utmost secrecy. He trusted his people—vampire and human—most of whom had been living in the *Fortalesa* for years, if not generations. They could still betray him. It *did* happen. Their lives would be forfeit, and the remainder of it brutally painful once he found them. Which he would, since the only way they could escape was to secure the protection of a stronger vampire lord. And there were none stronger than Xavier in Europe. Lachlan was possibly his equal, and Quinn was not only powerful, but had a truly fearful offensive ability. But they seemed to be content on their islands, and anyway, he couldn't see either of them taking on a vampire who'd betrayed his oath to Xavier.

The humans within the *Fortalesa* were another matter. He trusted them, too, but humans could be too easily forced to betray others against their will. Once confronted, he would know if they lied and could dig the truth from their brains. But the damage would be done. If one human knew a secret, it was no longer a secret.

"Any other issues?" he asked his most trusted aides. "The vehicle for tonight is set?"

Chuy nodded. "It's already checked out, parked in a space downstairs."

"Joaquim?"

"I'll cover the farm compound both nights, and call you with the necessary updates."

"Some of Layla's people are likely to be there tonight," Xavier cautioned. "So consider what you'll tell them."

"They'll never know I'm there."

"Good." Xavier stood and pushed back his chair. "Chuy, you'll bring sufficient arms for both of us."

"Yes, Sire."

"I'm going now to check in with Dr. Nowak. The two most seriously injured guards from the last attack are still hospitalized. I can't afford to be weakened before tomorrow night, but I'm more than strong enough now to at least assist in their healing." He thought of Layla's hot, delicious blood, which he'd feasted on twice in the last few hours, and knew he was about as strong as he'd ever be. Even so, he had to conserve that power for the fight he was likely to encounter the next night. Because Joaquim was right about one thing—they had no idea who or what might be stashed away in Sakal's Barcelona lair.

The sun was a red threat in the western sky when Xavier walked out of Dr. Nowak's small hospital and headed toward the ground-floor entrance to the vampire wing. He could remain awake until the sun had completely cleared the eastern horizon over the Mediterranean, but with every minute that ticked off before then, every burning slice of light that became visible, he would grow fractionally weaker. And the same instinct that was seared into the brain of every vampire warned him with a stab of heat at the base of his skull that it was time to seek shelter. For his part, Xavier preferred to be in his own secure quarters within the underground vault long before his strength was in any way diminished.

He was still under the covered walkway outside the hospital when a flash of movement caught his eye a bare second after he became aware that Layla was near. He pulled deeper into the shadows, not wanting to draw her attention. If he did, he'd seduce her into bed with him, which might end up with her waking next to him at sunset. The chances of that were low, since she had her own duties to tend to, but he couldn't risk it. If his plan was to work, he had to slip out of the *Fortalesa* with no one but Chuy and Joaquim even aware he'd left, much less knowing where he'd gone.

That didn't stop him from watching her, however. She strode for the stairs to her parents' apartment, walking with a casual grace that showcased the controlled lean muscle of her body. She swung around and climbed the stairs, ignoring the wrought-iron railing and everything else, except the ever-present smartphone in her hand. He almost winced, waiting for her to trip as she held the device in one hand and tapped away with the other while climbing. But of course, she never did.

The stairs split into two directions, with Layla going left, providing him with a clear view of her perfect ass moving smoothly from side to side as she climbed. He admired the view longer than he should have, then crossed the narrow, U-shaped courtyard to the door he sought. While he entered the complex digital code, he overheard one of Layla's fighters crossing behind him. Thinking he must have come from the vampire wing, he frowned, wondering what the human had been up to. But found his curiosity satisfied a moment later when his vampire hearing picked up the man's phone conversation, which involved female vampire stamina and how come no one had ever told him about it before.

Xavier grinned as the lock clicked and he pushed the door open. He didn't at all mind that Layla's crew included two strong men. Especially when those men knew how to take care of themselves, and were probably armed to the teeth. He didn't have nearly as many female vamps as male in the *Fortalesa*, but there were a few. And most of those were unattached. One of them had no doubt enjoyed the human's fresh blood, in more ways than one. A human had to be very strong indeed if they hoped to be a suitable bed partner for a vampire.

He went down the stairs and into his office with vampire speed, since there were no humans to observe him down here. Striding directly through the office, he entered the bedroom he'd so recently shared with Layla. He generally preferred the vault, but the time spent admiring his luscious lover had cut into his margin. And while he could easily make the vault before he collapsed into his daylight sleep, most of his vampires couldn't. He could key himself into the vault even after it was shut, but some of his people might hear the intrusion, and there was no need for them to fall into their own sleep with that worry on their minds. This sleep chamber was just as secure, if not quite as spacious.

Once in the bedroom, he stripped off his clothes, letting them fall where they would as he went to the bed and pulled back the blankets. Layla's scent rose to envelope him as he slid inside and lay back on the pillow. His cock went rock hard when the scent reminded him of everything they'd done together. Damn it.

His last thought before he dropped into his daylight sleep was how that fucking erection was going to make for a very unpleasant wakening at sunset.

XAVIER BROUGHT together the usual briefing group roughly two hours after sunset that night, which allowed time for Layla's team—and Joaquim, though she didn't know it—to observe Sakal's arrival at the farm compound. He listened to her report on their daytime observations, although she admitted that they'd seen nothing of any note. He was relieved to learn that there'd been no additional infiltration, on her part, of the main building. He had full confidence in her skill, but the risk wasn't worth any possible benefit.

Layla didn't—couldn't—understand fully yet, which was his fault. A good part of his reluctance was rooted in the ages-old vampire distrust of humans. He hadn't even shared completely with her father, who'd been his loyal retainer for decades. He'd never put her parents, or any of the other humans living in the *Fortalesa*, in danger. But there were things they simply didn't need to know.

As for his covert plans against Sakal, he reminded himself that by not telling her of it, he was keeping her out of danger. If the sorcerer had somehow discovered her importance to Xavier, he'd have spared no effort to kill her in the most painful way possible. He'd have done it in front of her own teammates, so they could know what he'd done, before he killed them, too, just because he could. And he'd have recorded the whole fucking mess, so that Xavier would know exactly how much she'd suffered, and know the raw helplessness that Sakal had experienced when Josep had ripped away his magic.

His reasons for keeping her in the dark were valid. But she would never have accepted them. Would never have accepted so much as the *idea* that she would be unable to defend herself against the damn sorcerer, or even that ignorance would keep her any safer. Hell, she wouldn't believe that *he* was any safer for not involving her, no matter his reasons. She was too damn sure of her own abilities and wouldn't accept the possibility that she, too, could be killed.

He, on the other hand, had been haunted by the too-real possibility of her death when she'd been away. The *inevitability* of it happening if she stayed away too long. And now that she was back, now that she'd been in his bed, he was *not* going to lose her to something preventable, when he could make her safer simply by keeping her in the dark about matters that involved only vampires.

"Sakal arrived tonight, within a few minutes of his arrival time last night," she was saying. "We hung around a little while after, just in case it was a *short* visit. But again, like last night, there was no movement in or out of the building for the time we were there. When we left, however, we took the long way around so we could see into the windows of the cafeteria, which they also use as a lecture hall. And we took some photos." She shoved six pictures to the center of the table. "That's two sets of three photos. They're not the best quality, since they were taken at the extreme high end of the long-range scope, and through the windows, too. But you can make out what sure looks like Sakal on the stage, especially since we'd just watched him arrive.

"One more thing," she added, and tossed six more photos onto the table. "We're confident that the three women who accompanied him tonight are *not* the same ones who were with him last night."

"I didn't know you'd photographed him last night," Xavier commented.

She looked at him with raised eyebrows and an expression that said, *"You're not the only one who can keep secrets."*

If it had been more important, he would have been furious. But since he already knew that Sakal was the one behind the attacks on his people, and most certainly the one planning even more and deadlier attacks, he let it go. For now. There would be a time for them to have a discussion about secret-keeping. Preferably when she was naked and in his bed—the one in his vault, so she would be unable to escape.

"You may be right," Joaquim said, sliding the six pictures over for Xavier to see.

Each showed a single woman, with enough detail to establish that there were no duplicates among them, despite similar, but *not* identical, builds and hair color. Which meant there'd been an entirely different *trio* of women last night.

"It's possible there are even more than the six, my lord."

"Possible," Xavier agreed. *"But still all human, correct?"* he added, in a telepathic aside to Joaquim who, unknown to Layla, had been there that night to see the women for himself.

"Yes, my lord. Definitely human tonight."

"They're probably still human," Layla observed, not knowing he'd already confirmed it. "But humans can be highly-trained and deadly, too." She lifted both hands palms up to indicate herself, then added, "Especially if they know they'll be fighting vampires. They'll come prepared."

"You're right." He pretended to ponder this news. "I'm not convinced they're a threat, but let me think on it later. If that's all for now?" he asked, eyeing each of them in turn. "Good. We'll meet again tomorrow night. Layla, if you would remain a moment?"

The two vampires, knowing why he was not offering further

consultation or planning for future operations, said their farewells without comment. Once they were gone and the door closed, Xavier pulled Layla from her seat and kissed her.

She resisted for a second or two, but then surrendered to the undeniable passion between them. *He* felt it, and was sure she did, too. It was like two parts of a whole that were inexorably drawn together to create the "one" where they belonged. She grabbed onto his neck, pulled at his hair, and pressed herself against him until he could feel every curve and swell of her breast, despite the athletic bra she wore under two layers of clothing.

She'd gone up on her toes to reach his mouth, but he tightened his arms and held her there, to prolong the kiss. He wanted nothing more than to carry her into his bedroom and spend the rest of the night there together. But he couldn't risk her getting curious about why he had to leave for a meeting in the wee hours before dawn, and then have her decide to spy on him in one of a thousand ways he could imagine her doing so successfully. And if he could come up with that number of vulnerabilities, with all the knowledge he had of his own abilities and the surrounding territory, he was damn sure she could figure out a sufficient number to make it possible.

But *fuck*, she was succulent.

He released her gradually, letting her slide down, with delicious, almost *painful*, friction, along his body until she stood on her feet once more, gazing up at him with a question in her eyes.

He met those eyes and sighed. "Business, *cariño*. I have a conference call with several of the vampire lords who share this continent with me. And once that is complete, there will be the inevitable individual calls which will certainly follow."

"Wow. You guys talk to each other? I thought vampire lords were all, "Don't set foot in my territory," she quoted in an extra-deep voice.

"We are, but aside from that, we have agreed, after the model of your American vampire lords, to cease aggression against each other's territories, in the interest of preserving peace. Which is better for all of us, especially now that humans are becoming more and more aware of our existence, and are prying into our affairs. We can no longer pass off ourselves as medieval lords fighting for land, or heeding the call of the Church to drive out non-believers."

"Well, hell, it's been a long time since you could do *that*."

"Ah, but you humans are such a violent and bloodthirsty lot.

There's been no shortage of very believable wars for us to camouflage our battles."

"I suppose I have to admit that, given the way I've earned a living for all these years."

He smiled, and though she once more tried not to respond to him, her smile, while grudging, lit her eyes with stars. She loved him. She wasn't willing to tell him yet, but he knew she loved him.

"What will you do with your evening without me?" he asked teasingly.

"Oh, you know, gambling. Sex. Maybe combine the two into a game of strip poker. There are two of each of us in the barracks. That works."

"I know you're joking, but I am not amused."

"How do you know I'm joking?"

"Because I know *you*. You don't fuck more than one man at a time."

"Crudely spoken, but regrettably true. No, I'm going to bed early, maybe read something that has nothing to do with fighting or war or *anything* violent. Not even sports. And then I'm going to go to sleep early and catch up on all the hours I've lost burning the candle at both ends."

Xavier had to think about that saying, but it clicked quickly enough. She was tired from getting up early to command the *Fortalesa* in daylight, and still contribute to the investigation in the evening, not to mention the much later hours she'd kept with him.

He kissed her again, needing to feel her soft and warm and *his*, before walking her upstairs to the outside door, and wishing her a good night's sleep.

IT WAS TWO HOURS after sunset the next night when Joaquim brought him the news he'd been waiting for. Sakal had arrived at the farm compound and had disappeared into the building, just as he had on previous nights. Joaquim had even copied Layla's maneuver and swung around the building before leaving, to sneak a look through the cafeteria windows, although he'd been able to get closer and hadn't required a long-range scope.

"He was there, my lord, just as before. Though I can't imagine what he has to talk about night after night."

"And the scouts in the city? Were they able to confirm his departure before that, from what we believe to be his daylight lair?" Xavier asked.

"Yes, they did, my lord. The building is not as . . . *golden*, as the prisoner described, but its location and description fit. They also agreed that the women are bodyguards, and *exceedingly* well-trained."

Xavier grunted a response. Human bodyguards were hardly a threat, but if his plan worked, they'd be more of a challenge than their master, Sakal.

Chapter Fourteen

LAYLA REMAINED in bed late the next morning, the first time she'd done so in weeks, it seemed. When they'd been on assignment in France as glorified bodyguards, she'd rolled her team out of bed early every morning for no reason other than to keep them on a schedule that would suit future assignments. They rarely had the luxury of more than a day or two to allow their bodies to adjust to any time zone shifts. And since her full team wasn't necessary to do the vineyard job, anyone not actively working had engaged in drills. She wanted them physically and mentally in shape for future assignments.

But this morning, though she was aware of Brian and the others thumping about, laughing and arguing over breakfast, she inserted ear plugs and went back to sleep. Or she tried. Her brain just wouldn't shut up about that fucking vampire. She argued back and forth with herself, reminding her of those cartoons where the main character had an angel on one shoulder and a devil on the other.

The angel, obviously, argued for her to stay the hell away from the esteemed Lord Xavier, even if it meant leaving the *Fortalesa* and bunking in town. Or worst case scenario, placing her team under Brian's command and getting the hell out of Spain altogether. He was just as capable as she was. Not quite as compulsive about knowing every damn thing, and more willing to trust other team members' judgment when it came to performing their assigned roles, but nonetheless quite brilliant and utterly committed to the safety of every member of their team. The devil, on the other hand, told her to stop being such a frightened little pussy and go after what she wanted.

Unfortunately, she didn't know what she wanted. No, she thought, shaking her head. That wasn't quite true. She wanted Xavier. She'd always wanted him, though she could admit now that he'd done the right thing rejecting her all those years ago. She'd been a child, and he'd been . . . well, he'd been a vampire lord. He might have looked like a twenty-something sex god, but he'd been an old man. So what had changed? Why did he now find her to be an acceptable lover?

She punched her pillow, trying to get comfortable enough to drift back to sleep, so she could stop thinking about this shit. Especially questions she already knew the answers to. Vampires didn't take human lovers their own age. For fuck's sake, there *were* none. Vamps were overwhelmingly male, so even if they'd wanted one of their own as a lover, they were mostly out of luck. They also happened to prefer human lovers, so they got a twofer—sex and food in one tidy package.

And she was letting her thoughts wander down meaningless paths to avoid dealing with the big question. Xavier wanted her. It was early in their relationship 2.0 to expect a commitment, though he'd definitely *said* he loved her. She didn't know if that had come out in the heat of the moment, or excitement because she was something brand new, or if he truly meant it. The problem—and she was honest enough to admit it—was that she wanted *him*. That had never changed. He was the reason she'd never managed to have a serious relationship with anyone. She hadn't been a nun, for Christ's sake, but the minute the guy started getting that soft expression on his face when he looked at her, she'd come up with a perfectly logical excuse for why they'd never make it. For why he wasn't "the one."

All those excuses had been pure bullshit, she admitted now. None of those men had qualified because the position had already been filled. Xavier had always been the *one* and he always would be. So why wasn't she grabbing onto him with both hands? Because he'd broken her heart, and the fact that he'd done the right thing didn't matter to her heart. She was afraid he'd break it again. And she didn't know if she could survive a second time.

Disgusted with herself, she let loose a low howl of frustration and jolted out of bed. What was the point of lying there if it served only to drive her crazy? She might as well join her team and recruit them to help her teach the daylight guards some new tricks. And keep them ready in case Sakal decided it was time for another surprise attack.

THE SUN WAS ALMOST two hours past setting by the time the necessary vampires had all reported for night duty, and Joachim had relieved her for the night. He didn't always. Sometimes it was one of the vampire commanders instead. But tonight, he made a point of not only being there personally, but taking the time to chat with her a little.

Contrarily, however, she didn't find that to be reassuring or friendly. She found it odd. Was it because they'd been in a few briefings together? Or was he there in order to assure her that the situation was under control, and she could relax for the rest of the night, with no concerns whatsoever. Telling herself she was being too suspicious, she returned to the barracks with her team, who'd waited with her until Joachim showed up.

When she checked her phone after showering, there was a message from Xavier. She couldn't remember him leaving her any previous messages, but since he had tonight, she listened.

"Layla, *cariño*. I'm still being hounded by my fellow vampire lords who are being nosier, and more neurotic, than usual. If it's not too late by the time I'm free of it, I'll call. If it is already too late, I will miss you, and dream of you, and definitely see you tomorrow night. Love you."

She played the message a second time, asking herself if she was being utterly paranoid to think he'd been shoveling some serious bullshit with that message. She thought about having a conversation with the unexpectedly chatty Joachim, but dismissed that idea immediately. He wouldn't tell her anything Xavier didn't want her to know. But between Joachim's unusual concern for her sleep habits, and Xavier's message, her suspicion that *something* was up had sure as hell been confirmed. Unfortunately, she couldn't storm into Xavier's office or, better yet, his bedroom and demand to know what was up. She didn't have the code, and as with Joachim, the guards wouldn't let her in if Xavier had told them not to.

"Son of a bitch," she swore and threw down the phone, which fortunately landed on the bed so it would be available when *someone* finally called to clue her in. She just hoped that whenever they got around to it, she wasn't being called because her team was about to be dragged knee-deep into a clusterfuck.

XAVIER PULLED ON soft leather pants that stretched easily around the hard muscles of his thighs, a padded leather vest that would do nothing to stop a modern bullet, but might slow down a knife thrust, and leather boots. The clothes were comfortable and wouldn't interfere with movement, which was why he wore them. He didn't worry about bullets or knife thrusts. When battle-driven adrenaline flooded his system, he'd barely feel those or any other wounds. Unless the knife was big and the strike true enough to hit his heart, or the bullet equally true and designed to shred flesh, he wouldn't much feel the injury until long after the battle ended. Even supposing his enemy had such weapons and ability, the damage would have to be massive to take him out of the fight.

He was a vampire lord—a title that indicated far more than a simple affinity for making tough decisions and persuading others to follow him. His power and strength combined to make him one of the toughest creatures on earth, *nearly* impossible to kill. Another vampire lord, especially one whose power equaled his own, might score a lucky hit and take him out. One whose power was greater than his might, theoretically, succeed in killing him. But the only vampire he knew who was likely to have power greater than his own was Raphael, and he'd left Europe to its own devices. At least for now.

What made Sakal dangerous was his sorcery, which had been returned to him in full the last Xavier had been aware, and now appeared to have grown.

Fortunately, whether it was fate or happy coincidence, Xavier was all but immune to magic. He didn't like to speak in absolutes, since fate was a fickle bitch, but he'd never encountered a magic user who could make sorcery work against him. He'd wondered at that particular talent of his. Every vampire lord possessed some unique power that was his, or hers, alone. A thousand years ago such an immunity would have been very useful, but in this modern age, when magic was thin on the ground, and sorcerers few and far between, it had seemed less so. But perhaps fate had known what she was doing after all, because Xavier was now prepared to face Sakal.

After tying his boots, he proceeded to arm himself with weapons new and old. An unassuming sword—short enough to be maneuverable in tight quarters, but long enough to keep his enemy from getting too close—was belted round his waist. It was simple in design, with a plain hilt, but the combination of modern steel and ancient techniques of folding and tempering had produced a blade that couldn't be found anywhere in the world, not even in the best weapons' markets. And while there were a few similar blades circulating among the vast population of earth, only this one had been tested in battle and proven to his exacting standards. After tying the scabbard to his thigh, he secured three knives of various sizes about his person, picked up the very modern, and very deadly MP5 submachine gun lying on the table next to him, and he was done.

He wasn't in his quarters in the basement vault or even his private office on the first floor of the vampire wing. Instead, he was in the small room near the loading dock where he'd met with Chuy and Joaquim. Chuy, who was at this moment beyond the *Fortalesa's* walls, had left this gear for him, depositing a piece at a time over the days since they'd settled on this strategy, in order to avoid notice. Absolute secrecy were the watchwords of the night. No one but Chuy and Joaquim knew of tonight's plan.

He experienced a small twinge of guilt, knowing Layla would be furious when she discovered his deception. He'd have told her, but he'd observed enough of her interactions with her team to know she trusted them absolutely. And while she *probably* would have honored a vow of silence when it came to the others, he knew without a doubt that she'd have shared with Brian Hudson. The relationship between those two was far more than simple professional respect, more even than friendship. No longer, perhaps, but he suspected that once upon a time, they'd been more than friends to each other, no matter how much she denied it.

And why the hell was he wasting time and energy worrying about such things at this critical moment? He needed to be ready, and that meant more than just strapping on weapons. He needed to get his fucking head in the right place for battle, and adopt the mindset to *kill* anyone who tried to stop him.

A quiet mental hail had him spinning for the door a moment before it opened to reveal Chuy, dressed and armed much as he was, his eyes already lit with a red-tinged lust for the coming fight.

"Sire," his lieutenant murmured.

"Everything ready?"

"Yes, my lord. The dock is quiet. The final deliveries completed thirty minutes ago. The vehicle you requested is waiting a mile outside the wall." He winced. "Though I do wish you would reconsider taking one with at least *some* defensive armament."

Xavier grinned. "We're trying to be subtle and commonplace. One of those black behemoths would all but announce our presence."

"Yes, my lord," Chuy agreed unhappily. "Even so . . . "

Xavier clapped his lieutenant's shoulder. "Do you have so little faith in me? I will defend us."

"I would never doubt you, Sire."

"I know. A little teasing, old friend. Nothing more. Shall we go?"

Chuy nodded once, then turned and, taking the lead, walked out into the hallway and discreetly scanned both directions before Xavier joined him.

They moved quickly and with purpose after that. There was no skulking about, no attempt to conceal their presence. They didn't anticipate running into anyone—vampire or human—but if they did, they wouldn't offer an excuse for their presence. Xavier was the Lord of Spain, and the *Fortalesa* was his. No one had the right to question where he went or why.

Nonetheless, he sensed Chuy's relief once they were beyond the walls and traveling through the trees to the narrow fire road where a small, ordinary four-door sedan of indeterminate age was parked. It was exactly what Xavier wanted for tonight's mission—dusty from the dirt road, with a back bumper that was dented as if it had suffered a rear-end collision recently. The only modifications to the unassuming vehicle were the windows, which were dark enough to conceal the occupants. Xavier was well-known, by appearance at least, in this area. And he didn't want to risk discovery if a driver happened to glance over and see him sitting in traffic.

The drive to Barcelona was uneventful, with little traffic until they drew closer to the city proper. Even then, it was late enough that most clubs and bars were closed, but not yet time for the earliest commuters to begin flooding the streets. Chuy did a drive-by of Sakal's lair and was circling around the block for another look when Xavier's phone rang.

"Joaquim," he answered.

"Sire, the sorcerer has departed the compound, accompanied by the three human females who guard him."

"Excellent. Return to the *Fortalesa*. You know what to do."

"Yes, my lord."

Xavier expected his security chief to hang up after that. There was nothing further that needed to be said, and Xavier was in the field and didn't want his attention diverted from the target. But he could almost *hear* Joaquim's reluctance in the silence as he waited. "What is it?" he asked finally.

"Only . . . take care, my lord."

Xavier was paranoid enough, or smart enough since the two were identical when living in vampire society, that he mentally stopped to consider Joaquim's response. Did the caution mean Joaquim was aware of a flaw in their plan? Was there some enemy movement against them that would make it unworkable? An unforeseen threat to the *Fortalesa* itself? He shook his head. No. Joaquim's loyalty was unquestioned, but the security chief had expressed doubts about this mission from the start. His concern had to do with that, nothing else.

"We shall," Xavier assured him. "And we will both be up on comms, if you need us."

"Yes, my lord. I will stand watch until your return."

"Problem?" Chuy asked, turning to meet Xavier's gaze when they stopped at a red light.

"No. Sakal is on his way with the usual three bodyguards. There may be more when we enter his lair."

"Humans," his lieutenant said dismissively.

"Yes, but well-trained and probably prepared to deal with vampire assailants, as Layla noted."

"Understood." Chuy drove into the building across the street from Sakal's lair, taking the ramp to the parking structure on top of the modest building. He followed the narrow up-ramp all the way to the last covered level, and slid into a spot overlooking Sakal's front entrance.

Xavier stared at the temple-like edifice of the building and wondered idly if the overwrought design had been a factor in its selection. The sorcerer had always had an inflated view of himself, which was why it had irked him so when he'd been reborn as a weakling vampire. Well, that and the loss of his power, of course. Even so, Sakal had never come out and said it, but Xavier was convinced the bastard had expected to wake up not only with his sorcery intact, but with the power of a *vampire lord*. That would have made him a super lord of sorts, first among them all, able to command not only other vampires, but other vampire lords.

Fortunately, that hadn't happened, and Sakal had been forced to reconcile to his new reality. Which thanks to Josep's unending ambition, had turned out well for Sakal, but not for Josep.

"Looks like a fucking temple." Chuy's mutter echoed Xavier's own thoughts so closely that he chuckled.

Shifting uncomfortably in the small car, Xavier did a quick but thorough scan of the area, and finding no other minds nearby, said, "Let's go, before this fucking car steals every bit of feeling from my legs."

"Yes, my lord."

And Xavier would have sworn there was an, "I told you so," hiding under the respect.

They opened their car doors at the same instant, and by the time Xavier got around the vehicle, Chuy was already sliding back the door of a white panel van that was the only other vehicle on this level, given the early hour. The open door of the van, which was parked on an inside row, away from the half-wall of the street view, revealed an interior that was not just comfortable, but a secure daytime resting place should they need it. This mission had too many variables that Xavier couldn't control and couldn't anticipate. For starters, they'd never been inside the damn building and didn't know who else might be hiding in there. Xavier's earlier scan had detected no vampires, but there had been humans. The number had been difficult to pin down, which meant they were underground and shielded from detection—most likely in a below-ground vault, like Xavier's own. Regardless of what story Sakal told his bodyguards to explain his vampire habits, he would have needed a secure daylight resting place.

Xavier hadn't liked this plan when he'd come up with it, any more than Joaquim had, but there'd been no other option. At least not one that didn't involve using his vampires to slaughter a bunch of lost teenagers whose only crime was having been conned by a homicidal sorcerer posing as truth-seeking philosopher. Chuy, on the other hand, had liked the idea of taking Sakal's lair by surprise, but he'd favored taking a squad of vampires himself, and killing Sakal when he arrived, also by himself. Since the only vote that mattered was Xavier's, and since he wasn't about risk vampire lives unnecessarily any more than he was human teenagers', his opinion had ruled.

Besides, *he* had to be the one who killed Sakal. He had to be certain that the sorcerer was *dead* this time.

"Let's go."

They didn't run, didn't make any attempt to conceal their approach to the building. They knew Sakal wasn't there, but Xavier kept his power up and scanning as they climbed the broad, cement stairs. "I'll enter first."

Chuy didn't object. Most vampire lords always led the way. Their power was so much greater that when confronting a dangerous enemy, it only made sense. Especially since Xavier happened to be the only one resistant to magical attack.

He grabbed the stylized handle of the metal door and tugged. Nothing. For all his strength, the damn door didn't move. He scanned the entrance from side to side, then stepped out to the sidewalk and scanned the building itself. "No windows," he commented as he walked back to the door. "Guess we'll have to do this the noisy way."

Bracing one hand on the frame, he pulled the handle once more, but this time sent a wave of power rolling up and down the connection between door and frame, measuring resistance, looking for weak spots, for vulnerability. His grin when he found it was more of a grimace as every muscle in his arms and chest strained, every tendon corded. The first squeal of metal tearing sped into the dark of early morning, breaking windows somewhere down the street. Xavier swallowed the roar of triumph that wanted to follow. No need to attract more attention, although the shredding metal was making enough noise that any humans inside would have to be deaf not to hear. But he wasn't worried about a few humans, no matter how well trained.

Recognizing signs of imminent give in the door, he tempered his hold so that when it finally surrendered to his strength, he wasn't knocked into the street like a hapless dummy.

"See what you can do with that, Chuy," he ordered as he strode into the building, every sense on alert. His lieutenant wouldn't be able to fix the door, but he could repair it sufficiently that it would function, and at first glance, would appear undamaged, especially in dark of early morning. It would open when pulled, and Sakal was far too weak to detect Xavier's presence, especially since once they were inside and the ambush set, he would shield himself completely.

The minute the door opened, Xavier was bombarded by the reek of sorcery. If he'd had any doubts that this was the sorcerer's lair, they vanished in that instant. Sakal had been living and practicing his magic here much longer than Xavier had guessed. It irritated him that he hadn't sniffed out even the softest whisper of the sorcerer's presence before the attacks. He'd been too confident that the city was *his*, too focused on problems and building alliances farther from home.

The air inside was frigid, as if the air-conditioning was set to run continually. Freezing air gusted down the short entrance way, caught by bare walls and a marble floor that was so cold, he could feel it through his boots. What the hell did Sakal have in here that he needed the temperature barely above freezing? Or maybe the question was who. He scowled, reminding himself that zombies weren't real, and vampires weren't *dead*, for fuck's sake. Maybe the asshole just liked it cold.

The freezing effect eased when he reached the end of the semi-enclosed entrance, roughly eight feet from the now-repaired door. He turned when Chuy came up next to him. "*I'm stepping out first. Give me five minutes,*" he telepathed. "*Then follow, if you can. No heroics, Chuy.*"

His lieutenant snorted his reply to that, and Xavier knew the vamp would go down fighting no matter what he said. As one of his children, Chuy was hardwired to defend his Sire with no regard for his own life. Although that cowardly fucker Dênis had proven, all those years ago, that the wiring could be overcome.

Xavier's expression split in a fang-bearing grin, not only ready for battle, but looking forward to it. Because Chuy wasn't the only one with hardwiring. Xavier was a fucking vampire lord. Violence was a beast that ran with the blood in his veins, and he was ready to set it free.

He stepped beyond the walls of the entrance and found . . . nothing. Not on this floor. No one breathed, no hearts beat, no scent gave away their presence. He straightened from the ready position he'd assumed, expecting *some* level of opposition to be waiting for him. "What the fuck?"

They were standing in a huge, wide-open space that wouldn't have been out in place in a cathedral or a palace. Or a bank, for that matter, which probably was what it had once been. The ceiling soared into a glass-topped dome that appeared as if it would admit light during the bright of day. It wasn't exactly the preferred arrangement for a vampire, no matter that he could hide downstairs when the sun was shining. The room itself echoed the domed shape. An open mezzanine made up most of the room, the circle split by the foyer in which he stood. A bank of two elevators was behind him to his left, and a narrow set of stairs on his right climbed to the mezzanine. Four elaborately carved columns, at least six feet around each, supported the mezzanine. Their design was repeated in much narrower posts which supported the half-height bannister providing safety for anyone walking around up there.

Not that anyone was. It was as empty as what he could see of the first floor. Which was most of it, judging by the layout.

"Why leave it deserted like this?" Chuy whispered, as if there was anyone to hear. Or maybe it was just the cathedral-like atmosphere.

"They're hiding somewhere. Check the upstairs," he said, indicating the mezzanine with a lift of his chin.

Chuy nodded, took a running start, and leaped upward, swinging over the bannister with graceful ease.

Xavier smiled and scanned the ground floor, walking over to where a simple wooden desk sat, with three chairs. Two in front, one behind. The incongruity of the inexpensive desk and chairs sitting in the midst of such conspicuous elegance stood out to him. It also surprised him, because Sakal had always been fastidious about not only his personal appearance, but the presentation of anything related to him. If he had a desk, it had to be an antique. If there were fabrics, they were the world's most sought-after, the most expensive silks and brocades available. The *room* suited him, with its soaring architecture and overworked columns, the gold and crystal chandelier. Even the marble was beautiful, a delicately inlaid circular pattern, that glittered with gold and other minerals.

But the desk apparently served a purpose. A quick search revealed basic tri-fold pamphlets, filled with pictures of the farm, along with happy faces enjoying communal meals and working in the fields and gardens. And then there were the prophet's own words—sayings so patently self-conscious that Xavier could practically hear Sakal's prim voice as he stood before his acolytes. What an ass.

So the lair doubled as a recruiting center. Empty for the night, but Sakal must have someone manning the desk during the day. He turned to study the elevators, and pressed the button to call one. The overhead display showed both cars locked in the basement, which had to be where the sleeping quarters were located, since his scouts had verified Sakal's pre-dawn arrival the previous day.

Chuy's soft footsteps announced his return via the stairs. "All empty up there, too, Sire. A lot of offices, but it doesn't appear any of them are used."

"There's a basement," Xavier told him. "Elevator's locked. We can't get there, unless there's another set of stairs going down."

"Not worth the effort," Chuy observed. "No one we care about should be down there yet."

"No, I sense humans. No one else." He shrugged. "This is essentially what we hoped to find. The only question is where to set up while waiting for Sakal to come home."

Xavier dropped his MP5 on the desk, irritated at having it around his neck when he wasn't using it. He'd have plenty of warning to reclaim it before Sakal entered the building, and even then, he doubted he'd need it. Chuy followed suit and the two of them walked back out into the big room. Chuy gave the glass dome an unhappy glance, but Xavier was focused on the mezzanine. It was a good hiding place, but what if Sakal went straight for the elevator car? He could very well be inside, with the doors closed before Xavier reached him. Or *maybe not*. Xavier was a hell of a lot faster than Sakal, but the logistics could be better. He spun on his heel, eyeing what looked like a bar set-up on the far side of the main space, and tucked under the mezzanine on that side. He'd just reached it when his senses blared to life warning him that humans and *something else* were on the move from below.

He ran for the elevators, with Chuy behind him, moving so fast that Xavier barely managed to grab his lieutenant's arm, stopping his headlong rush into the energy barrier that had suddenly appeared to surround the entire domed space, trapping them inside.

"Fuck." Xavier's curse was low and vicious. He couldn't explain how it had been done, but suddenly, that damn sorcerer strolled out of the elevator, surrounded by six female bodyguards, every one of whom was blond, beautiful, and firm with muscle.

He watched expressionless as Sakal approached the very edge of the marble circle, his gaze dancing with satisfaction, and his smile so smug that Xavier wondered if it hurt. He felt no fear. But then he'd never been afraid of Sakal. Magic was the sorcerer's only weapon, and it didn't *work* on him. The thought clicked over in his brain and he reached out with his power to barely brush against the enclosing wall of energy, testing its strength, its limits and vulnerabilities. He paid particular attention to the air *above* him and Chuy, wondering if the sorcerer had thought to make his spell all encompassing, or if he'd taken a shortcut and—Nope. The energy field curved over his head, surrounding him on all sides, and as far as he could determine, disappeared into the floor. He doubted the floor itself was included in the spell, suspected it was impossible. But tunneling through marble wasn't his first choice of escape.

Fucking Sakal must have been working on this spell for *months* before he ever arrived in Barcelona, and then it would have taken him weeks more to cast it.

Xavier didn't care about Sakal's pain and effort, other than as points of information to advise his own attack. He was already working on his first choice, which involved probing the field's magical energy with that part of his own power that deflected magic. What he'd discovered so far was that in addition to being obnoxiously all-encompassing, the spell had several layers, each of which seemed to be a separate casting. Without appearing to be doing anything, he began actively working to break through the barrier. Every layer demanded a fresh effort, which only mattered because of the delay. His plan had been to ambush and kill Sakal when he returned to his lair for the sunrise.

But right now, it was him and Chuy who'd been ambushed, stuck underneath a fucking glass dome inside a sorcerer's complex spell, with the sun only minutes away from rising.

Sensing movement, he shifted the focus out of his own head and onto Sakal, even as another of the spelled layers fell beneath his power, and he began working on the next. The sorcerer strolled closer, as if he had nothing to fear, despite Xavier's vastly greater power. His expression was one of such confidence and satisfaction that Xavier knew the bastard didn't realize his carefully crafted spell wouldn't hold much longer. Xavier wasn't the kind to taunt his enemies with details that could warn them, so he simply watched and waited, knowing Sakal wouldn't be able to stand the silence. He'd break first, driven by a compulsion to boast about his own cleverness and a deep-seated need to be the smartest one in the room.

"Lord Xavier," Sakal crooned. "What a surprise." The asshole was dressed in fighting leathers, which, had the situation been less dire, would have been laughable. He'd never been a warrior, had never learned even the most basic sword skills, claiming it was unnecessary since his magic would defend him.

Xavier simply stared, most of his attention still focused on breaking the spell.

"Nothing to say?" The sorcerer was pacing back and forth, moving leisurely, as if he had all the time in the world, despite the rising sun which was a growing fire in the back of Xavier's skull. Sakal stopped his pacing abruptly, and directed an angry glare at Xavier, probably frustrated that his vision of this moment wasn't working out as he'd hoped. Had he expected Xavier to beg?

The thought had a slow smile lifting Xavier's lips. Fury filled Sakal's expression, his eyes gleaming with the dull red light of a weak vampire.

Seeing that, Xavier's smile broadened into a grin, but he still said nothing.

One of Sakal's women stepped up with a whispered warning that had the sorcerer glancing at the growing light above the glass dome. With obvious effort, he relaxed his expression once again, and pasted an insincere smile on his face. "Did you ever meet my brother?" he asked casually, eyes narrowing when Xavier remained silent. "No?" he continued. "I had two of them, and frankly three boys were too much for my fragile mother to handle. Too many to love. So she picked a favorite. You'd think that would have been me. I was the youngest, my magic was evident at a very early age, and my brothers were both common laborers. Physically strong, I suppose, but it was *my* magic that had the potential to bring riches to the family and change our lives forever.

"And yet, it was my eldest brother she favored. The dullest of us all. But he was her firstborn, so perhaps that's all it was. She loved the first child, and didn't have any affection left for the rest of us."

Xavier had to fight against the urge to roll his eyes at this glimpse into Sakal's psyche. Was he actually trapped in this damn circle because the crazy bastard had mommy issues? "This seems like a private issue you need to work out for yourself, Sakal," he said finally. "I don't need to be here for this."

Sakal spun on his heel and glared his hatred.

"*If looks could kill,*" Xavier thought smugly, pleased that he'd gotten a rise out of the weasel. But he didn't say anything more.

"So clever, aren't you?" the sorcerer snapped, then visibly pulled himself together. "Unfortunately, you *do* need to be here for this," he said smoothly enough. "Because this is about revenge."

That surprised Xavier enough that he paused his digging at the spell, but only for a moment. "Revenge? For what?" He and Sakal had never gotten along, but they'd had very little to do with each other. He'd already left Josep's court by the time he'd returned to fetch Sakal for him, and his power had been so much greater than the sorcerer's that they'd had little in common after that.

"For what?" Sakal hissed, no longer making any effort to disguise his emotions. His lips were drawn back over his fangs, his eyes still gleaming red. "For destroying my life, *Ya Ibn el Sharmouta!*"

Xavier fought a smile at the Arabic curse, which reminded him that Sakal had been raised in what was now considered the Middle East. That might have accounted for his mother's preference for her first-born son, and in turn, for Xavier's current predicament. What a fucked-up world. But with the sun rising, he had no time to banter insults. And neither did Chuy. Feigning surprise, he said, "I wasn't the one who made you Vampire. That was our Sire, Josep."

"The great Josep Alexandre." Sakal all but spit the name. "He shredded my life for nothing."

Xavier raised his eyebrows in surprise. "You consented to the change. I was there. I heard you."

"For *nothing*," he repeated furiously. "A life of wealth and power, never growing old, never having to face the great unknown of death. Meaningless promises, when the price was my magic, and the vampire power I acquired worth less than nothing."

Xavier shrugged. Josep had made no guarantees. They'd discussed the possibility that Sakal would lose his magic. Some Sires wouldn't have bothered to warn him, but Josep had.

"All right," Xavier said agreeably. "You were angry, furious even, at Josep. But you killed him, didn't you? Not yourself, of course. You wouldn't risk your *own* life, but your assassin did his job well enough. So what's that got to do with me?"

"Because when I didn't come through the transition as a powerful vampire, when even my magical birthright was diminished, Josep discarded me like week-old meat. Rotted and useless."

"Not useless," Xavier corrected, as another spell layer surrendered with a lash of power that had him tensing for fear that Sakal would detect the change. "Though certainly not what he had hoped for when he chose you. He kept you at his court and even paid another sorcerer to restore your magic. Eventually."

"Yes. *Eventually*. And in the meantime, I was nothing. You *left* him, and *still* he favored you. He talked about you constantly. His greatest success, the golden one."

"I wasn't there. Hell, I wasn't even in the country sometimes. So why are you here? And why waste so much time and energy to acquire a pack of brain-dead acolytes who couldn't carry a conversation if you gave them a cart to hold it."

Sakal surprised him by laughing. "You're right about that much. Though they have been useful." He dismissed his absent followers with a wave of his hand. "They'll run back to the street when I'm gone from here. Or maybe they'll continue to play farmer for a time. I don't care which."

Xavier's attention sharpened, though he maintained an air of disinterest. "You're leaving?"

The sorcerer snorted in dismissal. "You think my revenge ends with *you*? You're an irritant, a fly in the ointment of history, one who's already demanded far more attention than he deserves." He drew close enough to stare into Xavier's eyes from only inches away. "But you *are* the one who delivered me to Josep. I only wish he was still alive to witness the agony of your death. Would he suffer along with you? Would he feel your pain? Did he love you *that* much?"

Before Xavier could answer, a soft chime announced the arrival of a second elevator, carrying another dozen female bodyguards. At first glance, they looked exactly like the others—blond, beautiful, and strong. No wonder his people had initially thought there were only three. Unless one paid very close attention, those he'd seen thus far were so identical as to be indistinguishable.

The new arrivals marched up to Sakal and bowed with admirable precision, before one of them—presumably their leader—murmured, "It is time, my lord." Her voice was low enough that she probably didn't intend Xavier to overhear, though of course he did.

"Yes. One of you seal the front door shut," Sakal ordered, then swung his gaze back to Xavier. "He'll sleep soon," he told the woman. "And when he does, kill him. But not until after the sun has him screaming in agony. The spell circle that keeps him in won't keep you out."

The woman's cold eyes scraped over Xavier. "A pleasure, my lord. Thank you."

Sakal grunted an acknowledgement, then spun around, heading quickly for the elevator. Xavier's voice stopped him.

"How did you do it?" Xavier waited until Sakal was facing him again. "How did you manage to be in two places at once? Not even *you* can do that."

Sakal's sudden grin was almost playful, a child whose trick had fooled everyone. "The eldest brother I mentioned, the one my mother favored? We look a great deal alike. When I knew what Josep had done to me, the centuries it would take for my sorcery to recover, I began plotting my revenge. So I turned my brother—"

"You don't have the power to turn anyone."

The hatred on Sakal's face was vicious. "You're right," he snarled. "Josep didn't even give me that. But I had riches, and the intellect to acquire more. I paid a master vampire whose personal wealth was dwindling. He turned my mother's beloved son for a pittance, really."

"Your brother consented, of course."

Sakal laughed. "He gave the same consent to being made a vampire, as I did to being the youngest unwanted child. Luckily, he's as weak a vampire as I am, but unfortunately for *him*, he still has *no* magic. So sad. I make good use of him, give his life meaning. He deals with matters that don't require my full attention, such as those pesky nightly visits to my devoted followers. He *enjoys* them, can you believe that? Hell, maybe he'll remain on the farm, too."

He walked forward until they were once more separated by only a few inches, and spoke softly. "He was also *very* useful in convincing old enemies that I was someplace I wasn't." He laughed, a harsh bark of amusement. "Farewell, *Lord* Xavier."

Then he crossed to the open elevator, surrounded by bodyguards as he stood inside, his gaze never leaving Xavier until the doors closed, blocking his view.

Xavier turned his back on the guards left behind and began to pace the circle, aware of the looming sunrise and what it would mean not only to him, but even more, to Chuy. He'd have to move fast once he broke the final layer of spell, which was one of only two remaining. He'd worried that Sakal would sense its vulnerability, but he'd been too sure of himself, too busy gloating.

Xavier needed a clear plan of action, and soon. His first order of business would be getting Chuy to a safe place. The damn glass roof would soon have sunlight beaming down into the circular room. There was shade under the mezzanine, especially behind the bar he'd been examining earlier, which was on the eastern side of the room, and would remain shaded the longest.

Before that, however, he'd have to deal with the guards, who seemed as devoted to Sakal as the young people gathered at the compound were. It irritated the hell out of him to admit it, but he needed help. *Human* help. He pulled out his cell to call Layla, surprised that Sakal hadn't taken it from him. Though on second thought, the coward would have been too frightened to confront Xavier himself, and if he'd sent any of the women in, their survival would have been measured in seconds, not minutes. He brought up the screen and discovered he had no signal. "Fuck. Energy from the damn magic barrier is screwing up cell reception," he added when Chuy gave him a curious look.

So he couldn't call Layla, but he didn't need a phone to reach Joaquim.

LAYLA AND HER team were already up on the wall with the rest of the daylight crew, and she was mentally plotting her strategy for wringing the truth out of Xavier who'd been mysteriously absent last night. No one had seen or spoken to him. Not even Dr. Nowak. And when she'd *casually* asked Joaquim how the various calls with the European lords had gone, he'd looked totally blank for less than a second, a mere instant. But she'd caught it, and she'd known.

She glanced at the call display and frowned. "Yes? Joaquim?"

"You have to get downtown. Sakal's lair. Xavier—"

"What? Slow down. Why am I going to Sakal's lair? He's a vampire, he'll be—"

"Xavier is there," Joaquim said and drew a deep breath, as if forcing himself to step back from the edge of panic. "He and Chuy went in early this morning, before sunrise, planning to ambush Sakal when he returned. But . . . Sakal was there, and—"

"Didn't Xavier check the farm before he left?" She wanted answers, but she wasn't waiting for them. Already running, she found Brian and gave him the hand signal for, "The shit's hit the fan. Time to go."

"Yes. I don't know how it happened, but there's too little time. You need to get to Barcelona—"

"We're leaving. Now!" Layla hit the stairs, jumping down four at a time, holding onto the wall with one hand, the way she had as a child. She caught up with her team in the barracks. "Full gear, including comms. And we'll need tents. Xavier—"

"—they're trapped," Joaquim was saying. "A spell keeping them in sunlight. Xavier can break the spell, but there are guards."

"Address, damn it. I need an address!"

He gave it to her, his words already slurring. Fool should have *started* with that.

"Got it. Hanging up now." She grabbed her gear and followed her team out to the SUV, talking all the way. "Xavier and Chuy are trapped in Sakal's lair, with the sun about to hit them. We have to get there, kill whoever stands in our way, and get them to safety. You brought the tents, right?"

"Got 'em," Brian said as he swung into the driver's seat and started the engine, while the others were slamming the cargo door and piling in. "What the fuck are they doing there?" he asked, spinning the SUV in a dirt-spewing circle before speeding for the gate, which was already rising.

"I don't know. Something to do with ambushing Sakal. Dumbass plan, but they'll be dead if we don't get there in time."

"We'll get there."

"No speed limit," she snapped. "I don't care if every cop in the city is on our tail."

"Roger that."

XAVIER PACED AS he worked to break the penultimate spell. Fucking Sakal. Forget the spell, which he'd clearly created before he arrived. But the rest of the scheme, recruiting young people to do his dirty work, to attack the *Fortalesa* as a distraction until he was ready for the final step. Kidnapping the children to make sure Xavier *took* that final step. And then using his brother as a decoy. How the hell had he known Xavier would choose to stage an ambush, or anything else, for that matter?

There had to be a spy among his people. But who? He'd been so careful to let no one but Chuy and Joaquim know the final plan, and he'd have sensed if either of them had betrayed him. Hell, Chuy would die with him if he failed to get them to safety in time. And Joaquim? Impossible.

But then who? Someone else in the *Fortalesa*, someone so far down the chain of command, or someone he saw every day, and so no longer noticed as he went about his nights was guilty. Damn it. They were so careful with the people they recruited to the guard force, and he always did the final interview personally. There was no way in hell a human could have deceived him that much and slipped by. But the daylight guards were only a small percentage of the humans living in his *Fortalesa*. And even they could change their minds once they'd been accepted into the ranks. There were also visitors all the time. A cousin coming to visit, a new lover spending a few hot nights. It was impossible for him to check everyone who passed through the gates. Although, now that he knew, he'd tear down his beloved *Fortalesa* stone by stone until he found the traitor.

The spell layer gave way with another snap of power that had him raising a hand to protect his face. Damn sorcerers. He hated every one of the fuckers. He wasn't old enough to have fought in the wars, but Josep had, and he'd met others who had, too. Ancient vampires who'd sworn fealty to him from the first, but who wanted only to be free to live quiet lives as artists and shopkeepers, even the occasional professional, a lawyer or a bookkeeper.

He walked over to check on Chuy, who'd withdrawn to a shady spot behind the bar. The sun wasn't high enough yet to shine directly through the dome, and indirect light only weakened Xavier slightly. Chuy was strong enough to remain mostly awake, but his strength was failing, trying to pull him into sleep as the fire in his brain urged him to find a safe place. Xavier, too, sensed the coming fire, could hear the clock ticking down the time he had left.

He crouched down to lay a hand on Chuy's arm and whisper, "Only a little longer." And then he hurried back to continue his work. If he fell before he succeeded, he might die where he stood. And if he was forced to seek the little safety remaining, would the spell stop Layla from reaching them? Would the fates be that cruel? To bring her back to him only to end his life?

No. He was no plaything for the fates, a piece to be moved on the chessboard of existence, subject to random chance or the mood of mythical beings. He was a fucking vampire lord and he would damn well determine his own fate.

He bared his fangs at one of Sakal's bodyguards who'd drawn close, unaware that while she studied him like some exotic creature safely caged in a zoo, he was about to break down the only barrier that kept him from ripping out her throat. Switching his gaze to one that was intentionally seductive, he waited until her eyes were locked with his, unblinking and hazy, and then moving far too fast for her human senses to follow, he bared his fangs, snapped the final spell, and lunged forward, slashing her throat while her gaze was still locked on his. Then he leapt on the others.

Xavier forced himself to ignore the panicked slam of bullets, the sudden heat of a lucky hit that passed cleanly through his upper arm and shoulder, as he moved too fast for them to follow. It hurt like hell, but it wouldn't do any permanent damage. He ripped the gun from the next guard's hands, tearing her arm off in the process, and then, drawing one of his knives, he stabbed it through her heart.

Stupid of Xavier to have abandoned his own MP5, but just as stupid of Sakal to have been so certain of his spell that he hadn't warned the women who protected him of just how dangerous a vampire lord could be.

The remaining women stared, too terrified to move, to react. Had they grown accustomed to Sakal and his brother? Had they believed no vampire could be as strong as the stories told about them? He stood there for a glorious instant, giving them that fang-bearing grin, and letting them see the arrogance and strength of a truly powerful vampire.

"Laugh, you fucker," one of them whispered, her voice hoarse with fear, as the others tried to hide behind her. "You'll be a pile of ash soon enough."

He shrugged. "Why wait? Are you *scared*?"

She glowered silently as they sidled like a herd of sheep toward the elevator. "My master has forbidden it," she muttered sulkily. "He wants you to suffer as the sun rises, as your blood cools and forces you to fall into sleep knowing you'll never wake."

Xavier laughed. "You think that's going to happen?" he said. "That the coward you worship can save you? You'll be dead long before me, girl, and your master with you."

And he attacked, killing four more when the rest abandoned their comrades, leaving them to face the monster while they raced into the remaining elevator, most of them bloodied and begging, crying to their God, to their impotent master to save them.

He would have given chase—he could have killed them all before elevator was gone—but the sun was still rising and with every degree of movement, his strength declined. Not enough to disable him, not yet. But he still had to save Chuy.

"Run. Hide if you can," he growled as the doors closed. "You will never escape my revenge."

He crossed to Chuy, cursing the heavens and whatever gods might still permit this good man to die. His concentration was wavering, his massive power reserves lower than they'd ever been, when he reached out and without slowing, grabbed Chuy's arm, forcing himself to keep moving until he collapsed against the shadow of the far wall, his lieutenant next to him.

His last sense of anything before he slept was the sound of a huge explosion filled with the shriek of tortured metal. And Layla's voice calling his name.

LAYLA ALREADY HAD her door open when the SUV slid to a tire-screeching halt in front of Sakal's lair. The building was just as Joachim had described in the briefing with Xavier, something that now seemed like a hundred years ago. She saw extensive damage as she ran up two steps to the big metal door, damage that appeared to have been repaired by welding the edges to the frame. Her first thought was that they'd used an odd choice of repair technique, since it sealed the door completely shut. But hard upon that observation, her brain was calculating the best way to blast through it. She called over her shoulder while she continued to study the barrier. "We need to blow through this thing *fast*. I don't care what's left, as long as you get me inside ten minutes ago."

"Roger that," came Brian's voice, as Layla rushed to the back of the SUV and yanked open the cargo door. "Kerry, help me get these tents out."

She leaned in to lend a hand, but said, "Tents, Cap? What—?"

"There are vampires inside," Layla snapped. "And the sun's up."

"Fuck!" Kerry raced to grab a tent, dropping it next to the one Layla had already propped against the building wall, well away from where Brian and River were getting ready to blow the door. Kerry dumped the two ground sheets on top, then yelled, "What's the delay on the fucking door?"

"On the three count," Brian responded.

The huge door crashed inward, nearly drowning out the ding of an elevator as it announced the arrival of four blondes with sub-machine guns firing on auto.

"Get rid of those assholes!" she shouted, but River was already tossing flashbangs and smoke grenades, while the rest of the team grabbed for the tents and belly-crawled into a short, narrow hallway, which got them inside, but provided shitty cover.

"Cover us," Kerry commed, and a moment later she and River were darting out, making for a curve of upward stairs to the immediate left of where the short hallway opened up. Once they were out of view and racing for better positions on high ground, Layla and Brian covered *themselves*, shooting wildly into the dwindling smoke while running behind a wall that curled right and ran under the mezzanine to form the damn circle.

Leaning against the wall, catching her breath before the blondes recovered enough to formulate a strategy, Layla studied the odd room. Other than the small area where the elevators landed, the room was one big circle, with a second-floor mezzanine hanging over all but a marble-floored section that was lit by a glass dome in the ceiling. The sunlight beaming through that damn dome had her stomach churning with dread, but there were still areas of shade deep under the mezzanine, and she thought she detected a boot sticking out from behind a . . . fully-stocked *bar* of all things.

There was no more time to sightsee, however. The smoke was down to wisps when the elevator opened and four *more* damn blondes raced out, panic firing as they ran, and not hitting anyone, because no one was in their line of fire.

They were in Kerry and River's line of fire, however, and soon there were only *three* left out of what had been eight blondes. One of the survivors was flattened against the wall of the open elevator, near the button panel, while two others huddled low to the floor, behind the curve of the stairs.

The huddlers were from the first charge into the smoke after Brian had blown the door. Their less lucky teammates were lying dead on the floor. Unfortunately for the two huddlers, they couldn't target Layla and Brian without stepping out of cover.

Elevator girl was the *only* survivor of the last suicide charge, but she also couldn't shoot without exposing herself completely. Her three friends had done that, and they were very definitely dead, their bodies all but shredded, parts of them actually stopping the elevator doors from closing.

While a *tiny* part of Layla's brain entertained the irrelevant thought of whether the damn bodyguards had bleach nights for all that blond hair, because no way it was natural, the rest of her was figuring out the best way to grab a tent and get to the *opposite* side of the circle, where she could still see that perfectly motionless boot behind the bar. With no warning other than a murmured "Cover me," and a glance at Brian, she stepped out firing, reached for one of the tents lying half inside the damn entranceway and ran for the other side of the room.

"Layla, damn it!" Brian's furious protest followed, but he changed his angle of fire to cover her movement, without *shooting* her, while at the same time Kerry and River opened fire from up above, making sure the remaining bodyguards couldn't risk exposing themselves to fire on her.

She was forced to dive to the ground, rolling for cover when a trio of shots smacked into the giant pillar next to her. But she managed to hold onto the damn tent when she scooted behind the damaged pillar and sent a hail of her own fire ripping into the stairway, destroying the wooden bannister, and taking out the remaining huddler. Someone else had killed the other one, probably either Kerry or River shooting from above.

Sakal's guards were fucking idiots Layla thought, when she scooted around to face the bar. They should have gone up to the mezzanine the minute they fled the elevator. Hell, at least the first group had tried to keep them penned up in that stupid entry hall, to stop them from entering the building at all. Too bad for them that her team had big guns and better tactics. But at least it had been smarter than getting boxed into a fucking *elevator*.

Clearly, bodyguarding one man didn't compare to fighting for your life in free-for-all war zones. Elevator blonde was still alive, but Layla wasn't worried about her, since the round room provided all the cover she needed.

Reaching the bar, she shot a quick look behind her position and was relieved to see two big bodies lying in what was clearly the darkest corner they'd been able to find. Fear swelled in her heart. No, not bodies, *vampires*. They were both old and strong, and *alive*. Scooting backward on her ass until she reached them, she experienced a dizzying rush of relief to find they were still breathing, followed hard by hot fury that they'd been forced into these circumstances, and even worse, that they'd obviously been meant to burn with the sun.

Sakal had tried to kill Xavier. Chuy, too. But Xavier was hers now, and she, by God, defended what was hers.

Rage took a backseat to practicality as she snapped open the tent, and taking Xavier first since he was covering Chuy, dragged and shoved him under its cover. Her back twinged at the awkward motion and Xavier's dead weight. He was a big fucking vampire, and doing a good imitation of a giant bag of sand.

"What the fuck?" That was Brian, sliding to his knees next to her, while Kerry and River were methodically taking single pot shots, trying to hit elevator blonde without destroying the elevator itself. It hadn't escaped anyone's notice that only one elevator seemed to be still working, and that none of the guards had appeared from any as-yet-unseen stairway going to the basement. Unlikely as it seemed, that there *wouldn't* be basement stairs, none of Layla's team were inclined to risk it.

Keying her comm, Layla spoke to Kerry and River. "I know you two probably have a bet going, but fun time is over. One of you get back down here and sneak up on that elevator bitch, while the other keeps her in hiding."

"Spoilsport," Kerry muttered. But a moment later, she slipped quietly down what remained of the stairs, edged along the wall, and the second, closed elevator, then ducked down, edged her Glock pistol around the open door, and fired.

The blonde screamed weakly as she fell face first to the elevator floor, unable to remain standing with what looked like a broken leg from Kerry's shot.

Kerry was on her feet in an instant, standing over the blonde before she'd finished falling. She shot her twice in the back of the head, then kicked her over onto her back, just to be sure. Staring down at the dead woman for a moment, she said, "Pussy. Nobody ever taught you, you've got *two* legs?"

Blowing out a relieved breath, Brian took in the situation with the vampires, then swore softly and immediately ran back for the second tent. Returning, he opened it quickly, gripped Chuy's limp body, then scooted backward into the tent, dragging the vamp with him.

He had to crawl over the limp vampire, since the one-man tent was too narrow to do anything else, but he managed to stand just as Layla snapped open one of the waterproof ground sheets and draped it over Xavier's tent. She then zipped the flap closed, while Brian followed suit to protect Chuy.

Layla didn't know if the sheets were necessary, but since they had them, she wasn't taking any chances, especially with all the bullets that had been flying. There was no doubt in her mind that once the sun rose high enough, no corner of this fucking circus arena of a room would be safe for a vampire, and the tents weren't designed to achieve blackout conditions. Usually, when she and her team fell into their tents after a battle, they were so exhausted they'd have slept anywhere.

With both vampires reasonably secure, she and Brian took up their weapons again, and edged slowly into the main room, where the only sound was chunks of wood hitting the marble floor. Kerry and River had already stacked the dead blondes like firewood in the open elevator.

With no way of knowing if enemy reinforcements were likely to appear from who the hell knew where, it made sense for them to clear the area, plus if the reinforcements tried to come up from the basement and called that elevator, they'd be in for a "bloody rude shock," as River would have said.

There remained the mystery of the second elevator, and the need to clear the basement. If they found that asshole Sakal sleeping down there, Layla was going to say to hell with the courtesies of vampire battle and dust the fucker while he slept. *She* wasn't a vampire, and she sure as hell wasn't bound by their rules.

Brian walked over and stood next to her, blood soaking through the upper part of his sleeve on one arm. "You okay?" he asked, his gaze raking her over, head to toe.

"Not a scratch on me," she said, which wasn't completely accurate, but close enough. "What's that?" she asked, lifting her chin at his arm.

"Well, my captain lost her fucking mind and ran into the open, so I had to cover her."

"What an asshole she must be."

"Nah, she's not bad. Will the vamps be okay?"

"I'd like to get them out of here, but I don't know how we can do it safely." She turned to stare at the elevators. "Maybe we could move them downstairs, but we'll have to clear it first. You catch sight of anyone except the blondes?"

"Nope. Who else is there? Sakal has to be in dreamland by now, right?"

"If it's really him," she complained. "How the fuck can he be two places at once? That sneaky bastard Joaquim was at the farm at oh-dark-thirty this morning, and he confirmed that Sakal was there until about an hour before sunrise. That's just enough time for Sakal to get back here and into safety. Meanwhile Xavier came here earlier, thinking to surprise Sakal when he returned for the day, and somehow found himself ambushed instead." She sighed. "That's all I got out of Joaquim before he couldn't form coherent words anymore."

"Would Joaquim betray Xavier?" It was River who dared voice the question they all had to be thinking.

Layla scowled. "I don't *know*, but . . . they've been together for a *long* time, like *centuries*. Besides, if he wanted Xavier dead, why would he have sent us here to save him?"

"Last minute guilty conscience? Or a nice alibi, if he hoped Xavier would be dead before we got here."

"Shit, you're right." She bit the inside of her cheek, thinking. "Well, we won't know anything for sure until sunset, so . . . "

They turned as one to face the elevators.

"Fuck. Shall we take a trip downstairs?"

"Might as well. If nothing else, it would be safer to move the vamps down there," Brian agreed.

"Your arm good to go?" she asked, nodding to where a fresh, white bandage stood out against the dark tan of his wounded arm.

"Barely a flesh wound. We should move the SUV into the parking lot across the street, by the way. Less noticeable by a mile."

"Good idea. What's the status on that fucking door? Is it useable at all?"

River joined her in studying the front door. "I could close it, Cap, but you'd never get it open again. We'd do better to block it with whatever we can find in this place, and set a guard."

"Okay, you and Kerry take the SUV, park it across the street. Brian and I will see what we can find to block the door. Did anyone find another stairway in here, like one that goes *down?*"

"Nah, I looked while Riv was playing Florence Nightingale to our Brian there," Kerry said. "Everything you see is all there is to this place, plus the basement."

"This sure is a weird-ass building. Don't they have fire regulations here?

"You Americans just aren't used to old buildings," Riv commented.

"Whatever. Let's get to work."

It wasn't long before Kerry and River were slithering through the small hole Layla had left in the mostly blocked front opening, just so they could get back in. And while she and Brian then worked to plug that, as well, with materials they'd already prepared for that purpose, the other two reported how they'd tried to circle around behind the building, to check for another door, but had found their way blocked by a police investigation that had sealed off the alley at both ends.

"That's awfully convenient," Layla commented.

"Yes, and we have more," Kerry mock-enthused. "There was a quite a crowd, including a few people who'd spoken to the person who was unfortunate enough to have found the body of a woman who'd been *very* brutally killed, her head practically torn off. And guess what color hair she had?"

"Blond," Layla and Brian intoned together.

"Sakal's losing his bodyguards fast," Layla said. "You think *he* killed her, left her there for someone to find? Maybe even had one of the guards clue in someone, who then rushed off for a look and reported it to the police?"

"Too many questions," Kerry answered. "And the answer's yes to most of them, but . . . does that mean there's no one in the basement?"

Right on cue, a sudden whoosh of sound had them all turning to stare at the floor display above the elevator door.

"Well, shit," Brian muttered. "Guess that's our ride. I just hope it's not filled with more bodyguards."

They all checked ammo, then guns ready, waited while the damn thing made its slow way upward, and the door finally opened on . . . an empty elevator car. They stared, until Layla said, "All aboard, I guess," and they walked inside.

With more than enough space for the four of them, they spread out, in unspoken understanding, so that they could all fire without worrying about hitting one another. It didn't take long, since the damn elevator didn't have to drop more than twenty feet, and that was being generous. Like the others, Layla had her weapon up when the doors opened onto a dark basement, but again there was no one waiting for them.

They stepped out to concrete walls and floor, and a hall—no more than sixteen feet long—that only went in one direction—left. At the end were two doors. The one on the right was an ordinary pedestrian door, with better locks than usual. But the leftward door was far more interesting. It was a vault, just like the one she knew existed in the basement of the *Fortalesa*'s vampire wing. She'd never actually *seen* it, but she knew it was there, and she'd overheard it being described by a friend of her mother's in very disappointing tones, as a bank vault. And that was exactly what this looked like. Hell, maybe that's why Sakal had chosen this building. Save some money on his hiding place.

Unfortunately, it was . . . Layla pulled on the door and jumped back when it responded by moving an inch or two outward.

"What the fuck?" she whispered, and glanced at Brian to find him regarding the door as if it was a live snake coiled to attack.

"Why would they leave that open?" he whispered back. "It *has* to be a trap."

She nodded in silent agreement, but they had to take a look. Turning, she studied the other, more ordinary door, then looked at Riv, who was closest to it. "See if you can get through that lock."

"Piece of cake," he said confidently, then knelt and pulled out a small zippered case, which held a set of lock picks.

Layla and the others took a few steps back and spread out. There was a strong possibility that one or more of Sakal's guards was waiting behind that ordinary door, ready to die for their master. But if that was true, then where was Sakal? *He* sure as hell wouldn't risk himself to take out Layla and her people. Not when he'd be too dead to enjoy it. But the vault was open, so where the fuck was he?

"Captain." She looked over at the sound of Riv's voice, when he stood and said, "It's done."

"All right. Usual precautions. Everyone stand back." She reached for the collapsible baton at her belt, but Riv beat her to it, snapping his own baton open as he took up a position on one side of the door. He waited until everyone else signaled ready, and then with his back to the wall, he reached out with one hand, gently turned the door knob, and with the same hand, used the baton to push it open about a foot.

Again nothing. Layla was beginning to think the whole damn place was empty.

Riv shoved the baton again, harder, until they could feel warm air rushing in through the open door. "Nothing there, Cap," he said.

"Let's see what's behind it, but slowly."

Riv didn't move away from his safe position against the wall, but stowed the baton and stretched out his arm, giving the door a hard shove with his hand. When it swung to a full right angle position, he crouched low and rolled through the doorway, moving fast, and coming up with his MP5 in position.

Layla was right behind him, her own weapon up and ready to cover him, if necessary. "It's a damn garage," she said. "Look at the door."

"You can smell it, too," River said. "Hot tires and diesel. I bet the bastard left hours ago."

"In daylight?"

"Why not? He's got his team of bodyguards to move him around, and if they have the right vehicle, he's in no danger. Not from the sun anyway."

"Well, shit," she hissed, then stepped back and over to the vault. "I bet this damn thing's empty, too."

"Let's not bet on that," Brian said, stopping her before she could pull the door all the way open. "Tactics 101, Cap."

"Yeah, yeah. Standard entry. You and me." She glanced at the others who didn't need to be told what to do. They moved to covering positions automatically, while Brian waited for her signal, then she pulled the door open and together they ran inside in a lethal rush. Or it would have been lethal, if anyone had been there to die.

The vault was on the small side, just big enough to hold an unkempt bed that stretched from wall to wall, and left a bare slice of room to maneuver along its foot.

"Looks like Sakal wasn't sleeping alone," Brian observed dryly.

"I never thought he was," she said absently, then found a light switch and flicked it on. There were two wall sconces above the bed that together emitted a low pinkish light. She sighed and said the obvious. "Sakal is officially in the wind. And I bet you were right, Riv. He left before we ever got here. Which means he could be anywhere."

"Except the farm," Brian said helpfully.

"Except the farm," she agreed. "But I doubt he planned on going back there." She kicked the stupid bed. "Fuck. Okay. Let's get Xavier and Chuy down here."

"I hate to think what might be on those sheets," River said, staring at the messy bed.

"Oh, for the fuck's sake. Fine. I didn't see curtains anywhere—"

"They'd be filthy with dust anyway," Riv commented in disgust.

"Riv, they're vampires. They don't *get* sick, okay? They drink blood. I'll strip the bed and flip the mattress. Happy?"

"No, but as I'm not going to be sitting on it, it's fine."

A HALF HOUR LATER, they had both vampires more or less safely resting in the vault—and yes, the mattress had been flipped. After that, there was nothing to do but wait. Unfortunately, they didn't have a comfortable place to do that, because everything resembling a chair had been broken into pieces to block the front door.

Layla texted Danilo to let her know that everyone was safe, without naming names, since no one but she and her team had even known why they'd rushed out that morning. And if there was a traitor, whether Joaquim or someone else, they didn't want word getting out that the vampires were alive.

So, throughout the day, they rotated from the first floor to the basement, keeping watch on both the vampires and the front door, which while *closed* in the strictest sense, definitely wasn't secure.

And while they sat—on the floor, because well, chairs—they speculated among themselves as to where Sakal might have gone, or what he might have been after, beyond Xavier's death. Had he planned to kill Xavier and simply go home? Or had he somehow convinced himself that Xavier's territory would be his?

Based on what Xavier had told her of his history with Sakal, Layla knew that was impossible. But maybe Sakal was sufficiently delusional to believe he could somehow rule vampires who were powerful enough to squash him like a bug.

"What are you thinking?" Brian asked, when she'd obviously been quiet for too long.

"When Xavier wakes—"

"He's going to be pissed as hell," he provided. "To say the least. Furious is probably closer. I'm not sure any of us should be here when—"

"He won't hurt *me*."

"Yeah? What about the other guy?"

"Chuy? I barely know him, but Xavier will wake first. He'll handle Chuy."

"Damn it, Layla."

"I know. I'm a pain in the ass. But you love me."

"Yeah. Okay, Kerry and Riv will stay upstairs, but I'm staying down here with you. Just in case."

"All right," she said agreeably. She had no intention of going along with it when sunset arrived, but she didn't mind company in the meantime.

"What about food?" he asked.

"Oops. I forgot about that. I guess Riv can go out through the garage and find something quick, while Kerry keeps watch on the front. You can rotate up and down until Riv gets back."

AT 1100 HOURS, RIV returned with a rather delicious assortment of tapas, including bread and dessert, of course, along with soft drinks and a fresh supply of bottled water, since none of them trusted anything about the building they were stuck in. Once he was back inside, they re-bolted and welded the garage door, just in case.

By 1300 hours, they'd gone through every crumb of food. Riv had found a trashcan upstairs to dispose of the rubbish, and as it was summer, which meant longer days, they were contemplating their next meal.

At 1400 hours, they tossed a bunch of smoke bombs into the elevator with the dead bodyguards, then closed and welded shut the doors, in addition to turning the air-conditioner to its lowest temperature, since the bodies had begun to do what dead bodies did—decay, which in turn made them smell.

At 1700 hours, the smoke bombs and the welding had worked well enough that they'd begun to seriously contemplate their next meal, while obsessively checking their watches and phones for the time.

"For fuck's sake," Layla finally said, after Riv, who was sitting next to her on the basement floor, checked his giant-can-do-everything watch for the twentieth time in as many minutes. "Sunset isn't until after nine, okay? That's hours from now. Set your super-duper watch to go off fifteen minutes before that. Then you can just stare at it until sunset, okay?"

Riv just looked at her. "What bug crawled up your ass, Cap?"

"I don't believe this." She opened her comm and said, "Brian, I'm coming up. He's all yours."

Brian was waiting when the elevator door opened. "What happened?"

"You'll see," she said tightly, then stepped out of the elevator and began doing laps of the marble circle, while breathing slowly in and out, in and out.

AT 1900 HOURS, everyone breathed a sigh of relief when they decided the front door didn't need to be *completely* blocked, and sent River out for more food. Which once again, they all enjoyed a lot.

And at 2000, with the sun still a pink glow above the glass dome, Layla made her way down to the basement for the final watch.

Since Brian still insisted on remaining downstairs with Layla, she explained to him what it would mean when Xavier woke to an unfamiliar and unsecured location after what had clearly been a pitched battle with Sakal's bodyguards, and possibly with Sakal himself. Xavier had been fighting not only whatever magic Sakal had used to trap him, but the power of the rising sun. That he'd succeeded at all, much less long enough for Layla and her team to finish off the enemy, was a textbook example of the extraordinary strength possessed by a vampire lord compared to every other vampire walking the earth.

"He saved both Chuy *and* himself," she told him. "But he paid a price for that, a price that is measured in blood. Which means he'll need blood to recover. No, not *need*. Demand. From me," she said softly. "Not only because I'm here, but because we're lovers, and he's done it before."

"You said he wasn't your boyfriend," he teased.

"Things change. But really, Brian, I should be down here alone. He won't hurt me, but he doesn't know you. And you're a guy."

"I am? When did that happen?"

"Ha ha. I'm serious. He's a guy, you're a guy . . . it could be problem. He won't be in his right mind, not at first. And I'm the only one of us he knows. It has to be me."

"I could stay," Kerry said as the elevator doors opened. "I'm not a guy."

"Thanks," she said, and hoped the other woman heard the deeper meaning in the words. "But, no. It's better if there aren't any strangers here. I'm going to go in there and close the door."

"How're you going to open it by yourself?"

Layla smiled. "I won't be by myself when the door opens," she reminded Kerry.

She chuckled. "Oh, right. Duh."

"Okay, see you all on the flip side. Casales out."

She stood and stretched, then walked over to the vault, where Xavier and Chuy slept in motionless silence beneath the tents which they'd had to be moved in. It was undoubtedly the most primitive daylight protection that either one of them had ever been forced into. She didn't know the name of Xavier's Sire, but she knew he'd been a Catalan aristocrat. And Xavier was *Chuy's* Sire, so as a vampire, he'd lived the same way Xavier did.

Closing the door on her well-meaning friends, she climbed onto the bed and unzipped Xavier's tent, the heavy metal teeth scraping her fingertips due to her awkward position. She sat in the opening, close enough to see him, to know that he still breathed, that his heart still beat. That he was alive. Because contrary to popular superstition, vampires were *not* dead. They'd never *been* dead. To the edge of death, yes. But not dead. As a matter of fact, from a vampire point of view, they were the new and advanced version of humanity. Their blood carried *something* that they were unwilling to talk about, that gave them enhanced strength and senses, power—for some of them—that could only be explained as magic, and virtual immortality. And Layla didn't see anything wrong with that, not as long as they consented to the change.

The chime went off on her watch, set as she'd advised Riv, for 2045. 8:45 p.m. Local sunset was at 9:10.

Twisting, she checked to make sure the door was shut. She felt almost guilty, she realized, because she was going to let Xavier sink fang and drink her blood. And she knew, although hopefully the others didn't *completely* understand, what would follow. "Fuck that," she decided, and crawling forward, did her best to reposition him so that he'd be a bit more comfortable. Although Xavier was so damn big, and it wasn't like moving a sleeping person. His arms and legs didn't want to stay where she put them, and moving his entire body was beyond her strength. She wondered idly if vampire bodies had a greater density than a regular human's. "Makes you think," she muttered, and finally gave up trying. The tent was designed for one person, but this wouldn't be the first time she'd shared one with a lover. So she lay down next to him, and maneuvered until they were face to face.

And then, suddenly, his eyes opened. And the next thing she knew, a big male body was crushing her into a too-soft mattress.

Chapter Fifteen

XAVIER WOKE, AWARE and awake in an instant. And didn't know where the fuck he was or who . . . No, he realized. He knew who was next to him. Layla. And he was starving.

He rolled, or tried to, but they were in some kind of tube. Reaching up, he tore away the flimsy fabric above him, switched their positions until he was half on top of her, with one muscled leg thrown over her lower body, trapping her as he lowered his head to sniff at the delicious scent of hot blood that flowed beneath every inch of her bare skin. Her eyes were wide with shock, but relaxed in a heartbeat, her hands cupping the back of his head, her body arching beneath him.

He licked her cheek, her neck, then burrowed his nose into the warm crevice beneath her jaw, while her soft moan fluttered over his cheek. Fangs slid from his gums without conscious thought, his body following instinct until he found what he needed. He was drained from a battle, from a struggle to survive, his power lower than it had been in years. Her blood was what he needed, what he craved. He whispered her name. "Layla."

He heard a soft inhalation that he might have called a sob from another woman, and then her voice. "How'd you know it was me?"

Bracing his arms on either side of her body, he looked down at her, making no attempt to conceal his fangs. This was who he was. "I would know your scent anywhere," he growled, his voice roughened by a hunger he was straining to control. "I would know the scent of your blood in a dark room filled with people, in a stadium of thousands," he told her, the gleam of his eyes highlighting the smooth curves of her face. "I know your mind, your soul. My body recognizes all of you."

"Is that good?" she asked, searching his face for answers.

He dipped his head and kissed her, forcing himself to go slowly, to gentle her mouth into sweet acceptance. "It is if you want it to be."

Her arms tightened around his neck, pulling him down and holding him closely. "I was so afraid," she whispered.

He lifted his head enough to give her a puzzled look, surprised that she'd admit to that, to caring that much about him. "Why?" he asked, waiting to see if she'd back away from the vulnerability of the truth.

She studied his expression for a long moment, as he waited for her gaze to shutter, to glance away. His heart tightened painfully when that didn't happen, when she said, "I thought we were too late. That you were already dead."

"If I'd died, *cariño*, you would have known." His lips curved into a crooked, deprecating smile. "All of Spain, and beyond, would have known," he admitted. "But only *your* heart would have known."

He claimed her mouth again, letting his hunger, his *need*, flavor the kiss as he lowered his body to hers, letting her feel his weight, his intent in the hard muscles of his arms and chest, the rigid length of his cock against her thigh. Without warning, he dipped his mouth to her neck again, his fangs grazing her soft skin, skimming over the thudding pulse of her carotid artery and coming to rest against the swollen vein beneath her ear.

Scraping his fingers through her hair, he pulled her head back to bare the smooth length of her neck. "I can hear the rush of your blood," he whispered, licking the curve of her ear. "I want you."

Her heart was thudding so loudly, he almost missed the words she breathed against his forearm. "You have me."

He bit down, his teeth breaking the skin of her neck before he stopped himself. "Not here," he snarled. He didn't want to stop. Wanted to take her right there, right now, and to hell with the consequences. But he wouldn't do that to her.

Her fingers clenched on his shoulders, digging into muscle with the strength of a warrior. "Here," she said, her hold going from a caress to a demand. "Right here. You need blood, you need your strength. We don't know what's waiting outside."

"Layla."

"Now," she insisted. "You can fuck me later—and you'd damn well better—but you need blood now."

He was weaker than he could ever remember being, but not so weak that he couldn't have resisted her if he'd tried. He didn't try. Sinking his teeth in her neck once again, he pierced her vein and moaned in a pleasure that was deep and heartfelt as the delicate silk of her blood flowed down his throat, heating his body like a furnace, while his parched cells stretched with new energy and eagerly drank up more. He could have lain there for hours, sipping the life-giving nectar from her vein, sliding first his fingers and then his cock into the succulent heat of her pussy.

But he forced himself to stop, to close off his senses against the temptation of her body. Withdrawing his fangs in a smooth glide that left the two small wounds already closing, he hastened the healing with a long, slow lick of his tongue. Then he stared down her.

She was still panting beneath him, overtaken by the chemical in his bite that had sped the most exquisite pleasure to everywhere blood flowed in her body. Which was everywhere. She cried when he stopped, bucking against his weight in demand, her glassy eyes staring up at him and filled with anger.

"How are you?" he demanded, biting back a groan as the soft heat between her thighs cradled his erection.

She finally seemed to focus on his face, stared for a moment, then said, "I'm . . . fine. How're you?"

He wanted to laugh at the polite, almost trite, response. "Feel that," he snarled, taking her hand and pressing against his unrelieved erection. "That's how I am. I *want* you. But there are several humans who I hope are your people standing just outside that door, and Chuy will wake at any moment. I don't think you want any of them to see us naked and entwined, to put it poetically."

She tried to conceal an amused smile. "I'm sorry," she said. "But you're right."

"Of course I am," he grumped.

She made a disgusted noise. "Good God, Brian just commed me. I told them I would be fine. How long before Chuy—"

Xavier sent his lieutenant a telepathic order, rousing him to wakefulness only slightly earlier than he would have on his own. "He's waking now," he told her.

"You'll have to open the door," she said as they rolled away from each other and sat up as much as they could before crawling off the bed to stand on the narrow strip of concrete floor at its foot.

"That won't be a problem."

"It's pretty well sealed shut, so—"

"Fix your clothes," he said, then stomped to the vault door, and with a quick glance over his shoulder to be sure she obeyed, shoved the door open to find three people standing in a concrete hallway, staring, as if waiting for him to start raving like a lunatic.

"Layla," he said in a flat voice.

"I'm here," she said and shoved in next to him. "I'm fine. I told you I would be."

The human male named Brian, who she'd insisted had never been more than a friend, was talking. He fought back an instinctive wave of possessive rage that was no more appropriate for the moment than it would have been to let the human fighters discover him balls deep in her pussy.

When the others stepped into the elevator taking Layla with them, he waited until the door was about to close, then reached out and pulled her to his side, his glare daring them to try and stop him.

"Go," Layla said calmly. "Send it back down. We'll be up in a minute."

Xavier bent to her ear when the door closed, leaving them alone. "You're mine," he murmured. "Tonight and every night."

She pulled back and gave him a searching look. "We'll see."

With an angry snarl, he yanked her against his chest and kissed her, his mouth hard. And as his tongue swept between her teeth, his fury filled her throat. "Decide now," he ordered. "You're mine or you're not."

She lifted her head with an angry glare to match his. "It has to go both ways. You're mine, too."

He grinned, flashing fangs that were still fully visible and dripping with hunger. "Of course," he replied silkily. "Just remember, *cariño*. I don't share, ever. Not for an hour, not for a moment."

"Same goes," she snapped.

His grin broadened as he took her angry mouth, rumbling with satisfaction when she softened into his embrace, when her arms circled his neck to hold him tightly.

They broke apart at the sound of furious howls from inside the vault, turned to see Chuy crawl from the shreds of his tent and flow gracefully to his feet, as if his bones moved differently than a regular human's.

"Sire?" he asked, gazing around the empty hallway, before looking to Xavier for guidance.

"The elevator, Chuy," he said when the thing dinged open. "We're leaving." When they stepped inside, he looked at Layla and said, "Sakal?"

"Gone." She continued speaking over his sharp curse. "There's a garage exit in the basement," she explained. "We think his remaining bodyguards spirited him out as soon as he went downstairs. It would have been a simple matter to park a shielded vehicle in there and take him out that way. Now we just need to figure out where he'll go."

"He'll run home, like the coward he's always been."

"Where's home?"

"I don't know, yet. Though I do have suspicions, and if necessary, I can contact my fellow vampire lords. After all, that's why I've spent so much time courting their friendship and alliance. It's time for them to step up and prove themselves.

"In the meantime, there's nothing we can do tonight. Let us return to my *Fortalesa*, have a shower, and change clothes, so we can all meet in a more civilized manner to consider the fastest way to locate Sakal. And then—and much more pleasurably—we can discuss in great detail how I will rip his guts open, watch him heal, and then do it again. Over and over, until he begs for death."

His voice had taken on a dreamy quality as he'd described Sakal's painful death, and when he turned, he found the elevator doors open, and the other woman, Kerry, staring at him.

"You're a scary motherfucker, you know that?" she asked.

He grinned. "Actually, yes I do." He clapped and said cheerfully, "So are we all traveling together?"

LAYLA DIDN'T KNOW what to make of Xavier's blunt verdict. Sakal? Yeah, sure, that bastard was guilty as sin and deserved to die. His own words had condemned him, so it wasn't the question of his guilt that troubled her. It was the torture. But the more she worried about it, the more she saw the inevitable logic. Vampire justice was very different than that of humans, for a good reason. Vampires were not only harder to kill, but they could tolerate so much more pain and heal so much faster. If you wanted them to suffer for their crimes ... well, that's where the torture came in.

One only had to look at Xavier and Chuy, knowing what they'd been through a day earlier, knowing the horrible death Sakal had planned for them, to understand Xavier's determination to make the sorcerer suffer. But that same evaluation of the two vamps demonstrated their resilience. Xavier, obviously, had taken Layla's blood, which explained his rosy health. But Chuy, too, seemed fully recovered.

She'd asked Xavier about it, when he'd been "helping" her gather her gear, mostly she thought, because he was establishing his claim on *her*. Like a dog, he was making it clear that she was *his* bone. She laughed to herself at the weird analogy, since really . . . he was the one with the *bone*, right? Ha ha.

Anyway, while Xavier was flexing his muscles, lifting her heavy gear bag as if it weighed nothing, Layla had glanced over to see Chuy in deep conversation with Kerry, and looking damn good. She'd leaned in to Xavier and whispered, "Is Chuy okay? He wasn't hurt by what happened yesterday?"

Xavier had studied her, as if wondering why she was asking, long enough that Layla had been certain she'd stumbled on another deep, dark vampire secret.

But then Xavier said, "Chuy is very well. As one of my own vampire children, it's easy to share my strength with him. He'll feed when we return to the *Fortalesa*, and restore his full strength. But I needed him capable and strong before we left this place. We can't afford to assume there will be no more attacks before we reach home."

"You think Sakal will hit us again so soon?"

"Not him personally, no. But he may arrange for some of his acolytes to do so."

"Right, I'll warn the rest of my team, too. They walked over to join the others by the front door, which was now a combination of the broken chairs and miscellaneous debris that had been used to block it, and the enlarged hole through which they'd been crawling whenever one of them needed to exit.

Brian dumped his gear bag and weapons in a pile, then turned to her and said, "The tents are a total loss, but we brought them along. Don't want to give the local cops anything more to wonder about. The damn bed in a bank vault is strange enough."

He shot a glance at Xavier when he made the comment about the bed, but the vampire lord didn't seem to hear. He was too intent on eyeing the exit hole.

"We're getting ready to blow that," Brian told him. "No need to secure anything that bastard Sakal owns."

"Yes. This will be faster, however." Xavier lifted both hands toward the door.

A moment later, Layla was gasping for breath as the short, narrow passage leading to the door filled with a wave of power that threatened to suck every bit of oxygen from the air. A moment later, barely in time to stop the black spots dancing in her eyes from becoming a complete blackout, she heard a sound like air being sucked into a vacuum, and then the heavy door frame and all the junk contained within it, were flying outward toward the street. She had the sudden thought that the damn door would crash into their SUV, which was parked a little too close. But before she could shout a warning, the door simply . . . stopped and hung in mid-air.

Her heart was pounding from the juxtaposition of fear and relief, but when she stepped up next to Xavier, she was grinning. "Show off."

He glanced down, one perfect eyebrow arched innocently. "I have no idea what you mean by that."

She snorted. "Yeah, right. It's all good," she added when Brian shot her a doubtful look.

They all moved fast after that, gathering up every piece of gear, anything that could possibly be used to identify them. As Brian had already made clear, they didn't want to waste time trying to explain what had happened to local law enforcement. The vamps could always wipe memories if necessary, but it was better to avoid that if they could.

River had been bored enough as they'd waited for sunset, that he'd succeeded in knocking out surveillance on the block, so there'd be no record of their departure. He'd taken out a good chunk of the electrical grid to do it, but city employees were already working on the unexplained failure, and had announced they'd have power restored soon. And that meant that both vampires and humans needed to be gone before that happened.

Loading was mostly finished, with the bundled up remnants of tents and various weapons shoved into the cargo space of the Mercedes SUV. The biggest problem, however, showed itself when the time came to load themselves. Xavier and Chuy had arrived in the small sedan, but there'd also been the white van, which had been prepositioned for them. Unfortunately, both vehicles had either been flat out stolen, or more likely, Sakal's minions had taken them both. The sedan had little value, but the van would have been a nice prize for a vampire. Especially one who didn't like to admit his true nature.

Xavier didn't care much about where the vehicles had gone, or with whom. But the loss meant they now had just the one SUV for all their gear, plus four big men and two women.

"Well, shite," Riv said, eyeing the single, back bench seat. Someone was either going to be taking a taxi, or shoved into the cargo space.

Kerry stepped up next to him and sighed. "I'll sit with the cargo," she volunteered. "I'm the only one who'll fit. But I want major points for this."

"You can sit on my lap, *petita flor*," Chuy volunteered, from where he stood in the open door of the front passenger seat. "There is more than enough room, and you can protect me." He gave Kerry a smile so charming and so fucking deceptively innocent that it was like looking at a completely different vampire than the one Layla knew.

She waited for Kerry to verbally rip his head off. Instead, the petite warrior who'd torn new assholes into every man who'd called her a *little flower* in the past, walked over to the vamp, placed one of her deadly hands on his chest, and said, "That's so sweet. Thank you." And then permitted Chuy, once he was in the seat, to *lift her* onto his lap.

"Were there drugs in that food you brought?" she asked Riv.

He turned his puzzled gaze on her. "If so, they were damn good ones."

"Load up!" Brian's shout from the driver's seat got them moving, with Layla wedged between Xavier and Riv in the back.

"You sure about leaving that open?" Brian questioned, eyeing the wide-open doorway.

"Leave it." Xavier's order was issued in a tone that softened it to a suggestion, but Layla saw Brian's shoulders tense.

"You had it right the first time," she told him. "I don't give a shit what happens to anything in there. It's Sakal's, and fuck him."

"Roger that," he agreed.

Ten minutes later, they'd left the city behind and were on the highway back to the *Fortalesa*.

Xavier turned to her. "Your cellphone, if you would, *cariño*. Joaquim needs to be updated. And I'll want to meet as soon as we return. You and Brian will join us. There'll be no move on the enemy tonight, but we need to evaluate and update the relevant information—especially anything dealing with Sakal's home estate, which I suspect is in France—and formulate a strategy. I specifically want to call the French vampire lord. He's still very much consolidating his power, but the country *is* his territory, nonetheless, and that's a courtesy I cannot ignore. Also, while Sakal is, as ever, a coward, he's also very shrewd when it comes to his own survival. We'll have a limited window before he scurries into much deeper hiding. If we're to attack tomorrow, which we must, we'll need to lock down his location, and develop a clear strategy before then."

Since she agreed with everything he'd said, she simply handed him her phone.

Chapter Sixteen

XAVIER TOOK TIME out for a shower before meeting with the others. At any other time, he'd have invited Layla to join him. Hell, he'd nearly dragged her in with him anyway. But there'd been such sensual hunger, such need in her eyes when he'd turned to her after their return. He'd recognized it, because his own gaze had certainly reflected that same desire, the same fierce longing. And once they came together, he doubted they would be capable of stopping until the fire was quenched—not even to plot revenge on his enemy. Not for anything. Stopping himself from having her when he'd awakened to find her next to him, when she'd fed him her blood . . . Shit. That had used up just about every ounce of control he possessed where she was concerned, where her *blood* was concerned. She was his, and he wanted to make damn sure she understood that.

But this fucking meeting had to take place first. They couldn't delay going after Sakal. The slimy bastard was too good at disappearing. Paradoxically, his weakness as a vampire made it easier for him to hide. Xavier was a powerful vampire and could locate virtually any one of his people if he set his mind to it. But if Sakal was no longer within Xavier's territory, especially when combined with his weak vampire signature, his presence simply wouldn't register.

There were other ways to spy on the bastard, but he had to be found first. In times like this, modern technology was very useful. Xavier would deploy every resource at his disposal to locate the coward, and then he'd dig him out of his hole, and kill him. Slowly.

Since thinking about Layla, and what he planned to do with her as soon as possible, had the predictable effect on his body, he finished his shower with a burst of freezing cold water that had him swearing the filthiest curses in every language he knew. Fuck, that had been cold. Cold enough that he feared his dick wouldn't recover in time to be of use later, with Layla, he thought while stepping out and scrubbing himself back to life.

Once all the parts of his body had recovered, however, he looked forward to the coming strategy session with anticipation. As always, the prospect of raining blood and disaster down on his enemy, of watching that enemy twist helplessly and beg for death, had his own blood running hot.

He was pulling on his boots when his cell rang, and Joaquim's name lit the display.

"Joaquim."

"Sire." His security chief's voice held such devotion, and such relief that he'd returned safely, that it almost made Xavier doubt his own worthiness. Almost. He was too much a vampire lord, too much an alpha male, to ever truly question his value.

"Where are you?" he asked Joaquim.

"On my way to your office, my lord. I've notified your senior military, and they're not far behind me."

"Good. Have you spoken to Chuy?"

"No more than to you, my lord. Layla provided an update earlier. It was waiting for me when I woke, so I know the essentials."

"And I know it was you who set her on our rescue this morning. You saved our lives, Joaquim."

"Layla and her friends did that. All I did was make a phone call."

"It was an important call, my friend. And we have an important matter to discuss. But not until you get here. Some discussions must be conducted in person."

"I am yours to command, my lord."

"Good. I'll join you shortly."

He considered his good fortune in having had Chuy and Joaquim beside him as the centuries unfolded. They were both more than the sum of their official positions. They'd been friends, too. Others among Europe's powerful vampires had commented on his ease in speaking to them—vampires who preferred to rule as human kings and queens once had, with formal courts and a lot of bowing and scraping, and justice that was arbitrary and unpredictable. Xavier, too, had been born an aristocrat, but he'd known too many verifiable idiots who'd been born to the kind of wealth that gave them power over others. He had no desire to be one of them.

He stood, then unable to stop himself, called Layla, half expecting her not to answer. She'd had her own cleaning up to do, her own team to debrief. But she answered on the second ring.

"Xavier."

"Are you coming . . . over?" He'd have sworn he heard her suck in a breath at his deliberate pause. Was her need as great as his? Was it taking every bit of *her* strength not to rush over and slam him to the bed? God, he hoped so.

"Bastard," she whispered, laughing. "You did that on purpose."

He grinned. "You're coming to the meeting."

It wasn't a question, but she answered anyway. "Yes. Brian and I are leaving now." She hesitated, then added, "Not a word!", warning him against making any comment about her second-in-command.

"I'm not worried about your Brian," he said dismissively. "Did you eat?"

"Yes. Lots of grilled meat and vegetables. Brian's ready, so we're leaving now. See you soon!"

She hung up without waiting for a reply, which he'd noticed she did often. He and his vampires did the same, but of course they could communicate telepathically, so it hardly mattered. He considered that for a moment. He'd never tried telepathy with Layla and wondered if she had any natural ability. It would help if she did, but soon, they'd be linked so thoroughly by blood that it wouldn't matter.

Opening the bedroom door, he strode out to his office to find Joaquim and Chuy settling at the table. Both stood when he entered, and he gripped each of their hands in turn—a warrior's grip that ended in bumped shoulders and slapped backs. Because they were vampires, the bumps and slaps were strong enough to have staggered, and maybe even damaged, a human.

Going to the bar, he poured a glass a quarter full with golden port, then opened the small refrigerator, took out the flask of fresh blood that was always there and filled the glass to the halfway mark.

"Before the others get here, there's a serious matter we must discuss. Sakal knew of our plan to ambush him. He knew sufficiently in advance that he substituted his brother, who looks very much like him, and who," he added for Joaquim's benefit, "was turned by a master vampire Sakal paid to do the job."

"Is it possible, my lord, that the brother was the one visiting the farm all along? That Sakal was alerted to your intrusion and simply took advantage?" Chuy asked.

"Perhaps, but he had a very complex spell waiting to capture us. I'm no sorcerer, but I know enough of magic to say that a spell like that would have taken several days to cast. It was not only multilayered, but covered a wide area."

"We have a traitor in our midst then," Chuy said, shaking his head in disbelief. "Sire, no one knew, except . . . . " He caught the wounded rage in Xavier's eyes, followed the direction of his gaze, and stared in disbelief.

"Why?" Xavier asked simply.

Joaquim's head was bowed, his eyes closed . . . in contrition? Or was it shame? "My grandson," he whispered.

"You would add lies to your treachery?" Xavier demanded, power rising within him, demanding to be released. "You have been a vampire far too long, have been in my service too long, to have a surviving grandchild."

Joaquim's head came up, his face stricken, though he knew what he'd done. Or perhaps, he truly felt that much regret. "Not from my own child, no. But he is descended from my daughter's line. I've told no one about my human family. I have no contact with them, either. None, my lord, I swear. From the first morning I woke as a vampire, I let them believe me dead. The sorcerer somehow discovered the boy—he is barely in his teens, Lord Xavier! I don't know how Sakal found him."

"Why didn't you come to me when he first approached you? Do you have so little faith in my power?"

Joaquim was on his feet, and then his knees. "No, my lord. I swear. I was desperate to save the boy's life and acted without thought. I . . . I called Layla at the last moment, hoping to save you. I didn't want them to succeed!"

"What you swear, what actions you took in the final moments to undo your treachery . . . it no longer matters. You served me loyally for many years, but in the end . . . You will never betray me again." His power lashed out, and in a moment, the vampire whom he'd considered a friend was gone, reduced to a pile of ash in an instant. There was no drama, no ripping his heart from his chest and burning it before his eyes. A traitor deserved none of that. Just the meaningless ending of a life and a pile of dust on the floor.

"Sire," Chuy's eyes were filled with tears, his face creased in sadness. "I don't . . . " He shook his head, unable to express the jumble of emotions inside him, which reflected Xavier's own.

"We'll move the meeting to the conference room down the hall. Take care of that, please, Chuy."

He bowed his head. "Yes, my lord."

LAYLA WAS LAUGHING at a comment from Brian when they walked into the vampire wing and started for Xavier's office. She looked up when the office door opened and Chuy came into the hallway, closing the door behind him. She smiled and raised a hand to greet him, but caught the look on his face and stopped. "Chuy?"

"Ah, Layla. And Brian. The meeting is being moved. The conference room down the hall is bigger and Lord Xavier has invited some of his senior military staff." He gestured to his right, presumably toward the new room.

It all seemed very normal, except for the wretched expression on his face, in his eyes. And . . . her head came up. Xavier was behind that door, and . . . Christ, his heart . . . there was so much pain.

"What the hell's going on?" she demanded. "What's happened?"

Brian was searching the area, looking for some threat. But Chuy only shook his head and said, "Please come with me."

"Hell, no. I need to see Xavier. Right now." She reached for the door. Chuy would have stopped her, but Brian stepped in.

"Don't touch her. What's going on, Layla?"

"I don't know, but I'm going in there. I like you, Chuy. But get the fuck out of my way."

The vampire, who was powerful enough to have killed them both on the spot, lowered his head in surrender. "Perhaps he needs you." Then glared at Brian. "Not you," he said in a hard voice.

"It's all right, Brian." She placed a hand on his arm. "I'll sort this out, and join you in a minute."

"You sure about this?"

"I'm sure. This is . . . " She frowned, trying to describe something she didn't fully understand yet. "Private. I think."

"All right. But I'll be close. If you need me, just holler."

She nodded, touched his arm in reassurance, then opened the door and walked into Xavier's office.

XAVIER'S HEAD SHOT up when the door opened, a furious command on his lips. He needed solitude in this moment. Needed to grieve for the loss of a good man who'd fought at his side for more than a century. He needed . . .

"Layla."

She came directly to his side, her face creased in concern, her emotions as tangled as his own when she took him in her arms. "Baby, what happened? What is it?"

Baby, he thought. Had any woman ever called him that before? "We spoke of a spy, someone who betrayed our plans to that filthy sorcerer."

"Did you find who it was? Was it someone . . . close?"

Tears fell then, warm tracks of wet heat on his cheeks. "Joaquim." There was disbelief in his voice still.

"Joaquim, but . . . he called me. He's the reason we were there to save you."

"Regret at the last moment," he said. His voice hardened. "That does not erase his treachery."

"It sure as hell doesn't," she snapped. "What the fuck? Why?"

He held onto her, soaking in concern along with the staunch outrage on his behalf. His Layla was a warrior. She understood the magnitude of his loss. The pain.

He would have dropped to the floor then, had she not held him as he stood, not guided him to a chair and settled on his lap, her arms strong around him. "Fuck him," she growled. "I don't care *why* he did it. It doesn't matter." Her head turned. "Is that . . . *him*?"

Xavier saw her staring at the pile of dust that was, in fact, *him*. "Yes."

"Good call on moving to a different conference room. Can you get someone in to . . . vacuum?"

He surprised himself by smiling. "Yes, *cariño*. It will be done."

"Did he know where the bastard is hiding, by any chance?"

"France. I was right about that, at least."

"What's he doing there?"

"Apparently making excellent use of his and others' talents in pursuit of criminal activities, most of which are aimed at building his fortune. He hasn't drawn much attention to himself, which is why I assumed he was long dead. Unfortunately, it's easy to hide in France, because it's in such disarray. Their current lord has been in power less than a year, and the two before him were both executed by Raphael, who's the *very* powerful vampire lord over the Western United States. You may have heard his name, seen his picture. He's quite the media star, though not by his choosing, I'm sure."

"If he's American, why did he kill vampires from France?"

"Because they tried to kill him first, the fools. It's a long story that I'll tell you some night when we're lying in bed exhausted from hours of sex."

"Hours?" she asked skeptically.

"Vampires have extraordinary stamina. Did no one ever tell you that?"

She laughed and squeezed him tightly. "I love you."

He stared at her. "I know that, but I never expected to hear it."

"Oh, well. Don't get too excited. This might be the only time."

He shifted his hold, so that he was the one doing the squeezing. "I love you, Layla mine."

She tipped her head to his, but said, "No mushy stuff during war councils." Then she kissed him, long and lingering. "You ready to go be a vampire lord?"

"I *am* a vampire lord."

"Annnd he's back. Come on, let's go kick some fucking sorcerer ass."

They walked together down the hall to the larger conference room, where the others were already gathered. Layla's stride was strong and confident by his side, where she belonged. Her heartbeat was a drum in his soul, the scent of her blood inside him, pulsing in time to his own heart. He'd worried for nothing about the strength of their connection. She was already a part of him and they weren't even truly mated yet.

They reached the open door to the conference room and she paused, indicating he should go first. "My lord." Her smile was amused, but in her eyes, he saw his own pain reflected. She was putting on a show for the others, but she knew his heart still ached with loss.

He nodded and strode into the room. "Let us begin," he said, then pointed to the chair next to him. "Sit." The last was more of an order than a suggestion. Her very presence was a temptation, but today, he needed her close.

She sat without a word, which anyone who knew her would know said more than any words how concerned she was about him. But now, it was time for war. Setting aside his grief, he reminded himself who, and what, he was and faced his military commanders. "As some of you know by now, just before dawn this morning Chuy and I set out to ambush Sakal in his own lair, and found ourselves ambushed instead."

His military staff, who were hearing this for the first time, reacted with concern tempered by the certain knowledge that he was well and whole, and plotting revenge.

"We had verified intel that Sakal was still at his nearby compound when we arrived at the lair to set up our ambush, so imagine my surprise," he added wryly.

"Was it magic, Sire?" one of his vamps asked.

"No. Sakal is a strong sorcerer, but even he cannot whisk himself from place to place in the blink of an eye. I've heard that there are at least two sorcerers capable of such magic, but they're living in North America. So they're Raphael's problem, not ours."

Every vampire present chuckled at that, though the humans didn't seem to get the joke. Probably because they didn't pay much attention to vampire politics and conflict that didn't affect them. Layla had spent considerable time in the United States or fighting abroad on their behalf, so maybe he'd explain it to her later.

"The answer was much simpler, as it usually is. Sakal has a brother who is virtually identical in appearance, and also a pathetically weak vampire. But unlike Sakal, he has no magic of his own. If Sakal is to be believed, it's the brother who's been most active in recruiting followers, although it was obviously Sakal's magic that permitted his fighters to approach undetected and seem to disappear when they left. And it was very much Sakal who attempted to kill Chuy and me this morning. I say 'attempted' because he obviously failed, and has now fled."

"Do we know his location, Sire? Is he still in Spain?"

"No, there was . . . one close to us who turned traitor, which is how Sakal was able to time his own ambush to foil ours. Fortunately, Layla Casales"—he gestured in her direction, then across the table to where Brian sat next to Chuy—"and the rest of her team discovered Sakal's plot in time to get us to safety."

"A traitor?" One of the commanders repeated, disbelief written on his face. "Sire, who would—?"

"His identity no longer matters, nor does he. However, before I executed him, I scoured his mind for any knowledge he had on the sorcerer—including the location of his current lair. It is in France, but close enough to my border that, knowing he was there, I was able to verify his presence. He thinks himself safe for having fled over the border. He's a fool.

"I will contact my fellow vampire lord in France. With or without his consent, we will be moving on the sorcerer and destroying everything he holds dear, before I kill him. However, I am confident we will be given leave to cross the border for this purpose, given the circumstances."

He activated a digital display hanging on the wall to one side of the table. "This is aerial drone footage of the estate where Sakal lives. As you can see, it is remote enough that a nighttime battle won't be detected by anyone except those who value their privacy too much to intervene. The estate is also separated from its neighbors by several acres.

"Now . . . " He zoomed into a close-up of the estate itself. "This will be a brutal, bloody, take no prisoners battle. A battle for *vampires*," he added, looking directly at Layla and her lieutenant, Brian. Her reaction was exactly what he'd anticipated, but before she could finish a sharp inhalation to power her even sharper protest, he cut her off by saying, "But first, I'm going to request the assistance of our human allies in scouting the location during daylight hours before we go in. Although these images are recent—"

"Acquired how?" Layla interrupted to ask. "And from whom?"

He regarded her for a long moment, not accustomed to being interrupted. She had certain privileges as his lover, and very soon his mate, but it set a bad precedent. Although not really for anyone in *this* room, except maybe her Brian. "Friends," he said finally, answering her question. "*Reliable* friends who own a fleet of drones for commercial purposes, and who are willing to turn them to *our* purposes instead."

He raised a questioning eyebrow in her direction, which she returned with an unapologetic shrug, before he continued. "As I said, these images are very recent, but they are prior to Sakal's recent escape and return to the estate." He paused. "Layla? Brian? Can we count on your assistance?"

She seemed surprised at his question. "Yes, of course. After yesterday, we all want that asshole dead. What do you need from us?"

He eyed her with some amusement, though strove to keep it off his face. She deserved respect as a military leader, just as much as he did. "Scouting. Before finalizing our attack plans, I want the latest information on defenses and troop placement, including vampires. Your people should be able to catch the first vampire movements as evening settles, and before we can get there. There are also human guards for daylight security, which you can see in the footage. I expect they'll fight for him, night or day."

"What of the sorcerer's magic, my lord?" Xavier wasn't surprised when Chuy asked the question. After all, he'd been with Xavier earlier when they'd both almost died as a direct result of Sakal's magic.

"I am, luckily, immune to sorcery and human magic," Xavier said, looking around the room. "I was too complacent, too certain of my facts, when we entered Sakal's lair this morning. That was my ego, my failing. It won't happen again."

Xavier paused long enough to sip from a small glass of warmed blood and wine Chuy had placed in front of him. Then he zoomed to a detailed close-up of the estate. "Layla, Brian, this is what I'd like you to do . . ."

TWO HOURS LATER, Xavier's blood hunger was a living thing inside him. He hadn't felt this way in such a long time that it had taken him a moment to reason out why he was not only hungry but could feel the edge of exhaustion creeping into his muscles. It was the fight in Sakal's lair, compounded by the sorrow of Joaquim's treachery that had drained him. What he wanted more than anything at this moment was to drag Layla to his bed and spend the rest of the night feeding and fucking. The combination would leave him fully restored and at the peak of his power for tomorrow's battle.

"Remember, gentlemen—and lady," he said, hoping it would signal the end of the meeting. "We will surround the fortress discreetly as soon as it's practical after sunset, and move as one on my command. Rules of engagement . . . we spare any humans who do not threaten our fighters, whether they were previously combatants or not. We're not in the business of slaughtering humans. That said, if they *do* threaten our people, they will be killed. And, of course, every vampire is fair game." He looked around, careful to meet the gaze of every person at the table. "Questions?"

When no one spoke up—much to his relief—he said, "Departures will commence by helicopter at one hour past sunset for my vampires. Layla, if you'll provide"—he stopped before he could speak Joaquim's name—"Chuy with your preferred departure time and any equipment you'll need, he'll arrange for a helicopter and a human pilot to be ready for you. Once sunset is past, all pilots will be vampire. For now, all of you should find what rest you can. The next time we meet, it will be war."

As the others stood, gathering papers or electronic devices, he said, "Layla?"

She gave him a private half-smile and said something quietly to Brian, who glanced at Xavier, then nodded his agreement and left. She strolled over to join him as Chuy followed the others out of the room and closed the door, leaving the two of them alone.

First, there was one more piece of battle planning that he needed to bring up with Layla. Looking down at her, his hands on her arms holding her body away from his so he wouldn't be tempted before he'd made a final request, he said, "I didn't want to say this in front of the others, since I'm not sure how many are aware, but I wanted to ask you something. You mentioned your Kerry has some magical sensitivity."

"She does."

"I'd like her to use whatever skill she has to detect any magical defenses Sakal will have deployed over the estate. He's not powerful enough to cast an overall defensive shield—"

"What about the shield that kept you trapped in his lair? Wasn't that a defensive shield?"

"No. First, it was a contained space, especially compared to an entire estate. And it was also indoors, which is more defined and easier to control, or at least that's how magic works in my experience. I'm also told by those who understand such things that few sorcerers are capable of casting several spells at once and Sakal isn't one of them. And before you ask, he must have been preparing his ambush for me for a long time."

"Okay. What if he waits until the battle starts tomorrow night to cast any spells?"

"He won't. Again, he can't cast several at once, so unless he is planning to use all of his power on a single trap—which is a risky proposition in war, as you well know—he'll be working tonight to lay as many spells as he can. His people escaped with him just before sunrise, which means he slept through the entire day, so he should be fully rested."

"All right. I'll brief Kerry before we leave, which should be midday. We'll want to assess the situation before we move in. But now . . ." She went up on her toes and kissed him. "It's time for *you* to rest and replenish."

He gripped her arms and, pulling her up to her toes, sank into the kiss. Her lips were so soft, her mouth so warm as his tongue stroked along hers, until desire had his fangs pressing against his gums for release, and he had to lift his mouth lest he slice the delicate skin of her lips. Because once he tasted her blood, even a single drop, he wouldn't stop. She'd be naked and spread out on the conference table in seconds. Unable to forego the taste of her altogether, he kissed her neck, her throat, while she spread her hands through his hair and wrapped her arms around his neck.

He pulled back, wanting her breasts in his mouth, and ready to rip apart the long-sleeved T-shirt she wore, until a voice from the hall outside the closed door reminded him this wasn't his office. He stopped and set her on her feet, then took her hand, opened the door to the hallway, and tugged her back to his office. He didn't stop there, but walked through the office to his bedroom, and farther, crossed to where a thick tapestry hung on the wall. Reaching behind it, he keyed in a ten-digit code, followed by his thumbprint on the reader.

Layla uttered a surprised, "Oh!" when the wall split along a previously invisible seam to reveal a set of stairs going downward.

Xavier pulled her in behind him, scanned his entire hand to close the door, then led her down two flights of stairs to yet another door, which opened to a second scan of his hand and a ten-digit code. *That* door opened in turn to reveal a short, silent, and dimly lit hallway that went nowhere, except to his private vault. One more biometric scan, this one of his eye and five fingers together, and he was pulling her inside before the door had finished its slow swing open. Still holding her hand, he shoved the heavy door shut, locked it with the same double scan he'd used to open it, and then turned to study her.

AS SOFT LIGHT slowly filled the room, Layla realized they were standing in another bedroom. A much *bigger* bedroom than the one upstairs, with a huge bed and very little else in the way of furniture. She'd had no idea that this place even existed. Hell, that this *level* even existed. She turned back to Xavier, to ask him about it, but found him studying her with the utterly focused gaze of a predator who'd just caught himself a tasty rabbit.

As if reading her thoughts, his lips curved into a lazy smile, while his eyes filled with a muted silver light, as if reflecting the gleam from another source. She didn't have to look around to know there *was* no other silver light, that this was a physical manifestation of Xavier's power, unique to him alone.

"I've never seen you really use your power, before today, with the door," she said, realizing it was true. Oh, there'd been the telepathy he used as casually as if everyone possessed the talent, and she knew he could heal horrible, even fatal wounds on others as well as himself. But she'd never witnessed an *explosion* of his vampire magic, never seen him—what the hell—never seen him stop a train, for example. Or anything equally dramatic and impossible. And yet, when they were close, when he was relaxed the way he was now, she could feel his power simmering just below the surface, like a static electric charge on her skin that was so strong it actually made the hair on her arms stand up.

"Most people don't *want* to see me use my power. They don't want to risk the chance that I'd be using it against *them*."

She closed the few inches of space between them, until she could slide her arms around his waist. "But I'm not most people, am I?"

He gripped her upper arms and yanked her even closer, until her breasts were crushed against his chest, her thighs pressed against his, and . . . . "Oh fuck," she whispered, as the bulge of his straining cock pushed right between her thighs.

"I can feel your heat," he murmured back to her, his breath warm, as his tongue explored the curve of her ear, dropped to nibble at the earlobe, and then farther yet as he sucked the skin of her neck and throat hard enough to leave a trail of bruises, before sliding his fingers under the fabric of her T-shirt and shoving it aside so he could kiss her bare shoulder. She was still shivering under the sensual onslaught when he gripped the hem of the shirt with both hands and stripped it off over her head so fast that by the time she registered what he was doing, he had the front closure of her sports bra open, and was pushing it off her shoulders, until she was bared to his gaze.

"Xavier," she said in what she meant to be a protest. She was sure it started out that way. But when he ripped off his own shirt to crush her against his gorgeously naked chest, she could only hum with pleasure at the delicious sensation of her soft breasts against hard male muscle, puckered nipples scraping the thatch of dark wiry hair that thinned to a narrow trail before disappearing into a pair of black, low-slung jeans that barely managed to hang on his hips and showed off the tight oblique V that seemed to point directly at his bulging cock.

"Layla," he breathed against her skin before his teeth closed over the delicate arch of her clavicle, hard enough to break skin.

Years of fighting had warning bells going off in her head, telling her that he could snap her fragile bones with a single bite. That with his strength, he wouldn't even have to put much effort into it. She silenced the damn bells without a care. If she knew one thing in this world, it was that Xavier would never hurt her. Not physically. Her heart though . . . .

The pain when he'd broken her young heart ten years ago was nothing compared to what he could do now, in this moment, this time they had together. But despite knowing that, she couldn't make herself step away, couldn't ask him to stop, to let her go.

It was too late. She'd lost any chance she'd ever had of walking away when she hadn't caught a plane and gotten the hell out of Barcelona after that first night. She tipped her head forward and licked the salt from his chest, detecting the very slight tang of iron that flavored his sweat. *Did it mix with his tears, too?* she wondered. She'd never seen Xavier cry, so she didn't know.

Opening her mouth, she pressed her lips to his skin, swirling her tongue in sensuous circles as she kissed her way to a nipple, closing her teeth over the tight male nub until she heard him hiss in pain, then moved to the other nipple and did the same. When she reached for his belt and began unbuckling, his big hands cupped her ass and once more ground the hard bulge of his erection right into the triangle between her thighs.

She gasped at the rush of wet heat that responded, cheeks blossoming when Xavier made an appreciative sound as the scent of her arousal rolled between them so strongly that even she could detect it.

Finally managing to undo his belt, she slipped the metal button open, dropped the zipper, and with her own groan of pleasure matching his, slid her hand into the opening and curled her fingers around his thick cock. Freeing his full length at last, she began working her fist up and down as she dropped to her knees on the deep carpet.

Xavier gripped her head, stopping her. "I'm very hungry, *cariño*. I won't last long if you do that."

She stroked her tongue along the vein on the underside of his erection, then slicked her tongue around the tip, while looking up with challenge in her gaze. The pewter shine of his eyes was no longer a reflection. They shone a deep gray silver when he stared down at her. She smiled, then brushed her wet mouth around his tip. "Then I'll just have to get you hard all over again."

"Fuck. Me," Xavier groaned when she sucked his full length into a slow slide between her lips and down her throat, then lifted her head and did it all over again. His fingers tore at her hair, twisting and tugging as she moved back and forth. It hurt. But the pain only magnified the utter wantonness of sucking his cock, of bathing it in warmth as she salivated with her own frantic hunger. And all the while Xavier groaned above her, the muscles of his abdomen and thighs turning to steel under her hands, against her cheeks.

A sudden snarl razored into the air like the cry of a wild beast when he came, his climax shooting down her throat as she swallowed over and over, his powerful hands pressing her against his groin while she gasped for breath. As if suddenly realizing what he was doing, he released his hold on her head and dropped to his knees next to her.

"Layla," he murmured, running his hands over her shoulders, her back as she drew long draughts of air. "*Cariño.*" He sounded worried now, head bent as he stroked her hair away and tried to see her face.

She coughed, then lifted her head and gave him a crooked smile. "You're even bigger than I thought."

"Fuck," he breathed and hauled her into his arms, stood effortlessly, and carried her to the bed.

Layla dug fingers into his shoulders, worried that he would drop her. She guessed that he had to be accustomed to having much daintier women in his bedroom, in his fucking huge bed. Still, she was proud of her body—she was strong and fit. But she was tall, and her strength came with muscles that weighed a lot.

But he didn't falter in the least. He strolled to the bed as if she was no heavier than a fresh blanket and laid her against the pillows with care, like a piece of fine porcelain. For some reason, more than anything he'd said or done, that bit of tenderness, of concern, hit her hard. Her heart literally ached with love, with longing. And when she glanced up and met his gaze, she found him watching her with the same emotion in his eyes.

"Xavier, I . . . " she whispered. She didn't know what she might have said next because he turned away, breaking eye contact when he reached for a decanter on the bedside table.

"You need to drink something," he said, as he poured some red liquid into a glass and offered it to her.

She *did* want something to soothe her throat, if nothing else, but when she took the glass, she eyed the red stuff suspiciously, and sniffed. "What is it?"

He laughed. "Wine. Nothing else. Do you think I'm trying to seduce you into vampirism with a taste of blood?" He took the glass from her, drank, then leaned over to kiss her.

His lips were wet with what she thought was a very nice Cabernet, although she was no wine expert. She did note that she'd never tasted a more delicious wine, coming as it did from Xavier's lips to hers. She slid her arms over his shoulders to circle his neck, to hold him close and prolong the kiss. He could have broken the hold if he'd wanted, but he just kept seducing her with slow, languorous kisses that told her they had all the time in the world to explore each other's bodies, to kiss and lick, to suck and bite every inch.

The wine glass hit the side table with a solid thump when the kiss grew more passionate, less patient. He slid onto the bed and stretched out on top of her, caging her between powerful arms, bracing his elbows on either side of her head while he slung a heavy leg between hers, his knee bent to rub right up against her pussy. Heat flooded her cheeks again when his knee encountered the wetness between her thighs, the slick juices drenching her pussy and soaking right through her pants.

"You're so wet," he whispered hoarsely. "So damn hot and wet."

"I can—"

He pressed his weight on her when she would have rolled over to do ... something. Take off her pants? Visit the bathroom? Clean up the evidence of just how much she wanted him?

"You're going nowhere," he growled, his expression fierce as he glared down at her.

She should have been terrified. His eyes were like twin spotlights, lighting not just his face, but her and half the bedroom. His fangs ... well, hell, his fangs were just *there*, gleaming white and deadly sharp where they pressed into his lower lip. And he looked like he wanted to devour her.

He stripped off her pants and panties with brisk efficiency. Nothing sexy or sensuous, her clothes were an obstacle to be gotten rid of and tossed aside. He studied her for a long moment, as if deciding which tasty morsel to sample next, then dipped his head to her neck, his breath hot and wet against her skin when he inhaled deep and slow. She waited for his bite. He'd bitten her before. She knew now what to expect and braced for the sharp pain ... that didn't come. Instead, he kissed her throat gently and glided his tongue in a slow, carnal path from her neck to her shoulders, her breasts. He paused there to suck one nipple—long pulls of his lips that had the soft tip becoming a hard, aching pearl, her back bowing with need when he sucked even more of the tender flesh into his mouth.

The bite was a shock. His fangs pierced the soft mound around her nipple, going deep enough to cause another spike of pain before something in his saliva sent a rush of heat into her veins, and pleasure stormed through every inch of her body, spreading downward to tighten her groin and stab between her thighs. Lust unfolded in its wake, and a ferocious craving filled her body when he took her other nipple, her other breast into his mouth, between his teeth, and bit.

She cried out, and her hips lifted off the bed searching for something to soothe the desperate need, the terrible emptiness between her thighs, something to release her from the scorching heat in his bite that left her hanging on the edge of climax. She didn't know if she wanted the pleasure to go on forever, or if she wanted him inside her, filling the emptiness, soothing this fierce longing that felt so good, but wasn't ... *him*. She needed his cock.

"Xavier," she cried. "Now, damn it."

He lifted his head from her breasts and glared at her, his fangs bared and gleaming while a terrifying growl rumbled from his throat and nearly stopped her heart. She stared, unable to look away, frozen in something very close to fear. He snapped his teeth at her in a show of dominance, and then with his eyes still locked on hers, still holding her in thrall, slammed his cock balls deep inside her.

She groaned helplessly as the first orgasm tore through her body, stoking the flame of her already scorched nerves, shocking every muscle with an ecstasy that she'd never known before. She clutched his arms, her short nails digging into his flesh when he pounded right through the first convulsive clench of her inner muscles, when he shoved his hands under her ass and *fucked* her. No mercy, no caution. But then, she didn't want any. She was tired of men who treated her as some fragile little thing. She wanted him to be wild and out of control. To drive into her body with all the strength and passion of the powerful creature he was. Vampire lord. Xavier. Hers.

Her orgasm was so unexpected, so stunning in its ferocity that she could only scream as her body writhed beneath his, while euphoria shot like a knife blade from her clit to her clenching womb, to her breasts, and finally to her brain. The last thing she remembered before her thoughts became a snowstorm of static was Xavier's deep voice against her ear rasping, "I love you."

She woke with his cock sliding lazily along the swollen lips of her pussy while she shivered in desire, as desperate for him as if he hadn't just knocked her into an orgasmic bliss a few . . . Well, hell, she didn't know *how* long ago it had been, and right now, she didn't care. She could barely feel her legs where they stretched around his hips, but she didn't care about that either. She *could* feel the hard pebbles of her nipples grinding against his chest. Could feel his *very* hard erection teasing her as it glided through the creamy warmth of her climax, tantalizingly close to her pussy. But what she *needed* was him *inside* her.

They kissed, their mouths as voracious as if it had been days or weeks, not however long it had been. His fangs were still out. She could tell by the blood flavoring the kiss, the slight sting of her lip where he'd cut her. His snarl rumbled down her throat this time, before he lifted his head enough to lick the blood from her lip, then stare down at her with those mesmerizing eyes.

"I need you," he murmured.

"You have me," she breathed, not quite sure what he meant. They were as close as two human beings could get.

"I need more." His gaze penetrated hers, as if willing her to understand what he was saying. "Say yes, Layla."

Realization struck. "Yes," she said fervently. "My God, Xavier. Yes, always!"

His eyes shut briefly as if in relief, and when they opened again there was nothing of the man looking down at her. This was Lord Xavier, the eminent vampire who had lived centuries and ruled thousands.

"Yes," she whispered again. "I want you, too."

He didn't rush, didn't shove his mouth under her chin, his fangs into her vein. He seduced her all over again with soft, lingering kisses against her throat and down to her breasts. With fingers that pinched tender nipples just enough to spark new thrills of desire skating over her body, before he kissed his way back up to her neck.

He tasted her first, with long sweeps of his tongue that had her blood pumping so hard, she could hear it pulsing in her ear. She speared fingers through his thick, dark hair—so soft and silky for such a fierce and deadly vampire.

He chose that moment to strike, giving no warning as his fangs sliced through her skin and pierced her vein. She whimpered as the first tendrils of heat licked into her blood, bringing that same exquisite pleasure that spread like flames through her body. Her breasts seemed to swell under the onslaught, sore nipples throbbing as they stiffened into firm peaks of lust, while a fervent need filled her womb and tightened her clit into a hard bundle of nerves that begged for his touch.

Xavier's mouth stretched her neck where the skin had been sliced, every sucking pull on her vein like a tug on her breasts, a stroke through her pussy, pleasure coursing through her in great swirls of longing. His hand caressed the length of her body, starting at her shoulders, lingering over her breasts, playing down her belly before flattening over her groin as one thick finger slipped between the lips of her pussy and with no warning, crushed the taut, throbbing nub of her clit.

Her torso came off the bed despite his fangs in her neck and his full weight pressing her down. She wrapped her legs around his hips and thrust upward, rubbing herself against his stone hard penis, while she drowned in waves of climax. She wanted him *inside* her, *needed* the relief of being filled by his cock, by the searing heat of his orgasm.

Xavier lifted his head with an unrestrained howl, his fangs dragging from her vein as he flexed his hips and drove into her with all the ferocity she'd longed for. He slammed into her once, twice, and then they were coming together in a fury of frenzied hunger, and a wild and passionate love.

Chapter Seventeen

LAYLA WAS SPRAWLED over Xavier's body when she woke. The room was pitch black around them, but she knew it was still nighttime because Xavier's eyes opened as soon as she sat up. Every part of her body ached when she leaned down to kiss him, and the sharp pain between her thighs reminded her that the (cough, cough) *delicate* parts of her anatomy had gotten more exercise than they'd had in years. *Ow.*

"I have to shower and get over to the barracks. I have to review the data and brief my team before we head out. And I'll want to talk to the helo pilot, too."

When he didn't say anything, she studied him a minute, *needing* to know the answer to a very specific question, but not sure she *wanted* it.

"What is it? What's troubling you?"

She bit the inside of her lip, then went for it. "Does Sakal have the power to kill you? *Could* he have killed you if he'd caught you unaware in that ambush?"

Pulling her into his arms, he kissed her forehead, and murmured her name. "Layla, *cariño*. No. I am immune to magic, and Sakal knows it. That is why his trap was designed to hold me there until the sun rose. Had I not escaped, had you not assisted with that escape, the *sun* would have destroyed me. But I will not make that same mistake again. In any event, the sun will not be a factor in the battle tomorrow night. And I remain immune to magic."

A new thought occurred to her. "Does Sakal know you *didn't* die?"

"I have to assume he does. He has plenty of human acolytes or other minions who would have reported to him."

"Which means he'll be expecting you to attack."

"Unless he's a total fool, yes. He may expect the French vampire lord to present some resistance, but I don't believe he'll trust a vampire, not even his own territorial lord, to protect him. I fully anticipate a vigorous defense on his part. Which is why I'm sending you and your team in to reconnoiter before we launch. That said, you are officially under orders to return to me unscathed."

Layla tipped her head from side to side. "I'll do my best, believe me. But that goes both ways, dude. If you're wrong about him, and he kills you, I'm going to be pissed as hell."

He chuckled. "When I die, it will not be at the hands of that fool. He's been begging to die by my hand since he murdered my Sire. But if I do die, I will at least go to my death knowing that my warrior mate will avenge me."

Her chest tightened with grief at the mere possibility of his death. How much worse would it be if that happened? "That's not funny," she insisted, her throat clogged with tears she wouldn't let him see.

He sat up and wrapped his arms around her, holding her tightly against his chest. "I didn't think it was. Having you by my side is a gift that I will defend with every shred of power I possess. I want lifetimes with you, and no sorcerer is going to take that away."

His words released the tears she'd been holding back. Not wanting him to see, she hid her face against his shoulder and fought for control. Her face was wet when she leaned back to look up at him, but she spoke lightly, needing to break through the weight of emotion surrounding them like a shroud. "Then I'll just have to make sure you don't die." She forced a smile.

"No, *cariño*. You make sure *you* don't die. I can take care of myself."

LAYLA THOUGHT of those words several hours later while sitting in the luxurious helo that had been sent to transport her team over the border into France. She wondered if Xavier knew how impossible it was for her to obey his command, even if she'd been inclined to do so. He'd gotten under her skin so deeply that she suspected he'd always been there, just waiting for her to grow up and return to claim him. *Sneaky bastard*. She sighed. He was that for sure, but he was *her* sneaky bastard and no one would be permitted to touch him if she could help it.

"Not our usual transport," Brian said, sliding the various maps and images of Sakal's estate back into the pack at his feet. They'd spent most of the trip checking and re-checking the plans they'd worked up for the coming recon operation. "Traveling with the boss's girlfriend has its perks."

"Ha ha. The pilot said Xavier only has two helos, and the other one is a Sikorsky transport. The vamps will be using that one later. It's too big for just the four us."

"Hey, I'm not complaining."

She wasn't going to complain either. Her team, together or separately, had ridden in a lot of helicopters over the years, but she could guarantee that none of those helos had been like this one. Apart from the seats, this thing was so soundproofed that they didn't even need headphones to talk to each other. She'd bet there had never before been weapons and well-used backpacks stacked next to the dusty boots using up all that nice leg room, either.

When the helo swept over the retail hub of Andorra la Vella, she glanced out the window for the first time. There'd been some pretty spectacular views during the flight through the Pyrenees, but this was mostly curiosity that a major shopping hub would be located in the mountains between the two countries. This was the only city, in fact, in the Principality of Andorra, which was under the joint sovereignty of Spain and France. Not easy to reach, but apparently profitable.

She turned away when the helo settled onto a bare stretch of land across the French border from the principality. This wasn't a sightseeing trip, and pretending it was would only jar her out of her combat ready mindset and cost lives—hers or someone else's. And luxury be damned, there was still the usual wash of air and dust when they finally settled to the ground.

Her team knew the routine. The door might have glided open silently, but they still ended up hunched over and hustling, heads down, toward the lone terminal of the small building that served as office and terminal both.

They were all equipped for recon, which meant no weapons beyond what they could run with. Their mission was to scope out the enemy's estate, to take pictures and write notes, not fight a battle. But that didn't mean they *couldn't*, or wouldn't. They were hunting intel, but their briefing materials had been very clear on one point. Sakal had plenty of human troops who were expected to be on full alert after his narrow escape the previous morning. They *knew* Xavier was coming, and odds were they had human spies of their own, either within the *Fortalesa* or down in the town, who could easily climb the hill to see and report everything that happened, including her small team of fighters boarding a helicopter.

Fortunately, Layla and her team were very good at what they did. She'd put them against Sakal's daylight guard any day of the week. Some of his were no doubt former military, but that didn't compare to her team, who'd been fighting in the jungles and deserts of the world just a few months ago. Frankly, the only real question was whether Sakal had any vampire fighters at all. Knowing he'd eventually have to go up against one vampire or another, it might be assumed he did. But the sorcerer hated vampires so badly, hated what he'd become as a vampire, that they hadn't been confident he would employ any in his own defense. Also, given his personal weakness as a vampire, he couldn't secure the loyalty of any vampire fighters he employed. At least not as a vampire. As a sorcerer . . . well, that was a different matter.

Either way, her team was charged up at the idea of entering into real combat after so many months in the vineyard.

A dark-suited bureaucrat met them inside the terminal. He confirmed her ID, saying only, "Captain Casales?"

When she nodded, he gestured for them to follow, and they did. This speedy transition was only acceptable because he'd been provided with photo IDs of both her and Brian, and she'd been given the same on him. He was one of Xavier's retainers, someone the vampire lord used whenever he or any of his people needed to slip into France, which apparently happened more often than anyone in that country was aware of.

Moving quickly through the small terminal and out to the parking lot, the man led them to a big black SUV in a model only available through private vendors in most of Europe. That didn't mean they weren't common, however, since they were the vehicle of choice around the world for criminals and the law-abiding rich who wanted to be perceived as criminals.

Brian took the keys, thanked the black-suited man, and that was it. The man strode back to the terminal and the team loaded up. Brian drove, with Layla riding shotgun, while Kerry and Riv sat in back. Continuing on by helicopter would have been faster, but while Sakal's estate was large, the area was still populated, and there was nowhere for them to land without being observed, especially in the middle of the day.

They stopped a mile away from Sakal's estate in the parking lot of a trailhead that branched into a few different hiking trails. Their vehicle wasn't typical, but there were enough passenger vans and busses that it didn't stand out any more than the four of them did when they headed down the trail with heavy backpacks, dressed for hiking. The day was warm, but it was midweek, which limited even further the number of possible witnesses.

Keeping to the tougher trails, and taking advantage of various ground dips and swells, they made their way without any interruption, other than the occasional barking dog, until they stood eyeing the sorcerer's estate. The several buildings sat on a slightly elevated rise, and were surrounded by a ten foot wall. It had been designed to mimic an aristocratic estate of old, or maybe it had begun its life that way and Sakal had merely upgraded. The question hadn't been in their briefing. The wall was constructed of irregular pieces and shapes of rock which, while attractive and in keeping with the design, was also much easier to scale. So, bonus for them.

Based on drone photographs and existing maps, they'd chosen to enter on the back side of the wall directly opposite the gate, which would give them a better view of interior operations. All four went over the wall with ridiculous ease, paused to exchange rapid hand signals, and then broke into two teams and headed off. Each team would cover half the estate, then return to the same point for withdrawal along the same route to their vehicle. Depending on the remaining time, they would copter back with their report, or if it took longer than anticipated, they would transmit digital copies of all data and maps they'd generated about the enemy estate.

Layla had specifically chosen Kerry to partner with, since their half of the estate included the main courtyard in front of a building which Xavier had been convinced did, in fact, house vampires. One of the conclusions from the previous night's discussions had been that Sakal, as the narcissistic and cowardly person he was, would want to ensure his own safety. And the best way to do that at night was to employ the best vampire fighters he could afford, since money was the only way he had to secure them in his defense. He was very likely, therefore, to exert the most effort to safeguard the courtyard closest to his own quarters. As Layla had told Xavier, there was no guarantee that Kerry had enough magical sensitivity to sense Sakal's sorcery at work, but it was worth a try. And if they found something, they could always notify the other team to look for identical or at least similar constructs. The two teams had their usual comm units, and had long ago worked out a shorthand version of clicks to convey most types of urgent messages. But if necessary, they could conduct careful and low-voiced conversations.

As they left Brian and Riv, the two women kept a close eye out for any daytime troops, scanning windows and roofs as well as any ground units. Daylight guards on vampire estates were typically more concerned with criminals and snoops, rather than armed invaders, but whatever the routine, Sakal would want to cover his ass against human intervention. The vampire quarters on Sakal's estate, as with most wealthy vampires, would be in an underground vault, much like Xavier's. The risk of human invaders penetrating such a vault was very small, especially in anything less than several hours. Therefore, while daylight security was generally strong, it didn't normally have to be strong enough repel a vampire's usual enemies, which in this day and age were other vampires. It was always possible that one or more of the guards on an estate could betray their vampire master and admit human intruders, as had in fact happened to Lord Raphael in California some years ago. But by all accounts, Sakal was more worried about daytime attacks, than those that might occur at night.

This was curious enough that Xavier remarked on it, but she already knew that Sakal acted more human than vampire. By far. He no doubt even saw himself that way. He so hated vampires and what he'd become under their tutelage that he simply pretended not to be one of them.

The two female fighters began their rounds, watching for anything, believing the greatest danger would be on the grounds, not on the short slope just below the surrounding wall. The slope had undoubtedly been intended to add a measure of difficulty should anyone attempt to scale the high wall. But that precaution had ultimately been ignored in favor of aesthetics, leaving the slope covered in medium-sized fruit trees, which provided excellent cover for anyone wanting to navigate the edges of the estate without being seen.

They stopped several times to snap photos of larger defensive sites, including camouflaged and surprisingly heavy gun placements, that hadn't shown up on the photos Xavier had shown them. If Sakal's soldiers let go with some of the heavier weapons, they could inflict serious casualties among even vampire attackers. Vampires were tough, but not invincible. Knowing about the weapons in advance, they could take them out before the real battle ever got started. Camouflage protected the placements from aerial reconnaissance, so it was possible Sakal hadn't considered their vulnerability to early targeting. Layla added it to her notes, then agreed with Kerry that they should search for ground-to-air placements next. The weapons would draw unwanted attention to the estate if they were ever used, but maybe Sakal considered his location sufficiently remote to favor security over practicality. Or maybe his plan was simply to abandon the estate, and its protectors, if the situation proved too dangerous to him personally.

They also noted guard routines, building entry points including whether they were guarded, barrack locations, and manned outposts, along with anything else that caught their eye. One of those eyecatchers, which they paused to study for some time, was what appeared to be two identical ammo dumps, watched over by two stationary armed guards each, but fortified with nothing more than sandbags. That wouldn't have been remarkable on a movable or temporary battlefield, when speed was of the essence, but on a permanent estate like this? Why wouldn't he have covered the ammo ditches with concrete bunkers?

Signaling Kerry to crawl to better cover, Layla did the same and huddled close enough to tap her head and whisper, "You getting anything?"

Kerry shook her head in the negative.

"We have to get closer, then."

Kerry shrugged and whispered, "Might help," and pointed at herself.

Layla understood that getting closer would not only let them get a better look, but would also give Kerry's magic a better shot at working. But such a move was arguably beyond the game plan they'd agreed on for this recon. Armed with compact but very high-powered binoculars and cameras, and with the high ground and all four quadrants covered, there was no reason to risk capture or worse for the sake of fixed details that they could ID from the satellite photos.

On the other hand, she and Kerry were already there. Wouldn't it be good to know if they were magical installations? What if they were more of Sakal's multi-layered traps, like the one he'd used against Xavier in Barcelona, but this time, designed to isolate large numbers of Xavier's fighters?

She'd already decided to do it, but spent several minutes arguing with herself, trying to find a flaw in her logic. Nothing came to her, however, so she signaled Kerry to move higher, under better cover. She wanted to reach out via comm to make Brian and the others aware of the situation, so they'd know where to look if something untoward happened to them.

She first signaled to Brian using mic clicks that they needed to talk and she was in a secure location—secure being relative in the situation. It took more than a few minutes, but Brian eventually voice-commed back.

"Problem?" he said before Layla had a chance to speak.

"Negative. A tactical adjustment. We need to take a closer look. Security status is doable."

"Is it worth it?"

"That's a roger."

"Shit," he said so softly that all she heard was the hissed "sh."

"Time?"

"Now. One hour estimated, start to finish," she said. She considered that to be the high end of what they'd need to complete the task, but didn't want the rest of the team to worry if they were late coming in.

"We're two zero mikes from your position," he said, indicating they were twenty minutes away. "I'm coming to you. Send Kerry in exchange."

"Negative. I need Kerry."

"Then you make the exchange."

"Negative." She didn't offer a reason, didn't fucking need one. She *knew* why he wanted her out of the danger zone, and it wasn't because they were friends. The whole team were friends. No, this was because if anything happened to her, Brian thought Xavier would go ballistic and maybe get a lot more of them killed. But if she thought that was true, she never would have come in the first place.

The silence on his end said he didn't like it, but knew she was right. "Roger that. We'll hold here until you're both out."

"Roger that." She'd give him that much, since it made tactical sense. "Out."

Layla turned the volume on her comm down to what she considered the "click" range, pushed the mic aside, then leaned close to Kerry. "That one," she whispered, pointing to the nearest of the strange ammo dumps. Maintaining their hidden location for the time being, she scanned for the most discreet path downward in terms of likely cover, considered what they'd seen of the relevant guard patrol, and finally decided on the best route which would avoid detection by both stationary and patrol guards.

By mutual agreement, she and Kerry waited until the current pair of patrol guards passed each other down below. Then with Layla in the lead, they began a cautious but steady descent that would bring them close enough to the curious site, while avoiding notice by the stationary guards.

It went better than she'd hoped, aided by the stationary guards who'd gotten bored enough to exchange a short conversation just in time to provide a convenient distraction. Layla reached for her camera just as Kerry tapped her leg. Jerking her head around, she saw Kerry gesture at her head and nod emphatically.

Magic. Damn it. She hadn't wanted to be right.

They were far too close to risk a voice comm, so they waited again until the patrol guards crossed each other's paths, wasted a few seconds wishing the stationary guards would get chatty again, then Layla gave the signal and they did a literal slow crawl back up to the safest hiding spot available, just short of the wall, where she called Brian one more time.

Brian and River were together, which saved some time. They both confirmed identification of the same type of installation. But while they'd questioned the battlefield experience of whoever had approved the design, they'd hadn't considered magic, and had no Kerry to sniff it out, in any case.

"We should take these out now, while they're still inactive. By the time our vamps arrive, Sakal could have activated them, and it'll be too late."

"Any way of accessing what we're dealing with?" Brian asked. "Are these things even worth the effort, much the less the risk we'll be taking by trying to neutralize them?"

Kerry shook her head. "I can't say. This is beyond me. It could be anything."

"The presence of guards says something about its importance to Sakal. We know that much. Anything important to him should be important to us."

"If we do this, how will we do it? What's the best way to blow up magic, without getting blown up along with it?"

"Just that, I'd think," Layla said, though she didn't know for sure. "Blow the fuckers to kingdom come, disrupt the spell or whatever, right?" She looked again to Kerry for an answer.

Her response was another shrug. "We're well outside my expertise here. I do know that spells can be disrupted by changing their physical elements, which would seem to apply here, but . . . " She shook her head. "I can't say for sure."

"Brian?" Layla asked. As much as she believed her assessment was right, it had to be unanimous. There were too many unknowns to permit one person's judgment to carry the day.

"I don't like it," he said. "But I like leaving it there even less. I say we go."

"I say what the bloody fuck are we doing here?" River grouched. "But yeah, we go."

Layla checked with Kerry, who added a simple, "Agreed."

"All right. We go in, and we get out. Rendezvous at our entry point. We wait no more than twenty, that's two oh mikes. If either team doesn't show by then, the other gets out and reports. Agreed?"

They agreed one at a time, until Layla said, "Let's blow some shit up. Out." She disconnected, adjusted her volume, and turned to Kerry.

Putting their heads together, the two women calculated their explosives supply and quickly decided on a plan. Ideally, all four dumps would blow at once, or at least within a minute or two of each other. But they couldn't guarantee that, didn't have the communications or the gear to time something that precisely. The best they could do was time their own two sites to blow more-or-less simultaneously, and hope the guys took roughly the same amount of time to set and blow theirs.

For Layla and Kerry, that meant splitting up and hitting one site each, which was far from ideal, but neither was carrying any timers, mainly because they didn't carry anything that could be triggered by one. The only explosives they carried were grenades, and the sites were too far apart to hit one, then run to the other without breaking cover and giving themselves away.

"All right," Layla said before they crept out of hiding again. "We stay together as long as these trees last, then split apart to reach each of our targets. I've got four grenades. You?"

Kerry agreed, holding up four fingers.

"Good. We toss three, arm and toss one, then get the hell out. Rendezvous at this point," she said, pointing her finger downward to indicate the spot where they were currently hunched down.

Kerry held up ten fingers, but Layla grimaced. Ten minutes could be an eternity on the battlefield. And once the first grenades went off, that's exactly what the estate would become. She held up seven fingers in a compromise. Kerry shrugged, but nodded her agreement.

They adjusted the heavy packs on their backs, made sure everything that needed to be reachable, was, and the rest was secure, then bumped fists and started down.

The first part of the descent was uneventful. The trees provided excellent cover and she and Kerry both wore clothes that had been selected to blend in to the expected terrain. When they reached the split point, they bumped fists once more and set off in separate directions, Kerry to the site they were just above, while Layla continued through the tree cover to the previous quadrant, which she calculated would take her five minutes more than it would take Kerry to reach hers.

She moved as quickly as she dared, climbing a few feet higher into the trees, so she could cross the horizontal distance faster. Either no one was watching, or she did a good job of it—probably a little of both—because she was above the dump spot with two minutes to spare. The next bit would be tougher. The site where Kerry was headed had considerable dried brush on the hillside above it, and the dump itself, with its surrounding sandbags containing the boxes of guns and ammo in tight circle, had been almost flush against the hillside. The one she was headed for had the same dried brush for cover, but only halfway down the hillside. After that there were two small . . . "shacks" was too kind a word for what she was looking at. They were sagging and weather-beaten, with peeling paint and, from what she could see, no windows. She couldn't fathom what they might be used for, but wasn't willing to assume they were abandoned or harmless.

Out of long habit, she touched her various pieces of gear like a multipart talisman, and left the security of the trees behind.

The shrubs had looked the same from up above, but were somewhat different than what they'd used for cover previously. These had fucking long thorns. Hell, they were like tiny needles that clutched at her clothes and dug into any bare skin, including her fingers in their fingerless gloves. Every time one managed to hit flesh, she had to bite her cheek to prevent cursing out loud. She couldn't risk making any noise until she knew for sure what, or who, was sitting in those damn shacks.

When she reached the first one, she moved with silent steps up to the back wall and just sat there for the count of ten. She'd have preferred to wait longer, but didn't want the delay. Eyes closed, she tuned out every other sense, listened, and heard nothing. No rustle of cloth to give away movement, no breathing to indicate a sleeping occupant. Pulling her knife—a gunshot would give her and all others away—she snuck around to the front, mindful of every footfall. Then crouching low, she slipped her head around the corner, caught a quick look inside, and covered her mouth to keep from retching.

It was a dead animal—a goat from the split second look she'd managed. It wasn't just dead, it was *long* dead and appeared to have been deliberately dried. Not mummified, but skinned and dried. Was it some sort of religious thing? Or just a weird and unsanitary way of making goat jerky? Who the hell knew?

More importantly, who cared? It was dead and posed no danger to her mission. She moved on to the next shack with slightly less caution, wanting to avoid detection from below, but not expecting to find anything different.

Another dead goat discovery later, she was back to creeping through a final patch of those damn needle plants before reaching the point where she could reliably throw a live grenade and hit her target. Settling herself behind a cluster of the despised shrubs, she picked her target within the dump, slipped three grenades from her vest, cocked her arm, and hearing Kerry's double explosion, she threw the first three in rapid succession, then picked her target for the fourth and last one carefully, pulled the pin and tossed it.

By the time it exploded, she was already running up the hill, counting on the enemy's confusion after the side-by-side attacks to give her a short head start. Unfortunately, while the two guards standing right next to the magical ammo dump were taken out by the explosion, one of the two patrol guards came racing around the building and fired on her as she climbed. Ignoring the needle plants for now, she concentrated on staying low, which meant doing all but a slow creep up the hill on her belly, while still trying to vary her path to avoid a tell-tale straight line. Two more shooters joined the first as they began randomly peppering the hillside with bursts from automatic rifles.

She was forced to a stop after one round came close enough to nick her calf just above her the boot, while another came so close to her head that she'd have sworn she felt her hair move when it flew by. She lay there unmoving, trying to control her breathing, trying to hear something—anything—above the uncontrolled gunfire. When it finally stopped, it was followed by something even worse—the sound of boots crunching the damn shrubs as someone climbed the hill.

Having only a few seconds to decide what she was going to do, Layla turned on her back and aimed her pistol, prepared to kill whoever appeared, then make a run for it. Her chances of escape were slim, but there *was* a chance she could get up the hill and over the wall before someone else managed to scramble up, check on his buddy, and start after her. Of course, that was assuming the guards liked each other well enough, and/or were poorly trained enough to stop and check their wounded before continuing their pursuit.

But when a lone guard, rifle pointed downward, appeared in the sights of her weapon, she fired, then jumped up and ran.

Chapter Eighteen

XAVIER STARED at the human male standing in front of him. Brian Hudson, Layla's lieutenant and longtime friend clearly understood the magnitude of what he was saying, and was just as clearly expecting Xavier to kill him on the spot for saying it. Layla and Kerry had not returned to the rendezvous site, nor had they communicated. Brian was of the opinion that the two women, while behind enemy lines, had not been captured, but were unable to contact him or anyone else for fear of discovery.

Xavier's thoughts went immediately to the worst possibility, which was that Layla was currently being held by Sakal.

"Did you at least *attempt* a rescue?"

Hudson's back straightened, his face going tight with anger. "We waited at the insertion point, though she'd ordered us not to. The estate was swarming with human fighters and dogs, which leads me to believe they're both still running free, probably together. If we'd gone in after them, we wouldn't have found them, and we would now be dead or taken. We came back here to deliver the intel we'd acquired, and to arm up for war. Now that's done, we're going back to get them."

Xavier was every bit as furious as Hudson seemed to fear. But that fury wasn't about to burst forth in a rage of violence against this human, who like it or not, had done the smart thing, the right thing even in reporting back. He needed the intel they'd brought, especially the destruction of the suspicious sites. He also, like Hudson, believed in Layla's skill and intellect, and thought it likely that she and the other woman had evaded capture.

His rage remained unabated, but was banked carefully inside him, saved for those truly responsible for this conflict, and for any harm that might befall his mate. It was possible Sakal didn't yet understand Layla's importance to him. But they were about to find out.

He let the cold violence of his nature fill his gaze as he studied the human once more. "You will return to where"—he forced himself to speak evenly, when all he wanted to do was howl—"where Layla was last seen. You will find her location *covertly* but make no attempt at rescue. Sakal will kill her if he knows she's important to me."

"We don't leave anyone behind. Ever. I'm not going to stand around and watch while they—"

"She is not being left!" he roared.

The door flew open behind them to reveal Chuy, fangs bared and ready to do battle in response to Xavier's outburst.

"We're fine," Xavier said with constrained calm. "I'm fine. Thank you, Chuy." He waited until his lieutenant had closed the door again, then continued. "I will see to Layla's safety. If, by chance, she has been taken, she will be under a vampire guard by now. If you went in, you would most likely be killed, and Layla along with you. So you will observe and report directly to me. I know you care for her, but know this . . . She is *mine* in a way you cannot understand. I will reduce Sakal's estate to rubble and kill anyone who gets in my way in order to find her, to keep her alive." He gave a slow blink and when he stared at Hudson again, he let the human see the monster in front of him. "Do you believe me, Brian Hudson?"

To his credit, Hudson didn't shrink back from the display of power, from the uncontrolled rage in front of him. His shoulders stiffened and his head came up to meet Xavier's gaze directly. "I do, Lord Xavier. But remember this, I love her, too. We all do. Not in the same way, but she is our sister and our friend. Whatever assistance we can render, we will. I'm going to brief my man, and we'll meet you on the battlefield." He punctuated that declaration with a sharp nod, then turned on his heels and marched out of the office.

Alone, Xavier closed his eyes and followed the pull of his blood, trying to find Layla. She was alive, he knew that much. But while he detected her determination and an accelerated metabolic response to danger, he sensed no fear. He touched her through their nascent blood link, wishing he could communicate more directly. But the link wasn't strong enough yet. Not at this distance. But once he arrived in France, once he'd taken Sakal and destroyed his fucking estate stone by stone, he'd find her easily enough. And then he'd let her watch while he showed the sorcerer what happened to those who thought to take him on.

He wasted no time after that. He and his vampires loaded into the Sikorsky helicopter he'd bought from a corrupt Russian general, who'd probably stolen it from his own government. Xavier didn't care where it came from, or what might have happened to the general who'd betrayed his own people. The helicopter was his now, and it was useful.

He was silent for most of the short flight, speaking only to confirm his attack plans with Chuy. It would be a brute force, frontal assault . . . with him providing the brute force. He'd left any idea of a slow, deliberate strategy on the floor of his office when he'd learned of Layla's disappearance. And nothing anyone said would dissuade him.

The Sikorsky didn't allow for a discreet landing, as Layla's team had earlier. It set down directly in front of Sakal's estate with its closed and presumably magically reinforced gate. His vampires piled out immediately. They had their orders and would soon be swarming over a wall that might as well have been half its height for all the good it did. Humans might have been deterred, but his vampires were only amused.

As for Xavier himself, he strode to the heavy front gate, with its curlicued designs and elegant wooden crossbars, then lifted his hands, and with a single, concentrated blast of power, blew the damn thing apart.

The sound was enormous—a huge concussive blast of noise that knocked over the estate's defenders and reduced the magnificent gate to rubble. As more of his vampires charged in his wake, Xavier remained outwardly calm and utterly collected. Human fighters lay everywhere, knocked unconscious by the explosion, while all around *his* vampires fought bloody hand-to-hand battles against the vamps whom Sakal had somehow persuaded to serve him. Most likely for money and for the simple love of battle. Vampires loved violence, loved the spray of blood from their enemy. It was a truth they tried to hide from the human population, but when it came out, as it did now, it was deliciously brutal and ultimately deadly.

With teeth bared and fangs on full display, Xavier gathered a far greater kind of power and bellowed his enemy's name. "Sakal!" The sound traveled into every building and room on the estate, sliding through windows and under beds, to every ear with the ability to hear. Xavier was confident the sorcerer would appear, although knowing the vampire lord's immunity to magic, would no doubt attempt to keep his distance, while still responding to the challenge. Xavier could deal with that. His power was more vast than Sakal could know, greater even than his Sire's had been.

It took time, but he was a patient man. Well, not truly, but his own vampire warriors were slowly destroying Sakal's army, clearing a path forward. The sorcerer could either present himself or Xavier would go hunting.

The human soldiers among Sakal's defenders had already dropped their weapons and stepped to the sides, where they knelt or sat in surrender, and the remaining vampires were few and not long for this life, when there was a stir beyond the immediate zone of battle.

"The coward comes at last," he thought and wondered if the sorcerer thought he could beg for his life. If he would even try.

Slowly, his vampires, covered in blood, violence still running high within them, began to step back, to clear a path. Xavier waited until he caught his first glance of Sakal, and almost laughed. It was the sorcerer all right, but he hadn't come to challenge anyone.

"Mate of mine," Xavier called, his heart soaring at the sight of her drenched in blood with more than a few injuries, but still whole and strong enough to stand and face him. "You brought me a present."

"We found him trying to climb over the wall. He's not terribly agile, I'm afraid." With all three of her fellow warriors ranged next to her, Layla shoved the bound and gagged sorcerer forward, where he fell to his knees, his eyes furious above the several strips of wide, silverish tape that covered his mouth.

Xavier grinned when he recognized it as duct tape—the American solution for everything, it appeared. Even muffling sorcerers.

"We thought about killing him," she said conversationally. "But decided you deserved his death, since it was you, and Chuy," she added with a glance at his lieutenant, "whom he intended to kill. Although his luck *does* seem to be somewhat lacking lately."

"Yes," Xavier agreed, walking slowly closer, enjoying the sight of Sakal's terror increasing with every step.

Standing before the kneeling sorcerer, he reached down and yanked away the tape, pleased at the raw skin it left behind, the tiny drops of blood that speckled Sakal's jaw when he howled in pain.

"You have no—"

He slashed out with his own power, shredding the sorcerer's vocal cords. "I should have killed you the first night I met you in Barcelona," he growled. "I knew then what you were. But at least now I can avenge my Sire's death, and the deaths of too many others who thought you were . . . *more* than the conniving worm you've always been. Burn in hell, Ori Sakal."

Holding out a single hand, he flexed his fingers and *pulled*. Sakal managed no more than a guttural noise as his sternum cracked and ribs shattered, freeing his heart from the cage of the cowardly body that held it, until it hung suspended in the air before his horrified gaze. "Die,"

Xavier said softly, and it burst into flame.

Sakal had never been much of a vampire, but he was old enough that he fell to dust in the dirt amid the ruins of his estate, where it mingled with the remnants of the vampires who'd made the mistake of thinking they could take on a vampire lord and win.

Going immediately to Layla—who he could sense was standing only by virtue of her unbreakable will and determination—he put his arms around her.

The pain in her eyes seemed to lighten when she grinned up at him. "Sorry to mess up your grand entrance."

"I was coming to rescue you," he said in an aggrieved tone.

"Aww, maybe next time." She pulled him down for a kiss, wincing when it crushed a torn lip. "I did bring you a nice present, though."

"Thank you for the gift, *cariño*."

She laughed weakly and said, "Well, it was really from all of us." She slouched slightly, but he took her weight, so no one would notice. "I'm really tired, though. Can we go home now?"

LAYLA WAS BONE-tired by the time they returned to the *Fortalesa*. When Xavier closed his office door behind them, he swept her into his arms and carried her through the office and into the first bedroom.

"Well, Sakal's dead," she said sleepily as he opened the second door and carried her down the stairs to the bedroom in the vault. "No more morning raids with heavily armed teenagers disappearing into the woods. No more kidnapped *children*, the *fucker*. He deserved to die for that alone. Whatever happened to those kids from the farm, by the way? Did they ever show up again?"

"No. Once Sakal left Barcelona it seems they did, too. In the middle of the night, apparently, taking Sakal's brother with them, or they with him. I'm not clear on that, and don't care. They were pawns, all of them, including his brother."

"His brother is a *vampire*, though. Didn't he betray you, too?"

He shrugged. "Another weakling, but without Sakal's sorcery, not much of a threat. If you want to kill him, however, I could find him for you."

He laid her on the bed and stretched out next to her.

"Nah. Everyone's going back to their lives, I guess. Which means my team and I should be heading back to France."

He rolled until he was mostly on top of her, her head caged in his arms, as they lay face to face. "Your team, perhaps," he said flatly. "But what of you?"

"Well, I go with—" She swallowed what she'd been about to say when she saw the pain in his eyes. She'd expected anger, a furious demand, but not this terrible hurt. "No, no," she said immediately, reaching up to touch his face, to sweep away the pain and betrayal. "I'm teasing, Xavier. My team isn't going anywhere. They're having too much fun here. If you're not careful, all the rest will leave the vineyards behind and show up here, too. They're jealous that the four of us got to fight with vampires, and they didn't."

"And you?"

"Oh, you're definitely stuck with *me*, I'm afraid. I do love you, so much. But honestly, dude, I'm too tired tonight. I have a headache."

He stared silently at her for so long that it scared her for a moment, but then he laughed. "Good one. But don't do it again. We'll settle the rest of it tomorrow night."

"The rest?" she mumbled, but didn't hear his answer, because she was already asleep.

Chapter Nineteen

LAYLA WAS COLD, but she didn't want to get up. Didn't even want to open her eyes. She was feeling lazy, and hell, she'd earned a day off. But she was cold. Scowling, eyes still shut, she reached blindly for the extra blanket that was always on her bed, and found . . . Heat. Hmmm.

Stretching farther, she patted the mattress until she found the source of the heat in a length of hard thigh, and smooth warm skin. Her hand moved higher.

"If you go any farther, *cariño*, you'd better have something in mind."

She froze at the sound of that familiar voice. Only her eyes moved, popping open to find herself in an utterly dark room. She knew that voice, however. She even knew the feel of his skin against hers. She *liked* the feel of that skin rubbing all over her, as a matter of fact. So rather than pretend otherwise, she said, "I'm cold."

Xavier responded as she'd known he would, scooping her up and bringing her closer, until she was tucked up against his side, with both of his powerful arms around her. God, she loved that. Loved the feeling of a strong man pulling her across the sheets to take her in his arms. No other man had ever made her feel that way. Feminine and fragile. And she loved it. She didn't care if it made her less than liberated, or not sexually actualized or whatever other tags some people would put on it. She kicked ass everywhere else in her life. But when she was in bed with her lover, she could feel anything she damn well wanted.

"So there," she muttered.

"There what?"

She wriggled a micro-fraction closer. "I was talking to myself."

"Should I be insulted that you prefer your own conversation when I'm lying right here?"

"The conversation was very flattering to you."

"Well. I feel better then."

She slid a leg over his thigh and said, "You feel *great*."

"You said you loved me."

She frowned at the seeming non sequitur, and had to think a

moment before answering, though that hadn't been a question at all, had it? "I do love you," she said cautiously. "What's going on?"

"And I love you. Would you like to get married?"

She sat up and stared, even though she couldn't see him in the pitch black room. "I didn't know vampires got married," she replied, then pinched herself to be sure she was awake and this was really happening.

"You grew up here. How can you say that?"

"I didn't pay much attention to who was married, or who was mated, or who was shacking up. It didn't matter to me then."

"But it matters to you now?"

"Well, yeah. I know the difference now."

"How? You've never been married."

This had to be the strangest conversation she'd ever had, and that wasn't even taking into account that she was lying in bed naked, with a vampire lord, in his bedroom vault beneath an ancient stronghold, in Spain. "No," she agreed, "I've never been married, but I know people who have. So I have a fairly good idea of how it works."

"Good. So . . . you want to get married?"

"Xavier, where is this coming from?"

"I love you," he said somewhat defensively. "I was lying here thinking about that while you slept, and I realized how much I wanted you to stay. Not just in the *Fortalesa*, but here with *me*, in my *bed*. And then I thought you probably wouldn't think the mating ceremony is official enough. Certainly not grand enough. No twenty-thousand-dollar wedding gown, no flowers, no church filled with flowers, with Ferran walking you down the aisle, and all the rest. I've never actually been to a wedding—I saw most of that on television. But I know it's an important day for women."

"For some," she amended.

"Not for you?"

"No. I never saw the point."

He was silent longer than she was comfortable with. At least in this conversation. But then he sighed, his deep chest moving up and down beneath her ear, before he asked, "What *do* you want, Layla?"

"What I've always wanted," she admitted, suddenly taking the entire conversation much more seriously. "You."

"Then stay with me," he said quietly. "*Be* with me. As my mate."

It was her turn to remain silent, but not because she didn't understand what he was saying. But because she *did*. And it had tears filling her eyes all over again.

"Layla?" He shrugged his shoulder, which had the effect of lifting her face so he could see her better. Which was great for him, since she could see *jack all* in the pitch black room. "Are you crying, *cariño*? Are you unhappy?"

"No," she said softly. "I mean, yes, I'm crying, a little. But I'm happy. Happy my father will soon be back home and well, but mostly . . . happy to be here, with you. Even though I didn't believe I would be when I first came back." She propped herself on one arm and looked up to where his beautiful face had to be, knowing he could see her, which was what mattered in that moment. "And yes, I want to stay here with you. And damn it, yes. I'll be your mate."

She'd swear his heart beat a little bit faster then, when he put his arms around her and rolled, until she was completely covered by his weight and warmth. Her arms circled his neck when he kissed her. It was the kind of kiss they wrote songs about, she thought. Warm and romantic and full of emotion. Full of love. And oh damn it, she was going to cry again. She *never* cried like this. Like a *girl*. But hell, if she couldn't shed a few happy tears now, when could she? The love of her life . . . *literally*, the Love. Of. Her. Life had just asked her to be his mate. That was about as serious as vampires ever got. Mating was for permanent. It was for life. She was going to be Xavier's mate.

When the kiss ended, he licked up her tears and kissed her closed eyelids, one at a time. "*Llàgrimes de felicitate*," he murmured. Tears of happiness. "Now," he growled.

"What?"

"I want to complete our mating now."

"I don't know what that means."

He made an exasperated noise. "How can you have lived here and not know?" he repeated.

"Because no one ever asked me before," she explained, just as exasperated as he was.

"I'm a vampire, Layla. Everything we do involves blood. The mating is blood. I take yours—"

"You've already done that more than once."

"And you take mine."

"Oh. That's . . . new."

He laughed. "It's ancient."

"New to me, then. Interesting. Okay."

"Okay?"

"Yeah, okay. Let's do this. I want to get my hooks into you, so I can give the next buxom beauty who glances your way a fully justified split lip."

The noise he made this time was nothing short of preening pleasure. "You're jealous."

"Uh huh. Just like *you're* jealous of Brian."

"*Pfft*. Certainly not."

She laughed, then rolled over and turned on the bedside lamp, so she could see. If she was about to mate with the most beautiful, most brilliant, and most *deadly* man on earth, she wanted to *see* him when they did it. She sat up, which had him reaching out to cup one of her naked breasts, his thumb rubbing idly over her nipple, his gaze fixed in fascinated attention as the soft nub hardened to a firm peak under the attention.

"Lovely," he whispered, more to himself than her.

She leaned closer, going in for a kiss, but biting his lower lip instead. He didn't curse and pull away as most men would have, most *human* men, anyway. Instead, he laughed and wrapped an arm around her waist, pulling her down on top of him and taking over the kiss, biting her lip in turn, then soothing the hurt with a stroke of his tongue that swept up the blood that spilled between them, a mingle of his and hers. His growl told her he liked it, and wanted more.

"It's time." His voice had gone dark and snarly, vibrating with the kind of hunger only a vampire knew.

"All right," Layla agreed, a little out of breath, a little scared, but determined and ready.

"You should take my blood first. It will make the rest far more pleasant, and besides, your blood is too intoxicating, and much too delicious for me to stop. Once I taste you, I'll want you in every way."

Every part of her body responded to the desire, to the *hunger* in his voice. Both her breasts had gone heavy with need, the nipples swollen and achingly hard, while her thighs had clenched over her pussy, and it felt *good*. Hell, it felt erotic, and fucking fantastic. "Xavier," she whispered.

"Come here, *amor meu*." He tugged her down on top of him again.

His fangs had emerged, and she watched with studied interest when he lifted his wrist to his mouth, gasping when he sliced open his vein and blood poured out. Her eyes met his for an instant, looking for reassurance that this was . . . normal. That the blood dripping down his arm now was a good thing.

He nodded and held it out to her. "Drink, Layla. And be my mate."

She licked her lips nervously. What would it taste like? But she'd never been a coward, never backed away from a challenge. Although this was so much more than anything she'd ever faced before. But if she wanted him, and God knew she did . . . She cupped his bleeding arm in both hands and lifted it to her mouth, intending to touch the tip of her tongue to the thick, red blood. What happened instead was driven by the raging need that small touch triggered in her brain, in her body. She'd never known such ecstasy, suddenly understanding for the first time what that word meant. Pleasure coursed through her body, hot and exciting, lighting up every nerve, every cell with lush passion and hunger. Her gaze swung to meet Xavier's in demand. She *wanted* him. She was going to *have* him. A soft growl rumbled in her throat as she licked her lips.

He growled back, deeper and louder, his power a living, breathing *thing* in the room, surrounding her, claiming her, wanting her as much as she wanted him. Moving so fast she didn't see him coming, he snapped up, and pulled her beneath him, his mouth at her neck, his fangs scraping her skin, his growl vibrating down her throat. A moment later, his fangs were slicing into her vein, her blood hot as it dripped over her neck to shoulder, while he drew long, greedy swallows. The growl became a rumble of satisfaction, when her arms tightened and her body bowed beneath him, as the euphoric in his bite sent wave after wave of climax cascading through her body, building to an impossible peak that left her screaming in helpless pleasure.

She was still trembling, still lost in the ripples of ecstasy rolling over her, when Xavier slid his cock deep inside her. Inner muscles stretched and ached in fresh need, welcoming his intrusion, sucking him in and holding him there, unwilling to let him go. Ever.

When he started to move, when he tried to pull his thick penis from inside her, her sheath clenched around him, and he groaned. "Your pussy holds me so tightly, *cariño*."

She thought, *"Because you belong there. You're mine."* She opened her mouth to say the words, but she couldn't remember how to speak. So she bit his jaw, opened the skin of his back with her nails, and didn't let him go.

He chuckled low and sexy and satisfied, then pulled his cock out and plunged it back in again, doing it over and over until Layla thought for sure the heat of his passage, the friction of his hard shaft against her clutching muscles would ignite them both in a fire of passion and desire. *Glorious,* she thought. What a way to die.

XAVIER SENSED HER surrender to the passion, the *heat* between them. Heard the first whisper of her mind speaking to his, welcoming the fire. But he wasn't ready to die. Not when Layla was finally his. He began moving, thrusting in and out, his erection growing, swelling until he thought she might get her wish after all. But then . . . sweet release, as ecstasy claimed him and a different kind of fire rushed from his balls to his cock, shooting deep into Layla's body and sending her into a final, powerful orgasm. Her legs tightened around his hips, holding him inside her, while her arms clutched at him, nails digging into his back in delicious pain, until they slowly collapsed in each other's arms, panting, limp . . . and mated.

They slept after that. Not daylight sleep, where he had no choice. But the two of them, sweating bodies twined together, sated and exhausted. They woke together. He didn't know how long it had been, but his phone was ringing.

He reached over and glanced at the display. He recognized the name, but his mate was warm and soft in his arms. So he put the phone down, flicked off the ringer, and slid back down, holding her tightly.

"I love you," he murmured, pulling the sheet over them both.

"Love you, too," she said softly, then kissed his chest and drifted back to sleep.

Xavier smiled, utterly satisfied, utterly content and happy for the first time in his life.

Epilogue

Porto, Portugal, present day

ANTÔNIO SILVEIRA, Lord of Portugal, scowled down at the phone in his hand when his call went to fucking voicemail. The curse of modern communication, he thought. It was well past sunset. Where the hell was Xavier? He'd never speak those words directly to the Lord of Spain, who also happened to be his Sire, but as his thoughts were *his;* he felt free to vent his frustration. When the damn *beep* filled his ear, he calmed himself and said, "Sire. A situation has come up here, and I could use your advice. If you could call . . . at your convenience, of course, I would be very appreciative. I trust everything is well with you, and look forward to speaking with you directly. *Muito obrigado.*"

He disconnected, then assured that Xavier, his Sire, could no longer hear, slammed the phone down hard enough to crack the ancient acacia desktop.

"Sire?"

He looked up to see his security chief and eldest child, Breno Soares, standing in the doorway, appearing worried. "Did you speak to him? What did he say?"

"Voicemail," Antonio snapped.

"Ah. Will he return the call?"

"Eventually," he muttered, but then remembered who he was, and *what* he was supposed to be. Breno would understand and never repeat anything that happened in this office, but others wouldn't be so discreet. He had to remember that, or someday he'd storm out of this office, forgetting he had a responsibility to his people. To be their leader—confident and sure—so that *they* at least felt safe and protected. Even if that that *bitch* was trying to destroy him.

"I'm sorry, Breno. Of course, he'll call. It's unrealistic of me to assume he would be sitting by the phone, waiting for me to contact him."

"Have you heard from the . . . *other* this evening?"

"Thankfully, no. I've had my fill of her threats and bragging. Fucking German whore. Why can't she take over her own country, and leave mine alone?"

"The weather is much better here."

His gaze shot up in surprise, before he realized Breno was jesting. Not funny, he thought. Since that probably *was* one of *her* reasons, assuming one could consider anything about her reasonable. She *was* beautiful, he admitted. But that was how he'd gotten into this fucking mess in the first place. Xavier had warned him, hadn't he? Told him his cock would lead him into trouble someday. But had he listened? No. No, he hadn't. He was Lord of Portugal. What did he have to worry about? She was nothing but an incredibly sexy, stunningly beautiful woman, after all.

He had a lot to worry about, apparently.

"Don't worry, Breno. Xavier and I have spoken of an alliance before. It's his goal for all of Europe's vampires, that we ally ourselves, much as they have in North America. This will be the first real test of his design. He'll call, and he'll come. Besides," he added with a grin, "I'm his favorite child."

To be continued . . .

(Read on for a preview of *Nicodemus*)

Somewhere in the mists of time...

IT WAS A TIME when gods walked the earth, when armies fought not for bits of land, but for the very existence of humanity. On such a battlefield, five formidable warriors stood against an evil greater than any the earth had ever seen. But evil is not an honorable foe. Betrayed by someone they trusted, the warriors were cursed, one by one, tossed into the maelstrom of time, imprisoned in stone, their freedom resting on nearly impossible conditions. Alone of the five, their leader, the sorcerer Nicodemus, was left free. His curse? To know that his fellow warriors remained trapped forever out of his reach, condemned to an eternity of searching for their stone prisons and the keys to their freedom.

NICODEMUS KATSAROS, the greatest sorcerer of his time, stared in shock at the battlefield before him, the desolation on the faces of victors and losers alike, the knee-deep mud colored red with the blood of the fallen, and beside him . . . nothing, no one. He stood alone in his victory. Aching at the lives lost, at the price he'd paid. A price that was so much greater than anyone could know. His warriors, the men he loved more than any on this earth, no matter that they were bound by friendship and loyalty instead of blood. They were his brothers.

And they were gone. One moment, they'd stood, the four strongest, bravest, most loyal warriors a man could ask for, had fought side by side with him until this final battle. The battle that would bring a long-sought peace to his world, would defeat his enemy Sotiris Dellakos, the rival sorcerer whose brutality and heartless pursuit of power had left misery and despair in its wake. They'd been enemies for decades, though it seemed longer. Nicodemus had been still a teenager when they'd first fought. Sotiris confident that his greater years and talent would easily wipe away this *child* who'd dared to challenge him.

It had been the bastard's first loss, but not his last. Nicodemus was far more powerful and drew strength from the love of his people, and above all, from the four warriors whom he'd called from the corners of the earth to fight by his side. Good against evil, light against dark. And they'd come, and they'd stood with him.

Until today, when Sotiris, in a last desperate stroke of evil, had stolen them somehow. Cast them into the sands of time and space, trapped in stone forever. Unless Nicodemus could find them, free them.

He swore that he would. That he would not rest—

A woman's scream soared over the battlefield, and he raised his head to listen. Had she been calling his name? Who would do that? What woman—

"Fuck!" Vaulting onto his horse, he raced not across the battlefield, but behind his own lines, past bloodstained tents where his medics toiled, trying to save the life and livelihood of those they could. Making heartbreaking judgments when faced with men and women who were too far gone to save. Medics and wounded alike watched with tired eyes when he rode past, his own gaze on the white peaks of his estate, where he'd left her behind, thinking her safer there than on the battlefield.

But he'd been a fool. What challenge was there for Sotiris in destroying one woman, when he'd disposed of four great warriors with a single blow?

Nicodemus slid from the horse's back as it loped through the gate, running on his own feet now, too agitated to call down a spell that would let him reach her faster, to open a portal and appear by her side in an instant. He climbed the stairs three a time, shoving past staff and courtiers alike. He had no time for them or their endless questions, he had to get to her, to . . .

"Antonia!" The door slammed against the wall as he screamed her name. But he knew. He *knew*. He was too late. She was gone, just as his brothers were gone. Everyone he'd ever loved . . . gone in the blink of an eye.

He'd won the war, the final victory over Sotiris. But he'd lost . . . everything.

To be continued . . .

Acknowledgements

I'm so fortunate to be able to write my stories, to sell them to a publisher, and have wonderful readers who make all the rest possible. But if I'm going to list my good fortunes, then chief among them must be working with my editor, Brenda Chin. She somehow gets inside my head, knows what I meant to write, and drags it into the eerie light of the computer, so that I can put it on the screen and create a story that others want to read and enjoy.

My sincere thanks also to my publisher, Debra Dixon at ImaJinn/BelleBooks, for her endless patience while I fought for creativity during a pandemic lockdown. I'm an introvert, but even I was going a little crazy . . . although some would say I didn't have far to go. I also want to thank everyone else at ImaJinn/Belle for their kindness and support in getting my books out on time and looking beautiful.

On a personal note, I want to thank my dear friend and fellow writer Angela Addams for late night/early morning conversations that kept me going when the book just kept getting longer. It's hard to believe that only a year ago, we were walking the streets of Toronto, without a care in the world. Thank you also to Julie Fine who beta read the longest sex scene in the history of sex scenes. Damn vampires and their stamina. Last, but never least, thank you to my very talented friend and contractor, Ori Sakal, who volunteered to be the evil villain in this book, even though he's the very opposite of evil in this or any other world.

And finally, as always, to my family who made sure to stay in touch and deliver safe, lockdown hugs while I wrote this. Because everyone needs a hug once in a while. Love you all. Don't know what I'd do without you.

About the Author

D. B. REYNOLDS arrived in sunny Southern California at an early age, having made the trek across the country from the Midwest in a station wagon with her parents, her many siblings and the family dog. And while she has many (okay, some) fond memories of Midwestern farm life, she quickly discovered that L.A. was her kind of town and grew up happily sunning on the beaches of the South Bay.

D. B. holds graduate degrees in international relations and history from UCLA (go Bruins!) and was headed for a career in academia, but in a moment of clarity she left behind the politics of the hallowed halls for the better paying politics of Hollywood, where she worked as a sound editor for several years, receiving two Emmy nominations, an MPSE Golden Reel and multiple MPSE nominations for her work in television sound.

Book One of her Vampires in America series, RAPHAEL, launched her career as a writer in 2009, while JABRIL, Vampires in America Book Two, was awarded the RT Reviewers Choice Award for Best Paranormal Romance (Small Press) in 2010. ADEN, Vampires in America Book Seven, was her first release under the new ImaJinn imprint at Belle Books, Inc.

D. B. currently lives in a flammable canyon near the Malibu coast. When she's not writing her own books, she can usually be found reading someone else's. You can visit D. B. at her website www.dbreynolds.com for information on her latest books, contests and giveaways.

Made in United States
Orlando, FL
22 June 2022